Banking on Reddy

a Craig Reddy investigation

Greg Butcher

Publisher: Voyagers of Fortune Inc., Montreal, Canada.

Contact: voyagers.of.fortune@mail.com

Printed and bound in the UK by Biddles, part of the MPG Books Group, Bodmin and Kings Lynn.

ISBN: 978-0-9881221-0-9

CHAPTER ONE

Just after dawn, Sunday 15th March 2009. South side of Ipswich, Suffolk, England.

Sitting comfortably behind the driver's wheel, the cocaine hit his bloodstream, increasing his level of awareness and sense of purpose. His breathing was steady and with that came a growing sense of calm. All around, the colours of everything took on more intensity. He felt good.

He had left his wife Elaine asleep in bed, taking his clothes downstairs and dressing in the kitchen to avoid waking her. When he stepped outside the front door there had been no one about. Using the remote control, he opened the garage door. The black Audi 6 purred quietly when he turned on the ignition. Manoeuvring it out of the garage, he swung the vehicle left into the tree-lined road. The digital clock, lit up on the car dashboard, indicated that it was 6.35am.

There were horizontal layers of yellow and russet spreading across the horizon, drowning out the grey dawn.

He drove without haste, knowing precisely the directions he needed to take through the town's south western suburbs. Traffic was sparse, it being Sunday. With his left hand he opened the CD cover lying on the passenger's seat and inserted the disc into the car's CD player. The album was Bill Evans' "You must believe in Spring". The choice of music had been planned the evening before, the CD placed on the passenger's seat in anticipation.

With his index finger he gently pressed the 'play' button and 'B Minor Waltz (for Elaine)' suffused the intimate space of his car. He considered Evans the key influence behind Miles Davis' classic "Kind of Blue". His impressionist style let the listener draw their own mental images. He appreciated the razor's edge that the music cut between hope and despair; between nostalgia and renewal. The razor's edge was where he felt at his best. It was where he had taken himself to in his own mind.

Evans' piano notes started to work their magic, corroborating his own calm sense of purpose and destiny. His driving became routine, allowing his mind to switch to auto control.

3

Experience had taught him that however convoluted life became, letting problems fester solved nothing. It was actions that got things done and problems resolved. Getting out early this morning was his definitive assertion of action. The hit of cocaine was mere intensification of the experience. Doubts that he may have had, he had cast aside some days ago. This morning, action would supremely express his freedom.

Having reached the last roundabout out of town, he eased the car left down a slip road onto the multi-lane arterial road that by-passed the town and headed for the coast. Traffic even here was still only very light.

Within a few minutes he was approaching the river estuary. The CD was playing Evans' 'We will meet again". Ahead, he could see the smooth rising curve of the suspension bridge with its immensely powerful vertical cables.

Checking his rear-view mirror for vehicles, he moved the Audi over to the nearside lane and slowly reduced speed. As the car passed onto the bridge, his view of the river was impeded by the concrete walls on either side, designed as a security measure to prevent drivers' attention being distracted. The bridge's incline was initially steep but lessened towards the middle. He knew the height at the top was 45 metres above the river.

As the car neared the summit, he again checked for following vehicles in the rear-view mirror. The next car was some way back. He braked, bringing the Audi to a halt and turned off the ignition. The music died. Opening the car door, he noticed the chill breeze but did not feel exposed. He walked quickly around the back of the vehicle and headed directly to the side by the concrete wall. Gripping the top of the concrete wall with both hands, he found a foothold and climbed. There was no need to look around as his purpose was defined.

He jumped into the void.

CHAPTER TWO

15.50 Friday 13th March 2009. Daily Courier Headquarters, Universal Tower, Canary Wharf, London

The Daily Courier's head office was in Universal Tower. A modern multi-storey office building, it was located in the Isle of Dogs, not far from the light rail stop at Crossharbour. The sharp-contoured edifice, whose exterior was dominated by concrete and tinted plate glass, powered into the dull winter sky. It had won an international architectural design award, fitting testament to its modernist mediocrity.

A bitter wind whipped around the streets. Craig Reddy grabbed hold of the front of his unbuttoned raincoat to prevent it being blown off his shoulders. Arriving at Universal Tower, he chose the middle of three ground floor entrances and pushed on the glass revolving door. It responded to his touch and he entered.

Inside, the atmosphere was frenetic with the ebb and flow of people across the marble floored reception area. The building was multi-tenanted and the Friday afternoon rush had already started as staff checked out for the week end. Some were intent on early departures for home on the tubes and trains. Others were destined for central London pubs and café bars to drink cheap alcohol hastily during 'happy hour'. Their 'happiness' growing in correlation with both their inebriation and the recounting of office woes and stresses to sympathetic ears.

Reddy headed across the reception area for the lifts. He gave a quick nod of acknowledgement to the security staff manning the reception desk off to his right, flashing them his ID. The Daily Courier's headquarters occupied the building's top four floors. Entering an available lift, he pressed a button for the thirty seventh floor, the penultimate one. The steel doors purred closed.

"Hello Craig, you're looking worried."

Pre-occupied with his thoughts for the impending meeting with Samantha his boss, Reddy was unaware of the frown furrowing his forehead. Nor had he seen the diminutive Mina Patel standing in the corner of the lift. A journalist at the Courier, she had been promoted recently to sub-Editor for the Business & City pages. In Reddy's opinion Mina was one of the Courier's 'good guys'. She even had a life outside

5

of journalism, playing women's hockey for a top Middlesex club. In contrast, most of the long term 'Courieristas' were wedded to the world of work and professional networking. Reddy felt an outsider. He was wary of most of his colleagues' incessant quest for political positioning and conformity.

"What brings you into the office at this hour?" Mina queried.

Reddy raised a lugubrious smile. "Off to see the Deputy Headmaster".

By which he meant his and her boss, Samantha Cavendish, Business Editor and Acting Deputy Editor at the Daily Courier.

"Probably get my knuckles rapped" he added.

 "Late with your homework again?" Mina volunteered, engaging with Reddy's role-playing.

"Something like that" he answered, evasively.

He gave her a theatrical long face, implying that it was nothing untoward. There was no point attracting attention to possible dissonances or disputes. Since the sacking of the previous Editor and the arrival of Sinclair Monroe, his replacement, rumours about power conflicts flared around headquarters like forest fires. In point of fact, Reddy was suffering a mounting sense of trepidation, following receipt earlier of a text message. It came from Samantha's personal assistant and read: "U R required 4 meeting with Sam 16.00 at HQ. Be there."

"Did you see" Mina continued "that I found space for that article you mailed to me yesterday evening ? The one about the bank with liquidity problems?"

Reddy had indeed seen it, hidden away in the back pages of the business section of this morning's edition of the Daily Courier.

"The Ipswich and Blackwater Bank. Yes, I did see it. Well done and thanks. Didn't Samantha comment at all about it?"

"No, I think she didn't read it to be honest. Too busy working on the leader articles. She left the filler materials to me."

Reddy logged this disclosure. Being relegated to 'filler material' was probably indicative of where things stood with him at the Courier right now. Intuition was telling him to be prepared for more grief from Samantha. Attempting to redirect the conversation, he asked:

"Have you had a conversion to working overtime? I would have thought you would be working from home on a Friday."

"Not when I have a new, top priority news assignment". She gave him a teasing smile, adding: "Sun Tsu says, 'know your enemy to avoid doing battle'. Craig, you should know by now that showing presence around the office is an opportunity to assess the political terrain".

Her cautious half-smile transmogrified into a huge grin. The lift decelerated and stopped at the 36th floor. With the briefest wave of the hand and a "Good luck", she spirited herself out and away. The lift doors closed and Reddy was alone.

He was disconcerted about the reference to Sun Tsu, the Chinese sage of military strategy. Was Mina already "in the know" about his wrangles with Samantha? Mina was bright as a button. She had a grasp of how to stay on top of the office politics. "She'll go far", Reddy mused. He wondered, ominously, whether the same could be said for his own longevity.

At the thirty seventh floor he alighted from the lift. Stretched away in front of him was a large open plan office filled with several rows of desks. Computers flashing sky blue coloured screens sat atop most of them. Off to the left corner there were a few Dilbert-like cubicles; minimalist last redoubts of individual privacy. These were hot-desking facilities afforded the Courier's journalists when needing to work at Headquarters.

On the far side of the office, large tinted glass windows ran along the entire length of the building. This time of year they afforded insufficient natural light and were supplemented by electric lighting, the fittings of which were concealed in the ceiling. Away in the office's far right corner a lounge area furnished coffee, soft drinks and comfortable leather chairs arranged in two rows. Banks of wide screen televisions hung suspended from metal rails in front of these chairs, permitting staff to follow top stories being retailed by the television media. Only a few staff were about; and no one noticed his presence. Most heads that were visible above their cubicles were bowed down as if mentally chained to their computer screens.

Reddy set off left to the other far corner in which was found the only independent walled-off office. The separation provided a deliberate

7

mark of distinction between journalists and managers. Samantha Cavendish, the incumbent, was a journalist but having become Acting Deputy Editor last year, was now unmistakeably also part of top management.

The door was ajar so Reddy pushed it open and went straight in to an office occupied by Samantha's personal assistant. To the left side of the room was a high quality varnished wooden desk; off to the other side were the tinted-glass windows again; and straight ahead was another door leading into Samantha Cavendish's office. Sitting on the front of the desk was a young man in his early thirties. He had one leg stretched out to the floor to keep his balance; while the other laid over it affording a ledge on which to perch his elbow and arm. Head down in concentration, Oliver Carrington was busy fiddling with the keypad on a hand held Blackberry. As usual, he was immaculately dressed. He wore a light blue signature shirt with gold cuff links, matching dark blue tie held by an elegant tie pin; tailored dark grey woollen trousers complemented by a black leather belt, and polished black brogues. Reddy detested the guy, and knew that the sentiment was mutual. Carrington was Samantha's hand-picked personal assistant; an Oxford graduate on a fast track career path. As the gatekeeper managing access to Reddy's boss, he exercised political power over all the journalists.

Carrington had something sinister and vicious in him. Reddy perceived him like Othello's Iago, smiling yet ever a villain. Carrington's métier was not journalism, it was spin; spin designed to protect and enhance the interests of his superior and, needless to say, of himself too.

Worryingly, despite his relatively tender age of thirty three, Carrington's mastery of the black art was already clinically precise. In the five months since he had been appointed to the post by Samantha, almost the entire cohort of journalists working for that part of the Courier's news business under Samantha's management had come to pay obeisance to prince Oliver Carrington's court.

Carrington caught Reddy's movement through the door in the corner of his eye. Ignoring him, he continued tapping at the Blackberry's keyboard until he had completed the text message. Thereby not only completing and sending the text message to Samantha indicating that Reddy had arrived, but also forcing Reddy to halt in mid stride and stand uncomfortably in no mans' land awaiting acknowledgement from the prince of darkness.

Reddy felt awkward but at the same time annoyed. He knew that by such techniques inter-personal power is gained; and that Carrington was gaming him. Eventually, Carrington looked up from the device straight into Reddy's face and beamed a Socratic smile. Reddy redoubled his conviction about this rodent's villainy.

"Craig ! Thanks for coming over" Carrington said insouciantly, staying glued to the desk. "Samantha's upstairs with Sinclair. Promises she'll be down in a minute. Why don't you take a pew?"

Reddy took off his raincoat and sat himself down in one of the black leather armchairs placed against the inner office wall. Seated there, he had a panoramic view through the windows across the river Thames to the Millenium Dome. Everything outside appeared as different shades of dismal grey. Slanting rain was splattering the huge windows.

"So, what's this about, Oliver?" Reddy enquired, apprehensively.

Carrington's Socratic smile re-appeared. He remained lounging comfortably against his desk.

"Oh, come on Craig, you know already. It's about getting with the programme. Samantha wants you to kick all this time-consuming investigative stuff into touch and take the "City Movers and Shakers" column that she offered to you. Its decision time".

"I see. Well, not much of a surprise there then. Join the revolution. Create celebrity status for City slickers. Help migrate the Courier downmarket to feed the public's voracious demand for gossip. That is our strategy for halting falling circulation, isn't it?"

"That's not even a parody of the truth Craig. You know very well that Damien wants to freshen things up content-wise. As well as have a clear strategic direction for us to compete against the twenty four by seven news cycle of the television news programmes."

Damien White was the Courier's owner. An American media entrepreneur, White had bought the newspaper cheaply in 2006. It was an ailing conservative broadsheet. For White, it was to be a vehicle that would promote his globalisation agenda on "this side of the pond".

When the financial crisis hit in 2008, he insisted the paper's focus remain international, supporting the "progressive" agenda of Brown's Labour Government. He had hired Sinclair Monroe as Editor a year ago to execute that agenda. Samantha naturally was on-board, having been promoted to Acting Deputy Editor when Monroe sacked the previous Deputy last autumn.

Reddy looked appraisingly at Carrington. There was no value in engaging in discussion with him on these matters, he reflected. Is Carrington himself "with the programme"? Probably only in so far as it suits his interests. Reddy suspected that Carrington's loyalty to Samantha was cast with his eye on the main chance.

At that moment of hiatus in the exchange between them, Samantha Cavendish walked briskly through the open door. She wore a tailored pastel yellow dress suit with matching coloured shoes. To an elegant gold chain necklace was attached a small pendant in which sparkled an opal-coloured precious stone. Her light brown hair, dyed with occasional subtle blond streaks, had a shoulder length cut. Ice blue eyes were set in a symmetrical face, one of almost of Florentine aquilinity. Samantha was a business woman for whom femininity was an asset in the service of business ambition.

"Hello Craig, let's go straight through" she said, indicating the door opposite to her own office with a wave of her right arm.

"Oliver, no disturbances please." she instructed, heading straight for her own office.

From the business-like tone, Reddy sensed the knuckle-rapping was imminent. He rose from the armchair, picked up his raincoat and, deliberately turning his back on Carrington, followed her into the other office.

Cavendish sat down in the chair behind her desk. She waved at the vacant seat immediately opposite. Reddy complied and sat, placing his raincoat across his knees. He noticed that her desk was immaculately tidy. Looking past her through the ceiling-to-floor windows, he again observed the murky-grey winter cityscape of the Isle of Dogs across to the Millenium Dome. The Dome's shape and spikes looked like a circus big top. Before Reddy could evolve this perception into an analogy, Samantha spoke for the first time.

"Well Craig, it seems to me you have reached a crossroads. The efforts that you've been expending on what you call your 'investigative' journalism are not in tune with the current Editorial strategy of the paper. The era of Bernstein and Woodward is long gone. I think I have made that perfectly clear to you on more than one occasion?"

"True." Reddy affirmed.

"What is more, your stance on the financial crisis is not shared by either Sinclair or myself. Why you persist in arguing that there is a systemic solvency problem in the banking sector is a mystery."

"If you're not looking, you won't see. Until the tsunami hits that is"

Cavendish cut Reddy off: "Be realistic. The Northern Rock and Lloyds Bank incidents are behind us, just as is the Lehman's failure in the States. They were based on investors' short term fears and imprudent lending practices. That's over now. The financial crisis is being tackled. Look, the US administration is launching a huge stimulus programme. Here in the UK the Bank of England has a huge new programme of twenty billion pounds' worth of bond buying. We've got new regulatory proposals for the financial sector due out from the Financial Services Authority. Not least, stock markets are recovering because investor confidence is returning. The Courier's Editorial policy is to support all that."

"Since when did the Courier become a mere cheerleader for the governing elites? No contrary voices any more Samantha? No critical analysis explaining alternative perspectives? Are we all Keynesian apologists now ?"

"We can't have you publishing articles explicitly contrary to the Editorial line. Period. You can take that from me or you can take it from Sinclair Monroe. As you please".

Cavendish paused, the embodiment of poise and self-control.

There having been no question asked, Reddy remained resolutely silent. He made a supreme effort to avoid his face betraying his thoughts. She gave him a cold smile.

"So the opportunity is there" she encouraged, "for you to take this new column 'City Movers and Shakers'. As I've explained to you before, I think the Business section of the paper will benefit from such a column. Features and interviews of the key decision-makers in the City."

"Gossip column" Reddy murmured.

"We want to bring the readership closer to the business people that matter. That will boost the return of confidence and trust in our finance industry leaders. I believe too that the human interest side will stimulate demand for the Courier. You would become a major beneficiary too Craig. Your by-line on the most read City column in the national press ?"

She had laid out the proposition crystal clear before him. As Carrington had prophesied, now was 'decision time'. Reddy held her gaze.

"Samantha, I appreciate that Sinclair has to get circulation numbers up. I understand too that we are competing against the twenty four hour television news cycle of CNN, CNBC, the BBC and others. However, I simply cannot see why you want to 'dumb down' the content."

He was regretting this last sentence the moment he uttered it. His thoughts nevertheless had gained momentum and involuntarily demanded expression. He continued:

"In my view the majority of the electorate are fed up with being sold a mess of potage. They are angry with the bankers for being negligent and greedy. They are disaffected with the political class for feeding themselves from the Westminster pork trough. They are alienated by the loss of sovereignty to the European Union. Not least, they are mightily worried about permanent debt enslavement for themselves and their offspring because of profligate levels of public spending and bank bail outs.

In my view the right thing to do at broadsheets like the Courier is to investigate these problems and expose them for our readership. That means taking a leadership role in the policy debates. We should shine light into the dark holes of the bankers' negligence. We can expose the hypocrisy and corruption of those in public service; make the case for returning controls from Brussels; hold Government to account for unsustainable public debts."

He sat back in his chair, hackles metaphorically raised. This really wasn't going well he told himself.

Cavendish leant back gently in her chair, her blues eyes coldly searching Reddy's face. For a few seconds she remained motionless. Then she glided effortlessly forwards.

"From that rant, it appears you're already an accomplished populist Craig. Maybe you would do well 'dumbing down' yourself. To the tabloids, for instance".

She placed her arms on the desk and asked sardonically:

"Shall I take it that's a 'no' then Craig ? Or do you want more time to think about it ?"

Reddy already regretted his outburst. In the cut and thrust of office politics, declaring yourself openly and emotively as he had just done, left you exposed and potentially vulnerable. But he wasn't going to retreat.

"Well, I don't see any shift in your position on this Samantha. From my point of view the investigative work that I am doing is valuable and justifiable. It does need investment of time though to dig out the facts and make the arguments. However, the benefit is found in the quality of the articles delivered. As regards your proposed new column, my views are unchanged."

Patience was not a virtue in Cavendish's world. To her, Reddy's intransigence smacked either of stupidity or naivety, or both. It had occurred to her too that it might be related to his refusal to accept her power to control what he should write. That, in her view, was beyond belief: she owned him. Nevertheless, Reddy was widely respected as a writer of business economic journalism. She still retained a last grain of reluctance to fire him.

"Craig, I'm giving you the week end to think it over one last time. But I'm handing your interview with the Minister Lord Preston next Monday, to Collins to do."

"But the whole thing's already scheduled. I've done my research for it." Reddy complained. He was keen to conduct that interview.

Lord Preston was the Government's Minister for the Banking & Finance industries. Reddy had already prepared much of what he wanted to cover in the interview with him. Questions would not only cover the likely impacts of the new Banking Act that had passed through Parliament a month ago, but also the article about the Ipswich and Blackwater Bank he had had published in today's Courier. Naturally, that meant conducting the interview on his own terms, not those constrained by the purposes of the 'Movers and Shakers' column. Reddy intended to provide an up close view of a Minister immersed in the Government's responses to the UK banking crisis. Whereas Cavendish wanted a tame profile of the Minister to burnish his and her reputation, steering well clear of any contentious policy details.

"Craig, this meeting's over. My decision on the Lord Preston interview is final. Go home and think about your situation please over the week end. Let me know by Monday whether or not you agree to the proposition available to you."

To emphasise that their discussion was terminated, Cavendish peremptorily shifted in her chair to face the screen of her laptop open at her desk.

Departing the headquarters and stepping outside of Universal Tower, Reddy noticed that he had a text message waiting on his mobile phone from Edmund Burleigh, an old friend and practicing lawyer based in Ipswich.

It read:

"Scoop ! Suggest meet 4 lunch 2morrow; Constable Club? EB. "

Curious what this might be about, and anxious to get the disaster of his meeting with Samantha Cavendish out of his mind, Reddy called Burleigh's mobile. Only an automatic voice response was available.

For Reddy, most Saturday afternoons during the football season were sacrosanct as he was an Ipswich Town fan and season ticket holder. But he knew they had no game this week-end. He tapped out a reply to Burleigh confirming himself for a 12.00 lunch.

His watch showed that it was 16.35. Simon Farley and the lads would already have finished their day's work at the 2012 Olympics site in Stratford and be downing their first pints at their regular pub near Liverpool Street station.

Reddy headed for the Cold Harbour rail station through the late afternoon gloom, intent upon joining them and perhaps drowning his sorrows.

Chapter Three

The Railway Tavern was Simon Farley's sort of pub. The public bar still had a "spit and sawdust" feel to it, even if the habitués were more often than not office professionals rather than manual workers. Simon, in his worn out work clothes, didn't feel at all out of place. On the contrary, the Railway Tavern was his 'office'. One that sported the advantage of selling Abbott ale, his favourite beer. Simon's dad had worked for the brewers when Simon was a kid.

The Tavern's bar stretched the length of the room. The bar, and the fittings behind it, were still the original hardwoods installed in the early Victorian era. The wooden floorboards, tables, stools, and chairs spread across the large public bar all had echoes of the same style. The whole was highly polished; an attribute accentuated by the bright lighting coming from the overhead lamps. These were in Victorian style and held to the ceiling by two enormous wrought iron light holders. The ceiling itself was painted a rich burgundy red. The overall effect was one of warmth, security and certainty. If in the street outside it was cold, dark and anonymous; inside there was fraternity and conviviality. Here, after a couple of pints and some friendly banter, the day's anxiety or fatigue could be placed in suspended animation.

At the far end of the room, held up high on metal supports, were two wide screen digital televisions. Both were tuned-in to Sky Sports, where a pretty female presenter with long blond hair was hosting the programme that previewed the week end sports fixtures. Below, ranged along the far wall, were four high tech games machines with flashing lights and techno noises. Simon still called them 'one arm bandits'.

He was leaning his large frame across the bar, with his body angled to look down the length of the bar, to attract the attention of the nearest barmaid. He refused to add "barista" to his lexicon. The pub was already busy and Simon, although a courteous soul, decided that it was time to impose his presence for service. As she was handing back change to a customer, he interceded:

"Hey, luv" he said, succeeding to catch the girl's eye, "that'll be three pints of lager; two of Abbott ale and two bags of peanuts please".

15

She acknowledged the order, took pint glasses from under the bar counter, and turned to fill them from the tap.

Waiting for the drinks to arrive, Simon found himself staring absently at a sad looking guy in one of the huge mirrors hanging on the back wall behind the bar. With a jolt of realisation, he found he was looking at himself. He ran a rapid self assessment. At thirty seven years of age he still had a full head of hair; which he kept shoulder length. Blue eyes shone out still but from dark holes that were the accumulated tiredness of years of hard physical work on construction sites. His old fur-lined bomber jacket, that he always used for work outdoors in winter, was a tight fit over his muscular upper body.

As a youngster, life had served up aspirations of sporting success that he had failed to fulfil. At the age of seventeen, Farley signed up as a trainee for Ipswich Town Football Club in 1989. However, the club's trophy-winning years under Bobby Robson were over. Farley never graduated to the first team and after eighteen months moved down a couple of leagues to join neighbouring club Colchester United. There he made a short career as a powerful centre forward until an injury forced him out of the game in 1994. Farley had long ago abandoned dreams of "what might have been". Today the remnants of his footballing desires were transmuted through his enduring support for the club that had rejected him, plus the occasional game on weekends playing for Manningtree Town as a non-professional.

He looked up again into the mirror. It reflected back the comings and goings of the customers in the room, giving the impression of a far greater space. Simon saw his work mates reflected over the other side of the room from the bar. Barry Moore, the two Polish lads Nikola and Kristof, and a Bulgarian hard case called Georgi Bourov. They were all seated on stools at a high oblong table which joined perpendicularly to the external wall with views into the street out the window. Barry caught Farley's eye in the mirror and signalled in theatrical exasperation that they were dying of thirst waiting for their drinks. As de facto leader of the group, Simon had agreed to buy the drinks while they staked out the seating.

The barmaid returned carrying the drinks on a tray.

"Hi, sorry I'm a bit late Simon"

Craig Reddy, wearing a dark brown overcoat, was hovering immediately behind him. Farley had not seen his approach in the mirror. Reddy patted his long time friend on the shoulder and offered his right hand. Farley took Reddy's proffered hand and shook it. The skin was softer than his own, which was hardened from handling bricks, scaffolding and the like over the past fifteen years. As Simon respected Craig both for what he did and as a long term friend, there would be no cheap jokes about his soft hands to his hardened co-workers.

"Craig, you've all but missed the first round." Turning back to the barmaid he said: "Make that another Abbot will you please?"

Turning around again to face his companion he complained:

"Where have you been ? What are you up to?"

Reddy pleaded vaguely: "You know , this and that. I got bogged down with some office bureaucracy."

Reddy looked carefully at his friend. He noted the physical tiredness, the dirty working gear and the hollowed out expression on Simon's face. Was that all down to the travails of outside manual labour over the years? The two of them were the same age give or take a few months, yet Simon looked at least five years older Reddy thought.

"Why don't you introduce me to your friends?" he suggested, glancing over at Simon's workmates who were now engrossed in lively conversation while staring at the sports programme on the television.

Having paid, Simon picked up the tray of drinks and they negotiated their way through the throng of standing customers over to the others. Simon placed the drinks tray on the table.

"Help yourselves guys."

Each beer was whisked away by it's thirsty owner.

There were no more seats available so Reddy positioned himself between Farley and his long time co-worker Barry Moore, a tall broad-shouldered man in his thirties. He turned to Moore.

"Hi Barry, we've met before haven't we? When you and Simon were working on the site near Colchester last summer ?"

"Right you are. Craig isn't it? We ended up having a few jars in the Horse and Hounds over in Manningtree."

Farley made the introductions to the others round the table.

The two Polish guys were younger and leaner; rough hewn with cropped hair. They wore identikit clothing as if in the same army unit. Heavy duty lace-up black leather boots and threadbare blue jeans with holes torn at the knees. Their thick jackets were camouflage green with black wool linings and hoods hanging down the back. Laying by their feet they had work bags in the same camouflage material.

Bourov, a Bulgarian, had the build of a weight lifter. Unlike the two Poles, his appearance was neater and cleaner. Reddy speculated that, even though he was still in his working clothes, he might even have had a shower somewhere before leaving work at the construction site. His face betrayed no inkling of what he was thinking. Yet there was something strangely supple about him. When he shook Reddy's hand, his grip was almost non-existent, while his dark eyes fixed Reddy with a penetrating yet expressionless stare.

"Cheers guys" Farley said, lifting his beer glass to the group.

The others followed his lead, and there was silence for a moment or two as they all imbibed man-sized draughts.

"TGI Friday, Barry ?" Craig asked Moore, trying to kick start some light hearted banter. He was unsure how fluently the East European guys spoke English.

"God damn right." Moore moaned. "Had my fill of crap at work this week."

"Barry operates the crane. He's been lifting the cladding units for the outer walls" Farley explained. "Spent half his time freezing his nuts off sitting waiting for other subbies to clear out".

Vehemently, Moore interjected: "Then they try to fucking blame us for the delays in the cladding going up. Those hard hat wearing tossers from Draper Forest Construction are pure CYA merchants."

"Draper Forest is the main contractor." Farley said, for Reddy's benefit.

"And there was me thinking that working life onsite was based on comradeship and cooperation" Reddy commented; following up acerbically with: "There's an epidemic of 'cover your arse' in my company's headquarters too. It must be contagious and spread up the road to Stratford by the sound of it."

Nikola and Kristof, the two Poles, had let their attention drift away from the conversation around them. They were watching the female presenter on Sky Sports.

Moore had noticed.

"Hey, Nikola, she's too classy for you mate. Not a chance." he teased.

"She's no good." Nikola retorted. "No style. Just peroxide hair. Polish girls are more beautiful. And they behave like real women too."

He grimaced at no one in particular, and resumed his expressionless assessment of the presenter. Besides him, Kristof smirked, wiped his nose on the back of his sleeve and drank some more beer.

Farley explained to Reddy: "Nikola has a corker of a bird. Long legs up to her armpits. Polish, of course. He keeps her well trained. Us lads here never get to see her."

Addressing himself to the Pole: "Isn't that so Nikola ?"

"Bollocks" came back the Pole's rejoinder.

Reddy was singularly impressed. Vernacular English was alive and well amongst the working immigrant community.

The conversation meandered nowhere in particular over the next few minutes. When their glasses were empty, Nikola, Kristof and the Bulgarian took their leave, departing out the door into the bustling commuter crowds of Liverpool Street.

"Don't worry about them" Farley said. "They'll be knocking back the schnapps at a night club tonight once they've cleaned up and found their girlfriends."

With the foreigners gone, the atmosphere between them changed. Farley and Reddy went back a few years together. They had been buddies since secondary school in Ipswich in the early 1980s. They had remained close despite Reddy's disappearance to university for three years at the London School of Economics. Both had remained Ipswich Town supporters over the years and that had proved to be the tribal cement that held them together. That, plus a shared history of war stories from being young and having fun together.

"Good bunch of lads?" Reddy ventured, not having met Farley's new East European work team before.

"Good workers Craig. Not afraid to put their back into it, not like some of the mollycoddled youngsters you find shirking on the dole these days."

"Construction work's not everyone's cup of tea Simon; especially not in this weather."

Farley put him straight: "These guys are just delighted to be here working. They earn far more than they could stuck in Poland or Bulgaria."

"Their English was good too. It's amazing how people with little formal education seem to pick up the lingo quickly." Reddy observed. "The Bulgarian was the muscular guy, right?"

"Yes, Georgi" said Farley. "You get to learn their differences soon enough. The two Polish guys think they're a bit superior. They say the Bulgarians are lazy and laid back. Georgi isn't though. He's as tough a nut as I've met in my time. Spends his spare time pumping iron . He told me he was a bodyguard back in his home country. One thing's for sure, when he gives the two Poles his 'pissed off' look, they quit the banter."

"So why are these guys working with you Simon ? What's the deal?"

"Simple. I get them the work and look after them. Remember Craig I've been in this contracting business now over twelve years. I've got some street cred where it counts and a good network of business contacts. These guys work hard but either get ripped off by unscrupulous subbies or else come to grief in onsite disputes with anti-foreigner British National Party guys. I got myself set up at the Stratford Olympics Village as a subcontractor not by offering jobbing labour like most guys but rather by winning a subcontract off the main contractor to do some cladding and scaffolding. That means I supply the plant to do the lifting, the crane operator – that's Barry here – and the Polish guys who do the scaffolding and brick laying."

"And what about the Bulgarian guy? He looks like he could hod a few bricks without breaking sweat " Reddy observed.

"The man pumps iron for fun Craig. He's small in stature but immense in strength. I've seen him in the gym lift nearly twice his own weight. He's our muscle literally. He helps me keep the predators at bay if we get any trouble onsite. He also does any work you ask of him. Great attitude. Just wants to do and get the job done".

"Where'd you find him?" Reddy asked.

"The fact is he found us. Or rather, I should say it was the Redwoods' boss who offered him to me."

"You mean Redwood Country Homes ? The outfit you were working for before you came down to Stratford ?" Reddy asked, keen to get clarification.

Redwood Country Homes was a firm he knew about. They were on his professional radar as they had commercial links to the Ipswich and Blackwater Bank which was at the centre of his current investigation.

"That's the one. Barry and me did well with them up in Essex. Until the bottom fell out of the housing market last year that is. The Redwoods boss closed down work on those sites before you could say 'Jack Robinson' ."

"So why did you take this Georgi guy?"

"Barry and I knew we could get work at the Olympics site if I offered a team doing a subcontract job, rather than just pitching up as experienced construction labourers. Georgi had been working for the Redwoods boss on different things including some construction work. Barry and I had seen him around from time to time on the sites where we worked. It was obvious he was a worker. Knew what he was about. Eventually, the Redwoods' boss offered him too us when we signed off from the site he was closing down."

"And its worked out since ?"

"Yup, he's been an asset. So too the Polish dudes to be fair."

"And how's the work going up there in Stratford, Simon ? Is it a big change from what you had before on the housing sites up around Colchester ?" Reddy inquired, curious.

"Its the end of another tough physical working week Craig. Don't get me wrong, the money's good, but there are lots of pitfalls that can mess you up financially. Having the contract is one thing, getting the work done on time is another. There's more responsibility for me on this London Olympics job in Stratford than there was just jobbing on the housing development sites out in Essex."

"Isn't that potentially to the good ? It offers the chance to graduate away from the coalface and develop your management skills."

"Forget the theory, Craig. Believe me, its tough. I have to manage the guys and pay them. Then there's the plant and equipment we're using. The rentals get paid up front, and the prices for renting are rising. Add to that the pressure of getting the work done. We are constantly being harassed by the main contractor to stick to the schedule. There are other teams of specialists whose work is dependent on ours. So you're in the dog house real quickly if the stuff you're supposed to complete is unfinished. If other suppliers are standing idle waiting for you to complete there are even penalty clauses in the contract."

"I see. I can imagine there can be some frayed tempers around. Work on large construction sites has become more organised and productive over the years hasn't it? There's far less influence of the Unions as well I would guess."

Moore chipped in: "Its incredibly strict onsite, Craig. You wouldn't believe it. There is tight access security. Then there are health and safety regulations that the main contractor is obliged to impose on all subcontractors. If you have deliveries that need to arrive on site, all that has to be signed off in advance with the site manager's logistics guys. I mean, you can hardly have a fart without first obtaining authorisation for it. "

Farley laughed, despite himself. He and Moore were tight buddies.

"Yeah, that's about right." Farley affirmed. "In addition to a full day's work onsite, I now have the headaches of the financial side too. I'm no accountant Craig and I hate book-keeping. I've given that to someone else. But when all is said and done I have to make all the decisions."

Moore had tipped back the last dregs of his beer. He banged the empty glass down on the table. Zipping up his thick jacket he said:

"Guys, this is getting too serious for my taste. Anyway, I'm off. Got a date for a game of darts later and then out with some lads to chase tail. Hey Simon, give me a call on Sunday afternoon and we can discuss the schedule for next Monday morning."

Moore took his leave of them. Reddy supped contemplatively at his beer. He tried a new line of conversation:

"Apart from the work up in Stratford, how is life treating you Simon ? You seem worn out to me. Is something getting to you ?"

Farley paused, and took a deep breath. He held Reddy's gaze with his blue eyes.

"Hey, its Friday ! No more of this depressing stuff. I've got an empty glass and its your round !" He pressed his case by putting the empty glass in front of Reddy, who responded by heading off to the bar with both glasses to buy refills. When he returned after a couple of minutes with the drinks, Farley was immediately onto their favourite subject:

"Craig, are you up for Town's home game against Burnley on Tuesday next week ?"

"Is that when its been rescheduled ? From last Saturday's postponement ?" Reddy queried.

"That's it. I'm going. You can get yourself freed up and out of London in time can't you ?"

"I should be able to, yes. Let's call it a date. Do you think they can first get a result this Saturday at Reading ? If they're to have any chance of the play-offs three points are a must."

"Personally, I can't see it." Farley admitted. "Reading have a good record this season and are better placed than us for a play-off finish."

Reddy countered: "There's away form in our favour though. The players seem to perform better away from Portman Road at the moment."

"Maybe. The bottom line is always which eleven players want it most on the day. Anyway listen. What are you up to on Saturday ?" Farley enthused. "I'm playing for Manningtree Town over at West Bergholt in the afternoon. But after that I'm spending the rest of the week end down at my folks' summer house. There's one or two things I'm doing up for them. Then, if the weather is fair, maybe go sailing on the boat Sunday afternoon."

"Simon, I'm pretty much a bachelor presently. Julie and I don't see eye to eye. At least, whenever we go out together it ends in a bust up of one kind or another. I haven't spoken to her for over a week. Sailing your boat and chilling out with a lazy Sunday breakfast and the newspapers sounds like the acme of a civilised week end. "No woman, no cry" as the song goes. Yes, let's go for it. Where shall we meet ?"

"The best plan for me would be if you could drive over Saturday afternoon to West Bergholt where the match is. It starts at three. I'll be arriving there on the team coach. We can meet up after the match and drive back directly to my folks' place."

"It's a deal. Although I'll probably arrive after the match has gotten underway, so don't go scoring too many goals early on." Reddy knew his friend still fancied himself as a prolific goal scorer, even if the flow had dried up over recent seasons.

"Come on, its just gone six thirty. We ought to head over to the station if we're going to catch the seven o'clock train for Ipswich and get seats."

They both finished the remaining contents of their glasses, picked up their bags and threaded their way through the throng of people to the exit.

Chapter Four

09.25 Saturday 14th March 2009. Reddy's Apartment, Ipswich Marina. Ipswich.

A thin stream of light was seeping through a gap in the curtains that had not been fully pulled together the night before. Reddy, having reluctantly opened one eye to peer at the outer world, realised that he was indeed in his own bed. He rolled over onto his side and stared at the alarm clock on the bedside table. It was already 9.25am. From outside the bedroom window, he heard the sounds of squawking seagulls.

Taking the available extra pillow on the other side of the double bed, he patted it on top of the one he had been sleeping on, rolled onto his back and slowly let his head fall into the soft material. Laying horizontal, he stretched some muscles; first in his legs then his back. No cramps took hold. He then considered his head. Although there was no thumping headache, he judged that he had probably consumed five pints the night before. This lite version of a hangover didn't merit a paracetamol, just coffee.

From the light issuing through the curtains, his eyes slowly adjusted to the dull shadows and shapes in his bedroom. He began to recall the later events of yesterday evening. Leaving the Railway Tavern, Simon Farley and he had taken the 19.00 train out of Liverpool Street station for Ipswich. On arrival, they had drunk a few more jars in a favourite pub near the town centre. Then, leaving Farley to take a taxi home, Reddy had walked back to his apartment at the Ipswich marina by around eleven.

With an effort of will Reddy overthrew his initial torpor, struggled out of bed and marshalled fresh casual clothes from the wardrobe. He dressed. Still bare-footed, he traipsed to the kitchen, where he found that disorder was the predominant motif. Dirty plates, pans and cutlery were piled to the left of the sink, like a 'life' sculpture on exhibition at the National Gallery.

Reddy wondered whether not buying a dishwasher was a false economy. The kitchen table was crowned with an unwiped bread board, bestrewn with crumbs; accompanied by a stainless steel toast rack in which were filed yesterday morning's burnt offerings.

In denial at his own shortcomings in house cleaning, he ignored the chaos. Instead, he conjured a filter paper for the coffee machine from a cupboard and sought to console himself by preparing strong Arabica coffee.

Waiting for the coffee to brew, he put on a pair of well worn trainers, went down to his mailbox at the building's ground floor entrance and collected the delivered morning papers and mail.

Back in the kitchen, with the smell of fresh coffee now reassuringly nourishing his nostrils, he poured himself a first cup of coffee and sat down at the table to peruse the newspapers' main headlines.

On the sports pages of the local newspaper, there were the usual pre-match commentaries and interviews regarding Ipswich Town's chances that afternoon away to Reading. The loquacious manager, while giving nothing away about team selection and formation, was his usual upbeat self at the press conference. Also, one of the players was quoted saying that the team had 'nothing to fear'. The league table positions printed on the opposite page told a different story, as Town were in tenth spot and Reading fifth. Habitually disappointed by his team's performances in recent years, Reddy did not let his heart rule his head: the best he hoped for today was a draw.

Replenishing his coffee cup, the contents of which had disappeared in short order, he turned his attention to the national broadsheet. It was one he liked to read as a useful counterpoise to the views expressed in the Daily Courier. The front page leaders covered two key subjects. In Northern Ireland, an atrocity had taken place yesterday with the killing of several British soldiers by the Real IRA. Audacious and brutal, the action was condemned on both sides of the political divide. Nevertheless, as the main article explained, the violence demonstrated that the IRA had no effective control over the Real IRA's 'military' actions. Hence the peace process itself looked in jeopardy. Reddy was appalled by the violence but felt unable to fathom the complexities of the problems involved. Like most people in mainland Britain he wanted to see a sustainable peace return, but the gap between here and there seemed intractable.

The other key topic was the upcoming G20 meeting of finance ministers scheduled for the coming week-end at a luxury hotel south of London. Since Reddy's journalistic specialty was business and finance, this was where he invested his own professional and intellectual efforts. Assessing how competing news media were reporting these topics was part of his job.

The perspective of the main articles was sceptical but hopeful. On the one hand, while stock markets were still very nervous and investor sentiment was risk averse, the recent initiative of the US administration in announcing a major spending stimulus of nearly $1,7 trillion had triggered widespread enthusiasm both on Wall Street and amongst economic commentators.

On the inside pages of the newspaper was a half page devoted to an interview with a well-known Nobel Prize-winning American economist who was lauding the initiative. Reddy was aware of his Keynesian views and so made a mental note to read the interview only later during the week end. He himself was highly sceptical of the purported remedies of Keynesian demand management. What piqued his interest more were the intense political and economic debates still swirling on both sides of the Atlantic about the efficacy or not of bank bail outs. These touched directly on his own current investigation into the Ipswich & Blackwater Bank.

Ruminating inconclusively on these matters, Reddy reflexively filled his coffee cup for a third time, and headed into the living room. It was bathed in bright light. Last night when returning home, he had gone straight to bed, not bothering to close the living room curtains. He took in the panoramic view across Ipswich Marina, one of the original reasons he had decided to buy the apartment.

The previous day's monotonous grey had vanished; replaced by sublime azure blue sky. Far out on the eastern horizon, a pale sun strived to give the impression of warmth. A multitude of sailing yachts was moored in the marina, sails furled. Their masts bobbed frantically, revealing that yesterday's wind was unabated. Intermingled with the yachts were occasional luxury boats, trophies of the rich. Circling seagulls, impervious to distinctions of wealth, alighted wherever they wanted and assumed temporary proprietorship.

Reddy turned back from the window and sat down on the sofa. It was one of several pieces of furniture that he had procured from a well-known Scandinavian retailer, not from a sense of preference for the style but rather a concern to live within his means. 'Isn't it good, Norwegian wood ?' he asked himself mirthlessly.

Budgetary discipline seemed wise in current circumstances: his acquisition of the apartment two years ago, now was looking less than propitious. Probably he had bought near the top of the market. Notwithstanding the marina location, the property had lost five percent of its value and the housing market showed no signs of recovery. Unlike some of his colleagues and friends living in London, Reddy prudently had avoided allowing the building society to sell him a mortgage at the full value of the property. But in consequence of having put up significant collateral for the apartment purchase, he had pitifully small savings to fall back on.

He reflected ruefully on his meeting yesterday with his boss Samantha. She had given him only till Monday for a decision to back off from his investigative work and take on the new 'City movers and shakers' page that she and the Editor planned to introduce. Was this a potentially fatal conjuncture for him? Had his short article in the Daily Courier on Friday about the Ipswich & Blackwater Bank's possible insolvency been the final straw ? Belatedly, Reddy realised that the subject had not come up at all during their meeting yesterday. Had she perhaps not even seen it, as Mina Patel had surmised ? In any case, Cavendish had canned his scheduled interview with finance industries Minister Lord Preston this coming Monday, handing the task to another journalist. That was a firm statement of intent from her. So dare he call her bluff? Being a journalist was a precarious existence at the best of times. The train of thought from there left him in uncharted territory: how would he pay the mortgage if he got fired?

His further examination of this danger was distracted by a flashing red light on the answer phone, which stood on a low table at the other end of the sofa. Messages awaited to be heard. He pressed a button for playback. There had been three calls yesterday. The first was from Julie Westwood his sometime girlfriend. She was emotional and angry. He was never available to meet she said. She had had enough and was calling it quits. The next message was Edmund Burleigh. He confirmed their lunch meeting for today at the Constable Club for 12.00. The final call was from Pandit Singh. Pandit, a British born Indian, was a colleague at the Courier who worked on the foreign desk. Reddy considered him as a trustworthy colleague and competitive squash partner. Pandit explained that he had bumped into Mina Patel at the Courier offices. She had mentioned seeing Reddy on his way to meet Samantha Cavendish. Curious to know what had happened, he proposed a squash game for early Wednesday morning at a sports centre on Bishopsgate near Liverpool Street station. He left his mobile number just in case Reddy had misplaced it.

Reddy tried calling Julie. Her mobile phone was switched off. Calling her fixed line, an answer phone responded. He left no message. He was not at all surprised by her decision; he had more or less seen this coming. He ought to talk to her. On the other hand, more time to think it through appealed. A voice whispered that his liberty was more valuable.

He sent Pandit Singh an sms to confirm the squash game for Wednesday morning.

Unwilling to mope about Julie, Reddy elected to prepare his meeting with Bernstein at lunchtime by reviewing his dossier on the Ipswich & Blackwater Bank. That might freshen up his thinking and raise new questions to the ones he currently had.

He decided first to put on some background music. From his trusted collection of CDs stacked in multiple black metal racks - he was not an early adopter of computer-based music - he selected Bill Evan's album 'You Must Believe in Springtime' and pressed 'play' on the CD player.

He then went into the spare bedroom which served as his office, and in which he had mounted speakers high up on two opposite walls. Opening his leather briefcase, he took out a file containing his typed notes plus other documents he had acquired in the course of his investigation and placed them on the table next to his laptop computer. Among the other documents were copies of the recent published accounts of the Ipswich & Blackwater Bank, the Celtic & European Banking Group; as well as those of Redwood Country Homes, the firm that Simon Farley had been working for until recently as a subcontractor. Finally, there was a broker's research report on Dominion Properties plc, a Footsie 100 company that had the largest single share stake in RCH.

From the pile of materials, Reddy picked up his own typed notes about the Ipswich & Blackwater that he had written on Thursday. Amongst them was a short descriptive history of the Bank's main phases of evolution. From its formation in the 1850s as a local building society making loans to Ipswich's artisans and skilled workers to buy their homes, it had grown steadily and expanded to have branches throughout East Anglia and the East Midlands. In 2001 it had demutualised and become a bank. Then in 2003 the Celtic and European Banking Group had taken a 20% share stake and put in place their preferred CEO from Dublin, Thomas Cartwright. He had executed a strategy for accelerated growth and profitability. By the end of 2008 the branch network had grown to 450, and assets under management were £ 185 billion.

Reddy recalled the interview with Cartwright earlier in the week. It had taken place at the Bank's modern Head Office on the outskirts of

Ipswich. His motive for requesting an interview was his assessment that all was not well at the bank. Since the 2008 banking crisis broke, during which major banks had been bailed out by the Government, there were new questions being asked in public about the solvency, business models and regulation of the sector.

His transcript of the interview was in his hand. Scanning the document, Reddy reminded himself of the Kremlin-speak the man had employed to answer his most edgy questions. The take away from the interview though, for Reddy, was simple. The growth strategy that Cartwright had executed since 2006 had started coming apart by 2008, as the US sub prime crisis and subsequent implosion of the world's financial markets had occurred. The result was a fall off in net deposits, increasing delinquency of mortgage loans and commercial property loans, and a decline in lending in all segments. Added to which, it appeared that these negative trends were intensifying, and now exacerbated by possible losses arising from the bank's new proprietary trading unit.

Reddy was convinced that there was more trouble coming for the banking sector. Confidence in banking and bankers had taken a palpable hit. Underlying that lack of confidence were high and rising indebtedness. Banks were wary of each other because there was no transparent way of knowing if their ability to repay loans was well-founded. This was creating systemic risks given the interconnected nature of the banking industry, not only in the UK but internationally. Reddy's investigation was on the look out for more 'unexpected' surprises amongst the banks. That was potential 'scoop' material he expected to uncover from a detailed investigation of the IB&B.

During the interview with Reddy, Cartwright had played his leadership role to perfection, conducting the interview in the Boardroom. He exuded authority, balmed by charm and quiet confidence. Clearly, he was at ease handling questions from a finance journalist at one of the national dailies. Yet, between the lines of his narrative, it was possible to discern fractures in the veneer. On reflection though, after re-reading his interview transcript, Reddy perceived that he had not pressed Cartwright with sufficiently penetrating questions to expose structural flaws.

Reddy concluded that the way forwards in his investigation had two axes. First, he needed to come up with firmer evidence of the Bank's insolvency risks. To achieve that he would dig deeper into the financial and commercial details of the Bank's own operations. Its' dealings with Redwoods Country Homes was his starting point, as a proxy for the Bank's exposure into higher risk lending. Second, he would explore the Bank's links with the Celtic and European Banking Group. Being both the single largest shareholder of the Ipswich & Blackwater, as well as six times larger in terms of assets, it ought to bring into tangible relief the hot questions of systemic risk and 'too big to fail' that the regulators, government and policy gurus were grappling with.

Given the wealth of documentation he already had accumulated about these, more forensic analysis could yield greater insight into the dynamics of the IB&B's financial health. However, what he really needed to bring the whole story to life, was some account of what was actually going on inside the bank itself. That would require finding either a courageous 'whistleblower' or obtaining more confidential information. He hoped that he had recently found such a source in the person of Natasha Medvedev, a young woman who had already furnished him with some insights into the IB&B that he had used in the article published in the Daily Courier on Friday.

He looked at his watch. It was already 11.28, time to depart for his lunch appointment. Reddy opened his briefcase to return the various documents but they were blocked from falling fully into place. Opening wide the briefcase, he discovered a small plastic object jammed at the bottom. It was a press pass to next Monday's "UK Banking in Crisis" Conference in London. He smiled to himself, having forgotten that he had already received this pass before the contretemps with Cavendish. An unexpected windfall then ! He would attend the Conference. Samantha Cavendish may not want him to interview the Minister, but the press pass was valid so there was nothing to stop him going there. Perhaps even to have an informal conversation with him anyway ?

In his bedroom he threw a few clean clothes and shaving kit into a bag ready for his overnight stay at Simon Farley's parents' house near Manningtree. Collecting his car keys and Burberry's coat, he headed out of his apartment to the lift and the ground floor residents' parking to drive his car to the meeting with Edmund Burleigh.

Finding that press pass had summoned a new sense of purpose.

CHAPTER FIVE

12.05 Saturday 14th March 2009. Constable Country Club, south of Hadleigh

The Constable Country Club was for members and guests only. It had an enviable reputation for providing traditional East Anglian hospitality, comfort and service in a tranquil sylvan setting. Its long membership waiting list paid testament to its desirability as an exclusive social venue, imbued with understated class and authenticity.

The Club was hidden in its own grounds of twelve acres off the B1070. The Clubhouse occupied a converted half-timbered farmhouse dating back to the early 17th century, which was Grade II Listed. Surrounding the main building were a number of other farm outbuildings, each of which had been variously but tastefully transformed. There was an indoor swimming pool, a wellness spa and library cum reading room. At the back of these buildings were 4 clay-surfaced tennis courts, gravelled car parking spaces and a wide expanse of well tended lawn giving way eventually to woods.

Reddy had arrived punctually, but more by luck than judgement. Although he had been here before as a guest of Burleigh's, on that occasion it had been Burleigh who had driven and as a passenger Reddy hadn't paid attention to the precise turnings.

He parked his Mondeo next to a sleek silver-metalled Jaguar SJ6. Then he walked along a paved footpath around to the main entrance. Opening the thick oak door, he had to duck slightly as he went inside to avoid cracking his head on the overhead timber beam.

The old farmhouse's traditional interior was still intact. There were oak-panelled walls and low timbered ceilings throughout. In the main corridors the walls were decorated with leather workhorse harnesses and brass horseshoes, as well as occasional oil paintings of pastoral scenes reminiscent of the Constable period that gave the Club its name.

At the reception, he announced himself to a delightfully attractive black-haired young woman whose accent betrayed the soft cadences of a Spanish origin. She informed Reddy that Mr. Burleigh had not yet arrived but he was welcome to make his way to the bar and wait.

Taking the direction described, he found the main bar off to the left of a long corridor. It was well-appointed with leather armchairs grouped around low tables, oak-panelled walls, and fitted lighting softly illuminating wall-mounted etchings and period lithographs. Thick carpets and a low half-timbered ceiling helped further to make the ensemble cosy and intimate.

At the bar Reddy ordered a tomato juice with a generous addition of Worcester sauce. While awaiting his drink, he cast an appreciative eye around the bar lounge. He identified a well-know Turner painting of Venice and some excellent seascapes and marine compositions. Lastly, a replica of a portrait of Cardinal Thomas Wolsey, possibly Suffolk's greatest son, hung on the wall to the right of the doorway into the bar. The portrait had Wolsey dressed in imposing Cardinal's scarlet robes, while looking indomitably askance at the viewer. Wolsey, in his time, had reached the pinnacle of both religious and political power in England, managing meticulously the affairs of state of Henry VIII and keeping the Church under control. Who was today's equivalent of Cardinal Wolsey in Britain, Reddy mused ?

The half-formed thoughts evaporated as his drink arrived. He paid and looked around the room for somewhere to sit. The bar lounge was as yet sparsely populated. He spotted a couple of upholstered leather armchairs across the room besides the period paned glass windows. They afforded privacy so he went and sat there. Looking out the windows over the tended lawn he could observe the entrance road and so watch for the arrival of his friend.

But with no immediate sign of Burleigh's arrival, Reddy's thoughts turned to the man himself. Edmund Burleigh had been a close friend of Reddy's father – Ralph - when the latter was alive. They had studied law together in London in the nineteen sixties. Ralph Reddy then returned to Ipswich to raise a family, and joined the Ipswich branch of a major legal practice. Burleigh remained in London, specialising in commercial law and based in the City with Toze McNulty & Tully, with whom eventually he became a partner. In 1998 when he was fifty five, Burleigh abruptly decided that he had had enough of the London legal scene. That decision came only two months after a stressful separation from his wife who, after eighteen years childless marriage, took off with a French businessman ten years' her cadet. Chastened and seeking fresh impetus to life, Burleigh convinced Ralph Reddy to set up a new legal partnership and practice together. Ralph's initial reticence to leave a tried and trusted employer was quickly worn down once Burleigh revealed his idea to settle in Ipswich, Ralph Reddy's home town.

Reddy's father met an untimely death from cancer at the age of 62, some five years ago. Burleigh had continued to operate the legal practice, with some major commercial customers benefiting from his commercial law specialisation. He brought in new and younger people, adding a highly successful notary business handling conveyancing work. This proved to be a buoyant source of additional revenue.

Since Ralph's death, Craig Reddy had kept in close touch with Burleigh. He provided Reddy with a willing ear; listening to his periodic professional troubles. Reddy appreciated his composed, avuncular style and had enormous respect for his intellectual strengths and professional integrity. Burleigh was a master of wise counsel.

On a lighter note, they had in common an abiding passion for Ipswich Town Football Club. Both were season ticket holders; the difference being that Reddy preferred the lively North Stand whereas Burleigh was with the older crowd in the Cobbold stand. Like all avid fans, their exchanges of views on their team's performances provided an inexhaustible source of diversionary entertainment. Especially, as the gods of misfortune invariably visited disappointment on their team's talent-challenged players. Their most combustible debate presently was whether or not the manager should keep his job if the team did not make the end of season play-offs. Reddy smiled to himself at the memory of their last excursion on that subject.

Glancing out the window, there were several cars arriving for lunch but Burleigh's did not appear to be among them. Sipping his tomato juice, Reddy reflected on his investigation into the Ipswich & Blackwater. Would Burleigh be able to offer assistance ? Burleigh's conveyancing specialists often handled large land transactions deals, not just house properties. Burleigh also had plentiful contacts amongst auctioneers and liquidators. Reddy speculated that, in the current downturn in the property market, Burleigh would be involved in the murky world of selling off distressed assets. He wanted to ask him about this. In particular, he was keen to discover if Burleigh or people at his practice had had any dealings either with the Ipswich & Blackwater or Redwood Country Homes. Reddy suspected that the relationship between the bank and the house builder was more than just a standard one between creditor and borrow, but currently he had only circumstantial evidence. He suspected too that there was something less than transparent in the way that RCH succeeded in gobbling up distressed land assets in the region.

"Aha, there you are Craig !"

Reddy turned his head away from the window. Edmund Burleigh was standing directly next to him with an affable smile, hand extended to shake his in greeting. Reddy rose from the armchair, and shook his hand welcomingly.

"I must apologise for being late. However I wanted you to meet my good friend here who I went to collect before coming on to the Club. May I introduce you to Mitchell Havering? Mitchell, this is a close family friend of many years' standing, Craig Reddy."

Havering extended his hand. "A pleasure to meet you Mr. Reddy. I understand you are at the Daily Courier ?"

"Yes, that's correct. I write articles for the business section. Please call me Craig".

As he shook hands with Havering, Reddy felt confused and disconcerted. He had had no forewarning of someone else joining his meeting with Edmund. Given the private and confidential nature of their intended topic of discussion, the presence of a third party was undesirable so far as Reddy was concerned.

Discerning Reddy's ambivalence Burleigh said "Don't worry, my boy, there's method in my madness. Mitchell is here for a very good reason. You'll see in a moment. But first of all, let's get ourselves some drinks and move next door into the snooker room. There's usually no one in there at this time of day. We can have complete privacy."

Havering offered to go to the bar and buy drinks, then join them. Having given their orders, Reddy and Burleigh strolled out of the bar together down the corridor and into the snooker room on the right. There was indeed no one else there. Two full size snooker tables filled most of the room, both completely covered with protective cloths. Attached to the far wall were two wooden scoring charts and in one corner a row of metal clips which held upright a number of snooker cues. Daylight entered from three large windows offering views out to the tennis courts and lawns. The room's walls were oak panelled. A traditional wood and coal-burning fireplace decorated with coloured tile surround occupied the centre of the interior wall. Around it in a half circle were placed four high-backed wine red leather chairs, each accompanied by a small wooden side table. The two men headed for these and sat down.

Reddy pounced somewhat abruptly: "Edmund, what about the 'scoop' you've been tantalising me with ? Can we talk about it now before Havering returns ? By the way, why did you bring him along ?"

"Patience, patience" Burleigh intoned soothingly. "Let me put you in the picture about Mitchell."

Quietly and assuredly, Burleigh proceeded to recount to Reddy a few germane facts. Mitchell Havering was the local Tory party constituency chairman. In his late 60s, he was about the same age as Burleigh. After many years of running an effective and successful Constituency organisation, he became fed up with the persistent interference of the new regime running Tory Party headquarters. He had no faith in the new party leader either. For many years he had been managing director of a major insurance company. He was still a non-executive member of the Pensions Committee of the County Council as well as a non-executive director of the American Internation Investment Bank, a US investment bank with European headquarters in London. Naturally too, he was one of the oldest members of the Constable Country Club. In short, he had not only clout and widespread influence in the area; he was disaffected and looking to cause political damage. So too was his brother, Neill Havering.

"You mean Havering the MP ?" Reddy queried, his curiosity now piqued.

"None other. MP for Amersham, and one of the most senior backbenchers in the House. Also on the Tories' 1922 Committee. Used to be a Queen's Counsel at the Inns of Court."

"So the brothers are in league to mount a coup of some kind ? Are they the players behind your 'scoop" ?"

"Coup no; scoop yes. And that's why Mitchell is here. He's better-placed than I to put you in the picture." Burleigh explained.

The door to the snooker room half-opened and Havering walked in holding drinks on a tray purloined at the bar. Reddy observed him carefully as he advanced towards them. Tall; still with a good head of grey hair for his age, Havering was of strong build. His facial features were pronounced: a long nose, firm mouth and tufty eyebrows sheltering big brown eyes. His posture was upright, his demeanour confidently outward-going. The sort of person who, on entering a crowded room, would quickly act as a gravitational pull.

Mitchell first invited Burleigh to take from the tray the glass of white wine he had requested , then turned and offered a tomato juice for Craig. He placed his own half pint of beer on the table, put the tray on the floor, and eased down in the armchair next to Reddy.

"Mitchell, I was just giving Craig some background intelligence on you and your brother while we were waiting" said Burleigh. "So I've whetted his appetite but left the scoop story entirely for you."

"Thanks Edmund. Cheers, good health gentlemen !" Havering toasted, and took a gulp of the local brew. "I still drink our own home grown product" he enthused, referring to the beer which came from a major brewing firm headquartered in the county.

He then turned his body around towards Reddy, giving him a firm regard from under his bushy eyebrows. Having claimed his undivided attention he began:

"Craig, the terms 'scandal' and 'crisis' are pretty much common currency in the UK these days. What with MPs' outrageous expenses, bankers' avaricious excesses, and bank bail-outs at the public's cost. So on a Richter scale of one to nine, what I have here is not going to cause a tsunami. Not yet at any rate. But it is seismic in its potential. By the way, did Edmund mention to you that my brother Neill is Tory MP for Amersham ?"

"Yes, he did" Reddy affirmed.

"Well then. Neill sits on the House of Commons Select Committee for Home Affairs. In that capacity he and his Committee colleagues have the right to enquire into many UK public institutions. Unsurprisingly too, he has even more access 'off the record' to informal sources from such institutions.

Neill and other older heads in the Tory Party are concerned about public expenditure growth. As the economic environment deteriorates, it is rapidly becoming unsustainable and risky. The government's credibility to pay its debts could become a big issue soon with the markets. The total public debt has increased significantly under this Brown government. That is the big issue that we on the right of the party think is the key differentiator in the national political debate. We think that we Tories can defeat the government at the next election if we get back to sound money policies and prudent levels of public spending. We are building a campaign to win the hearts and minds of the electorate with that single strategic aim in mind."

"'The best laid plans of mice and men…. ?" Reddy offered aphoristically. "Mr. Havering, what is the scoop please ? I'm a journalist not a politician."

Hearing the sarcasm, Havering reflected that the younger generation were destined to repeat the mistakes of the past due to their poor appreciation of history, but kept the thought submerged.

"Here's the scoop, Craig." he announced, raising his voice momentarily.

"Accessing one of his 'informal' sources, Neill has fortuitously stumbled upon a relevant story. It could provide the first step to raise public awareness of the problem in a direct and practical manner. The story in question is likely to have negative consequences across the country for local authorities' spending and is intimately linked to the crisis in the banking industry.

However Neill himself cannot be at the centre of the breaking news. That would compromise his sources and his own role. Which is hopefully where you come in as a standard bearer of the Fourth Estate. I'm offering you this 'scoop' story because you are one of a handful of genuine investigative journalists still operating on the national dailies. By the way, one who has quiet respect among my brother's colleagues in Westminster."

Reddy had been listening carefully to Havering's exposition. Like most people accustomed to the cut and thrust of political life and arguments, Havering possessed the art to convince. Reddy was unsure though to what extent he was divulging the true motives for this project.   Even if he was, did Reddy want to be the packhorse carrying this faction's political campaign to the media market place ?

"Mr Havering, before you get to the details, let me say I'm flattered that you and your brother have identified me as someone who you think could accomplish this task. On the other hand, let me be frank with you. My reputation as an investigative journalist is built on protecting my sources and also on demonstrable integrity and truthfulness in the quality of my reporting. The two form an inseparable whole. I do not compromise either.

What that means in practice is I am happy to examine the details of what you and your brother have to disclose. However, if I am to write about them, that will be my decision. Additionally, the content will be verified for accuracy before publication. Those are my immutable conditions for any cooperation with you. By the way, I would be saying the same to others, so please don't take it personally."

Havering's demeanour was unchanged by Reddy's intervention. He remained straight-backed and alert; his eyes fixed carefully on Reddy like an eagle watching its prey.

"I would expect nothing less from a reputable investigative journalist" he avowed. "Your conviction to apply rigorous standards simply underwrites the reason why my brother and I agreed that you are our first address to call for this opportunity. The fact too that you are an old friend of Edmund here reinforces the confidence that we have in your integrity."

Reddy was unsure to what extent this praise was flattery. Nevertheless, he decided he would give Havering the benefit of the doubt. He said:

"If you accept my conditions, then let's continue."

"Good, yes. Let me explain. There is a report by the Audit Commission pending publication within the next couple of weeks which will be highlighting irresponsible financial management by many Local Authorities. The Commission has uncovered that many Authorities across the country have been putting their cash funds into foreign banks to earn higher interest. The problem is that these included banks that went bust in Iceland and Ireland. My brother's 'source' is close to the situation and has made a copy of the final draft of the report available to him.

Substantial sums of money, possibly as much as £ 500 million, have therefore been lost. My brother and I are firmly of the opinion that "leaking" this news anonymously now is in the public interest. We want to ensure that the facts are published in one of the national dailies before the Commission publishes the report. That way the government is unable to bury bad news during the forthcoming G20 Summit in London."

Havering paused and supped his beer, awaiting to hear Reddy's reaction.

"That definitely sounds a 'public interest' subject" Reddy affirmed. "But how big a 'scoop' it is will depend on how big the losses really are and what political capital can be gleaned from it."

"Which is why" Havering interjected "it should be brought early to the attention of the public. That way, on publication, the Commission's report is likely to obtain wider and higher profile coverage than otherwise".

"Look" he continued "we agree on anonymity of all sources. We agree too that you have *carte blanche* for the reporting of the scoop, subject to its' focus being on the losses of public monies. The publication needs to be within the next week though. Can we reach an agreement on that basis ? If so, then there is a copy of the report available for you locked in Edmund's car outside."

Reddy turned to look at Edmund who had been silent throughout these exchanges between them.

"Craig" he said "there is a local angle to this too. Word in the report is that both Stour and Blackwater Borough Councils are up to their eyeballs in trouble over this story. It is likely that their Finance chiefs will be asked to resign. As you know Stour is Labour controlled, and Blackwater Tory, so there would be no accusation of bias if you focused on those."

At that moment, across the room the door opened. A young woman member of staff dressed all in black entered the room. She crossed to where the three men were seated and gave her attention to Havering:

"Mr. Havering, your guest has arrived and is waiting you at reception. Shall I bring him through ?"

"Thank you, Cynthia" Havering replied. "No, I'll be there in a couple of minutes. Please ask him to wait." The women called Cynthia smiled, turned and departed with the instruction.

During this interruption Reddy surmised that, despite lingering doubts about how important this 'scoop' might turn out to be, on balance it was worth a shot. He might not yet trust Havering, but the fact that Edmund Burleigh had brought them together was good enough for him as a proxy to cover those doubts. On top of that, he had an intuition that this story might play in his favour in some as yet unforeseen way.

"Mr. Havering, it's a deal." he pronounced emphatically, and offered him his hand.

Havering smiled and grasped his hand in both of his.

"I'm most pleased that you have accepted, Craig. Thank you. As I said, the report is available to you in Edmund's car. Here is my business card. Please give me a call if you have any questions. And let me know of course when you will have your article published in the Courier. Please, not later than next week end."

"I'll do that" Craig said.

Showing a sprightly agility for his age, Havering sprung up from his armchair.

"Edmund, thanks to you for making this introduction possible. Now, if you will excuse me ? " he asked "I do have a business guest waiting. We have lunch booked for one o'clock. So I shall take my leave of you."

He gave Burleigh a broad grin and shook hands. They parted, Havering swivelled around briskly and was on his way to the door.

The Constable Country Club's restaurant was excellent for two reasons: the quality of the cuisine and the ambience.

The dining room was beautifully appointed. The traditional half-timbered beam walls were hung with paintings depicting a variety of maritime scenes, including one by Turner as well as a magnificent portrait of Admiral Lord Nelson. In the middle of the exterior wall were two sets of double French doors which opened onto a broad paved patio and then the manicured lawns beyond. At this time of year, although closed, they afforded plenty of natural light into the restaurant. The round dining tables were all perfectly set with high quality cutlery, table cloths and delicate snowdrops in small crystal cut glass.

Burleigh and Reddy were seated opposite one another at a table in the far corner with a window. Burleigh had already enjoyed an excellent *sole meuniére* with fresh green beans and potatoes, all steamed, with a sauce hollandaise. Reddy had let his head be ruled by his stomach and indulged himself with a *roti de boeuf saignant*, roast potatoes, echalottes, parsnips and horseradish sauce.

During the main course, Burleigh had listened attentively and sympathetically to Reddy's description of his present travails at the

Courier. When Reddy finally asked him for some advice on the best course of action, Burleigh was typically forthright.

"Craig, the matter is clear; at least at the level of principle. You can't buy integrity. I think I know you well enough to understand what makes you tick. That is your independence of thought and action. You adhere to the core tenets of classic journalistic practice. If I'm right, then don't compromise those."

"You mean then that I should continue to refuse the new column being offered to me, at the risk probably of being left to rot in a corner, or even sacked ?" Reddy articulated. As a question it was indeed the thought that had been niggling him ever since Friday afternoon's calamitous meeting with Samantha Cavendish.

"No; 'it ain't necessarily so' " Burleigh sang the line from Porgy and Bess, knowing Reddy was familiar with the song.

Burleigh was aware that the additional twenty five years or so of age and experience separating he and Reddy were also an algorithm for the more nuanced analytical astuteness that an older head can often bring to resolve a problem. Burleigh could still tell black from white. But in deciding how to proceed in practice, he knew *profoundly* that there were only shades of grey.

"I would recommend Craig that you play a long game. Try to find some avenues of dialogue with your boss that allow you not to say 'no' outright, but which still keep you on track in terms of what you believe is right. That may require some compromise. Including taking the column but subtly tuning it to your perspectives"

That advice had given Reddy pause for thought.

Their waitress had arrived again at their table. She was, at least so far as Reddy could tell, Polish. He marvelled at the extent to which the country had become a magnet for young people from all over Europe looking for jobs, not least from Eastern Europe. It looked as if the Club had no qualms in hiring such people eager to work, so long as their English was fit for purpose. He didn't fail to miss either that their manners and behaviour, in the round, appeared better by a considerable margin than those of many British youngsters.

Reddy held in front of him a small card on which was printed the day's menu. Above the menu was a delicate artist's sketch of the Clubhouse buildings.

The waitress stood patiently at the table holding a small notepad and biro, awaiting their orders. Reddy noted that she was left-handed, like him. Burleigh removed his metal-rimmed spectacles slowly and placed them beside him on the table.

"I'll take the fresh fruit salad" he said, looking up at the girl to check that she had registered his request.

There was panacotta amongst the listed desserts. Reddy was sorely tempted, but sensing that he had already attained alimentary sufficiency, he copied Burleigh and opted for the fruit.

With the waitress departed and no food on the table, Burleigh decided that now was a good moment to learn more about what Reddy was up to with his investigative efforts.

"So Craig, let's get to the bottom line of your current investigation. You've been examining the connections between the IB&B and housing developers regarding land deals ? Tell me what you have come up with so far. My law practice has extensive dealings with land transactions in the region. We know a fair amount about the 'who' and 'what' that goes on in the land market. Is there anything I can perhaps do or explain for you off the record ?"

Is the Pope Catholic ? Reddy thought to himself. Edmund Burleigh rarely failed to fulfil Reddy's expectations of him.

"Edmund, there may well be some information that you can assist me with in that area, yes." said Reddy. "Let me say first though that my fundamental interest is in the IB&B itself. I have concerns about its' solvency. You know, these days the bank is no longer the staid demutualised retail bank that it was a few years ago. Its growth these days is fuelled by all manner of financially leveraged products. They even have a proprietary trading desk."

Burleigh raised his eyebrows and nodded his head in studied surprise. He observed: "How times change. I remember them more as the old Ipswich & Blackwater Building Society, Craig. You know, my father opened my first savings account for me with them back in the 1950s. Anyway, how then do you want to tie up the IB&B's story with that of some house builders ?"

"Simple. The Bank is going progressively into riskier and riskier lending operations in search of profits. That will have potentially negative implications for them in due course. Equally, if you look at it from the viewpoint of the law of unintended consequences, then I expect to be able to show too that massive doses of easy credit can fragilise and endanger the real economy as well."

A tolerant man, wise in the ways of man's cruelty to man, Burleigh cautioned:

"That's maybe simple to you Craig, but not self evident to others. You'll have to elaborate your story step by step if you want to take the public with you !"

"Point taken. Thanks for the advice. It's why I want to focus on a specific case. I hope that way to demonstrate clearly the argument. You know, with the collapse in the stock market and the housing market, development land prices have tumbled. Several housing developers have been bankrupted. Nevertheless, that hasn't stopped a lot of potentially developable land changing hands. Especially around here on the Suffolk and Essex borders areas where long term prospects for population growth are good."

Burleigh nodded his concurrence. Despite the downturn, land with potential for residential building was changing hands. In some cases it was distressed sales of assets or company liquidations.

"Quite right. For those with the capital to buy and the ability to hold and wait, this is a once in a lifetime opportunity to grow a sizeable land bank for future development"

Reddy enquired "One company that has particularly attracted my attention: Redwood Country Homes. They've been busy acquiring in this region. Probably you have heard of them ?"

"Surely" Burleigh responded, " During the boom years you would see their corporate logo on flags flying on many of the housing developments around the Ipswich, Colchester, and Chelmsford areas. They brought a lot of jobs for people in the building trades. They priced their new-built houses mostly at levels affordable for aspiring middle class folk. That won them a lot of friends and a good image in these parts."

"They are smart not only with their image and marketing" Reddy elaborated, "but also with their operations. They saw the housing market downturn coming in 2007 and cut back on all new housing production. They focused on selling those that were being built. That way they ran down working expenses to a minimum. Now, with land prices having taken a knock, they have been adding significantly to their land bank with astute purchases at bargain prices. Clever businessmen."

Burleigh feigned surprise at Reddy's anti-entrepreneur sentiment: "That's what the market place is about Craig. It rewards those that calculate correctly what the customer wants and when; but punishes those who fail. No 'scoop' there I'm afraid"

"I agree" Reddy conceded. The waitress returned to their table and served them their desserts, retiring discreetly from whence she came. Burleigh, spoon in hand, began to eat his fresh fruit salad.

Reddy continued: "I'm more interested in what RCH have been up to since the end of the boom. Edmund, these guys seem to have an uncanny ability to hoover up all the developable land coming onto the market. It's as if they wave a magic wand. What is also disconcerting is how they obtain the capital to fund their purchases."

Burleigh interjected, "Well, on the last point, if my memory serves me correctly, aren't they part of the Dominion Properties Group that is listed on the Footsie ? I suppose that the parent firm provides RCH with long term loans ?"

"No; not any longer." Reddy replied. "Dominion *were* the major single shareholder with twenty five per cent. The CEO of Dominion Properties is Sir Peter Westlake, father of Russell Westlake, who heads up RCH."

"Family businesses are often the best run." Burleigh suggested.

"And the least transparent" Reddy countered. "Dominion's published accounts show that they sold most of this holding on the open market during the summer of 2007. So they took profits before the stock market cratered. Now they hold only 5% of the stock."

"Not much paternal protection or filial faith there then, it would seem."

"You may be right there" Reddy replied. "But here is the really interesting fact. Having parted from his father's protection, there is a new mystery holder of nearly twenty per cent of RCH which is a nominee company. It is registered in Panama. Due to secrecy rules in Panama, it seems not possible to identify who the beneficial owners are. My suspicion is that this anonymous backer is the significant source of funding. I was wondering Edmund whether you, with your network of contacts in the City, might know how to get around this barrier in identifying the persons involved ?"

Burleigh pursed his lips in a sign of scepticism. "I'll see what I can do for you Craig, but no promises about a result. I can contact my old partners at Toze McNulty. They have specialists who deal with offshore companies and the like. They may be able to offer some insight into the regulatory environment in Panama and who to contact there."

"I'd really appreciate that" Reddy enthused.

"Closer to home, what I can tell you Craig are some facts about Redwood Country Homes that probably are unknown to you."

"Go ahead".

Burleigh continued: "My law practice has been involved in two cases of land developments being disposed of cheaply to them. Both were the result of other firms' bankruptcies and the liquidators seeking buyers for the distressed assets. They come to us to run due diligence on the land banks of these bankrupt firms – do they have proper title, are they mortgaged, and so on – before doing deals with buyers.

As a commercial law lawyer, I also get involved in drawing up contracts with potential purchasers that the liquidators choose to sell to. Of course, the liquidators' concern is to recover as much money as possible from the asset sales to pay off debtors and the like. They are not too worried about how transparent or fair the process is so long as they can proceed quickly and get the money. Curiously, Redwoods has been very quick off the mark in these cases. It invariably succeeds in being the first caller at the liquidators' door when there are developable land assets for sale."

"It all sounds a little too good to be true ? Maybe insider information ?" Reddy speculated.

"I don't know Craig. To be honest it is not something that, until now, I have given serious thought to. But their success does appear on the face of it to be more than coincidental. There is another case involving Redwoods that looks curious too."

"Is this another of your scoops Edmund ?"

"Possibly. Listen, have you heard of the proposed new residential development that is being planned to the north west of Colchester ?"

"Of course. A huge thing. Over three thousand houses plus community facilities and shops. There's some controversy though between Colchester Borough Council and the outlying local Councils isn't there ?"

"Exactly. Most of the land concerned is situated within the boundaries of Blackwater District, outside of the Borough. Yet it is the Borough Council that wants to see the expansion and is pushing for massive infrastructure investment to support it. I know the senior Tory on the District Council. It seems they now have a blocking majority on the District Planning Committee. They will use it to vote down the application before them on the grounds of deteriorated economic circumstances. They're arguing that demand for new owner occupied housing has dried up."

"If they vote it down that will bloody a few noses" said Reddy "but its surely not the end of the world ?"

"Ah, but that is where it starts to get really interesting" said Burleigh indulgently. "You see, much of the land that is under consideration for this development – around 200 acres – belongs to a young aristocrat by the name of James McAuley. James is the son of the late General Sir Robert McAuley of the Royal Anglian Regiment. James inherited the land on his father's death but by then also had a liking for cocaine. He now has a drug habit that apparently he cannot kick."

"That's sad but what does it have to do with RCH ?" asked Reddy

"McAuley already took out a mortgage on the land over nine months ago. I guess he has financial problems and figured that the site, which has been favourably promoted by the Borough Council, would be granted outline planning permission. If that happens, he would be many times richer overnight. Land prices per acre for land with outline planning permission are far higher than land without. The current market has cut prices but even so McAuley would be a very wealthy man once permission is granted."

Reddy saw now where this story headed: "So when the Planning Committee votes down the application, McAuley can kiss goodbye to his prospective fortune. Let me guess: he probably doesn't then have the means to pay back his loans ?"

"Unless his Sugar Daddy pays for him." Burleigh riposted; adding the coup de grace: "And that is none other than RCH."

"RCH are lending money to McAuley ?" This was news to Reddy.

"They have been financing McAuley's re-payments on the mortgaged land for at least the past six months, in anticipation of a positive decision on the planning permission. My sources are impeccable." Burleigh explained.

"That defies market logic" Reddy objected. "Who wants to be involved in a huge residential development right now ?"

"No one, of course. But that doesn't prevent RCH from taking on more distressed assets at bargain basement prices. They will simply buy out McAuley's land, paying only a fraction of the price once the Planning Committee reject planning permission. It then gets written into their books at perhaps only £15,000 per acre. They hold onto it for three to four years waiting for market demand to return. The Planning Committee then comes back with a reversal of its earlier decision and RCH stands to make millions on the development. "

"Nice work if you can get it" Reddy observed. "So we have RCH with deep pockets able to make handsome profits when the market is up. And then when the market is down they reap rewards of cut price land disposals by distressed competitors or others who come up short because of planning decisions."

"A little like the parable of the talents isn't it ?" Burleigh suggested mischievously. "Unto those that hath shall be given."

"Except that in RCH's case they also do it with borrowed money. Did I mention that my researches of the company's finances also threw up the fact that they have had substantial loans from the Ipswich & Blackwater Bank ? The last published accounts say over £750 million."

"Was that something you raised in your article in yesterday's Courier ?"

"No. That was focused solely on my preliminary thoughts on the Ipswich and Blackwater Bank" Reddy clarified. "My next article will bring up the subject of the wide links between the Bank and Redwoods."

The conversation between the two men started to meander. Reddy sensed that Burleigh had exhausted his interest in the topic for the time being. Both men had finished their desserts. Neither had enthusiasm for coffee so Burleigh called for the bill. As they waited, it occurred to Burleigh that they had failed to touch on their perennial favourite topic: Town.

"So what's your prediction for Town's game at Reading today Craig ? We need three points really. I can't see it myself" he professed.

"Well there's no consistency in the results is there ? We blow hot and cold from game to game. But I'll plump for a draw. Will you go to the evening game at home next Tuesday ?" he enquired.

Burleigh said he was otherwise engaged. The bill arrived and they left the restaurant together companionably. Burleigh paid the bill at reception. Once outside they walked to the parking area. Burleigh fetched from his Mercedes the report Havering had provided and handed it over to Reddy. They gave parting farewells to each other. Driving away from the Club at the wheel of his Mondeo, Reddy felt far less stressed. Good food and company had much to be said for it.

CHAPTER SIX

9.55am Sunday 15th March 2009. Home of Lord Preston, between Amersham & the Hertfordshire border

Lord Preston – aka James Sturridge – leant back in his chair, ran his hand through his wavy brown hair and frowned at the report laying open on his desk. The sun's morning rays streamed through the doubled glazed windows of his private study providing an additional source of warmth to that provided by the central heating. Raising his eyebrows quizzically, he looked over at his visitor.

Across from him, wearing an open-necked blue-checked shirt and black slacks, was his private secretary Blessing Hall. Known to all as "Wes", on account of his being a keen cricketer and having family hailing from the West Indies, Hall was seated cross-legged on the comfortable settee opposite. He had the look of a former athlete about him too, although with middle age his midriff was starting to fall prey to gravity. Open on his knees, Hall was balancing a copy of the same report that the Minister had. It's title was: "Ipswich & Blackwater Bank plc liquidity crisis: policy options and risks." It was marked "strictly confidential".

Hall had driven out earlier from his home in Chorleywood to join the Minister at his large country residence outside Amersham. Lord Preston himself had been up before 7.00am in order to read the report. It had been prepared for him by a small team of Treasury Ministry civil servants on Friday, using confidential data supplied by staff at the Bank of England and the Financial Services Authority. Matthew Lowther, the Permanent Secretary, had sent it to him encrypted on Saturday by email.

Preston and Hall were waiting to initiate a conference call at 10.00am. This would be over a secure telecommunications link with Matthew Lowther, who was working from his Whitehall office. Also expected to join the call was a senior economist from the Bank of England representing the Deputy Governor of the Bank who was himself unavailable; plus an official from the Financial Services Authority whose remit was oversight of banks' risk management models relative to their loan books.

The Treasury's report consisted of two parts. The first, analytical, part provided a summary of the financial problems afflicting the bank. The second part offered options to the Minister what steps to take.

The first part of the report said that in the retail mortgages side of the bank's business, bad loans had increased substantially in recent months and net deposits had fallen. In commercial properties' lending, loans to some major firms were rumoured to be in default. The bank's own access to borrowing on the inter-bank lending market was in difficulty. Interest rates being charged the bank were thought to be much above market rates. Mention was made too of a new proprietary trading department within the bank. Whilst small by comparison with most investment banks, the report took the view that the department's early successes had brought profits to the bank far in excess of its' relative size in revenue terms. Questions needed to be asked though about the department's governance and risk management controls. An appendix at the back of the report included a scanned copy of an article published the previous Friday morning in the Daily Courier under the by-line of a journalist Craig Reddy. This made reference to 'sources close to the regulators' admitting that there were deeper concerns about non-performing loans. The journalist speculated that the last published book value of assets of £140 billion at year end June 2008 might be worth only two thirds of that today. The article ended disconcertingly with the claim that rumours were now circulating in the markets about the bank's solvency.

Part two of the report offered three clear options for action in regards to the Ipswich & Blackwater Bank. They were available before the Minister for evaluation. It was his decision which one to prefer and advocate approval for from the Cabinet.

The first option proposed was to request the Bank of England to provide temporary lending to the Ipswich & Blackwater to assure effective liquidity. An amount of between £1,2 and £1,5 billion was thought to be necessary. Option two was for the government to bring quiet but firm pressure to bear on the main shareholder, the Celtic & European Banking Group, to take a majority stake in the Ipswich & Blackwater and then recapitalise it. The CEBG was a Dublin-originated bank which had expanded its footprint not only into the UK but across central and eastern Europe and held assets in excess of 1,000 billion euros. It was considered to have the scale and resources necessary to takeover the Ipswich & Blackwater. The third option, in line with previous government interventions in the banking sector with Northern Rock in 2007, the Halifax Bank of Scotland and Royal Bank of Scotland in 2008, was to take the bank into public ownership. However, the latter of the three options might involve triggering application of the new Banking Act.

Lord Preston and Hall had already had breakfast together. They had used the time to discuss the political situation the Government was in and the constraints that placed around the policy options. Lord Preston had himself been involved in having a new Banking Act pass onto the statute books last month, which provided new tools for managing banking institutions in danger of failing, so-called 'Special Resolution'. However, these legislative tools were still unused and awaiting further precision in the form of a Code of Conduct that had to be prepared by the Treasury and approved by Parliament. He knew that the civil servants in Whitehall were reluctant at this stage to touch this untested arsenal.

Further, both Preston and Hall were fully aware of the upcoming G20 Summit in London in a week's time. As host, the Prime Minister would want to be seen in statesmanlike form, taking a leadership role in any decisions regarding international economic policy coordination to address the ongoing financial crisis. Translated to this present situation that meant : "no cock ups" on the domestic front in the run up to the G20

With the time now at ten o'clock, and the scheduled conference call imminent, Lord Preston said: "So, we are agreed then, that on balance it should be option two ?"

By this stage, the question was merely a rhetorical one of summing up a debate that he and Hall had already parlayed before the call with the others began. In any case, the Minister didn't use Hall as his Private Secretary for any heavyweight contribution to the economic and policy debates the Minister had to grapple with. Lord Preston himself had the experience, capability and gravitas to handle those. Rather, "Wes" was there for his loyalty, scrupulous honesty, discretion and, above all, his uncanny ability to read people. Hall was a people skills guy *par excellence* and as such, worth his not inconsiderable weight in gold to Lord Preston.

"Agreed Minister." Hall replied. "If the CEBG's Board agree, then the announcement of that would send a clear signal to the markets that the Government has no intention of indefinitely bailing out the banks. Which would also be a very popular decision, I think, with the voters. Recapitalisation and clearer ownership of the Ipswich & Blackwater under the umbrella of the CEBG will bring reassurance for the markets."

Lord Preston swung around in his chair back towards his desk. He had already pushed his laptop computer to one side and placed the telephone on the middle of his desk. He dialled the Ministry special conference call number. When it rang, he responded to the automatic voice response by entering the unique ID he had received for this call.

"You'd better grab that wicker chair over there in the corner Wes and pull it up over here so we can both follow what's going on here once the conference starts."

It was already 10.02 and Matthew Lowther was ready and waiting on line from Whitehall.

"Good morning Minister, you're the first to arrive on the call. I trust you received the report and it is satisfactory as background for this meeting ?"

"Morning Matthew. Yes indeed, received thanks. Read before breakfast. Well done to your chaps for pulling this together in short order. Oh, by the way, I've got Wes Hall with me here too."

"Good morning Wes. Always happy to have you along for the ride" Lowther enthused, without evident trace of deceit in his voice.

Wes Hall, being off-screen and so out of Lowther's line of sight, caught his boss' eyes and raised his own to the ceiling as if to summon the Gods as witness to the implausibility of Lowther's blandishment. The Minister, himself onscreen and in sight of Lowther, betrayed no response.

There was noise on the line interrupting further exchanges and then: "Hello, this is Fraser Campbell from the Bank joining the call. Who is there please ?"

Lowther then took charge of ensuring that the necessary formalities and introductions were made between them all, since Lord Preston had never met Campbell. There was no sign of the representative from the FSA joining the call so Lowther got the meeting underway. As the official senior civil servant this was indeed his legitimate role, enabling the senior party to the call, the Minister, to remain above the fray until the moment of decision.

The "no show" of the FSA man provoked an acerbic comment from Preston:

"Matthew, these fellows are a law unto themselves. Unaccountable and too big by far."

"Well Minister, the FSA Board is appointed by the Chancellor as you know, but as we all saw the other week in their submission to the Treasury Select Committee, they are indeed unaccountable in how they conduct their operations."

Lowther was fully aware that Lord Preston was less than enchanted with the FSA's performance in the financial crisis – notably their lack of oversight over the Northen Rock building society which had been taken into public ownership. He also found the continuing triumvirate approach – the Treasury, the Bank of England, and the FSA - for managing the financial industries cumbersome and ineffective.

"Who is it that is supposed to be on this call ?" Preston asked

"A rising star from their Supervision Department Minister, by the name of Arthur Cornwallis. Top chap according to his boss."

"Not in my book." Preston rejoined. "Please be sure to convey my displeasure at his absence to his boss Matthew. Now, let's get down to business. Matthew, take the reins."

Lowther's exposition of the key points in the report before them all was persuasive, calm, and sure-footed. His delivery was with a firm but reasonable voice. Like a good diplomat he left open to the Minister the decision but offered significant signposts as to the pros and cons of each option. He then invited Fraser Campbell from the Bank to speak.

Campbell spoke with authority as one of the most senior economists from the Bank of England. More crucial, he confirmed that he was representing the view of the Deputy Governor himself whom he had met with briefly late on Friday to discuss the subject.

"Minister, the Bank is in a position to make temporary emergency liquidity available, if the Ipswich itself requests help or is encouraged to request it by the Government. The problem with that approach though may be a re-run of the Northern Rock experience. You may remember Minister that what happened with them was that the market and the public interpreted the BoE's provision of liquidity as a sign that the bank was bust, causing a run on their deposits."

"Yes, indeed. I remember all too clearly. We got the opposite result from what was intended. The bank's customers rushed to their local braches to withdraw their savings. We absolutely must avoid a recurrence of that mess."

Campbell continued:

"The BoE's strong view is that, in light of recent experience , both the Government and the Bank risk creating serious moral hazard if further bank bail outs are undertaken. So a condition of the Bank's intervention would be that the Ipswich & Blackwater not only repay the loan in full once its liquidity difficulties are resolved, but that there is also a premium paid in terms of the interest rate. That would signal to the market not only that the authorities have confidence in the Ipswich turning around its financial position, but also that there are real costs to banks that do not proactively and prudentially supervise their own risk exposures. Finally, we suggest any actions to assist the Ipswich & Blackwater should be accompanied by a statement from the Government that it will continue to provide guarantees for retail depositors. It might even go so far as to signal that it is not in the business of indefinitely socialising the debts of private banks. The BoE considers that the Government needs to signal to the banking industry that it must get its own house in order."

Lowther, sensing that the Bank's man was crowding out the picture, smoothly interjected himself as Campbell paused.

"Fraser if you will allow me ? Minister, just to be absolutely clear, this position of the Bank of England is contingent on an interpretation of the Ipswich & Blackwater's position indeed being one of illiquidity and not insolvency. Please be aware that the BoE and we at the Treasury are both highly concerned that apparent illiquidity issues for the Ipswich and Blackwater may be a precursor worsening rapidly into insolvency. Probably you read the article to that effect in the appendix to the report ?"

"Indeed I did", responded Lord Preston. "Troubling news if true, but how accurate is it ? I see Reddy from the Daily Courier was the journalist that wrote it. He's interviewing me next week. Has he done his homework properly, Matthew. ?"

Lowther, not unaware of the Minister's forthcoming meeting, took his cue:

"Minister, for a journalist I suppose Reddy has a good reputation for reasonably accurate reporting. Although I doubt he has access to our own impeccable sources. The article in question was buried deep in the back pages of the newspaper so it has not attracted much attention. The low profile for the article may indicate the attitude of the Courier's

Editor too. However, as our colleagues at the BoE have been able to attest through the data they have made available to us, and that we have presented in the report, there are indeed worrying signs in the Bank's latest financial indicators.

Minister, I am sure that the Government wishes at all costs to avoid another Northern Rock-style collapse. A major run of deposit withdrawals at the Ipswich & Blackwater would have a further unsettling effect that would have repercussions in both banking and political circles."

Lord Preston "heard" the inference from his civil servant that the Government's preferred line to assure a neat and quick resolution might be another nationalisation.   Similarly, he had understood that the Bank of England, although it would act to provide temporary funding to the Ipswich & Blackwater after a firm nudge from the Government, was signalling nevertheless its discontent with the Government's policy of banking bail outs. The Bank of England already had its work cut out buying Treasury bonds in the markets to bolster demand and keep yields down. Nationalising more private banks, thereby inflating the public sector's liabilities still further, could render the government itself insolvent unless the BoE printed hundreds of billions of sterling. Lord Preston knew the Governor well enough that he would never forego the basic principles of sound money, even if he was susceptible to Keynesian tinkering with effective demand.

"Gentlemen, as you all know there will be the G20 Summit held here in London in two week's time. What is essential is that the Prime Minister is fully focussed on that, without the political cost of a failed bank generating flak. We are not in a position today to know for sure whether or not the Ipswich & Blackwater is at real risk of becoming insolvent. It is also not in the government's interest at this time to bail out another bank. As Fraser aptly explained, there are already many critics arguing that we have been creating 'moral hazard' in the banking industry with these nationalisations. It's time to signal to the rest of the banking industry that it must start to take responsibility for it's risk taking. That is why I will propose to Cabinet that we act on the report's option two."

Off screen, Wes Hall gave his boss a thumbs up sign of approval.

"Matthew, that is the approach I expect to take to the Prime Minister before the Cabinet meeting on Wednesday. However, first of all I'm going to have Wes take contact confidentially on Monday with the Chairman of the Irish & European Banking Group, Declan Moroney.

Wes will explain to him my position and that I would like to hear back from him and his Board latest Tuesday morning. Wes, I need confirmation from them that this is a flier. If not, I will want to talk to him directly about this on Wednesday. "

"I'm on the case." Wes nodded affirmatively.

"Very well Minister. I hope that plays out well. Of course, should you need my assistance, please let me know." Lowther acquiesced.

"Meanwhile Gentlemen" Lord Preston added ominously, "this is strictly confidential. No leaks. I repeat: no leaks ! Thank you all for your time and efforts on this matter. Enjoy the rest of your week end"

There were unanimous murmurs of assent all round. Lord Preston and Hall heard two consecutive beep sounds as the lines went dead from the other participants.

Whitehall, London

Lowther's direct boss was the Chancellor, not Lord Preston. Sitting alone now in his Whitehall office, Lowther switched off the his desk, he smiled to himself languidly. Lord Preston, he speculated, was probably putting a noose around his own neck.

Lowther knew that the absence from the conference call of the FSA representative was significant. He had a rumour from Downing Street that the Prime Minister would want to nationalise the Ipswich & Blackwater. Arguably, nationalisation of the vulnerable banks in 2008 had prevented a meltdown. So, the 'rumour' went, the PM still saw this as the safest course of action for protecting jobs, depositors and mortgage loans, in the event that the Bank was becoming insolvent.

Lowther also knew that the task of getting the CEBG Board to agree to the Minister's preferred course of action would be fraught with complications. He picked up from his desk a photocopied article recently published on the financial pages of an Irish national daily. It's title read: "Senior bankers resign in loans scandal". While it did not mention the Celtic & European Banking Group, Lowther had good sources in Dublin civil service circles telling him that, as an Irish bank, the CEBG was possibly not untainted from improprieties.

"What a shame !" he thought with schadenfreude.

Lord Preston's home, near Amersham

Having let Wes Hall leave for home, Lord Preston turned his attention to his speech for the Conference on the Banking Crisis next Tuesday morning. A draft text had been prepared for him by the Ministry's civil servants. Now he had to tune it.

Have read through the draft, he was sensing a growing unease. The message in the speech was that the Government's policy priority was to settle markets by protecting depositors, jobs and banks. "Too big to fail" was uncritically implicit in the argument. Moral hazard was not given a mention.

"How", he asked himself "am I going to be able to make a speech like this on Tuesday while pursuing a no bail-out solution for the Ipswich & Blackwater ?"

James Sturridge – aka Lord Preston – felt a cold chill down his spine. His intuition told him that something was distinctly amiss. He was not a career politician. He had been brought into the Government because of his many years of senior experience in the financial services industry. While he was broadly sympathetic to the 'New Labour' of Blair and Brown, his business instincts were still entrepreneurial.

"Was this a set up ?" he pondered.

Chapter Seven

10.15am Sunday 15th March 2009. Summer house of Simon Farley's parents, near Manningtree, Suffolk

Simon Farley was already up and outside fixing a broken window pane at the back of the house. Earlier, he had driven to the newsagents and bought Sunday papers, one a broadsheet, the other a tabloid. When Reddy came into the kitchen having eventually woken up and dressed, the papers were left still folded on the edge of the round wooden table.

Reddy headed straight for the coffee machine which was on. In the cupboard overhead, he chose a mug depicting the Ipswich Town club insignia one side and 'Championship Play-off Final Winners 2000' on the other, and filled it with the black elixir. A strong aroma wafted up, infiltrating his nostrils as he put the cup to his lips and sipped.

Peering through the kitchen window, he saw Simon striding down the garden path to the tool shed at the far end of the property, his hands holding his denim jacket closed against the squalls of wind. Overhead, dark inky clouds scudded low across the skyline and the fruit trees and bushes around the back garden's perimeter swayed drunkenly. Reddy was not a nautical man but he surmised that the likelihood of going sailing later today in Simon's small sailing boat was scuppered by this weather.

He turned his back on the unsettled conditions outside. Sitting down at the table, he opened up The Sunday Messenger. Although a broadsheet, its Sports pages provided extensive match reports, not only of the Premiership but also the Championship games. Like millions of football fanatics the length and breadth of the country, Reddy's first reflex with the Sunday papers was to find the result for his team and read the report.

Town had won at Reading 1-0 with a spectacular scissors-kick goal from Jon Stead, but their league position was unchanged in tenth position. The three points were more than Reddy had predicted at lunch with Edmund Burleigh yesterday. Still, that did not alter his scepticism about Town's chances of reaching the play-offs. The team's performances were too inconsistent; although results like yesterday's kept hopes alive for diehard fans that the unlikely was a probability.

Reddy paused from reading further. Savouring some more coffee, he reflected that the fascination of football for true fans – those that supported a team year after year regardless of results – was to wilfully indulge in emotional rollercoasting. 'Fan' was a shortening of "fanatic". In everyday life, fanaticism is dissuaded as it invariably leads to danger. Yet in the surreal world of football it is glorified as unalloyed allegiance to dreams believed. Football was the UK's largest religion. Did football fans compensate for the mundanity of daily life through an emotional fixation to a football team ? Similar to the world's religious faithful who hang on to the dream of God in the face of relentless evidence to the contrary ?

That thought reminded Reddy of Simon's emotional outburst yesterday afternoon. Reddy had gone to meet his friend at West Bergholt FC football ground. Farley was there as a squad member of Manningtree Town FC. Reddy arrived at the ground late, so the entrance gate was unmanned and he entered freely. A dilapidated stand with rows of wooden benches filled the near-side of the ground to his left. A majority of the spectators, a couple of hundred at most, were seated there absorbed in the match. The pitch was ringed by a barrier of white-painted metal poles and a few punters were huddled here and there in small groups, using the barrier's horizontal pole as a prop. A large electronic scoreboard mounted on the front of the stand showed that the home side were ahead two nil and that the game was in its last ten minutes.

Checking the players on the field, Reddy tried to identify Simon Farley. He was not there. Casting his gaze back to the low dug outs used by the two teams' managers and substitutes, Reddy saw his friend. Wearing a dark blue track suit over his playing kit, he sat motionless on the bench, his elbows on his knees and chin cupped in his hands. The grim expression on his face spoke of frustration at not having been brought on.

The home side scored again before the match ended, their players celebrating triumphantly as they left the field to the appreciative applause of their fans.

Afterwards, Farley had showered, dressed and bid a disconsolate farewell to his team mates. He studiously ignored the team manager. Reddy was waiting in his Mondeo in the car park outside. They drove together in Reddy's car to the east side of Manningtree to stay the rest of the week end at Farley's parents' summer house. For the first ten minutes or more of their journey Simon vented his spleen for the three nil defeat on his manager's failure to use him as a substitute. Farley had always been a goal scorer and even in the twilight of his career, had the self belief that he could unsettle defenders and find the back of the net. Reddy suspected that hurt pride was at work. Not getting on the pitch when the team were in desperate need of goals was a travesty. If anger had still lingered, then Sunday with Farley was going to be a long day.

Reddy was jolted back to the present when a door banged. Then there were sounds coming from the corridor outside the kitchen and Simon Farley appeared in the kitchen. He still wore his thick working boots and blue denim jacket. His long blonde hair was tousled from the wind outside and he was rubbing his big hands to warm them.

"Ah ha. Up at last Craig. Good morning. I see you found the coffee; I left it on for you deliberately. I know you're an addict" he enthused.

He was in a big hearted and Guyarious mood; not one to let a grudge or disappointment drag him down for long. Anger at the Manningtree Town manager for not having brought him on to play, evidently was history. Reddy stopped reading the sports results and looked up at his friend.

"That was an unexpected three points for Town at Reading yesterday. Maybe we shouldn't yet write them off for the play-offs ?"

Farley responded with a dismissive shake of his head. Although he continued to pay to watch his team, he had lost hope for this season at least. He helped himself to the last of the coffee and cold toast.

"Damned if I know what caused that window pane to break, unless it was already loose" he said, ignoring Reddy's useless speculation. "I've got it fixed though. Luckily I keep spares out in the garage, just in case."

"A pity you didn't do the same for some bricks too" Reddy responded sarcastically, but with a tongue-in-cheek grin to signal that he was teasing. If Farley's current disposition was not entirely robust, better not to push its' limits.

The quid pro quo for Farley's use of this house was that he do the occasional repairs and minor improvements for his parents. The promised delivery of bricks for yesterday morning, from Dears' the local brickmakers, had not happened. Farley had explained to Dears' that he would not be present for the delivery but that they should stack the bricks out of sight from the main road as a precaution.

Immediately Reddy and Farley had arrived yesterday evening, Simon had walked around the side of the house to check for the bricks. He came stomping back to the front of the house hands on hips and frustrated that they were not there. It was too late to phone Dears' office as they closed at mid-day on Saturdays. Simon however was a close friend of the Operations manager Elvin, and so phoned him at his home. The upshot of that conversation had been that he and Reddy were due to go out to the brickworks this morning and meet Elvin to resolve the matter. Whether or not that meant working to load and unload the bricks was not clear.

"Listen, Craig the weather isn't fantastic. I don't think we can take the boat out in these conditions but I'd still like to get down to the mooring and check that she's okay. First though we need to drive over now to meet Elvin at the brickworks. I don't know what he's doing there on a Sunday morning but it was his suggestion. I'd like to get to the bottom of this story why the bricks haven't arrived. Maybe he has got a truck ready and wants us to load up."

They finished their coffees and left the house in Reddy's car. Simon directed him to drive through the centre of Manningtree and then take the A137 in the direction of Ipswich. A few kilometres later they came to a mini roundabout, followed by a long straight road past bungalows and small houses built probably in the 1930s. There was hardly any traffic.

"Its just up the road from here" Farley explained. "There's a turning off right into a lane and the brickworks is at the end."

The lane proved to be an unsurfaced and bumpy track wide enough for only one vehicle. On one side was a grill fence, on the other some well-appointed houses partly hidden behind trees and bushes. Reddy silently cursed Farley for having to bring his Mondeo down here.

The lane was straight and came to an end after about half a kilometre. Large rusty security gates were open at the entrance to the brickworks. Ahead of them a track continued up to some low buildings on the left hand side. Off to the right were other unprepossessing structures that Reddy assumed to be the brickworks. Newly-made dark red bricks were stacked at the far end of the property.

He was not quite sure what he had expected to find, as he had never before seen one, but the ensemble had the character of artisan works rather than an industrial scene. This impression was underwritten by the splendid view that spread out before them beyond the boundaries of the property. There was a huge expanse of lush green water meadows running down to the river Deben. The river was dark grey-blue, its surface serrated by the gusting wind. Cumulo nimbus clouds towered above.

A flock of birds flew in squadron formation across their line of sight as Reddy drew the car to a halt near to the first building on the left that he assumed to be the office. As he did so, the main door opened and a man stepped outside. Probably in his late fifties, he was rotund and short in stature with a chubby, jovial face. Stubble protruded from his ample chin and a bushy unkempt moustache vegetated in the space between upper lip and nose. He wore baggy corduroy trousers, a green waterproof jacket under which was a shabby pullover. An old peak cap sat jauntily on the back of his head, revealing a predominately bald pate. The cap looked like an all-weather perennial, keeping off both rain and shine whatever the season.

"That's Elvin, the guy who manages the kilns." said Farley, opening the car door and energetically getting out to greet him. Reddy followed cautiously.

"Elvin you rascal, you've let me down" Farley chided, shaking his hand. "What's happened to my delivery of bricks ?"

After a silence, in which it looked to Reddy as if Elvin might be too disinterested to respond, the man replied softly: "Like I told you son, not ready are they ? I'm not responsible for what the office staff told you on the phone. Wouldn't be the first time those youngsters have got the wrong end of the stick."

Persisting, Simon waved his hand expansively at some stacks of bricks on pallets at the other side of the property next to the perimeter fence. An open-backed lorry with mounted automatic crane was parked alongside. It too was loaded with pallets of bricks held tight by high strength wire.

"Plenty of bricks ready and waiting over there Elvin. Any chance of having my small order delivered from that lot ?" he asked.

"Not from that batch. They're a committed order for delivery tomorrow to a new housing development near Ipswich" Elvin explained. "Anyway,

63

they're not the type of bricks you need. Your folks' place was built in the 1930s."

Still baffled as to the real story why his bricks were undelivered, Farley chose to change tack.

"Elvin, let me introduce my good friend Craig. Craig, this is Elvin Brown, the man who knows everything about brick-making and a lot else besides." He grinned infectiously, as he encouraged them both to shake hands. Reddy had been admiring the view across from the brickworks.

"Pleased to meet you Elvin". Reddy shook the offered hand. He felt the hardened skin but the handshake grip applied was light. "Marvellous location to be able to work at, with nature right on your doorstep". He motioned with a broad sweep of his right arm off towards the wetlands and river Deben in the distance.

Elvin gave Reddy a wary appraisal. "You get used to it quickly enough" he said. "They don't pay you to look at the view. It's all about productivity and costs these days. Not that this place has seen any investment these past years."

Reddy had an intense interest in the immediate surroundings of the brickyard and works. It was true that the buildings all around were somewhat ramshackle and in need of maintenance. They had an air of being in terminal decline. His curiosity was piqued how big an operation they ran here. This certainly was not industrial scale production.

He sensed that Simon was in no undue hurry to sort out the mystery bricks, and wished to avoid a confrontation with Elvin. To Reddy, Elvin looked the type of character that would shut up shop and become defensive the moment he felt wrongly accused.

Reddy took the initiative: "Have you got a moment or two free ? Could you show us around Elvin ? I've never seen a brickworks in action. "

A spark of light appeared in Elvin's eyes. His taciturnity ebbed as Reddy's evident interest in the place triggered his pride in his work.

"No problem. Sunday there's no one around to complain. Better you see it now 'cos I doubt it'll still be working a year from now the way things are." Pride perhaps, but mitigated by a heavy dose of morosity.

He turned and led them away from the office towards the low-built structures opposite. They were modest timbered outbuildings, open at the sides. Approaching them, Reddy saw iron rails running along the ground from the inside away towards other nearby brick structures that he assumed were the kilns. Elvin led them inside. It was very dusty but dry.

Elvin waited for their attention, then explained: "This is where the process begins. The prepared clay comes down from above there" he said, pointing upwards to the ceiling from where a funnel was poised above a large well-worn round wooden table. "The table here rotates on its base. Two guys work here with standard moulds. As the clay descends from the funnel they mould the clay into individual bricks with the moulds. Then the bricks move automatically over to there." He pointed again. "Two more guys are busy stacking them onto those wheeled metal pallets. Then each full pallets is transported down the rails to the kilns."

The wheeled pallets reminded Reddy of trolleys used in large kitchens to pile used plates. It was basic, unadorned; but apparently effective. He marvelled that in the era of high tech it was still possible that such a simple mainly manual process could exist and be commercial in the UK.

Meantime Elvin had ambled off down the rail tracks to the kilns twenty metres away. Simon and Reddy silently followed.

Elvin stopped at the entrance to the nearest kiln. It was open, currently empty and rose to about two and a half metres in height. With both hands stuffed into the depths of his jacket pockets Elvin conveyed a calm proprietorial air.

He explained. "The bricks are first unloaded manually and stacked inside here. Then we seal up the entrance and also the roof. Once that is done the firing starts. This is kiln number one and there are four in all. The bricks get fired in these kilns."

Simon gave Reddy one of his wicked grins.

"Not the only firing that might be getting done soon, *n'est-ce pas* Craig ?" he quipped. Reddy chose not to be drawn by his friend's verbal swipe at his job predicament, opting instead for a disconsolate shrug of his shoulders. This was not the time or place to rehash the conversation the two had had last night.

"Follow me." Elvin instructed, oblivious to the meaning of the two's exchange.

He led them round to the side of kiln number one. He bent down and removed a brick from the wall just below knee level. It was loose. Reddy could see that there were several similar places along the length of this wall with just one brick loose.

"When the firing is underway, these are the places where you can check on what is happening inside." Elvin said.

A broad metal pipe ran horizontally along the length of the wall at about waist height. At regular intervals vertical pipes ran up perpendicularly from them, attached to the kiln wall. Each had a tap.

"That is the valve for turning the fuel oil supply on and off. The temperature in the kiln during the firing is kept stable at 1,200 degrees."

"It takes a couple of days to fire the bricks. Then a couple more for cooling before we can unload the bricks. And that's about it really. We get four thousand bricks fired from each kiln, and operate them in a cycle so that one is being loaded, one doing the firing, one cooling and the fourth unloaded."

"Simon, the bricks we have for you are over there in kiln number three, still cooling down. That's why they weren't delivered. There was a delay in starting the firing to Thursday evening. No way we could unload them by the week end. I reckon we'll do that on Monday afternoon or Tuesday morning. So the bricks can be delivered probably Tuesday or Wednesday. But you'll need to talk again to the staff in the office, as they're the ones running the deliveries."

"Understood Elvin. I suppose I can start work on the folks' place next week end then."

"I guess I'll miss it if they close the place." Elvin had confided to them in the car on the way down from the brickworks to Manningtree town centre. To Reddy's surprise, they had departed leaving the site's security gates wide open. "We only lock up if the kilns are firing" was Elvin's explanation to his inquiry if he was going to lock up.

They dropped Elvin off outside The White Horse Hotel where he had arranged to have a bar meal with an old friend. Simon then directed Craig to drive them eastwards along the length of Manningtree's main street and off towards the estuary where his small two berth sailboat was moored at the Yacht Club a couple of miles away.

Breaking the silence, but with the memory of Elvin's remark fresh in his mind, Farley commented:

"Elvin lives alone. His wife died a few years back, so I guess he's lonely. The job at the brickworks keeps him going. If they do close it down I don't know what he will do with himself."

"Different people live with loneliness in different ways." Reddy replied. "What seems most difficult for many is the loneliness of old age when your partner has died."

"Well I'm well and truly single at the moment Craig. Its not sexy being a guy in the building trade. Women these days only want glamour and celebrity. No commitment."

"Really ? I thought it was money and power ?" Reddy said acidly.

"That as well" Farley accepted.

 "Talking of money, it must be a stretch funding the boat, isn't it Simon ? You were fortunate being able to switch over to the work in Stratford, but times are pretty uncertain economically."

"True. But I don't have a mortgage to pay 'cos the flat in Ipswich is rental, as you know. I also paid in full for the boat while the good times were good. The bad news is I've got some other financial commitments that are getting ugly. Listen Craig. This is just between you and me, right ?"

"My lips are sealed. You know you can trust me. Nothing you say to me will go anywhere."

"The fact is that I've got additional stress from another source too. My business is suffering from financial problems. I've been running another activity on the side until recently."

"Which is ?" Reddy asked. Apprehension was welling up inside him, as he sensed that his friend was about to reveal damaging news.

"Importing timber roof trusses from the Continent into Ipswich docks and selling them on to building materials merchants and sometimes direct to housing developers."

Reddy had no clue about the commercial attractiveness or otherwise of such an initiative.

"Is there much profit to be had in that Simon ?"

"There was in the early days. The regional housing market was booming. Added to that there was a favourable exchange rate. It was cheaper to buy on the Continent and ship the roof trusses over."

"You never told me about it. How long have you been into this ?"

"It all started back in 2007. I was working on the new housing developments up in Essex. Eventually I got to know the guy who ran the firm, Redwood Country Homes. He used to come over to the sites regularly and made a point of getting to know who was doing what onsite."

Reddy's ears pricked up instantly. Again, mention of Redwood Country Homes, a firm on his radar in his investigative dossier. He decided to say nothing on this score to his friend for the time being, preferring to let him recount his story.

"He and I came to an agreement" Farley continued. "His firm committed to buying up about half of the load from each shipment. My business had to fund the rest and find buyers.

The problem Craig, was that the bottom fell out of the house building market last autumn. Yet I had contractual commitments in Antwerp to keep taking monthly supplies of roof trusses through to the end of this month. The last shipment is due next week. While the housing market was buoyant, that wasn't a problem as I could easily shift the goods. But the writing was on the wall 6 months ago. Buyers started reducing their orders. So now I've got stock lying unsold in a warehouse at Ipswich Docks. I'm bleeding money there too, paying a fortune to keep them securely stored."

"The guy at Redwoods also cut his orders ?" Reddy asked.

"Of course. He had a deal only with me, not the Antwerp supplier. He's walked away, because he had no long term deal with me, just month by month. The trade started out as a nice little earner supplementing

68

income from the building work. Now it's an albatross round my neck. I don't seem able to shift them and I have a big loan to repay."

Reddy, caught up in reflection about his friend's novice's mistakes, missed the content of Farley's last sentence. His curiosity was peaked at the same time as he was genuinely concerned that Farley might have fallen into deep water. Farley continued:

"It was Elvin that helped me get my first independent order for the roof trusses. I had a cooperation deal with Westlake. He accounted for about fifty percent of the consignment of trusses shipped from Antwerp. The rest were mine to find buyers for. Elvin still had contacts among the building materials suppliers from the days he used to work in Ipswich. Without the orders from his old contacts I don't think I would have made enough money to fund the purchase of the boat."

"Elvin is a true yeoman of England. Cut him open and there is a heart of English oak" Simon said.

Chapter Eight

13.15 Sunday 15th March 2009.   A12 eastbound, bypass around Chelmsford

There was only light traffic on the eastbound lanes of the A12 but the wind was gusting in from the north east. Fast moving dark clouds raced across the sky. Russell Westlake could feel the wind's occasional tug of resistance against the car as he drove.

He was in a black S series Mercedes. Wearing sunglasses even though it was dull, he was carefully casually dressed in expensive designer clothing. He had preferred the Mercedes, the company car, rather than his own Porsche. The latter, plus a 500cc. Kawasaki that he rode from time to time up at the Snetterton race track in Norfolk, were playthings to indulge his mania for speed.

The Mercedes however fulfilled another function entirely. It announced to those in his business network that he had prestige and money. For Russell Westlake was the CEO of Redwood Country Homes, a company that he had grown rapidly over the past three years to rank among the top five house builders in the UK. Money, and the trappings of power it brings with it, was the second great pleasure in his life.

There was a third; the one that really made the adrenalin pump through him and which was, in reality, an addiction. Westlake was compulsively attracted to risk. In all its forms.

Not understanding risks and how to manage them, can lead to serious, even fatal, trouble very quickly. Westlake had learnt about risk at an early age, while riding powerful motorbikes in competition during his late teens. Once he had broken his collarbone during a race; a painful experience that was chiselled in his memory. Competitive racing was now a thing of the past, but it had given him both his thirst for speed and a stage on which to play with risk.

He had since evolved strategies for managing risk and avoiding serious accidents. He accorded respect to risk; but refused to be mastered by it. He was a seasoned practitioner of evaluating both impacts and likelihood of risks, both in his business and his personal life. At least, that was his self belief.

In business dealings, he hid his risk taking as far as possible from others. He cultivated the persona of a smooth operator, one with the golden touch of genuine entrepreneurship. Yet the truth was different. Addiction to risk meant that, in weighing the options for a course of action, Westlake invariably chose the higher impact risks but those which he calculated would have a low incidence. After all, wasn't that what being an entrepreneur was all about ? Acting where others feared to act; but knowingly, and after having calculated the risk-reward and defining tactics for combating risks should they rear their heads ?

There was just a nagging feeling he had, a poorly defined perception that perhaps he was allowing himself to ramp up too many risk-taking adventures in parallel. Like the alcoholic who over a long period of time blindly but progressively allows himself to intensify the dosage, Westlake vaguely sensed that he might be at some tipping point in his obsessive love affair with risk.

He did not think of his risk taking in terms addiction; after all, he was a strong man and at thirty eight had energy and determination on his side. Nevertheless, he was smart enough to understand that immortality was an illusion. That very thought gave him a *frisson* of excitement. Life lived close to the edge was the only life he cared for.

Westlake loved the S series Mercedes for its teutonic precision engineering, soundlessly potent motor and immaculate interior comfort. He always drove the vehicle with due care; never exceeding speed limits, and always mindful of the rules of the road. This overt behaviour, the polar opposite of his psyche, was rational. It left him free to extemporise his wildest thoughts and risk laden actions; turning them around in his mind to savour which might yield him the fullest flavour of satisfaction.

Today's sedate drive out from London in the Merc had proved again its excellence as a fertile seedbed for germinating Westlake's prolific imagination. Time had been suspended by a constant flow of absorbing reflections on options to the subplots that populated Westlake's mental chess games.

He was on his way to visit James McAuley at the latter's hereditary home of Loxwood Hall located north west of Colchester. Westlake viewed McAuley as a useful if unreliable pawn in the game of making more money at RCH. McAuley was unreliable because he had a cocaine habit, which was a risk. However, that weakness was Westlake's opportunity. McAuley was unable to hold down a job yet needed money to finance his extravagant lifestyle and cocaine addiction. Several months ago, Westlake had enticed McAuley to take on debt by mortgaging some of the land on his inherited Estate. Not just any piece of land. Westlake had delicately manoeuvred McAuley to mortgage land that was incorporated in their joint partnership proposal to the local planning authorities to build a new private housing estate. The mortgage itself was easily arranged. Westlake leveraged his business relationship with the head of the Ipswich & Blackwater Bank to broker a deal for McAuley.

Ostensibly the loan was a means for McAuley to finance his expenditures. What Westlake calculatingly foresaw had now transpired: McAuley was behind on his loan repayments and he, Westlake, was already subsidising the repayments. Westlake having responded to his cry for financial help, McAuley wrongly assumed that his occasional visits were mercy missions.

Russell Westlake smiled to himself knowingly. He was not in the mercy business.

He turned his attention to another plot, one that was so far proving far less malleable. This was his desire to disassociate his RCH business entirely from any influence of his father Sir Peter Westlake, CEO of Dominion Properties plc. It was his father who had helped him set up RCH originally, using his position as CEO to create an associate company and installing his son as Managing Director. Dominion Properties took a 25% share stake. However, father and son being hewn from the same stone, they had clashed vehemently over the direction of the company.

Russell's independence plan was presently off course. He had schemed that a break up would be on his terms: a nominee company, owned by a Bulgarian businessman that Russell was actively cultivating business links with, had on his encouragement accumulated a 10 per cent stake in RCH. However Sir Peter, being no slouch himself at the game of corporate warfare and having fallen out with his son, had had no compunction to sell out most of Dominion's RCH shareholding at a profit before the collapse in the housing market last year.

Whether the shares had been sold to an interested party or simply on the open market was unclear, as Dominion had refused to be drawn into any public pronouncement. Sir Peter himself had avoided talking to Russell for the past six months, playing his own cards close to his chest.

Russell suspected his father of subterfuge. The problem was that the, from his perspective, untimely divestment by Dominion left RCH vulnerable to takeover. For while Russell effectively controlled 15 per cent of the company's shares, 5 per cent himself and the 10 per cent of his Bulgarian associate, the rest were out in the market. With RCH's share price severely depressed, Russell's business intuition told him predators were lurking; probably with discreet support from his father. Somehow he had to get his plan back on track, but so far he had not fathomed a clear strategy.

Was it that which frustrated him or rather the molten anger that he was unable to vent towards his father ?

Now driving north west around Colchester, he saw ahead the exit that would lead him to McAuley's home at Loxwood Hall. He eased the Mercedes left up the slip road to a small roundabout.

His smart phone, hung in a purpose-made holder below the dashboard, was ringing. Westlake looked down momentarily at the device's LCD screen to check the number. It was Elaine's private mobile. He had recently bedded her while her husband was away on business. In the marital bed at her home no less.

The memory of it infused Westlake with piratical amusement at having possessed the wife of a business associate. Perhaps hubby was again away and Elaine in need of further entertainment ? His senses tingling as this new risk opportunity seized hold of him, he accepted the call on hands free.

With deliberate recklessness, he did not wait for her to speak first.

"Hi Elaine. Did you want me ?" he asked sensuously to insinuate the *double entendre*.

The voice on the other end was distraught.

"Its Thomas" she wept, ignoring his question.

Evidently she was crying and her words were inchoate. Westlake realised immediately that there was something seriously wrong. His exultant mood vaporised.

"What's the matter ?"

"He's dead. He committed suicide."

Elaine's voice broke up again.

"That's unimaginable Elaine. I'm really sorry. If it's true, my sincere condolences." Westlake was genuinely stunned.

His fast-moving thoughts concluded that he had to put some solutions in place immediately. However, it would be better to pursue this conversation from a phone box rather than his own phone. He pulled over and stopped at the entrance to a concrete road. It led fifty metres away to an hotel of a national chain with a pub restaurant alongside. He decided to drive up and see if he could call from a phone there.

Inside the pub, a quick enquiry at the bar elicited access to a payphone located at the back in a corridor leading to the toilets. There was no one much around. He put through the call. Elaine responded almost before the phone even rang.

"Elaine, listen ! Try and calm yourself " he advised. "Are you alone ?"

She again ignored his question. "The Police were round here. They told me that Thomas committed suicide. He jumped off the Orwell Bridge around dawn this morning." She was blurring her words.

"Are you alone ?" Westlake insisted. This was treacherous territory.

"Yes. They offered a woman police constable to stay with me but I told them to go." She stammered. "Russell, I'm scared. They said that they don't know why he did it."

Westlake's mind raced through a number of possibilities why this had happened and how to manage Elaine. She was indeed scared even though she didn't know what he did about Thomas Cartwright.

"What else did the police say Elaine ?" he solicited, trying to sooth her.

"Nothing really. They thought I could tell them why he might have done it. I said I had no idea. He didn't leave any note or anything. He'd told me on Friday he was going to the airport for another business trip. They advised me to get friends in. Russell, what shall I do ?"

There was a plaintive desperation in her voice. Westlake put a tone of instruction into his voice.

"Elaine, I want you to phone your mother as soon as I hang up. Tell her what has happened and arrange for a couple of days' stay with her. Can you do that ?"

"Yes, I can" she replied, lifelessly.

He knew he had to get her to think straight and commit to everything he wanted her to do.

"Stay there until I get in touch again. Whatever you do, please don't phone me on my private mobile number. Is that agreed ?"

"OK"

"Good. Now, Elaine. I'm going to make a quiet visit to the house. You know I have some things that Thomas stored for me ? They're in the safe. I'm going to collect"

Elaine knew there was a safe, but had no idea what was in it. Mechanically, she concurred again.

"Elaine, be easy on yourself. I want to help you. You don't want to know what is in there. But if anyone found out it might cause you trouble. So please let me deal with it. Okay? I'll be in touch again as soon as its done."

They concluded the call. Westlake was concerned for Elaine. She sounded as if her actions could be unreliable. Knowing he had to act quickly, Westlake countenanced someone he thought reliable and with the expertise to do the job he needed done. Under no circumstances did Westlake himself want to be caught doing it. He placed a call to the man's mobile phone. When it answered, Westlake said:

"I've got some business that needs conducting. Can we meet this evening to arrange it ?"

The man understood discretion and avoided asking questions on the phone. They fixed a rendez vous at a pub car park outside Ipswich that they both knew.

Westlake restarted the Mercedes and headed down the short drive to the junction with the main road. He turned the vehicle right in the direction of James McAuley's mansion which was still a few kilometres away.

75

Westlake sensed that his blood pressure had risen slightly as a result of dealing with Elaine. Her husband's death would bring some unwanted complications into his business dealings. Nevertheless he needed to put this episode out of his mind for the moment and focus on his next challenge: McAuley and his 'mercy' mission.

As his thoughts returned to McAuley, Westlake observed that his attitude had been affected by the intrusion of the events with Elaine. He began to play with the idea that McAuley was an unnecessary liability. Why should he keep funding repayments of his loans to the bank ? Perhaps there is no commercial reason to have McAuley as a partner at all ? Perhaps there was a way to obtain the land RCH wanted without paying development value prices ?

Westlake smiled to himself. What was it he had been thinking earlier ? That he might be at some tipping point in his obsessive love affair with risk. He continued driving to his destination. Or was it his destiny ?

CHAPTER NINE

9.05am Monday 16th March 2009. Police HQ, Civic Drive, Ipswich

Detective Inspector Pauline Wright paced impatiently around her small office on the first floor at Police Headquarters. She was awaiting the arrival of her assistant, Detective Sergeant Adam, and had left open the office door to the corridor outside as if willing that he would appear.

Tall and lean as a lamp post, Wright cut an athletic figure; which was unsurprising given her past as a AAA County champion at fifteen hundred metres and occasional All England finalist. Although those achievements were some years past, at thirty four years of age she still kept herself highly toned as a result of a rigorous track and gym training programme, and was a regular participant, work permitting, in competitive running events across the south east of England.

She was wearing a narrow-cut dark blue trouser suit which accentuated her height and slimness. Her long straight black hair was tied back tightly at the back of her head, giving prominence to her facial profile. Unlike some of her colleagues, Wright was diligent about how she looked at work, believing that care and attention to personal presentation was integral to accomplishing the same approach to work. Anyway, it worked for her, and that was what counted.

It worked for others at HQ too. Her performance was widely, if not universally, appreciated. Her fleetness on the athletics track might have diminished marginally with age, but at work she was definitely on a fast track. She had joined the Force only seven years ago, after taking a first class degree at Sheffield University in criminal law and then completing the Police Management Academy at Hertford. Since then, she had been promoted twice already. With her boss Chief Inspector Haddock now 59 years old and expected to retire within the next two to three years, there was speculation that Wright might be his successor.

Wright walked over to the sole available window, pulled the blind aside and peered through. Outside, the sky was a monotone grey. The usual incessant traffic was passing along Civic Drive, generating a permanent low hum of background noise. The pavements were devoid of pedestrians. Police headquarters was situated in an urban landscape of depressing and unremitting ugliness.

This negative view was born of Wright's current mood, which arose because of her new assignment to a suicide case. The event had occurred yesterday. A man by the name of Thomas Cartwright had driven his car onto the Orwell Bridge soon after dawn on Sunday morning, parked it and then jumped off the bridge to his death in the river Orwell forty five metres below.

The emergency services had dealt with the case initially following a 999 call. A jogger who at the time happened to be running along the B1080 near the bridge had witnessed the tragedy and phoned it in on return to his hotel. The body had been recovered and transported to the morgue. Road transport police had organised the removal of the deceased's parked car to the Police compound for forensic inspection.

Wright had received a call on her mobile phone early Sunday afternoon from her boss. Initial police analysis of the vehicle, an Audi 6, had turned up some disquieting evidence. The investigators had brought these facts to Chief Inspector Haddock's attention. Haddock had concluded that, on balance, they warranted further investigation. He called DI Wright to allocate her the case. Mercifully, Wright had been spared the task of visiting the deceased's wife to inform her of her husband's tragic end. That unenviable task had been the responsibility of the police sergeant handling the matter yesterday.

Rain started to fall outside, spattering the window that Wright was standing at. The drops became rivulets flowing down the glass. Eventually she was spurred out of her reverie by the sound of approaching footsteps in the corridor. She straightened up and turned towards the door just in time to see Charlie Adam surge through.

A diminutive five foot seven, Adam weighed sixteen stones of pure steel. With shaven head and a thick neck poised on muscular shoulders Adam was not to be messed with. At thirty one years old he still played club rugby as a scrum forward for Ipswich. He had a physical likeness to Brian Moore the former England rugby hero. There the similarities stopped. Adam was a Scotsman from Ayrshire. Although he had moved south in search of work, he was Scottish through and through.

Marching confidently through the open door to Wright's office, he pulled up adroitly once inside. He felt a black pall of despondency settled on the room like an unwanted oil spill on a sandy beach.

Wright moved back to her desk. On it were placed a beige folder and a large transparent plastic bag containing several objects each of which was itself bagged and labelled. She had obtained these at an earlier meeting that morning with her boss. That had been the formal handover of the investigation to her, and hence these objects were now in her possession.

She retrieved and opened the folder, withdrawing a set of typed pages. These were the notes and reports prepared yesterday evening by the colleagues who had handled the initial emergency call response and subsequent analysis of evidence. In one swift movement she glided into the seat behind her desk. Picking up the opened report on the table she gave her full attention to Adam.

"OK Charlie. You've had time to read a copy of this ?"

"Yes, I have."

"Good. Let's run through the facts as reported and then brainstorm what we have. Bear in mind that Haddock will be breathing down our necks within forty eight hours. Either we come up with arguments and evidence to keep the case open or we'll have to report that no credible criminal or suspicious circumstances are in evidence.

First, as regards immediate cause of death. His lungs were filled with river water so he may have drowned. However he also suffered multiple bone fractures, including to the vertebrae, presumably due to impact with the water. That too could have been sufficient to kill him. No other apparent signs of violence to the body that could rule in possible aggression by a third party. Blood tests are still awaited but may reveal ingestion of cocaine.

Second, evidence taken from his Audi," she gestured towards the transparent plastic bag full of contents. "We have the following. A set of five keys, one of which is the car ignition key. The uses for the other four remain to be discovered. Then there is a woman's small vanity mirror, with black plastic cover and hinge. That was found lodged down the side of the front passenger's seat. Cartwright's wife has denied that it is hers. Then, several music CDs found in the glove compartment, and one in the CD player. Also in the glove compartment, a small snuff box in which has been found traces of cocaine. That's why the colleagues expect the lab to report later today that cocaine is present in his blood. Then there is a smart phone thrown on the floor of the car, driver's side. Our technical guys have already accessed the device and listed out the stored call numbers as well as last calls made and received. Those are in the report. Last but not least, amongst some road maps of England and Ireland there was also a street map of the city of Sofia. Oh, and nothing of note in the boot of the car."

"Last, we have the rudimentary details about Thomas Cartwright. He was Chief Executive Officer of the Ipswich & Blackwater Bank for the last six years. He was married, and living here in Ipswich. No children. No criminal record. No known credit history difficulties, although background checks with his credit card companies are ongoing since his cards were retrieved from the wallet found at his home yesterday."

She came to a halt with her summary and sat motionless looking expectantly at Adam.

"No suicide note either it seems." he observed.

"None found in either the car or at his home. That's not unusual in suicide cases. At least, so I understand." Wright replied.

"Trouble is, it leaves us floundering for a motive."

"Which is why I want us to brainstorm this Charlie. After all we have a married man with a good job and no apparent economic worries. Why is he so desperate that he kills himself? What is the underlying motive here and is it in any way linked to criminal activity ?"

"From the information at hand, I think we have only a few disconnected pieces of the jig saw." Adam surmised. "By the way, the report says that there was a street map of Sofia ?"

"Right. What do you know about Bulgaria Charlie ?"

"Former nasty communist country that brought down Ceauscescu to bring back democracy." Adam asserted.

"Ceauscescu was Romania, not Bulgaria" Wright chided him. "But the communist part is correct. Now Bulgaria is part of the European Union though."

She perceived that their collective ignorance of this East European country would take them nowhere in this investigation without assistance. Was it even relevant ? she mused. Adam broke into her silent thought:

"Berbatov !" he exclaimed.

"Who ?" she quizzed, nonplussed.

"Bulgaria's greatest export Paulie. Plays for Manchester United."

He grinned winsomely at his colleague, knowing that Wright had no time for football or footballers. She shot him a threatening stare.

"OK. Let's quit this Bulgaria line while we are ahead. Maybe he just went on holiday there ? Let's leave it for the moment."

"Cocaine. Is there a useful starting point with the cocaine ?" Adam suggested, trying to reignite the brainstorming. "Was he just an occasional user or did he have a dependency ? Who knows about his habit and did they use it to their advantage ? I mean, a little blackmail could wreak havoc with a CEO's life."

"Agreed, that is one area to explore, particularly if the blood test results show up positive." Wright concurred, then added: "Another avenue is the vanity mirror. If his wife is adamant that it isn't hers, who is the 'other women' ? "

"You're surely not suggesting that love lorn angst drove him to despair ?" Adam scoffed.

"Its not at all impossible" Wright countered, "if the female was making increasing demands on him."

"Sex or money ?" Adam queried brazenly.

Wright shrugged her shoulders. "Perhaps both. Throw drugs into the mix and you have a befuddled middle aged man unable to manage a demanding job and an even more demanding mistress."

"Could be. Did you notice the music that he had in the CD player was Bill Evans ?"

"Never heard of him. What does that tell you ?"

"His state of mind. Evans was himself a coke addict. If you look at the tracks on this CD – they're listed in the report – track seven is called 'Suicide is Painless'. How's that for mood music when you are about to jump off a 45 metre high bridge ?"

"I don't know. Is it the blues or something mournful like Leonard Cohen ?"

"MASH !" Adam exclaimed. "It's the theme tune to the hit TV programme MASH. Surely you must know it ?" He was incredulous that Wright might not be a paid up fan of actor Alan Alder.

Lack of recognition stared back at him from his colleague's face. He gave up and extemporised to another track:

"Paulie, if we want to get behind what was going on in this man's life then I suggest we need to find out who were the key players in it. So why don't we contact the mobile phone company and find out who owns the numbers that are stored in his mobile phone ? That might throw up some leads."

"I support that. Can I leave that task to you ?"

Adam nodded his assent. He was a team player and was keen to help Wright get this investigation on a roll.

"What I want to do right now though" she said, suddenly becoming animated and pulling open the plastic bag on her desk "is learn what these keys are for."

"Is that really top priority ?" Adam didn't see that it was.

"Yes. Look carefully at these keys, Charlie" she instructed placing them before him on his side of the desk. "What's special about those two there ?"

She was pointing at the two middle keys on the key ring which were the same type and unusual in form. Not standard door keys. Adam stood up and moved closer to the desk, then whistled through pursed lips and gave an admiring glance at Wright.

"These babies are safe deposit keys. You could be onto something. Maybe he meant to throw them out and forgot ?"

"No idea. What I do know is that safe deposit boxes are usually found in Banks. Cartwright worked at one. I think we should pay a visit ! We'll try the 'element of surprise' approach, unannounced, and see if we are welcome."

"I'll catch up with you in the parking bay, Paulie."

With her facial expression DI Wright threw him an unspoken question what he was going to do.

"I just want to get the back room lads on the case, identifying those phone numbers" he explained. "Give me two minutes".

It stopped raining during the twenty minutes' drive that took them from Police headquarters to the main office of the Ipswich & Blackwater Bank. Before leaving, Adam had instructed a colleague to put in calls to the mobile phone companies as well as British Telecom requesting they run searches on the numbers found in Cartwright's mobile phone memory.

The Ipswich & Blackwater's main office occupied a new four storey building situated on a modern commercial estate in the north western suburbs of the town. The location benefited from regular transport services which was useful for their staff, as well as attractive shopping facilities that drew in consumers needing banking services. The Bank's flagship bank branch was the main tenant of the ground floor level of the building. The other floors housed all the Bank's back office functions for its many branch bank outlets across eastern England and the Midlands.

Wright was driving an unmarked police car. While passing in front of the bank branch, she remarked a queue of customers gathering outside the main doors.

"Since when do people queue at a bank on a Monday morning ?" she pondered, looking askance at her colleague.

Adam mimed ignorance. He had no ready answer. Wright turned the car off the road to enter an underground parking in the adjacent shopping centre. They found a parking space two levels underground and then took a lift to street level. Returning back along the pavement to the Ipswich & Blackwater's building they avoided the queue outside the bank branch and found the main entrance to the Bank's Headquarters. Inside, they announced themselves to the female receptionist, showing her their police IDs.

The young woman, disconcerted and flustered by their unscheduled visit, nevertheless responded proficiently to their request to "see immediately whoever is now in charge here". After a minute on the phone explaining their presence to persons unknown she replaced the receiver.

Offering her most polite smile, she explained: "Please wear these ID badges and take the lift to the fourth floor. You will be met there by the personal assistant to the CFO who will take you to meet her. Her name is Mary Donoghue."

Having been chaperoned from the lift exit down a corridor and through security doors by a young woman named Nancy, Wright and Adam were now both seated across from Mary Donoghue in her office. They had all made their respective introductions.

Donoghue, her figure framed against the dull grey light entering through the windows behind her, remained standing behind her desk. Natural red hair, a freckled face and emerald green eyes gave her a vivid presence, accentuated by a judicious application of make up highlighting her eyes and firm cheekbones.

Wright noticed that Donoghue's eyes exhibited very quick movements, a sign perhaps of a highly active mind. She judged that, although Donoghue was not agitated, she was definitely stressed and in a hurry. Adam, on a different cognitive track, judged that she was about thirty five and a woman with impulsive appetites.

"You must excuse me" Donoghue confessed, attempting to disarm her unscheduled guests. "There are important new matters that I am having to take charge of. Dublin handed me the job of acting CEO this morning because of Mr. Cartwright's suicide."

Wright thought that this added responsibility might account for the woman's apparent stress. But she wasn't sure. In addition, she was unsure also of Donoghue's reference to Dublin even if she had an Irish name.

"We appreciate your time Mrs Donoghue" Wright began.

"Miss, not Mrs." Donoghue corrected, with a brief smile.

DS Adam took mental note of her single status but kept silent. Wright acknowledged the correction with a slight nod of her head, then pressed ahead.

"Miss Donoghue, my colleague and I have a couple of matters we need to discuss with you regarding the death of Mr Cartwright."

"Yes, of course. Naturally." Donoghue hesitated momentarily. She sat down at the chair behind her desk and crossed her legs, trying to compose herself. She said: "Mr. Cartwright committed suicide, I was told ?"

"Mr. Cartwright died yesterday morning from injuries sustained jumping off the Orwell Bridge" Wright confirmed. "We are now making enquiries into the circumstances surrounding his death. Amongst other things we want to check the pertinent aspects of Mr. Cartwright's life immediately leading up to his suicide. We would like to know what Mr. Cartwright was like at work. Was there anything erratic or unusual in his behaviour recently ?. What was he like to work for ?"

"I've worked here as Chief Finance Officer reporting directly to Thomas for just over three years. I was sent over by Dublin." Donoghue's voice had a lilting Irish accent.

The repeated reference to Dublin caused Wright to interject: "Could you explain that Dublin reference to us please Miss Donoghue ?"

"Yes, Dublin is the headquarters of the CEBG. That's the Celtic & European Banking Group. They are the major shareholders and investors in the Ipswich & Blackwater Bank. Their influence is important as regards who takes the Board-level jobs here."

She paused, waiting for a follow up question from the police. There was none, so she continued.

"As CEO, Mr. Cartwright was accountable for the performance of the Ipswich & Blackwater. Under his leadership we've experienced very successful results in recent years. I would say his management style has been firm but inclusive. He was respected and liked by most of the staff here at headquarters. He couldn't have an open door for everyone; however he did understand the business thoroughly. He was comfortable dealing with staff at all levels. I mean, he had the human touch if you like. He invested particular efforts in building working relationships with the back office management here at headquarters as well as with our branch managers."

"So everything was hunky dory ?" suggested DS Adam sceptically.

Donoghue glared at him, in rebuke.

"Every organisation has its problems Detective. We are no exception."

"So what problems do you have that might have been unsettling for your boss Miss Donoghue ?" Adam persisted, undeterred.

Donoghue ignored Adam and turned to Wright: "Do you assure me that any information I share with you is strictly confidential ?"

"It will remain confidential within the terms of this investigation, Miss Donoghue" DI Wright confirmed. "That means it is confidential so long as there is nothing unlawful."

"Then I can tell you that Mr. Cartwright and I have been monitoring closely certain trends in the performance of the Ipswich & Blackwater's business. There has been a progressive fall off in the level of net deposits over the past six months. On the retail and commercial lending side, we are also seeing a worsening in loan repayments. It's all reflective of the deteriorating economic climate. As I am sure you are both aware many households have falling real incomes and the rate of business closures is rising."

Wright asked: "How nervous was Mr. Cartwright becoming about these trends ? Could it cause difficulties eventually for the Bank's future ?"

"We have forecasts for the Bank's financial position under a number of different scenarios. If you simply extrapolate the recent trend, and do nothing to change it, then the Bank would encounter liquidity difficulties eventually" Donoghue admitted; adding hastily: "Mr. Cartwright and I were of course working hard on taking corrective measures to ensure that would not happen."

These revelations made Wright remember the scene in the street below.

"Miss Donoghue, as we arrived here we couldn't help but notice that there was a queue of people outside your branch on the ground floor. Is that a normal volume of customer traffic for a Monday morning ?"

"No it is not. As I explained to you, we are very busy this morning. The death of Mr. Cartwright has been communicated widely through the local media this morning. That and some poor sentiment expressed in one of the week end newspapers has unnerved some of our customers. Our branches this morning have been handling enquiries and offering reassurance that the Bank is solvent and our customers' deposits secure."

"Are they really ?" Adam cut in, more than a little dubious.

"Yes. After the Northern Rock failure the government did a review and one thing it has changed is to provide unambiguous depositor insurance. So the public can have confidence, even if rumours or the market try to undermine an individual bank."

"So your customers have no need to worry at all ?"

"Officer, banks operate on the basis of trust and confidence. That is why these matters that I am divulging to you must rest absolutely between us please. Deposit insurance is in place but one cannot legislate for what customers might do regardless. The last thing we need now is a run on our deposits because of baseless rumours."

"We fully appreciate that. But please can we return to my question how this affected Mr. Cartwright ?" Wright probed.

"He handled himself professionally on all matters Detective. He was profoundly committed to finding solutions to our issues." Donoghue stonewalled.

"But you say that you yourself worked closely with him recently on this sensitive topic. Surely you must have picked up on his state of mind ?"

"Look. I am not a psychologist. My function is to manage the Bank's finances efficiently and in conformity with accounting and regulatory rules. I was unaware of any particular psychological difficulty that my boss might have had. On a professional level though I know he was concerned about it."

DI Wright was unimpressed with Donoghue's dimensionless reply. She ratcheted up the pressure: "Miss Donoghue, did your relationship with Mr. Cartwright extend beyond the workplace at all ?"

"You mean did we mix socially ? Well, of course I have met his wife on occasions. Apart from that, no. Our other activities together outside the office were related to business engagements and relationships."

DS Adam was observing and listening to Donoghue. She was aware of his attention but ignored him. He sensed that she was aware too what was behind DI Wright's question.

"I understand then Miss Donoghue that your can throw no light on the matter of Mr. Cartwright's suicide. Your knowledge of him was restricted to your work with him at the Bank or for the Bank. You have no insights afforded by other means."

"None, that's correct" Donoghue was adamant.

Wright, dissatisfied but not seeing any obvious route through the woman's armour, decided it was time to raise the matter of the keys.

"In that case, may I ask you to take a look at these ?"

She withdrew from her jacket pocket the set of keys found in the suicide's car and laid them on the desk in front of Donoghue. Their presence generated no discernible reaction from her.

Wright continued: "They were found by our colleagues in Mr. Cartwright's car soon after his suicide. The two larger keys would appear to be security keys probably for safe deposit boxes. Does the Bank keep deposit safes here at headquarters ? If so, do you know if these keys might open them ?"

Donoghue quickly appraised the keys.

"We possess a strong room protected under high security here on the top floor. It is used mainly for holding overnight cash balances from the branch bank downstairs as well as emergency reserves for the branch network. All that money is held in an industrial strength safe which does not use these types of key. There are however a few safe deposit boxes, but they have nothing to do with the Ipswich & Blackwater Bank. They are used for private clients of the CEBG. That was an activity managed solely by Mr. Cartwright since he was also a Director of the CEBG. So I have no idea whether or not the keys you have there would open any safe deposit boxes in the strong room."

Wright's intuition was sending her a loud signal to persist.

"In that case, I would like to find out. Can you please authorise us access to the strong room ?" she insisted calmly.

DS Adam had the impression that Donoghue momentarily weighed refusing. Instead, she acquiesced.

"Let me phone through to our head of security. He has authority to provide physical access to the strong room, if I permit it."

Harry Keogh wore a well-tailored dark blue pin stripe suit with matching tie and blue and white striped shirt. His head was shaven and shining. Head of security at the Bank he was, he informed Wright and Adam, an ex-policeman in his early fifties. For his age he was fit, with not an ounce of visible fat. DS Adam was impressed by the man's fitness, given his age. "Still one of us" he surmised.

Keogh had collected Wright and Adam himself from Donoghue's office. He took pride in his work and was keen to use this unscheduled meeting with the police to impress them with his credentials and capability. Recognising the need for discretion, he had asked them no questions about the keys while passing through the office with them towards the strong room.

They retraced their steps down the corridor along which they had originally arrived at Donoghue's office. DI Wright this time noticed that on one of the closed doors lining the corridor was the sign "Authorised trading staff only". She asked Keogh:

"Some top secret activity in there is it ?"

"That's the prop desk guys" Keogh replied.

"Which means ?"

"They're an elite bunch of youngsters working directly for the CFO. Their sole purpose is proprietary trading. It's new at the bank. Since a couple of years. Set up by Mary. But apparently these guys make oodles of money. The rest of us have no clue how they do it. We call them the Irish Tigers, as they're all Irish and fiercely loyal to Mary."

"They're traders ? Buying and selling commodities and foreign exchange ? Stuff like that ?"

"I suppose so, yes. Look, you're really asking the wrong person. I'm security not a finance buff."

DI Wright conceded the point. She and Adam followed Keogh in silence. After turning a corner, he led the two police officers through a security door, which had required entry of a code, into a small room. It had no external windows and was unfurnished. Security cameras were positioned in two corners of the ceiling focused on a metal door in the middle of the opposite wall. A round swivel lock was set in the door. Keogh again entered a code. Slowly, with a low electrical whine, the thick heavy door automatically opened.

Ceiling lights came on automatically in the room inside. The three of them entered. It was windowless and small. Embedded in the far wall was a large safe. Along the wall to their right, there were four rows of small safe deposit boxes, about forty in all. They were fixed by sealed metal fittings, the whole bolted into the floor and wall. Each deposit box was numbered. To their left, there was a varnished wooden table and two upholstered wooden seats.

"The inner sanctum" Keogh said, waving a hand around at the security infrastructure and giving a brief, proud smile. "Not many people get to come in here."

"I assume that the bank's cash reserves are kept in that safe ?" Wright asked, indicating the large door in the far wall.

"That's correct. Access to it is restricted to authorised personnel from our security firm who transport money to and from our branches. They can only come in here once I have verified their identities and received the green light from the CFO who manages treasury operations. Of course, they are always accompanied by someone from my team."

"So the safe deposit boxes over there" Wright indicated with her right index finger, "are the ones belonging to the Celtic & European Bank?"

"Correct again. As Miss Donoghue told you, they were managed under the responsibility of Mr. Cartwright. We in Security have no copies or access to those boxes' keys. They are held exclusively by the private clients who have rented the boxes."

Wright was anxious to proceed. Once again she removed from her pocket the set of keys. Selecting the two that appeared to be safe deposit keys, she looked closely at them. One had the number eighteen stamped into it, the other had none. She handed the key set to Keogh:

"Number eighteen. Try it please" she requested.

With a hint of conspiratorial cooperation, Keogh accepted the key and paced purposefully over to the rows of safe deposit boxes and examined the numbers. Box eighteen was located near the far right end of the second row down. Angling the key to the lock, he slowly inserted it. There was no evident resistance. He turned it gently to the right. The door clicked softly ajar. Opening the front of the deposit box fully, he bent down to peer inside.

From behind him, Wright's and Adam's view of the interior was blocked by the bulk of Keogh's back. However from the movements of his arms it was evident that he was lifting something out.

Keogh slowly turned around to face the detectives. He was holding a small black velvet bag tied by a black cord woven into and around the top. From the way that the bag hung down it contained some heavy object.

"Let's take a look" Wright said, indicating to Keogh with her arm that he take the bag over to the table on the other side of the room. Keogh did so. He sat down in one of the chairs, carefully opened the top of the bag and then by holding one corner of the bottom with the tips of his thumb and forefinger gradually upended the bag. The contents fell out and spread across the small table. Keogh withdrew the empty bag from above, like some magician having succeeded with his most elaborate trick.

DS Adam blew an involuntary whistle through his front teeth. Keogh stared at the stones as if stricken and transformed. DI Wright stepped forward, delicately selected one of the stones and held it up to the ceiling lights. It sparkled. She asked Keogh:

"I suppose you don't know who this box belongs to ?"

Keogh, still sitting down but beginning to fidget in a nervous manner, looked up at her:

"No, I'm afraid I don't, and I had no knowledge of these being present."

"OK. I want you to gather them up, return them to the bag and lock the lot up again. I will sign for the key. It will remain in police possession until the owner is identified and verifies their legitimate ownership."

DS Adam, recovered from his initial surprise, had been busy counting. He said:

"Paulie, I make that about twenty five uncut diamonds !"

Chapter Ten

10.55 am Monday 16th March 2009.   Conference Centre, Euston Road. London

Reddy walked purposively up Euston Road past St Pancras station. It had stopped raining. There were glimpses of blue sky as the clouds progressively thinned out and broke up. Despite himself, he was in good humour. The week end respite from his ongoing predicament with Samantha Cavendish had produced positive results.

He had caught the nine minutes past nine train down to London Liverpool Street in order to attend the Conference for which he still had an invitation as a journalist representing the Daily Courier. Right now he didn't give two hoots about the interdict placed on his participation last Friday by Samantha. The possibility that Headquarter's bureaucratic wheels had been turned on a Friday afternoon to cancel his attendance were extremely low.

"Take a hike, Sam" he said out loud to no one in particular, provoking a stare from an oncoming pedestrian.

Although the rain had gone he persisted in wearing his Burberry's mackintosh as protection from a chill wind. In free-wheeling mood, he had time and inclination to look around at the many marvels of a metropolitan Monday morning. He was delighted to observe the exuberance of St Pancras' gothic features; its' decorative red brick walls and pinnacled slate towers recently having been cleaned and returned to their original pristine colours.

Reddy might feel purposive, but in honesty he had no precise plan of action. Would he be able to talk to Lord Preston ? Certainly not in the capacity of interviewer from the Daily Courier. That task had already been re-assigned by Samantha to Ted Collins, another Courier journalist. Nevertheless, he might steal a few minutes if the Minister was not overly chaperoned by minders and monopolised by media groupies.

Apart from the chance of getting a word with Lord Preston, Reddy was genuinely curious to have access to the presentation materials from the Conference itself. Themed as "The UK Banking Crisis: Risks and Reform", it had numerous speakers from the banking industry itself, the financial sector regulators, and some academic economists. It was due to last two days.

On the train down from Ipswich he had perused the programme. The Conference's first guest speaker, for a brief twenty minutes, was Lord Preston. He was scheduled to talk on the Government's policy for the UK banking sector in light of the recent bank bailouts. Reddy did not expect anything revelational from that. The Minister's speech no doubt was drafted by some mandarin and designed to reaffirm the official government line as cemented in the new Banking Act that had just passed through Parliament.

On the other hand, Reddy had identified a presentation from an academic on "Systemic risks in the banking sector: illiquidity or insolvency ?" , that had attracted his attention. The presentation was scheduled for the second main working session, after the lunch break.

In order to put his investigative work about the Ipswich & Blackwater Bank on a sounder footing, Reddy wanted to have a firmer grasp of the economics underpinning the policy debates. Perhaps naively, he hoped to find here at the Conference some sources of enlightenment. He did not countenance enduring two days of talk fest. Yet he might just obtain value from listening to experts like the academic making this presentation, Professor Bernstein from London University.

He turned right off of Euston Road through an iron gate into an open space situated in front of the British Library. The traffic noise from Euston Road abated. A public seating area with shrubbery spread out before him. It was devoid of occupants due to the cold and damp.

Directly in front of him was an imposing statue in bronze of a seated naked man created by the sculptor Paolozzi. Reddy read the plaque. The sculpture was in homage to Isaac Newton. The man was leaning over his knees and holding opened dividers in his left hand while with his right he held steady a piece of paper. Reddy was perplexed.

He mused about buying a coffee at "The Ultimate Taste", an outlet selling food and drinks just in front of the Conference Centre but thought better of it and headed straight for the front doors. Before diving inside, he had another excellent view of the gothic Disneyland of St Pancras station towering up behind the Conference Centre building. The sunlight played on the bright red bricks cleaned of their decades of encrusted grime.

The atmosphere inside the Centre was surprisingly quiet. The first

Conference session was already underway so most attendees were by now seated in the main auditorium. In the entrance lobby Conference workers sitting behind a row of elongated tables were available to cater for arriving participants. Large printed signs pinned to the front of each table section indicated that participants' badges were obtainable in grouped alphabetic order.

Reddy took off his mackintosh and approached the two ladies sitting behind boxes for surnames beginning R to U. With casual confidence, he smiled at the nearest young woman before him. She was idly interrogating her brightly varnished nails. He patiently waited for her to deign to give him her attention. When she did, he showed her his Daily Courier press pass and Conference invitation confirmation letter. The young woman searched deftly through the array of badges, demonstrating the usefulness of her long nails. She retrieved his name badge and handed it over, together with a copy of the Conference programme and a thin transparent plastic folder containing some of the presentations. She offered him a thin smile and directed him towards the main auditorium off to her right.

He left the entrance area and strode up the wide carpeted steps leading to the set of multiple swing doors that hid the Centre's auditorium. Quietly he pulled one door open, but then someone called from close behind him.

"Craig ! Craig Reddy. How are you ?"

Reddy didn't recognise the voice. He glanced over his shoulder. Approaching him with adroit jumps two at a time up the steps was Stanislav Cerny. An old acquaintance from the London School of Economics, Reddy hadn't seen for over five years. Cerny was smartly attired in a well fitted light grey suit, tailored white shirt and blue tie. His fair hair, receding at the temples, was neatly combed. The man looked in excellent condition.

Reddy recalled that the last time they had met, Cerny had recently left his academic post to take up a new job at a London-based US bank. He couldn't remember which one, but Cerny's work had something to do with the bank's business in central and eastern Europe.

"Stan, I should have guessed that I would meet you here. How's the world of high finance ? Are you still with that American investment bank ?"

"Craig, its great to see you again. Yes, I'm still at American International Investment Bank."

Cerny took out a leather wallet from his jacket's inside pocket, withdrew a business card and handed it to Reddy. "I'm now a senior vice president responsible for central and eastern Europe. That means I have to bring in more money and clients. By the way, I enjoy reading your articles in the Daily Courier. You have an edge in comparison with other financial journalists. I mean, you come across as a contrarian; someone not at ease with the party line. Wherever or whoever it comes from. Am I right ?"

"I'll take that as a compliment Stan. With your upbringing in communist Europe I don't doubt you know well enough both the benefits and dangers of the party line."

Stan grinned and his lean face crumpled up into a multitude of little ridges, curves and crevices.

"Working for an American company my motto now is 'Liberty and the pursuit of happiness' " he confided, with a touch of irony. "That translates with my employers as "more profits", and with my former communist clients as "more influence and leverage". It's the same thing, just different sides of the coin."

Reddy decided to exploit this unexpected meeting with Stan to his advantage. Serendipity strikes ! he said to himself. He could query Stan about the CEBG's activities in Eastern Europe.

To Stanislav he said: "I'd really appreciate it if we could have a more detailed chat Stan. There's a coffee break coming up soon. I'd like to listen first to the end of the Minister's speech. Can we hook up again after that ?"

On that understanding they parted through separate doors into the auditorium.

On entering the main auditorium, Reddy found himself at the back, behind the main audience. The place was enormous with terraced rows of seating for perhaps five hundred people and a high ceiling. All the lighting had been dimmed, except for at the far end where a carefully targeted light beam from high above shone down onto an elevated stage bathing a solitary individual who was standing behind a wooden lectern. This was Lord Preston. Behind him, on a huge white canvas, were emblazoned the title of his speech, his name and the Conference subject. The Minister was speaking.

"And so in conclusion ladies and gentlemen, let me summarise this Government's policy stance. First, we will enhance consumers' protection in the form of deposit insurance. Consumers can rest assured that their savings - up to the legally defined threshold - are not at risk. Secondly, with regards to the banks that have been taken under Government control, this is an exceptional but temporary measure. It was necessitated by the impacts of the financial crisis last year. However, as soon as the Government deems that these banks' balance sheets have been adequately cleansed, they will be returned to the private sector as responsible buyers are found; if possible, at a profit to the taxpayer. We have sought to protect bank employees' jobs but we do not envisage that the taxpayer will suffer. Third, it is not the Government's policy to provide unlimited protections to the banks. Banks must behave prudently and the Government has introduced a new Bank Act to improve regulation of the industry. Thank you ladies and gentlemen."

There was a round of polite but unenthusiastic applause from the floor. The session chairman stepped up onto the stage and shook the Minister's hand. Lord Preston stepped away from the lectern. Unpinning the tiny microphone from his lapel, he departed off the platform to join Blessing Hall. His private secretary had been waiting for him in the aisle, ready to assure his smooth transition to the next appointment, which was to be interviewed upstairs by a journalist from the Daily Courier, Tom Collins.

Cordless microphone in hand the session chairman addressed the audience: "The Minister apologies but, owing to his tight schedule, he will be unable to take questions now from the floor. Please once again, join me in thanking him for giving us his time today. Thank you Lord Preston."

This time the applause might just have registered on the Conference organiser's recording of proceedings.

"There will now be a fifteen minute interlude before the next main session begins at eleven twenty. Refreshments are being served on the first floor."

Attendees began to file out en masse from the Hall.

Alone, Reddy too joined the stream of people headed upstairs through

97

exit doors off to the left of the Hall. By the time he arrived in the refreshments area it was awash with movement and noise as people fought for access to the self service drinks and snacks.

Across the room, standing with a group of journalists around a high table, Reddy spotted Natasha Medvedev. Tall, elegant and assured she was anchored next to Adrian Cornwallis, a rising star at the Financial Services Authority, where they both worked. Cornwallis was due to give a presentation to the Conference later in the day. The FSA's Turner Review was due for publication later in the week, and Cornwallis eagerly lapped up the attention from copy-hungry news hounds.

Seeing Natasha reminded Reddy that he should have thanked her for the help she had given him with information for his article about the Ipswich and Blackwater in last Friday's Daily Courier. When they had last spoken, Natasha had advised Reddy that they to act in public as if not to know one another. She did not wish to lose her job being accused of leaking information to the press. Reddy had agreed; self-interestedly, if he were to be honest. Nevertheless, he decided to send her a text message later on anyway saying thanks.

He was curious also to ask her what her motive was in assisting him with his Ipswich and Blackwater investigation. He'd have to find an appropriate opportunity next time they met. She had shared some personal thoughts with him, notably regarding her boss, Cornwallis. He perceived her as his protégé. In reality, he was infatuated with her, she claimed. He had also convinced himself that she was attracted to him too. That wasn't at all the case. Cornwallis, she told Reddy looking him in the eyes, was an arrogant dolt.

Reddy looked across at the group of journalists and others, with Cornwallis and Medvedev apparently collegially cordial. The echo of Natasha's firm put down of Cornwallis amused him. Cornwallis looked like a strutting peacock Reddy thought.

The journalists' centre of attention was now another journalist, Guy Almond, from one of the national broadcasters. Almond had developed something of a cult status amongst the coterie of economic and financial journalists who had privileged access to the political elites. Reddy referred to him as "the nut", both because of his name and his reputation for being impervious to criticism.

Quietly drinking a coffee at the outer edge of the group, Reddy also identified Peter Houseman. Reddy suspected that his peripheral position indicate his lack of interest in the conversation. Houseman was a rare fellow professional whom he respected and enjoyed exchanging political and economic views with.

Reddy wanted to speak to Houseman. Since last week end's unexpected meeting with Neill Havering, he had been trying to fathom how to publish quickly an article about the financial investment mismanagement practices of local authorities. Using the Daily Courier under present circumstances was not an option. Houseman was an old hand at The Messenger, and a confidante of Arthur Givens, its Editor. Reddy hoped he could leverage the relationship to have his article accepted as a freelancer.

He was about to approach the court of King Almond, with a view to discreetly peeling off Houseman from the group when, looking up, he saw that Houseman himself was roused to action, hailing him from afar and already en route towards him.

"Craig, what a pleasure to see you" Houseman enthused. He had left behind him the coffee cup and offered Craig his hand to shake. In a confidential tone he continued: "Great opportunity to unburden myself from the Oracle over there." Houseman too was unimpressed by Almond.

"Morning Peter. How are you ? I wouldn't have thought that this place has much to offer you ?"

Houseman these days wrote all manner of opinion pieces, and was not tied down by his Editor to any particular focus. That liberty had been hard won after some thirty years' journalistic career. Reddy was easily fifteen years Houseman's junior. They nevertheless had a mutual respect for one another and were easy conversational partners.

"Always expect the unexpected Craig. Particularly in politics. A word out of place and you are toast. Prime Ministers, whatever their characters on entering office, all become autocrats. Wielding power is better than sex. Just when some Minister or other thinks they're on the up, they're cut down and out."

It occurred to Reddy that Houseman might not be talking in the abstract: "There's only one Minister here today Peter. Is he the object of your attentions ? Or, should I say, the Prime Minister's ?"

Houseman beamed benevolently at Reddy. "Craig, if you think that I have any access to number 10 these days you're wrong. I've not been on this lot's Christmas list since I wrote favourable reviews about Maggie back in the eighties." He chuckled, presumably at some personal Maggie Thatcher memorabilia.

To the best of Reddy's knowledge, Lord Preston was very much "onside" with the Government's work and policies. Concluding that his question was obviously off the mark he chose to raise the matter closer to his own interests.

"Listen Peter, just briefly if I may. I have a favour to ask."

"Ask away. I'll help if I can." Houseman's chuckles had induced an expansive mood.

Reddy explained. "I'm in need of an outlet urgently to publish an exposé article. I've been given privileged access to some sensitive information that will see the light of day later in an official report from the Audit Commission. I have the chance to put it into the public domain ahead of the report's publication and so obtain a scoop."

Houseman's demeanour changed visibly. He now folded his left arm across his chest, rested his right elbow upon it and began stroking his chin; all the time pinning a penetrating look at Reddy. He raised his eyebrows inquisitively.

When Reddy had finished, Houseman was silent but held his gaze a moment. Then he smiled and said:

"Well. This sounds entertaining Craig. Let me guess. First, for one reason or another, your Editor at the Courier is not enamoured of the subject matter of this supposed "scoop" and has refused publication. Second, your scoop has been garnered from some politician who in all truth probably stands to gain more from its publication than you ever will. Now tell me I'm wrong." Houseman was amused; adopting a theatrically world weary stance.

"Pretty near the mark to be honest." Reddy conceded. "Samantha Cavendish and I do not agree on some fundamentals. She's placed a roadblock in the way of my investigative journalistic work. Instead she wants to label me as a gossip columnist. Writing a bland column about the captains of industry. That's why I'm looking for an alternative outlet for this piece."

Houseman was a sympathetic listener.

"I'm aware of Samantha's ambitions. She's notorious. Her boss Monroe had better be wide awake. I wouldn't be surprised if she's after his job. Do you know her husband, Colin ? He's a junior minister at the Treasury. They make a formidable power duo. You'd better watch out Craig. She's unscrupulous and love's busting guys' balls too. So, just to help raise the temperature, yes I can help."

He smiled, just a tad too malevolently for Reddy's comfort. Then added ominously: "Far be it for me to curtail a fight to the death Craig. Let me have a word with our Editor Arthur Givens. I'm sure he'll accept to publish you on a freelance basis in the Messenger."

Reddy felt a strange vibration on his chest. He had forgotten that he had put his mobile phone on vibrate when he had first entered the auditorium. He quickly pulled the device from his inside jacket pocket and signalled to Houseman that he had to take the call.

Houseman affirmed and concluded their business: "Unless I call you, consider it done. Send me a mail later today when you want to publish." With that he melted away into the crowd.

Because of the noise in the refreshments area, Reddy retreated out onto the adjacent mezzanine overlooking the entrance lobby. He failed to recognise the calling number but pressed the accept button and placed the phone to his ear.

"Hello, Reddy speaking."

A man with a Scottish accent said: "Good morning, sir. Am I speaking to Mr. Craig Reddy ?"

"That's me, yes."

"Sir, I'm Detective Sergeant Adam, Ipswich Police."

What in hell's name is this about ? Reddy wondered, desperately running through a list of things he might have done wrong.

"Yes, is there something wrong ?"

"Sir, we are making some enquiries relating to the death of a Mr. Thomas Cartwright, who committed suicide over the week end."

Reddy absorbed the news silently. He didn't know of any suicide. The name was familiar. He had interviewed Cartwright, the IB&B CEO, only last week.

"I see, that's tragic news. But I hardly know Mr Cartwright. You think I can help you in some way officer ?" Reddy thought it best to remain diplomatically cooperative.

"That may well be so sir." Adam replied.

"I'm at a loss to know what to say." Reddy said tamely.

"Well you could help us by meeting my boss and I here at headquarters in Ipswich tomorrow to answer a few questions. I understand that you live here in Ipswich, is that correct sir ?"

"Indeed I do."

Reddy had intuited that a reply of "no" to this invitation would have been the wrong answer.

Adam was quick to seize the opportunity and close out: "In that case Mr Reddy, tomorrow morning, ten o'clock at HQ Civic Drive. I know I can count on you to be punctual. Ask for me, DS Adam. Thank you very much for your cooperation sir. Good day."

The line went dead.

Reddy exhaled. Blow me, the 'Old Bill' are sharp nowadays. Next thing you know they can be waking you up in the small hours and you disappear without trace.

Knocked off balance by the unexpected call, Reddy decided he needed a strong coffee. He went back into the coffee bar. The Conference attendees had for the most part already left the refreshments behind and descended again to the ground floor where proceedings were about to recommence. The huge space was almost empty except for the staff clearing up the empties.

Reddy wandered past a collection of dishes with curled up sandwiches to the far side of the room. Low tables covered in white cloths still sported stacked clean cups and saucers. Coffee was available self-service from huge aluminium containers. Reddy retrieved a cup and poured himself a black coffee. His mind still toying with the phone conversation, he turned around absently and just avoided pouring coffee all over a tall man's immaculate suit.

"Whoops ! I'm terribly sorry" Reddy lamented, secretly relieved that nothing untoward had in fact happened. He looked up into the face of Lord Preston.

Lord Preston, with a schoolmasterly mien, looked at him. An anxious expression evaporated from his face as he too realised that an accident had been averted. There were two other men close behind him. One Reddy knew and this depressed him. The other was a solid looking black guy, perhaps security.

"So this is where they have you hiding out Reddy" the Minister intoned. "I was expecting to be interviewed by you. Instead I got....." He stopped, looking heavenwards for inspiration.

"Ted Collins, Minister", the entity known to Reddy offered helpfully, at the same time staring dully towards his journalistic colleague.

Collins was Samantha's "on the programme" replacement for Reddy. For Reddy he was just another careerist. Not having expected to meet Lord Preston under these precise circumstances, Reddy was at a loss for some extenuating pleasantry to put himself at ease. Before he could summon up a face-saving formula, the Minister waded in.

"Listen to me Reddy. If you've been fired don't be embarrassed about it. Getting fired is just part of the training ! Its happened to me in the past. If it happens, take it in your stride. Don't lose any sleep over it."

"Its not exactly that, Minister. Rather just incidental office politics." Reddy said, recovering. He was annoyed that this worst case scenario was playing out before him, with himself as the likely victim should Collins traitorously communicate all this proceeding to Samantha Cavendish.

 "I'm sorry that I was unable to do the interview with you myself. I had a number of important issues I was hoping to query you about concerning the banking crisis and the Government's response to it."

Reddy was regaining his *sang froid*, irrespective of Collins' unfortunate presence. Inappropriate as it may be, Reddy began to hope that this spontaneous meeting with Lord Preston, although inauspicious, could turn into an impromptu interview.

Lord Preston, was not to be fooled. He effortlessly extracted himself.

"Wes, can you please give Mr Reddy here your phone number. He may want to ask a few questions."

Addressing himself again to Reddy he adopted his politician's best *noblessse oblige* graciousness. "Sorry Reddy, I have a tight schedule. I'm due in ten minutes at a Select Committee in the House of Commons. It's about bankers bonuses and why the government has done nothing. In front of the television cameras so the back benchers can grandstand. This Ministerial game is not all it's cracked up to be, you know. Bye. Another occasion will present itself, I'm sure."

He whirled away, heading for the exit stairs and the waiting chauffeur-driven Ministerial car parked outside on double yellow lines in Midland Road. He forgot to acknowledge Ted Collins before leaving.

"The name's Blessing Hall" said the presumed security guard, handing Reddy a business card. "I'm Lord Preston's private secretary. Please call me if you have any questions."

He smiled with genuine charm. Then he too pivoted around on his highly polished leather shoes and followed in his boss' wake.

Reddy was now left face t o face with Ted Collins. The man gulped down the last dregs of his coffee, unsure what to say. Putting down the cup and saucer on a nearby table, he made to depart keen to avoid any embarrassing interchanges with Reddy. Reddy said amiably:

"Hope the interview went well Ted ?"

Collins was unprepared for jaw jaw. He looked back confusedly at Reddy, unsure of his motives and aware that in work terms he was highly toxic. He jammered:

"Yeah, well, thanks. Not too bad. I'll pull something together from it. Got to go now. Bye Reddy."

Reddy, watched him traipse uncomfortably from the large room.

Alone, it occurred to him that he still hadn't talked to Stan Cerny, whom he had promised to meet during the coffee break. Using the business card that Stan had given him earlier, Reddy sent him a text message to ask if he was free. Cerny fired back an immediate affirmative reply and within a minute had come out of the main auditorium to join him.

Reddy apologised for having missed him during the coffee break. Cerny cheerfully accepted:

"No problem ! Anyway, I've been following the presentation about the main recommendations of the Turner Review on financial sector regulatory reform. Interesting, but only time tell whether or not these latest reforms are the real deal. You know, the industry is global and very dynamic. I think the regulatory authorities are always one step behind, fighting yesterday's battles."

"There are costs to more regulation too Stan. Isn't there also a more market-based solution ? If you're a failing business in industry, then you either go bankrupt or you get bought out and broken up. What's wrong with the same market logic for banks ?" Reddy challenged. "Building more and more safety nets for banks miscalculations is pure 'moral hazard', isn't it ?"

"I tend to agree, Craig. The counter argument is the one about 'systemic risk' and 'contagion', I suppose. Global interconnectedness of the large banks means that you can't protect counter parties. If one bank goes down it can take others with it."

"That's a politician's argument for interventionism. I think it simply needs standing on its' head. Individual banks should be prudentially managed which means understanding risk. Amongst other things, from counter parties. The problem is that you have a dozen or so colossus banks who are all buyers and sellers of derivatives products to one another. Its casino banking. Let banking go back to first principles. They're all drastically over leveraged. Let them put their own house in order, that's the view I'm steadily coming to myself. Let the buck stop where the accountability lies."

"It sounds to me as if you've been doing some homework" Cerny chuckled.

"I rest my case, Stan. Go back to first principles !" Reddy concluded, with prosecutorial gusto.

Reddy now changed tack. He wanted to pick Stan's brains. Tentatively, he asked:

"Stan as you're working at a major international, would you indulge me a little ? It's for my current investigation into the Ipswich and Blackwater Bank. They look to me as if they're in financial difficulties."

Cerny was gregarious: "Sure, Craig. Anything to help an old buddy."

"I need help to identify the beneficial owners of a Panama-registered nominee company. It's a secretive investor in the shares of Redwoods Country Homes, the big private house builder ? You may have heard of them ? I'm looking into Redwoods' links with the Ipswich and Blackwater, who've been extending them substantial amounts of credit. This Panamanian company has been on a spending spree over the past few months buying up Redwoods' stock at dirt cheap prices."

"That might be a smart move. Some stock market forecasters are saying that the worst of the crisis is now behind us. I'm not sure Craig if I can get a result for you, it's a difficult request. I'll see what can be done. Maybe I can get one of the trading desk staff to run a search on the share trading patterns of Redwoods, using our Reuters service. If he finds regular buying by the same broker, perhaps we can shed light on who is the end purchaser ? It's a long shot though."

"Anything you can find would be greatly appreciated. Thanks. One other thing. This is also for my investigation. I'm sure you know the Celtic and European Banking Group ? They're one of your bank's competitors in the region aren't they ? I'm interested in their activities there."

"Yes, they're huge. Been expanding big time into mortgage lending and commercial property lending. Very aggressive. Operations in places like Poland, Czech Republic, Romania. Bulgaria."

introduces Reddy to Prof. Bernstein. They exchange observations on the crisis and Reddy ask for a meeting with him to discuss in more detail.

"Could we have an extended discussion about them some time soon ? There's not time for that now I know. But I'd appreciate your insider's view. I'm working on the activities of one of the CEGB's Directors. Thomas Cartwright. He was in the news at the week end ? He unaccountably committed suicide."

"It's tough at the top" Cerny lamented, melodramatically.

"He was also running the CEGB's activities out of their Vienna office ? It has a business footprint covering eastern Europe."

"Sure, I'm aware of them. Not in granular detail, but if you want to talk just get in touch."

With that, they closed out their conversation and left the mezzanine, returning together to the auditorium hall to listen to the end of the presentation that Cerny had left earlier. Reddy's mobile phone rang as they approached the auditorium's entrance doors. He signalled Cerny his desire to take the call. Cerny waved a goodbye at him and disappeared through the swing doors.

"Hi Craig, it's me again". It was Peter Houseman's voice.

"Yes Peter. Is there a difficulty with Arthur accepting the article ?"

Houseman had said he would call if that were the case.

"Not at all. On the contrary, he likes red meat. He says if you want war with your boss he's happy to assist you with the materiel ! No, I forgot a couple of points before we terminated our chat. First, just in case you're not aware. This is important given what you want to write about. Did you know that Samantha's husband's area of responsibility at the Treasury is for local authority finance ?. Like I said, those two are a formidable team. I wanted you to know."

"I wasn't aware of that Peter, thanks. So I can expect pushback. What's the other point ?"

"You failed to elaborate on your investigation's source. Or is that hush hush ?"

"Sorry Peter. It's hush, hush."

Chapter Eleven

10.15am Tuesday 17th March 2009, local time. Patisserie, Kaletski Hotel, Lozenets, Sofia, Bulgaria.

Radomir Angelov had completed his regular morning work out in the fitness centre located at the back of the Kaletski Hotel. He was feeling vibrantly alive, quietly satisfied with his work out. Gently, he pushed open the glass door partitioning the inside of the hotel with the adjoining patisserie that faced out onto the street. The patisserie was almost devoid of customers; most locals could not afford the prices. Angelov discreetly surveyed the interior.

Seated languorously at a table in the opposite corner awaiting his arrival, and radiant in the sunlight that bathed through the external windows, was his favoured mistress. She sported Gucci sunglasses, long straight black hair tied in a pony tail; a tight-fitting décolleté white body stocking topped with an elegant diamond necklace and matching diamond earrings; hipster white satin drainpipe trousers, and Ferrari red high-heeled Italian shoes. To match the shoes, her leather handbag, thin trouser belt, lipstick and manicured nails were flaming red. She was so ice cool she could make a man's blood boil. Angelov called her Lolita, because she was his audacious and dedicated sex kitten in the bedroom. She was twenty six, Russian, and her real name Anastasia.

Angelov was himself fifty two years old, but felt more like forty. He kept himself fit and healthy as a matter of policy. He never smoked or consumed drugs; and drinking was restricted to the rarest of special occasions, and then only the very best Scottish whiskey. His one weakness was women. Or more exactly, women who enjoyed sex and were aware of its artistry. His latest mistress fitted the bill perfectly. She was trained to stay silent or be absent while his "business meetings" were in progress; yet encouraged to perform all the dark arts of feminine eroticism when alone with him.

She saw him approaching her table. Angelov was tall and strongly built. He walked with a relaxed air of confidence that was attractive to women. Nevertheless his eyes, which had dark pupils, gave nothing away. Unless of course you were his lover. She was aware of her power to arouse and captivate him. Equally, she understood that he was ultimately unattainable. He kept his deepest emotions to himself.

Angelov pulled up a chair from the adjacent table and sat down on it next to Lolita. He called a waitress from behind the counter and ordered himself an espresso. Lolita had finished a fresh orange juice but declined anything further. She began talking to him, but his attention was elsewhere, his eyes seeking out his trusted personal bodyguards Vladimir and Igor. He saw one of them, Igor, outside leaning against Angelov's spotlessly clean and gleaming black C series Mercedes. The car was parked less than five metres away from the entrance to the patisserie.

As Igor bathed in the Lozenets sunshine, a police car drove up and stopped. The driver opened up his side window and engaged him in conversation. The bodyguard maintained zen-like equanimity. Watching the exchanges anonymously through the patisserie windows, Angelov smiled inwardly at his evident control of the situation. The Sofia police force's wages were inordinately low. Courteous patrols around Lozenets minding one's own business was an essential part of the harmony and security that coexisted between the forces of law and order and the 'business community'; which had its reward in the form of wage supplements paid monthly via attaché cases delivered to the district police chief. With some pleasantries and humour having been dispensed, the policeman waved goodbye and slowly pulled the patrol car away in search of nothing in particular.

After a few minutes desultory conversation with Lolita, she deftly gathered her bag, effortlessly extracted her long legs from beneath the table and stood up to her full stiletto-ed height. Pirouetting towards Angelov, she bent her knees sufficiently to bring her lips level with the crown of his forehead and her breasts provocatively close to his face. Then taking his chin with the outstretched index finger of her right hand, she lifted up his face, ovalled her red lips into a pouting "O", and carefully branded his forehead with her feline version of a red hot iron. She smiled momentarily at her work and then stared icily and indifferently into Angelov's eyes as a defiant sexual challenge. Before he could respond, she covered her eyes with the Gucci sunglasses, elegantly swung herself around and walked to the exit, letting her rear do the talking. Angelov gazed on appreciatively until she disappeared out the door.

His mind drifted for a few moments. Then the door from the street opened once more and the sunlight streaming through it framed the menacing form of a huge figure dressed neatly in black from head to foot. He had a shaven and waxed cranium, the nakedness of which revealed that the man was wired for sound behind his right ear. Not revealed, but nonetheless present, was a leather holster strapped beneath his left shoulder hidden by his smartly tailored black Armani jacket. The pistol occupying the holster was fully loaded. Its owner had a successful record of using it. This was Vladimir. Earlier that morning he had been at the gym with Radomir. After that session, having followed Angelov through the hotel to the patisserie, he had temporarily removed himself from his boss.

As soon as Vladimir saw Anastasia depart, he had disengaged from his observation post in the shade of the opposite side of the street from Igor and quickly moved inside the patisserie.

Angelov nodded almost imperceptibly at the muscle man; just enough to acknowledge his presence. Vladimir said nothing. He understood from his boss' muted behaviour that he wished to remain alone for the time being. Walking over to an empty table next to the wall, he adroitly manoeuvred his black granite form into a comfortable chair. From this position he had a clear view of his boss and both exit doors, the one partitioning to the hotel and the other giving onto the street outside.

Whilst working out earlier in the gym, Angelov had determined that this morning he had to have a "business strategy" meeting. He was facing formidable challenges in his strategy to expand and switch away from criminal pursuits to legitimate ones. The most recent phase in this push to clean up his business interests involved trying to expand into the UK construction sector. In the past, his activities outside the law had seen him come close to physical liquidation; risks thankfully avoided through pragmatic accommodation with kindred Mafioso bosses. "Honour amongst thieves" was a sound principle, one Angelov knew to be a life saver. That is, until honoured in the breach.

The patisserie now served as his "office". He had no need of either a corporate organisation or an office. He also had no need for others. Trust being a rare commodity in matters of deep import to his own survival, the only dialogue he deemed safe to have was one with himself. He sipped his Italian espresso and savoured the pleasing bitterness. Easing himself back further into the upholstered chair he reflected critically on the historic trajectory of his business affairs.

During the Communist era he had worked as a State intelligence agent during the eighties and early nineties. That experience had served him well. Many of the techniques he had then assimilated for self defence, interrogation, surveillance and psychological control served him eminently well in his new guise as a first generation Bulgarian businessman and entrepreneur.

In 1996 he had left the security services and started work for one of the Sofia-based mafia bosses. His job was in the "insurance" industry as a collector of premiums from clients; "insurance" being a pseudonym for taking protection money from shopkeepers. It was a cash-only business.

In those pioneering days of the late 1990s, his role model had been Vladimir Putin. He believed that strength and intelligence equated with leadership; and that to be successful in the "wild west" economies of Eastern Europe you must possess both.

Then in 2001, his boss was taken down in a daylight hit operation in the centre of Sofia while being chauffeured away from a meeting with the Deputy Minister of the Interior. His alleged crime was to have extended the reach of his insurance business outside of Sofia into the Black Sea resort of Varna. His summary killing on home territory was a signal reminder to other Sofia-based bosses that their entrepreneurial talents were not welcomed in Varna unless first invited.

To reinforce their message, the Varna mob audaciously blew up his bosses' head office building in Lozenets. The site was out there across the street from where Angelov was now sitting. To this day, it remained a vacant lot; a subtle testament to the unwritten truce that had thereafter grown up between the gangs.

After this chastening experience, Angelov had worked carefully to avoid direct power conflicts with other Bulgarian mafia bosses. While most of the others had been murdered usually by other mafia bosses' hitmen, Angelov had made staying alive his overriding preoccupation.

Exiting the insurance business, Angelov used his accumulated earnings to opening a string of small casinos in Sofia. The night life scene was hot for laundering money and also providing cover for drugs and prostitution. Around that time he befriended a German he met in one of Sofia's foreign-owned hotels. The German was working on a project to improve the Bulgarian customs service ahead of the country's entry into the EU. He kept his nose clean, coming in from Turkey.

By 2002 he had begun to see the bright future beckoning Bulgarian mafia bosses astute enough to re-position their businesses towards more legitimate pursuits. For a while he became an assiduous reader of Western management books with the aim to teach himself the best practices of capitalism in order to be a "businessman". However he had long ago concluded that those who wrote books about getting rich were neither capitalists nor, for the most part, rich. They simply wanted to sell their book.

The one book that he had read that had left a lasting impression was one about IBM by an ex CEO of the company. Angelov had read it slowly in the original English. It had some crazy title like "Elephants can dance". Aside from that inanity, what he had admired was the way that this CEO had gone about imposing himself. He destroyed all the regional fiefdoms of a global organisation employing at the time over 200,000 people. That guy had balls ! Not only had he sacked the bureaucrats who were running the organisation in their own interest, he had turned around the company and made it profitable and successful by re-inventing what its core business was about. Angelov didn't care too much for the technology part of the story. Instead, what held his attention was that this guy had come in as a rank outsider – hell, from some credit card company or something ! – and not only rescued the outfit from bankruptcy but completely transformed its business. That took ruthlessness, discipline and perseverance. Qualities that Angelov, as a former Bulgarian intelligence agent and now seasoned mafia boss, both appreciated and applied.

In 2003 his company had metamorphosed. Backing off from confrontation with the Varna mafia started to pay dividends. Over the years he had been able to build bridges with some of them. These relationships, although always at risk of drifting onto the shoals, were sufficiently robust to allow him to buy development land on the Black Sea coast. His company began rapidly scaling up profits from hotel and holiday home construction as well as property management.

Unexpectedly but fortuitously, he was invited to join forces with a foreign partner. He first met up with Thomas Cartwright when visiting Vienna. Cartwright, a senior executive of an Irish bank, was searching for property development opportunities in Eastern Europe. The opportunities for bargains in Central Europe – places like Prague and Budapest - had already been snapped up in the late 1990s. By 2002, Bulgaria and Romania were among the few remaining locations offering cheap prices, low development costs and attractive climate.

Cartwright had proved his worth to Angelov many times ever since they had first grown acquainted over five years ago. Indeed, it was he who had brokered Angelov's first foray outside of Bulgaria by introducing Angelov to a young businessman developing residential estates in the east of England. Characteristically for Cartwright, this new business acquaintance also came with a certain quotient of 'baggage'. Well versed in the politics of survival from his Bulgarian mafia roots, Angelov had played along with this business man, always with an eye to his own self interest.

If Angelov was 'ahead of the curve' in seeing the opportunity to move out of Bulgaria altogether, what he had never imagined was what had recently happened to him. On his last trip to London for a property industry exhibition last January, he had had the good fortune to be introduced by Westlake to his father, Sir Peter the head of Dominion Properties.

While talking together during a coffee break about the UK property market and the financial crisis, Sir Peter mentioned that he had set his sights on winning construction contracts for the 2012 London Olympics. Spending on infrastructure for this event was just starting to ramp up with contracts being progressively put out to tender.

Angelov saw an opportunity to progress his own agenda. He manoeuvred their conversation towards an agreement to meet again for a private lunch together, to examine potential avenues for co-operation. Westlake, unsurprisingly, evinced initial scepticism to the idea. Nevertheless, before they parted company, Angelov succeeded to have him agree in principle. Yesterday, he had called Sir Peter's personal assistant and set Thursday 17th March at the Excelsior Hotel on The Strand for evening meal with Sir Peter. His flight was already booked. He was excited by the prospect and looked forward to celebrating there with Lolita should he pull of a coup.

For the heart of Angelov's 'business strategy' scenario for expanding into the UK, envisaged leveraging the forthcoming discussion with Sir Peter to offer him a supply of low cost but skilled and hard working Bulgarian construction workers for new projects arising from the massive spending in London linked to the preparation of infrastructures for the 2012 Olympics . The quid pro quo being that he would want to become a junior partner in the venture, bringing his share of capital to the partnership.

Angelov's train of thought was interrupted by the vibrating noise emanating from his Blackberry which lay on the coffee table in front of him. He lifted the device and recognised the calling number displayed on the LCD. It was Georgi phoning from the UK.

"Dobre den boss".

"Georgi, dobre den. I was planning to call you later. You know I'll be flying into London on Wednesday. I want us to meet. I need to hear from you how things are evolving on the ground."

"Yes boss. But listen, this is urgent. I'm calling you because there's bad news."

Angelov was alert immediately, shifting himself upright in his seat. Vladimir, ever the instinctively aware bodyguard, caught the abrupt change in his bosses' comportment and planted both his feet forwards ready to move should Angelov signal action.

" Go on" Angelov said, apprehensively. He had seen Vladimir's reaction and put the palm of his hand up towards him as a sign to wait.

"Its Cartwright. He's committed suicide. I got a call from Westlake about it yesterday. He said he had learnt about it from Cartwright's wife. I was suspicious but just now confirmed it in this morning's local newspaper."

Angelov's thoughts spun momentarily out of control. He didn't understand. Nevertheless, he knew that this meant danger.

"How did it happen and when ?"

"According to the news, he jumped off a road bridge into the river near Ipswich. Early yesterday morning, Sunday. But that's not the end of it."

"Why ? Anything suspicious about his death ?"

"Not sure boss. The local paper says that the police are still making enquiries into the circumstances of his suicide. I thought you ought to know. Anything you want me to do ?"

Angelov breathed deeply to regain his calm; inwardly he was angry.

"Not for the moment. Don't call me again from that number. I'm on my way to the UK."

Angelov quickly placed money on the table to pay for his own, and Anastasia's, drinks. He rose from his seat. Opposite him Vladimir did the same and approached him.

"Vladimir, there's a crisis. That was Bourov. Cartwright is dead. He committed suicide yesterday in the UK. We need to get over there."

114

Control of UK operations was at risk of slipping away. He began to have suspicions. Was there double dealing by Cartwright ? Or indeed Russell Westlake ?   In any case, this was no territory to have a woman in tow.

He opened the glass door to exit the patisserie.

"Another thing, Vladimir. Cancel Anastasia's air ticket to the UK. I don't need the extra baggage".

Vladimir said nothing. Economy with words was a golden rule when his boss was angry.

Chapter Twelve

13.45 Monday 16th March 2009.   Dominion Properties PLC, Hammersmith, London

Sir Peter Westlake was in a thunderous black mood. He was in the CEO's suite on the top floor of Dominion Properties' head office together with his Finance Director. Before him on his table were two documents. One, the unaudited annual accounts of the company, which were urgently due for external audit prior to final publication in April. The other, a short report produced by the Finance Director addressing the matter of interest rate swaps that were responsible for a 50 per cent share of the losses stated in the unaudited accounts.

Sir Peter had received these documents first thing in the morning at 7.00 am when he started work. He had instructed the FD last week that that deadline was not to be missed, or else. Having read the two documents, Sir Peter weighed his options. The 'or else' struck him as at least one step in the right direction. He was now at the tail end of a meeting with the Finance Director. The man had effectively buried himself, lamely attempting to sanitise the results and distance himself from any responsibility:

"Those are the facts. The annual accounts will have to report a loss of over £ 400 million, and that's mainly down to the negative impact of the interest rates swaps that we have on the books. It was, as you know, the CEGB that arranged the swap deals for us."

Sir Peter, who had taken off his jacket at the start of the meeting, stood bellicosely behind his desk with huge hands on hips. Dismal grey light came through the office windows and there was a low permanent hum of traffic coming up from the Great West Road below. From the Finance Director's perspective, seated in front of his boss' desk, there was a monster of a man blocking out the meagre light and breathing fire. He feared the worst.

Sir Peter shot back: "The CEGB may have brokered the deal, but who analysed its terms ? Who was responsible for assessing the risks ? Who selects the appropriate financial instruments for structuring our leverage and controlling our cash flow ? Who approved it ? Who ?" His voice had risen a few decibels and the whites of his eyes flashed.

The Finance Director, a seasoned and qualified professional but a weak hand at corporate politics, remained silent. Sir Peter himself was of course accountable; he had signed off on the interest rate swap deal. The FD's own level of delegated authority within Dominion's corporate governance did not extend to single-handedly signing off on such a large deal. Sure, he had made a recommendation to go ahead. That was back in summer 2007 when they had obtained a fixed rate of interest of 4.5%. The problems only started last summer when the Bank of England started to reduce rates. Since September they had come down from 5% and to a mere 0.5% now. He and his team of financial analysts simply hadn't projected such rapid and dramatic change over a space of a few months. The crash in the financial and stock markets over the same period, which precipitated the Bank's change of policy, had been predicted by virtually no one. He certainly wasn't alone with his dilemma. All over corporate London other Finance Directors were in the same boat, desperately trying to find ways to shore up their firms' finances, profits and share prices.

Sir Peter, exasperated by the man's capitulative silence, had 'You're fired !' on the tip of his tongue but held it back. Instead he chose to make him sweat a while longer:

"Get me proposals how to address this mess. I want to know our options and I want them on my desk by Wednesday lunch time. Meeting over. Now get the hell out of my office !"

"I'll certainly do that. You'll have it Wednesday" the Finance Director acquiesced, submissively.

He stood up, avoiding eye contact with his boss, and attempted to retreat from the office with dignity. The five or six steps needed to reach the door out to the PA's office seemed to him to take an age. Within seconds of his departure, Sir Peter's personal assistant phoned through to him:

"Just to remind you that you're scheduled to meet Declan Moroney of the CEGB in the Board room at 14.00 I understand from reception that he's just arrived at downstairs."

"Jessica, please don't let that Finance clown near me again until Wednesday. Set up a 30 minute meeting for him here in my office some time in the afternoon will you ?"

Jessica wondered to herself how long the 'clown' might survive. She knew Sir Peter probably better than he knew himself. She had been his personal assistant for over ten years. He relied heavily on her, appreciating her calm effectiveness; not least, her profound discretion as regards office politics. She was never a source of rumour but always an accurate observer. One thing Sir Peter failed to understand though was that she influenced him, more than he her. She replied:

"I will. By the way, there was a call earlier from a Mr. Angelov ? Calling from Sofia. He's arriving in London Wednesday for a few days. Requests a meeting with you this week. Possible cooperation on contracts for the London 2012 Olympics ? Claims you've promised to meet him. I wasn't entirely sure whether you wanted to talk to him or not, so I didn't commit anything. What would you like to do ?"

Sir Peter paused. Angelov and he had met once last January at a property exhibition held down the road in the Earls Court Exhibition Centre. His son Russell had made the introductions. At the time Angelov had expressed enthusiasm for entering the UK construction market. He explained that he was already doing business with Russell's company on the Bulgarian Black Sea. At the time, that had been news to Sir Peter. Since then, he had neither seen nor heard from the man. Letting his business instincts rule, he made a snap decision:

"OK, Jessica. Set something up for me with him. Maybe out of the office somewhere ? I need to find out more about this chap and what he's about. A relaxed atmosphere is more likely to get him to open up. Say for Thursday evening if you can find a slot in my agenda."

"Will do. Is there anything you need in preparation for your meeting with Mr. Moroney ?"

Under normal circumstances, given that this meeting involved discussions about loan financing, Sir Peter would have included his Finance Director. But just the thought of the man raised his hackles. He had already determined over the week end that he would take on this challenging rendez vous with the chairman of the CEBG on his own.

"Jessica, please check for the refreshments to be ready in the Board room. Other than that, I'll handle this on my own. No one to disturb me unless you yourself consider it necessary. By the way, Moroney has come alone ?"

"I'll make sure everything is ready. I was told by the receptionist that there's Mr. Moroney present. No one else."

Sir Peter replaced the receiver. Strange that Declan Moroney had come alone. Was there something afoot from the CEGB side that favoured a private one-on-one? , Sir Peter speculated.

The purpose of the meeting was to review the progress of their partnership agreement for a commercial property development in Dublin. Agreement on the next round of multi million euro funding was supposed to follow. However Sir Peter was aware that the Dublin commercial property market appeared had peaked. Hence he had had second thoughts about committing to the development even though it was a prime city centre site. Much more interesting UK construction contracts opportunities were beginning to flow from the Organising Committee for the London 2012 Olympics.

With the losses that Dominion's unaudited annual accounts revealed, together with the severe weakness that had overtaken the property market in Ireland, Sir Peter's challenge today was to negotiate a tactical postponement of the project without at the same time destroying the business relationship with the CEGB. While blasting his Finance Director for the debacle over the losses attributable to the interest rate swaps, Sir Peter also saw that the CEGB's participation in negotiating the swaps deal could be turned to his advantage. He planned to turn up the heat on the bank's chairman for having allowed Dominion to accept what had proven to be highly risky terms on the swaps deal. Quid pro quo, he would then extricate Dominion from its commitment to the Dublin project as the price paid for the CEGB's lack of prudential oversight.

Sir Peter smiled to himself. Even at the age of sixty four he had lost none of his fox-like cunning. He remained a risk-taker at heart. That's what had taken him to the top in business. 'Who dares wins' was an adage he firmly endorsed from personal experience. Risk was everywhere; you had to learn how to deal with it. Accurate forecasting of the future was impossible. So making mistakes was inevitable. The key thing was learning from them. The more times you win, the more times you are likely to win.

He remembered once advising his son Russell, whilst helping him set up Redwood Country Homes, that the secret was not to risk too much of your own money. Use other people's ! Leverage was the oxygen of successful businesses.

Recalling that conversation with his son reminded him painfully of the fact that he and Russell had hardly spoken since soon after that visit to Earls' Court back in January. They had fallen out over the question of

Redwood's expansion overseas to the Bulgarian Black Sea. Sir Peter had been unconvinced by the location, the opportunity and the enduring communist legacy. Russell, on the contrary, was gung ho. He had waxed lyrical about the Black Sea coast, believing demand for holiday hotels and second homes presented major opportunities. This was partly the cause of their falling out. The other was Angelov. Sir Peter couldn't figure the guy, so didn't trust him.

His phone rang, breaking his train of thought.

Jessica announced: "Sir Peter, it's 14.00. Mr Moroney is waiting for you in the Board room"

As Sir Peter entered through the double doors of the Boardroom, Declan Moroney chairman of CEBG. arose from the chair he had taken at the head of the table and approached him, smiling warmly. He had a ruddy face and a full head of silver white hair. The back of the large hand he preferred to Sir Peter had liver spots, evidence of his partiality to Irish malts.

They shook hands vigorously and then Moroney clasped Sir Peter's hand with both of his, as if putting the seal of approval on the solidity of their friendship. The two men were roughly the same age and hewn from the same rock in terms of business acumen and zest for life. Their business relationship had evolved over the years into genuine friendship. A mutual interest and pleasure in Rugby Union had transformed into the institution of a joint annual pilgrimage either to Twickenham or to Croke Park for the Six Nations' match between England and Ireland. Regardless the result, post match Saturday night celebrations and entertainment in Dublin or London were *de rigeur*.

Sir Peter was about to formulate a rugby story reminiscence but Moroney beat him to the ball. He opened with a tongue in cheek observation about England's losing performance in Dublin last month which they had attended together:

"Sure, the score was close Peter. But the England boys were an indisciplined crowd. The lad who got yellow carded and sin binned, Care wasn't it ? Obviously he didn't care did he ? With one player off the park England were goners."

Sir Peter was content to concede the point. Lack of discipline had probably cost England the match:

"It was a scrappy affair, I'll grant you Declan. But did you see the England coach's reaction to the player getting carded ? He was incandescent. I'd be surprised if the player makes the England line up again for a while."

Moroney exploited the opening in Sir Peter's weak defence:

"Ireland are up for the big one now. Unbeaten. Last game of the season against Wales in Wales. It's a tough call but I think we can do it. The Irish boys have the quality and the *esprit de corps* to do it. That would be our first Six Nations title in fifty years."

Sir Peter recognised the quality and passion in the Irish side and had an inkling that it was indeed to be Ireland's year. He chose to go along with Moroney's forecast to see if it might soften him up for their business discussion.

"You may well be on the money with that call Declan. The current Irish side have got the experience and quality to beat the Welsh. Let's wait and see. It should be a titanic encounter in Cardiff that's for sure. Talking of which, what about our own ? The Dominion and CEGB partnership ? Shall we get down to business ?"

He waved with his arm for Moroney to be seated again, since they had been standing since he entered the room. Sir Peter took the chair next to him, first pulling it back from under the conference table to give himself ample space.

"I'm surprised you've come alone today Declan. I expected you'd bring over at least Seamus your Finance man ? What's with this streamlined approach ? Don't get me wrong, I prefer small meetings. You don't need a committee to get things done. Still, with the financing aspects on the table.........." he deliberately let his sentence trail to encourage Moroney's response.

Moroney shifted the position of his chair so that he was directly facing Sir Peter rather than the table. He said

"There's a reason for this, as I'm sure you've guessed Peter"

"I'm listening. Go ahead." Sir Peter encouraged, with diplomatic charm.

"Well, back in Dublin we've been hit with a triple whammy of problems. Collectively, they're causing us severe difficulties. First off, we have a housekeeping issue that could potentially hurt our reputation. Myself and Brian the CEO have had to dismiss one member of the Board. We had no choice, the man had arranged unauthorised loans to a company in the name of his wife. The amounts involved weren't insignificant. The really bad news was that it came to our attention via the supervisory boys at the Irish Central Bank. What should be an in-house disciplinary action now risks to mushroom out of the Board's control. The Central Bank have investigations ongoing already into the activities of some of our competitors. They're threatening now to widen their investigation to us. We've got a fight on our hands to keep our reputation intact."

"I've got sympathy for you Declan. Once these regulatory bodies get their teeth into you they don't let go, even if they fail to unearth anything. " said Sir Peter, with empathy. He suspected nonetheless that this was the least critical problem Moroney would raise.

Moroney shifted his body position again, as if adjusting his weight ready to dive into a scrum. He continued:

"The second problem is part tragedy, part political conflict. Over here in the UK our man Thomas Cartwright, who was CEO at the Ipswich and Blackwater Bank, committed suicide at the week end. In itself that's a tragedy because the man was important to us. It also raises the question of the leadership succession at the bank. We do have a CEGB person in place as Chief Finance Officer, and we've used *force majeure* to name her acting CEO. But the problem is that, although we are the single largeest shareholder we're not able to control the bank through that holding. It's not a controlling share. What we did in the past in order to have effective control was to have Thomas voted CEO by the institutional shareholders."

"What's to prevent you doing the same with a new candidate Declan ?"

"Two things. First, this time around, we're not sure we can get enough insititutional shareholders to vote for her, due to her relative inexperience. Second, we've received a call from a UK government Minister – Lord Preston – asking us urgently to consider to buy out the Ipswich and Blackwater. He's waiting for my reply 'as soon as possible' I was told."

"And why wouldn't you take effective control ? That could strengthen your presence here in the UK banking sector."

"We would like to, but for two things" Moroney countered. "First, we do not presently have a banking license in the UK. The Ipswich's banking licence is one that they themselves obtained years ago. If we seek to take control we'd be vetted by the FSA. That wouldn't be easy at a time when the Irish Central Bank has got its' eye on us. Second, there's a rumour that was put about in the UK press last week that the bank may not be in good financial health. That's apparently what ruffled feathers in Whitehall and initiated the call to us this morning from the Minister. You can understand that with these issues not under control we must conduct our own internal due diligence. We can't commit a huge injection of capital to take a majority shareholding in a bank that might suffer from a lack of confidence in the markets due to rumour."

"I fully agree. But what's the rush ? Can't you and the Minister come to an arrangement ? It must be in everybody's interest for 'due process' to take its course. That way the eventual decision is more likely to be the right one ? I mean, is the bank basically sound or isn't it ?"

"Your voicing a rational approach Peter. But you know as well as I, once the politicians get involved there are other interests in play and rationality is the casualty. The fact is, your Prime Minister has already nationalised any UK banks that look likely to be insolvent. So he's got form. And with a G20 Summit to be hosted here in the UK soon, do you think he wants a return of the UK banking crisis to embarrass him ?......No, its ok, you don't need to answer. I rest my case. The point is this. The CEGB Board are between a rock and a hard place as the Americans like to say. As chairman, this problem is on my plate and I have to get it sorted."

"I suspect that I know where you're headed Declan but I don't want to steal your fire. What's the third issue burdening CEGB ?"

"As you well know Peter, news like this inevitably leaks into the markets. If they suspect that the CEBG is going to have to raise significant capital to acquire the Ipswich and Blackwater, then imagine what that will do for their appetite for more CEGB debt ?"

"Lending money is your core business Declan. Why would you need to borrow ?"

"Our Chief Finance Officer now says that we need to raise over Euro 600 million to realise the Dublin City centre project. Your finance analysts share that view. That's up 35 per cent from the original estimate of last December. It would probably require going to the wholesale markets for the money."

"You're saying that the planned investments by the Dominion CEBG partnership are terminally impacted by the revised investment costs ?"

"It isn't simply that, but basically, yes. You see, in addition, our property market analysts are advising us that the commercial property market in Dublin has already peaked. Bringing on stream more commercial office and shop floor space in two years' time might be suicidal. They've showed me a scenario with unlet floor space in excess of 30 percent and per square metre rentals down 20 per cent from current levels that would push the payback period out another three years. That would inevitably knock on negatively to our profitability."

Moroney's expression was taut and anxious, uncertain of his business partner's reaction to this negative assessment, yet at the same time determined to find a formula that would avert a potential financial meltdown for the CEGB.

Sir Peter was secretly delighted by this turn of events. Unexpectedly, Moroney was laying before him an escape route from a commercial commitment that he himself no longer wished to respect, at no cost or compromise to Dominion. He could devote his attention to more lucrative construction contracts for the forthcoming London 2012 Olympics.

He began to relax, knowing that the rest of the meeting would be a walk in the park. Dominion were off the hook. He might even weigh in with a demand to Moroney for compensation for CEGB's miss-handling of Dominion's interest rate swaps. A fair price to pay, Sir Peter thought, for freeing them up to pursue their interests with the Ipswich & Blackwater Bank !

Chapter Thirteen

9.20am Tuesday 17th March 2009.   Police HQ, Civic Drive, Ipswich.

Because of its orientation towards the south west, Chief Inspector Haddock's office did not benefit from the sun's rays early in the morning. At least, not in March. On the plus side, being located on Headquarters' top floor meant that Haddock had a panoramic view across much of the south side of the town.

His office was large, befitting a senior policeman, but spartan. All furniture and fittings were of basic functional quality. Luxury was absent; comfort obsolete. Not even a soft upholstered chair for guests; just bare wooden seats with upright backs. The most decorative item visible was a large scale map of the town of Ipswich and its environs, which hung across the inner wall of the room.

The cool temperature and muted morning daylight were much to the Chief's liking. He was at his best first thing in the day. He could think and decide clearly, assessing only the key elements that made up the particular problems or investigations before him. The pettifogging routines and administration that increasingly bedevilled police work only encumbered his approach. 'Old school' or not, Haddock's sole allegiance was to the tried and tested practises that he knew kept the police force honest and effective. Which meant staying alert and prepared for front line operations.

Rumours circulating around headquarters of his imminent retirement were premature. True, his mortgage was paid off and he enjoyed an occasional round of golf. But it was his daytime job that still created. the enthusiasm to perform. As he had no illusions about further advancement, there was no resentment to distract his commitment to the cause.

This morning he was dressed in full uniform. A meeting later that day with some panjandrums at the County Council offices beckoned. He figured that the most likely way to have done with this unwanted event was to offer his most imposing uniformed presence and keep discourse as laconic as possible. He had learnt long ago that controlling a group of people was a relatively easy thing to do if you subordinated them to your will from the outset with quiet authoritative strength. Talk was cheap; authority was priceless.

Because he still loved the operational side of policing, Haddock remained an unreformed and unapologetic meritocrat. Which profile he sought to convey persistently and consistently to his staff in the not forlorn hope that it might rub off.

"So what to make of this young woman ?" he mused to himself, taking care not to look directly at DI Wright. "The best policewoman on the Ipswich force by a country mile. Probably merits another promotion. Let's keeps her busy delivering results, lest she gets ahead of herself". Haddock knew his own failings with people skills, but beguilement by an energetic ambitious female officer was not one of them.

DI Wright and DS Adams were seated next to one another on one side of an oblong wooden table that was positioned close to the inner wall that supported the map of Ipswich. Both were looking up directly at Haddock waiting for him to direct proceedings. His massive physical presence blocked out a portion of the meagre light that attempted to insinuate its way into the room.

In the silence DS Adam noticed that the Chief's bald forehead was a little too shiny. DI Wright, ever the sorcerer's apprentice, took note of her bosses' ability to impose his personality even when tight lipped.

"Go ahead please Inspector. Keep it succinct please. I want to know what your lines of enquiry are and your reasons for taking this further."

"Thank you sir." Wright began confidently. "We do not rule out that this suicide may well be just an act of desperation by a stressed or disillusioned man. At his age, because of the weight of responsibilities at work and at home, he may have concluded that life was not worth living."

DI Wright paused and looked patiently at her boss. He showed no desire to interrupt. Perhaps her reference to age had touched a raw nerve.

She continued: "We have not yet interviewed his wife. The officers who went to her on Sunday confronted an overwrought woman. On psychological grounds, we were advised by them to wait another twenty four hours before questioning her in detail."

Haddock's nose twitched and he swallowed, but he maintained a stoic silence.

"To the best of our knowledge, Cartwright left no messages for anyone explaining his actions. However, amongst suicides that is not unusual. DS Adam and I consider that there are two key avenues of inquiry. First, we have identified a list of people who were in contact with Cartwright in the days immediately prior to his death. Some of them stand out as strong candidates for interview as they could shed light on Cartwright's interests and actions at the time. Second, we have learnt that two of the keys found in the suicide's car are safe deposit box keys for private clients at the IB&B. Having opened them, one has yielded a stash of uncut diamonds. We're awaiting expert opinion on their value. We intend to discover who the diamonds belong to. So far, no one at the bank has admitted any knowledge."

DS Adam said: "Chief, that is our 'follow the money' line of inquiry."

Adam's unsolicited intervention won him the distinction of a grimace from the Chief.

DI Wright continued: "Another line of inquiry relates to a woman's vanity mirror found in Cartwright's car on Sunday. Mrs Cartwright was unable to identify it when it was shown to her later by our colleagues. Our assumption is that Cartwright might have had a mistress or at least some significant female 'other' secretly involved in his life. DS Adam and I have already met with Cartwright's acting successor at the Bank, sir. She's an attractive woman and very tight lipped about her relationship with her boss."

Haddock stretched himself ominously to his full height and came to life.

"We infer to a widow that her husband had a mistress hours after he commits suicide ? No surprise that she is 'overwrought' Inspector ! Then, the first woman you meet in his professional life, you want to suspect of being the cause of his adultery ? It sounds to me that you are clutching at straws."

He prevented DI Wright from replying with an upraised palm of his hand. "Be that as it may. What about the drugs angle ? I understand that traces of cocaine were found in Cartwright's bloodstream."

"That's correct, Chief. We've had confirmation from the autopsy report. What we intend to follow up there is whether Cartwright was a casual user and if so who was supplying him. Or, less likely, was he himself involved in any way in selling cocaine. A street map of Sofia in Bulgaria was also present in his car. We need to find out what the significance of that, if any, might be."

"Be sure that you do. The Chief Constable is sensitive to any publicity that this town is becoming a drugs capital. Why is it that it is now the white collar classes mixed up in it ?"

"Maybe it always was, sir ?" DS Adam conjectured, "It's called a 'recreational' drug these days."

DI Wright raised a disapproving eyebrow at Adam, out of the Chief's line of vision. Did Charlie deliberately want to court Haddock's wrath ?

Haddock had gotten restless. He looked at his wrist watch then said: "I agree you keep the investigation open till next Tuesday. No additional resources though without my approval. A last comment from me on the subject of drugs, DI Wright. I want you to lend a hand also in this sad story of McAuley's suicide. Sergeant Clarkson has briefed both you and Adam I understand ? One suicide is unfortunate. Two inside twenty four hours begins to look careless. Moreover there's a pattern: both involve the use of cocaine. Be sure that you to cover that aspect of it please. The Chief Constable is expecting feedback. McAuley was from a well-connected local family. The CC knew his father."

Their conversation was broken when the phone at the side of Haddock's desk started ringing. Haddock arose, paced to the desk and lifted the receiver on the third ring. He listened briefly, then raised the receiver towards Wright: "You have a visitor awaiting you at the front desk, a Mr. Reddy. Nine thirty o'clock appointment"

It was nine thirty five.

Wright took the phone receiver and gave instructions for Reddy to be taken into the ground floor conference room. This was used for members of the public requested to assist the police at HQ but who were not suspects.

Without Haddock requesting amplification, Wright explained: "Mr. Reddy seems to have been an acquaintance of Thomas Cartwright. His mobile phone number made a call to Cartwright a few days before his death. Reddy's a journalist at the Daily Courier. DS Adam and I decided to interview him."

"I don't need the details." Haddock admonished.

He moved over towards the office door and turned the door handle.

"You're running the investigation Wright. Get to it. Bring me the results by this time next week, or before if you have them. If you need me for anything you know I'm available any time."

He stood back and opened the door in one movement. As Wright and Adam filed out into the corridor, Adam imagined that he had caught the shadow of a valedictory grin on the face of the Chief.

Wright and Adam passed side by side down the long corridor. It was lit solely by artificial light from recessed light bulbs in the ceiling. As the three storey building had no lifts, they had to take the stairs leading to the ground floor.

"A penny for them ?"

"Huh ?" Adam grunted, absently. He was still unsettled by the impression he had that the Chief had grinned at him as they departed his office.

Wright tried again: "Your thoughts, Charlie. A penny for them. What did you make of the meeting ?"

"He gave us a week's time to pursue an investigation. That's tight, but at least it's something." Adam counselled.

Wright was not to be easily consoled. "It's absurdly tight. The Chief is ratcheting up the pressure on us. My guess is he's in dialogue with the Chief Constable. That stuff about white collar crime and the CC personally knowing the McAuley family ? The local power elites won't take lightly bad publicity about the Town becoming a haven for cocaine dealers and a locus for middle class suicides and delinquents."

"Maybe you're letting your sociological theories get the better of you ?" Adam observed, adding before Wright could offer a derogatory retort: "Nevertheless, if you agree, then at some stage during this interview with Reddy I'll also raise the subject of McAuley's suicide."

"Yes, do that. Let's see his reaction."

Adam, still with the nagging mental image of the Chief when opening his office door, blurted out: "You know something ? This may sound crazy, but I'm sure I saw the Chief grin at me as we left his office."

"In your dreams, Charlie, in you're dreams. The day the Chief grins is the day he's lost it. Never forget, he's 'old school'. Grinning's not part of the rulebook."

They had reached the ground floor. In silence they headed left past the reception, and walked down the tiled corridor to the Conference room. Adam took the lead. Grinning mischievously at Wright, he opened the door into the Conference Room, permitting the Detective Inspector to enter first.

A varnished wooden table occupied the centre of the room. On one wall was a white canvas screen used for projecting videos. Reddy was seated behind the table. He had placed his Burberry's mackintosh over the back of the seat next to him. Off to his right, aluminium framed windows afforded a view out into the street.

Reddy rose to his feet to acknowledge the arrival of the two officers.

"Mr Reddy ?"

"Craig Reddy, yes. Good morning."

DI Wright introduced DS Adam and herself. She smiled at Reddy but without warmth.

"Please sit down. Thanks for coming in at short notice."

Reddy sat back down. He adopted a forward posture with his hands clasped together. Casting an appraising look at DI Wright, he immediately sensed her lively presence. The idea half formed in his mind that perhaps he had met her somewhere before. He dismissed it as a distraction.

DI Wright took a chair opposite him while DS Adam selected a seat off to the window side of the room where he would be but a silhouetted figure from Reddy's position.

Wright, relaxed in her interviewer role, was curious to see how her visitor would behave. He was not a suspect, yet her professional instincts inexorably drew her to define the man before her. He was, she sensed, decidedly uncomfortable. She ought to discover why.

Reddy had come willingly to the meeting knowing that he had done no wrong. Nonetheless, he was suffering from an unhealthy sensation of guilt. It had started at the Conference Centre soon after Adam's call.

Returning to Ipswich that evening, he read that day's local newspaper which ran an article on the death of Thomas Cartwright. The news item deepened his sense of shock. That night, in his dreams, Reddy's imagination created a phantasmagoric fiction with a ghoulish disfigured Cartwright at its' centre, operating some illicit crime ring. Reddy was somehow implicated in the affair and the police knew about it. This morning, while on his way to this meeting, Reddy had decided that he had to set the record straight at the top end of the interview to avoid misunderstanding.

"Mr. Reddy I understand that you are a journalist at the Daily Courier ?"

"That's correct."

Reddy intuited that journalists at the national press were not, in all probability, unambiguously appreciated by the rank and file police officer. Wright went on the offensive:

Are you are aware Mr. Cartwright has committed suicide ? It has been reported in the local media."

"Yes, I am. Most disturbing, the last thing I would have expected. May I ask though, how it is that you know I have a connection to him ?"

"Simple sir. Your mobile phone number was registered in the deceased's smart phone memory. The police obtain quick cooperation from the mobile operators to requests for phone owner identification in such circumstances. Now, could you please give us an account of your relationship to Cartwright ?"

"Of course. The fact is that I have met him only once. I arranged to interview him for an investigative dossier I am writing. The interview took place last Wednesday at his office. I requested his personal number from his personal assistant beforehand just to be absolutely sure that we would meet as scheduled. I suppose you've found my call on his phone from last Tuesday ? That was when I double checked his availability directly with him."

It was evident to DI Wright that Reddy's account matched their information. Nevertheless, in her experience telling the truth could be part and parcel of carefully constructed lies.

"You were not friends ? You had no business relationship ?" she inquired.

"None at all."

"So your only connection to Cartwright was this interview you conducted ? Could you tell me about the purpose of that and what you learnt ?"

"Sure I can. Let me first put it in context for you ?"

"If it will help, please do."

"At the Daily Courier my work is focused on the economy and financial markets. In addition to regular reporting of events, I undertake occasional in-depth investigations into topics that deserve exposure to the public. When the financial markets cratered last year, there was huge interest from the public for insight into what went wrong and why. There's continuing concern today. As I'm sure you know, public sentiment is highly negative about the banking sector. The government's bail outs have not reassured the majority. So what I've been doing is looking for news stories about the potential risks still out there."

"And you found one involving Mr Cartwright ?" Wright interrupted, with a dose of scepticism.

"Not immediately, no. At the outset I was searching for examples of UK-based banks or other lenders that might have gotten themselves into possible insolvency difficulties through reckless lending. The premiss was to demonstrate that banking is not out of the woods in terms of potential systemic risks."

"OK, Mr. Reddy, let's keep it simple here. DS Adam and I are police officers not economists. How did all this bring you to Mr. Cartwright's doorstep ?"

"By going local ! " Reddy enthused, beginning for the first time to feel expansive. "I live in Ipswich and know the area well. I was born and brought up here. The region has experienced a boom in business activity these past years. It seemed a fruitful approach to take the investigation local. Find evidence locally and then build from there to a broader argument about the clear and present dangers in the banking sector. I started the local investigation by researching who was involved in large scale lending around Suffolk and Essex. In that context, I kept coming across the name of the Ipswich & Blackwater Bank."

"Which eventually led you to its CEO ?"

"Precisely. My researches revealed that the Bank was expanding very quickly. Its loans book grew alarmingly, notably by expanding lending away from its traditional segment of housing mortgages towards funding commercial property and land purchases by speculative house builders. At that point, I felt that I'd hit upon a candidate of a bank vulnerable to insolvency. So I decided to obtain an interview with its CEO. That was Thomas Cartwright."

"Excuse me, Mr. Reddy, but I fail to see that the head of a bank would grant an interview with a journalist from a national daily to discuss the bank's possible insolvency." Wright interjected.

Reddy laughed involuntarily, appreciating DI Wright's incredulity.

"Indeed not Inspector. That's where the tricks of the trade come into play. First rule as an investigative journalist: never divulge your ultimate goals. Simply establish a rationale which makes your target want to talk to you. Second, and this is just understanding human nature: tickle their egos. Encourage them to feel important. I convinced Mr Cartwright to talk to me because I impressed upon him that his knowledge and understanding was invaluable, and that confidentiality would unquestionably be respected on matters that he identified as off the record. That combination yielded the desired result. He acceded to being interviewed."

"So, have you published anything arising from your discussion with Mr. Cartwright ?"

"I've written an article that uses elements of the information garnered from the interview plus material from other sources. It wasn't a major piece. The Courier published last Friday, buried in the finance pages somewhere."

"Were there any follow up communications between Mr Cartwright and yourself subsequent to the meeting ?"

"Not with him no, but I emailed his personal assistant a copy of the article requesting that he comment anything. She replied by return that she would see to it that Mr. Cartwright had it on his desk. Of course, I've heard nothing since."

"Is there any insight you can bring to us about possible reasons why Mr. Cartwright has killed himself sir ? During your meeting with him did you learn anything about his situation either professional or private that could infer he would take such a course of action ? I know that those are tough questions to answer, but now with the advantage of hindsight, can you think of anything of that nature ?"

Reddy gave this question some considerable thought before he answered.

"I met a man who appeared in control of his life. He was forthright in his views, not at all cagey. He was demonstrably well informed about the bank's business. On the other hand, I think he showed me the person that he wanted me to see."

"You think that his real state of mind was perhaps less confident ?"

"There were no abnormal behaviour traits that I noticed. Of course, I can't speak about his personal life."

"Is there any information you can share with us that confirmed your original hypothesis about the bank being in financial trouble Mr. Reddy ? I appreciate this is a highly sensitive subject. Nevertheless we too can and do operate under strict confidentiality rules in these circumstances."

"Let me put it this way Inspector, I have not unearthed definitive evidence of illegal activity. Which isn't to say that I wont."

"That reply is elliptical, if you don't mind my saying so. Candidly, what is your professional view of the state of health of the bank, sir ?"

"I think it is definitely suffering from liquidity difficulties. Its' net deposits are dwindling. Some of its lending looks highly risky. The published data from the bank's last annual accounts are now out of date, but I'm sure that their delinquent loans have increased significantly over the past six months."

"Is it possible that there could be a run on the bank ? Could it be insolvent ?"

"There you are headed onto thin ice Inspector. At this stage, I can't give you a firm judgement on questions of that kind, although I have serious concerns. I understand your hypothesis though. High insolvency risk equates with a bank head at the end of his wits ?

Nowhere to turn ? In desperation takes his own life ? Would that be the logic ?"

"The toxicologist's report shows that Mr. Cartwright had cocaine in his blood at the time of his death. People usually take strong drugs for a reason. Cocaine helps the depressed or psychologically weak feel good. We do not rule out at this stage that such a 'logic' as you call it might apply."

"That's the first I've heard of drugs in connection with Cartwright." Reddy said, in exculpation. "What I do know though is that Cartwright was not only CEO of the Ipswich & Blackwater, but also a Director of its parent, the Celtic and European Banking Group. So he had two jobs. Maybe he was in over his head in that respect ? I have only looked at his local activities up till now. What he did to fulfil his other role I'm about to research."

DI Wright and DS Adam had themselves learnt the same thing about Cartwright during their talk yesterday to Mary Donoghue at the Ipswich & Blackwater's headquarters. Although she appreciated that Reddy might be painting on a broader canvas than just locally, DI Wright chose at this juncture not to explore this. With an unobtrusive nod she caught the attention of DS Adam who had been sitting listening in brooding silence.

"Do you know or have you ever heard of James McAuley, Mr. Reddy" Adam inquired brusquely.

Reddy turned partially towards the silhouette with the Scottish accent. He could just make out his craggy facial features. He sensed that the interview was at a turning point. He sensed too déjà vu, in that he found himself full circle faced again with a question about his knowing a person whom the police had an interest in. Giving the wrong answer would be an act of folly. On the other hand, he was reluctant to divulge what he had learnt from Burleigh about McAuley's dealings in the development land market. DI Wright, observing Reddy minutely, noted his hesitation before answering.

"I do not know him personally; in fact, I've never met him. However, I am aware of who he is to some extent, yes."

"Could you elaborate on 'to some extent', sir ? DS Adam mimicked.

"Well, McAuley inherited a huge estate at Loxwood near Colchester when his father died a few years back. I understand that he has been

135

involved recently in dealings with a housing estate developer trying to get a portion of the land approved for planning permission. If that happens, he stands to make a tidy sum."

This was news to Wright and Adam. However, their interest was to assess the possibility of a linkage between the two deaths of Cartwright and McAuley via drugs.

"Are you perhaps aware that young McAuley had a drugs dependency ?" DS Adam persisted.

"Not at all" Reddy asserted, genuinely surprised. "As I said, I have no knowledge of him personally."

"Nor will you ever, sir. Mr. James McAuley is dead." DS Adam announced with telling finality. "He died last Sunday night from an overdose of cocaine. The news will be released to the media later this morning by the police team investigating his demise. It is assumed at present that it was suicide or death by misadventure."

DI Wright watched Reddy's reaction. It was genuinely spontaneous. His eyes widened involuntarily and his jaw slackened.

"I'm stunned. I don't know what to say. Really."

DS Adam and DI Wright exchanged glances. DI Wright had decided to take back control of the meeting.

"Mr. Reddy we simply wanted to assess the possible linkages here between the two deaths, given that they are both suicides, both more or less contemporaneous, and both associated with cocaine consumption. As the media are being informed later this morning, I would appreciate it that you treat this information as strictly confidential until then."

"You can rely on me."

"Then I think that we can terminate proceedings there Mr Reddy. At least, for the time being. We may need to come back to you in a day or so to ask follow up questions. I trust that we can have the same easy availability and cooperation from you sir ? We are on a tight schedule from our boss either to close this case as a tragic suicide or else open it up into a more thorough investigation."

"Yes, count on me." Reddy rejoined.

DI Wright stood up. The two men followed suit, Reddy first having reclaimed his mackintosh.

"You're continuing your own investigations into the banking sector sir ?" DI Wright threw out as an afterthought.

"Certainly, yes. But I have bosses who need to be managed too" he quipped.

They all filed out of the Conference room. DI Wright took her leave after shaking his hand and departed down the corridor to her office. DS Adam accompanied Reddy back to the front desk to assure his authorised exit from the building.

From her office on the first floor standing besides a window, DI Wright observed Reddy depart down Civic Drive, now wearing his Burberry coat. She had known while interviewing him that she had seen him before somewhere. Only now it came to her where. He was an occasional visitor at the Sports Centre where she habitually trained twice a week after work.

At that moment, DS Adam stormed into her office, extinguishing any half-formed reflections. In his right hand was a copy of the morning's local paper. He brandished it at Wright, pointing with his index finger at an article on the front page.

"Some bugger has let the cat out of the bag !" he exclaimed irately, "Look at this."

He slapped the newspaper flat on Wright's desk, standing back to let her read.

Wright peered down and studied the article. Under a headline "*Mystery diamonds discovered at Bank's headquarters*", the story described the bare facts of the diamonds' discovery in the vaults of the Ipswich & Blackwater Bank. It omitted to provide any source for the information but claimed that "*officials at the Bank were mystified, and unable to offer any explanation*".

The article ended with the sentence: "*Last week end the chief executive officer of the Bank, Mr. Thomas Cartwright, commited suicide.*"

Having insisted to the Bank's head of security, who had been with them at the time of the discovery, that the discovery remain undisclosed until they had satisfactorily cleared the matter up, DI Wright felt chagrined. She turned and looked up at her colleague.

"What do you make of it, Charlie ? Just loose tongues ? Sensation-seeking journalism ?"

"Money and mischief, that's what I think" Adam responded acidly. "That Bank security guy ? He was playing up all pally with me yesterday with the "I'm an old cop" routine. He was the only one who saw the diamonds. I'll swear it was him."

"Motive Charlie ?"

"Money would be my guess. Listen, let me get onto this at once. I'll make some enquiries about him. Harry Keogh was his name ?"

"Correct. I thought you liked him ?"

"I've changed my view." He wheeled around and was gone.

Alone, DI Wright re-read the short article. She found it odd. Particularly the last sentence. Was it, she wondered, just tagged on as a journalistic afterthought ? Or was it a deliberate signpost drawing attention to the proximate connection of the two events ?"

The investigator in her told her that it would be worthwhile learning which of those two interpretations was the valid one. She picked up the phone and dialled the internal switchboard.

"Hi Pauline, how can I help ? "

"Hi Maggie. Listen, can you get me the local newspaper offices please ? I want to speak to the Editor."

It was chilly outside on the street. Vehicles streamed past incessantly. Reddy put on his mackintosh for warmth. He checked the time on his watch. It was just gone ten twenty, so he had been interviewed by the two police for about half an hour or so. Remembering that he had switched off his mobile phone prior to the meeting, he took it from his mackintosh pocket and turned it back on. Someone had been trying to reach him but the number was withheld so he was unable to return the call.

Uncertain of his thoughts about the police interview and given that it was not raining, he selected to walk back to his apartment at the Marina via a route that would allow him to meander through the southern section of the Town centre. He hoped that a little distraction and fresh air would provide an antidote to the oppressive atmosphere of police headquarters.

More importantly, he needed time to distil the contents of the meeting with the two police officers. Performing another activity unconnected with the events or information recently experienced, invariably led him to valuable conclusions or new insights.

He was walking along Museum street, vicariously observing the comings and goings of shoppers and small groups of indolent youngsters. Suddenly, he recalled where he had previously seen DI Wright. She used the same gym as he did not far from the train station. He remembered her using the running machines. Seeing her today for the first time out of that context, wearing professional attire, had thrown him off balance.

This realisation immediately powered another. People have many 'disguises'. They reveal personas tailored to specific needs and relationships. Wouldn't that explain the fact that, when individuals commit suicide, family friends and acquaintances invariably comment that they never expected it ? That the person they knew was stable and level headed, and other mundanities of that ilk ? No wonder then that he had no clue who was the 'real' Thomas Cartwright.

Reddy made a mental note to contact Thomas Cartwright's wife. Who did she think her husband was and what he was doing ? Additionally, he determined to put more effort into examining Cartwright's other job as Director of the CEBG.

His mobile phone was ringing. The withheld number again. He took the call.

"Reddy here. Who's calling please ?"

"Craig, this is Samantha Cavendish." Her tone was thunderous.

"Good morning" Reddy offered neutrally, as if playing his first pawn in a chess game.

"It is *not* a good morning ! Why haven't I heard from you already this week ? Last Friday I gave you a deadline to provide me with your decision. You have breached it. I take it from your silence that you reject my offer."

From Samantha's adamant delivery, Reddy inferred that that was not a question but a firm conclusion on her part. Belatedly, he realised that he had made a mistake with Cavendish. Procrastinating with his decision, or as Edmund Burleigh had advised on Saturday "*playing a long game*" with his boss, wouldn't work. Samantha was a woman in a hurry to succeed. Buoyed by her unrelenting ambition, clearing out the debris and deadwood from around her was her default posture.

"I think we should discuss……" Reddy began hesitantly, but was interrupted.

"No discussion. You have cooked your goose. What in hell's name were you doing at the Banking Conference yesterday ? I took you off that assignment and gave it to Ted Collins."

"I still had a valid invitation. There was no point in foregoing an opportunity to gain insight into the latest debates. There were some excellent speakers."

A red warning light was flashing in Reddy's head. What had that bacillus Collins said to Cavendish to incriminate him ?

"You used the Courier's press pass. You were unauthorised to attend. Collins initially was refused entrance to the Conference. He had to call me in order to be accepted by the organisers."

"Samantha I am not responsible for the Courier's inability to manage its administrative duties" Reddy fired back.

"Craig, this was an egregious error on your part. No. It was deliberate insubordination. Your actions and lack of co-operation take this relationship to breaking point."

"Stuff and nonsense. Any sensible….." The riposte was too vague, even for his own satisfaction. Cavendish, impervious, cut him off. She crossed the finishing line at a canter:

"I have to inform you that the Editor Sinclair Monroe has agreed to your suspension. With immediate effect. It's on full pay pending an

140

inquiry by Human Resources into possible breach of contract. Until the outcome of that inquiry you shall under no circumstances conduct any business in the name of the Daily Courier; nor enter these offices unless specifically requested to do so by either myself or Cranshaw, the HR director. Is that understood ?"

Reddy cut the line in exasperation. He didn't bother to reply. No time for remorse. Get back to work at the apartment, he reflected.

As he set off again along Princes' street he passed a decorative building with authentic half timbers and white plaster probably dating from the late seventeenth century. His eyes took in the beauty of it. Then they fell to street level and he saw who occupied the premises.

It was a branch of the Ipswich and Blackwater Bank.

Chapter Fourteen

On the top floor of Universal Tower, Sinclair Monroe and Samantha Cavendish had taken a working lunch together in the meeting room next to Monroe's office. They had not been disturbed for the past ninety minutes, under instruction from Monroe to his personal assistant.

Monroe, fit and strong for his sixty one years' age, revelled in his role as Editor, feared but respected by his staff. He had become a household name in UK journalism since moving to the capital in the early nineteen seventies. His earlier journalistic experiences as a young reporter at the Scottish Clarion stood him in good stead in the combustible environment of Fleet Street.

A decade or so later, Monroe won his first editor's job. Subsequently, he had been editor of two other national press titles. The longevity of his tenures, according to apocryphal stories, arose directly from his skills in navigating around the egos of their respective owners.

Prior to taking up the editorship at the Daily Courier, he had ventured into television. He anchored his own Friday evening programme interviewing politicians and other prominent persons in the news. His signature interviewing style involved deploying a carefully crafted granite Scots persona asking blunt, 'no nonsense' questions. This was theatrically dressed with brusque interruptions of his interviewees if their replies were evasive, vacuous or 'sound bites'.

Audience figures for the programme soared because of its entertainment value. The public adored seeing politicians being contradicted, cajoled and castigated. Since all publicity, good or bad, is oxygen to those in the public eye, Ministers and opposition figures alike fell over themselves to be invited onto the programme. A "Minister mauled by Monroe" headline in the front pages of the week end papers was a valued prize for members of Westminster whose media profiles had been slipping.

However Monroe himself, ever the unpredictable and effervescent Scot, tired of his television success after a year or so. Curiously, this disillusionment coincided with the arrival of Damien White an American, as new owner of the ailing Daily Courier.

Monroe put it about that he had a hankering to return to 'real journalism', meaning a prestigious Editorship. White, keen to find a thoroughbred Editor able to fulfil his goals, saw in Monroe both a feisty media master and a walking address book with unparalleled access to the highest echelons of government. Monroe took up the editorial reins at the Daily Courier in early 2008, reportedly on the highest salary in the UK print media.

Samantha Cavendish, applying a mix of feminine guile and hereditary intelligence, had learned quickly to work effectively with Monroe. She saw behind his 'granite' persona. She saw his contradictory conceits and compassions; his pragmatism laced with charm; his authority architected on practiced mannerisms. She respected his epic ability to recall instantly people and events; his sure fire command of the language. Above all though, she was obsessed by his ability to prevail. He possessed an unmatched tenacity. Samantha saw that, to Monroe, winning an argument was a matter of will, more than of intellect.

Spending time with Monroe provided Cavendish with an accumulating store of understanding and rare insight into the world of contemporary power. It was not for nothing that Monroe was White's chosen media voice. He had rapidly disabused his acting Deputy Editor of the pretence that there were different fundamental choices in government. In command performances of scathing oratory, Monroe trashed the pluralists' apologias for the demise of Left and Right in politics. Left and Right were anachronisms in the age of transnational power elites, he explained. The imperatives of globalisation and interconnectedness drove the power elites to cooperate. He dismissed nation states as "relics". National power elites were merely "the sherpas". Policy today was ineluctably transnational. For what was at stake was the maintenance of five hundred years of western economic and cultural dominance.

To her astonishment, after six months' exposure to Monroe's influence, Cavendish discovered that her professional focus had switched away from the traditional beliefs that she had had about the 'fourth estate', 'pluralism', democracy and the like. These classical liberal assumptions were replaced with recognition that government, the state, the media and many satellite institutions were primarily means for harmlessly 'churning' dissent amongst the masses while retaining power for the global elites.

143

The final nail in the coffin of her liberal ideals had been hammered in by her own husband, Colin. One Sunday afternoon in late January they had taken a walk across Wimbledon Common. The weather was dry but overcast, the predominant colours everywhere sombre and grey. They were immersed in conversation, oblivious to the surrounding bleakness. The facts and fictions of their respective jobs absorbed them both.

She had unburdened her ideas to him, expecting to meet opposition and denial. Instead, he expressed sympathy. As a junior minister at the Treasury, he was depressed to learn how much automatism was imposed on a Minister. He had almost no room for manoeuvre on policy. He was anxious about an independent Audit Commission study being conducted into local authorities' financial investment management activities. At the Treasury, local government finance was part of his portfolio of responsibility. Whispered word in Whitehall was that the Commission was already unnerved by its interim findings. Although he didn't expect their report to be published until the spring, he was intending already to sound out job opportunities in the City. He might be axed as the scapegoat.

Monroe and Cavendish's "not to be disturbed" working meeting had been to determine the best way forward for the Daily Courier's reporting on the economy and the government's handling of it. With a critical G 20 Summit in London in two weeks' time, Damien White had left Monroe with no illusions that the editorial line to follow must be a pro-US, pro-stimulus agenda. How Monroe played those cards was up to him. Hence the meeting with his acting Deputy Editor.

Spread before them on the table were copies of competing daily and Sunday newspapers, including some overseas titles. Monroe was a firm believer in understanding the competition. That enabled him to plan better how the Daily Courier's own voice could be distinctive, incisive and dominant.

Beyond that, they had also co-ordinated their respective media exposure for the next days. Monroe had secured for himself an interview with the Prime Minister for the coming Friday. It would be published in the Courier's Saturday edition. For his acting Deputy, he had leveraged his contacts in broadcasting to obtain for her a first appearance on a Sunday morning current affairs television programme discussing the financial crisis and the forthcoming Summit's likely responses.

They had now over-run the allotted time for the meeting. Monroe's personal assistant had called through to announce that Oliver Carrington was waiting outside to join them when they were ready. Monroe, shirt sleeves rolled up to his elbows, launched into a final summing up.

"Look at it this way Samantha. Leadership is the essential ingredient that will get the West out of this crisis. This clearly isn't just another recession. It's the worst collapse in economic activity since the Great Depression of nineteen twenty nine to thirty two.

"That is agreed by most economists and political commentators Sinclair. The question is......."

Monroe, not having paused for breath, ignored Cavendish's interruption. He continued:

"The opportunity is there for the US administration to take the lead by adopting massive economic stimulus. Roosevelt succeeded back in the thirties. The current administration is intent on the same thing. Damien is adamant that the Courier's editorial line must be supportive. He sees the reticence of many on this side of the Atlantic as damaging. The Courier must lead opinion in this direction. The Prime Minister can build a strong platform from this too."

"I'm with you, Sinclair. I do have a concern though."

"Which is ?"

"That we risk becoming cheerleaders for the present UK government. It's unpopular with the electorate. Surely Damien doesn't want the Courier uncritically identified with an administration that may lose the next election ?"

Samantha, to her own surprise, found herself echoing the sentiments she had heard last Friday afternoon from Craig Reddy. Intellectually, she had graduated to the Sinclair Monroe school of governance; yet emotionally and culturally, she had not wriggled out of her old pluralist, liberal skin.

"Damien is concerned with influencing the influencers Samantha. If this administration is voted out, the new government is voted in. Damien requires that the Daily Courier be there in the forefront. Not just for the glitz and television camera events like G20; but more for the behind-the-scenes deal-cutting and bloodletting."

"Making sure the decision-makers are 'with the programme' ?" Samantha asked.

"Yes. We at the Courier can leverage the arguments of the economists and policy wonks who are endorsing calls for Keynesian demand side stimulus by governments. Make sure our column inches are stuffed with their thinking. Crowd out the opposition until the public has either forgotten them or sees them as nutters."

"So in the context of these preparatory coordination efforts with the US administration, Damien wants unalloyed editorial leadership from the Courier ?"

"For Damien, anything else is an 'un-American activity', Samantha" Monroe intoned with finality.

Cavendish picked up on the reference to Senator McCarthy's inquisitions of the 1950s. It jogged her memory that she wanted to raise with Monroe the subject of Lord Preston's surprise resignation from the Government that morning. She heard about it while talking to some of her journalists before lunch. It had been a breaking news story on one of the tv news channels switched on downstairs in the Business section's news room.

"Sinclair, before I forget, have you heard the news about Lord Preston's unexpected resignation ? You know I had Ted Collins do an interview with him yesterday ? I was intending to publish it in tomorrow's edition. I suppose I'll just have to pull it."

"Yes, of course, can it. Lord Preston is simply a victim of his own stupidity. Samantha, I was on the phone this morning with Downing Street coordinating with the PM's people on the interview I'll be doing with him this week end. Lord Preston's departure was no surprise to them. He wanted to push something through Cabinet that the PM categorically objected to. So he had to walk to keep face or accept being squashed in front of the whole Cabinet at their Wednesday meeting."

"You're well informed, I see. Did you discover what the subject of conflict was ?"

146

"Obviously to do with his portfolio. Other than that, nothing was forthcoming. Anyway, let's close the book on this planning session. Your young man Carrington is outside waiting to join us. Samantha, one thing I forgot to mention. Just before we have Carrington join us. This is definitely between us."

Involuntarily, Cavendish moved closer to him. Perhaps this secret was to be communicated in hushed tones.

"Damien has pulled strings with friends at a big US investment bank to have an exclusive interview with the US Treasury Secretary while he's over for the G20. I've recommended to him that you do it." He beamed a rare smile at her.

"Thanks Sinclair. I'd be delighted to have the chance."

"You deserve it lassie" he said, paternally. Before Cavendish could respond he continued, enthusiastically: "And there's more. White has hired the banqueting salon at the Excelsior Hotel down on The Strand. He's preparing to invite the great and the good to rub shoulders together immediately after the Summit. You and Colin must be there. Damien's personal assistant has the details and will go public with it tomorrow."

Without more ado, Monroe was on his feet and headed for the door connecting to his office. Opening it, he decorously held it open for Samantha to pass through. Like Samantha's office, Monroe's boasted a panoramic view across this part of east London, the Thames and the Millenium Dome. Floor to ceiling windows, instead of an outer wall, dramatised the effect.

Monroe went directly to his desk situated at the far side of his office. He speed dialled his personal assistant and told her to send Carrington through.

Oliver Carrington entered confidently and calmly into Monroe's office. As usual, he was immaculately turned out. Today he sported a medium grey three piece wool suit over a sky blue cotton shirt and plain marine blue silk tie.

"Take a seat Oliver" Monroe instructed.

Carrington obeyed, gliding into one of two comfortable chairs positioned either side of the Editor's desk. Cavendish took the other. Unlike most Courier employees, Carrington was at ease in Monroe's company. His sense of entitlement and self-assurance was profound. Anxiety and self-doubt were alien to him.

Monroe opted to remain standing behind his desk. Munroe drew himself up to his full height. Then he looked down towards Cavendish.

"So let's decide about our problem person. You spoke to Reddy as we agreed and told him he is suspended, correct ?"

Samantha and Carrington had earlier agreed on the briefing they would make to Monroe about the phone call to Reddy suspending him from work. Carrington had been on speakerphone with Samantha when she delivered her suspension message to Reddy.

"That's right. I spoke with him on his mobile phone this morning. I explained there will be an internal inquiry administered by HR."

"How did he respond ? Is he likely to become a serious liability? We don't want rebels, Samantha. History shows they tend to become martyrs."

"Reddy wasn't at all pleased Sinclair. On the other hand, he knows his options are limited. My guess, since he's obstinate, is that he'll walk."

Munroe was decisive: "Let's be strategic about this. It's time to cut his lines of supply and prevent further damage. Carrington, I want you to make sure that we know exactly what information he has collected. I also want you to uncover who is feeding the information to him. Results by Friday, please."

Carrington, keen to oblige, keen to go for the kill, suggested:

"As he is suspended already we can simply recall his notebook computer. It's company property after all. I can ask Human Resources to request he return it at the same time as he attends for the inquiry. Or, for instance, require the I.T. boys to call it in for maintenance or software upgrade ?"

"Do it" Monroe sanctioned, " but on condition that its secret and no trace of any intervention be evident."

Carrington smiled malevolently:

"Sir, I'll deliver the results. Just don't ask me to explain their means."

Munroe eyed Carrington dispassionately. He understood that the young man was providing him the freedom to remain innocent.

He remembered the phone call he had received yesterday from Declan Moroney, from the CEGB. Moroney grumbled about the "intrusive and unsettling" article published last Friday by Reddy on the matter of the Ipswich and Blackwater Bank. Munroe hadn't even seen the article himself and took a dim view of Moroney's compliant. The CEGB should mind their own damn business. Still, in the bigger picture, he saw that Reddy wasn't part of the Courier's future. Let Carrington pursue his fratricidal aim.

Back at his desk, Carrington got to work on what, in his own mind, he had named the 'Reddy redundancy project'. He was on a mission to see the back of this maverick. He placed an internal call through to the head of IT service management. After three rings the line was answered:

"Williams, IT service management."

"Hi Ambrose, this is Carrington, Deputy Editor's office ?"

"OK; but you know standard procedure for IT problems is a request logged through the service desk. I'm not your man" Williams drawled, disinterestedly.

"Right Ambrose, but I'm not your average IT user. I've got a job for you" Carrington insisted, with relish.

After a pause on the line Williams replied hesitantly "What is it you want ?"

"Craig Reddy, who works on the Courier's Finance and Business section, is suspended from work pending an inquiry. We want back his notebook computer immediately. Have your service maintenance team leader send him an instruction by email within the hour. It is to say that the machine is required urgently for software updates, or something similar that doesn't raise any questions. Then he should call Reddy to impress upon him that the notebook must be returned within 48 hours. Say he had been overlooked and is now late? Is that clear ?"

"Clear as mud, Carrington. Who the hell do you think you are ?" Williams challenged. "You have no authority. Go through the proper channels."

Carrington smiled to himself. Williams was a typical IT guy. Clueless about the politics of the business and the court of prince Oliver ! In a suavely authoritative tone Carrington said:

"Listen Ambrose my dear fellow, I am relaying to you instructions that come directly from Monroe. You can have it my way and keep your job. That means have that email sent out within the hour. Or you can have it your way. That means phone Monroe's office yourself now. I would caution you that that would be a terminally career limiting experience for you. Which is it to be ?"

In the following silence he could almost hear Williams' grey matter struggling with his predicament.

"OK. Fuck you, I'll do it. But I'm emailing you confirmation and copying my boss."

The line died.

Chapter Fifteen

Simon Farley unlocked his Ford truck using the vehicle key's infrared button. Opening the driver's door he flung his worn out leather holdall containing his work clothes and lunchbox onto the passenger's seat. He hauled himself into the driver's seat, switched on the ignition and drove the vehicle out of Manningtee station car park. The car park was packed still with commuters' cars silently awaiting the homecoming of their beleaguered owners.

Farley had taken a half day off work from the Olympics construction site at Stratford. He had caught the fast train out from Stratford for Norwich, which stopped at Manningtree at three twenty five. In truth, he could ill afford the time off given the pressure of work. Fortunately, he trusted his pal and workmate Barry Moore to run things smoothly in his absence.

He recalled their conversation first thing this morning. Moore and he stood huddled together on muddy terrain near the site 'office', a bright yellow Portakabin. It was damp, dull and damned cold. The two were sipping hot tea from plastic cups filled from Farley's thermos.

Moore had said: "Go for it Si. I'll keep the ship on an even keel. If you need to get stuff sorted back at Manningtree, the sooner you get to it the better. I'll call you if anything here needs your attention. Trust me." They had both grinned broadly and shaken hands firmly.

Apart from his parents, Farley only trusted two other people in his life. Moore was one of them. Craig Reddy was the other.

Farley directed his Ford to the A137, and then in the direction of Ipswich.

A number of problems were bugging Farley. They circulated in his mind as he drove. Foremost of these was the money he was losing from the roof trusses business. Since divulging this to Craig Reddy last Friday, he had received further bad news yesterday. Another of his builders' merchant clients had called to say that sales were down and he intended to discontinue stocking them. Farley offered to talk to him the following day, face to face. This particular client happened to be the

151

one who had first taken up the trade with Farley through the encouragement of Elvin. In Farley's own mind then, failure to keep him would be a highly symbolic defeat. He was desperate to convince the man to hang on. Farley had phoned Elvin last night and had him agree to join the meeting today. Elvin and this guy – Mark Hancock – went back a few years together. Elvin's acceptance was conditional on being picked up directly from Dears' brickworks fronting onto the river Deben near Cattawade.

That was Farley's present destination.

The second matter also involved money. Not only that, but it required him trying to enlist Mark Hancock's help. Hancock's brother in law – David Morley - supplied the plant and equipment that Farley used for heavy lifting work on his contract at the Olympics site in Stratford. Hancock had recommended Morley to Farley. He was 'family' and his business was conveniently based south of Walthamstow, not far from the Stratford site.

Sure enough, Morley had done a deal with Farley. Farley's request to hire out the equipment on a month by month basis was accepted. That worked well for Farley because his own subcontract could be terminated on equally short notice. He hadn't wanted to be caught in the same error he had committed with the contract for importing the roof trusses.

Morley was threatening now to raise his hire prices fifteen percent with effect from next month. He claimed that the east London construction plant market was hotting up with the increase of Olympics-related infrastructure projects. Farley figured now was the time to leverage the relationship with Hanley to obtain concessions from his brother in law.

To pile further trouble onto his litany of misfortunes, Farley was also concerned that Georgi Bourov had not shown up for work. Barry Moore had phoned him earlier with the news. This was exceptional. The guy never missed work. Yet he had not called in either to say he was sick or offer any explanation. All efforts to reach his mobile phone had failed. It was switched off.

Mulling over his problems, Farley's driving had been reflexive. The route was one needing almost no conscious effort on his part, such was the number of times he had driven it.

Suddenly, he saw ahead that he had was approaching the exit from the A137 to Elvin's brickworks. He indicated right, and turned the Ford truck off the road onto the bumpy track. At the far end he drove through the open security gates at the brickworks' entrance. Ahead he saw the burly figure of Elvin. He was standing stock still waiting for him outside the office, hands in pockets. As was his habit, he was dressed in his baggy old working clothes, topped off by a scruffy peaked cap.

Farley executed a wide U turn so that the vehicle was pointed again for the exit. Time was short so they had agreed to depart at once for Hancock's merchants yard a couple of kilometres back down the road. Once the vehicle halted, Elvin opened the passenger's side door and clambered inside. His weather-beaten features resembled the ravaged Tennessee basin of the 1930s.

"There's good news and bad news" Elvin announced, even before Farley could welcome him aboard.

"Let's hear it, then." Farley had his own troubles enough, but he owed Elvin due consideration.

"Good news first. The bricks you ordered were delivered to your folks' house this morning."

"That's great. Do you know if they stacked them safely around the side of the property as I asked ?"

"Is what they were told to do Simon, but you'll have to check."

"OK. So the bad news is ?"

"The owners told all the staff yesterday that they're definitely closing the brickworks for good. According to them, it's no longer profitable because of the energy costs."

"Shit. Elvin that is bad." Farley commiserated. "No possible buyers ?"

"Come on ! The place is almost a ruin. It works fine but they haven't invested here for ages. So no; no trade buyers. They're going to keep operating only 'till the end of the month to complete outstanding orders."

While Elvin was talking, Farley had driven the Ford away from the brickworks back onto the A137. Cattawade was just a couple of kilometres down the road. He said to Elvin:

"The way my luck is going, I'll be joining you on the dole queue myself. What with the losses on the roof trusses and Morley raising his prices on the construction plant equipment."

"No dole queue for Simon. I'll simply retire. Had enough to be honest. Even if I don't know what I'll do with myself. You shouldn't be so negative. Let's see what leverage we can get with Mark in a minute. Maybe he'll play ball."

Farley wasn't willing to be optimistic. His mind was full of his woes:

"They say troubles come in three's don't they ? 'Cos my other crap is that we're getting ourselves a bad name now down on the Stratford site. Did I tell you by the way that Geogi Bourov, the Bulgarian strong man I have on the team, has gone awol ? Simply disappeared. Unreachable and hasn't been to work this week ?"

Elvin had been introduced to Bourov when he accompanied Farley up to Catterwade once. They'd all ended up having a couple of pints together in the White Horse in Manningtree. Elvin surprised Farley with his comment:

"Strange that, Simon. I had Bourov visit me at the brickworks yesterday. Gave me a call on Sunday and asked if he could come over. Naturally, I said 'yes'. Assumed he'd okayed it with you !"

Farley couldn't fathom what he heard, giving Elvin a puzzled look:

"What the hell did he want Elvin ?"

"He was interested in the brick making. Asked me to explain the whole process to him. I didn't need an excuse. It was a pleasure to find someone genuinely interested. He asked lots of questions too. He's a good lad is Georgi. I've got time for him. Old school temperament if you know what I mean. Wants to do the right thing."

Exasperated, Farley cut off the eulogy: "Elvin, you sound like you're giving him a bloody recommendation. The man's awol so far as I'm concerned."

The Ford arrived at a mini roundabout and Farley turned it left onto a road that was a cul de sac. They passed through a residential zone of nineteen thirties bungalows and semi-detached houses. Beyond these, the road made a sharp ninety degree turn left. The straight road, empty of traffic, led past dilapidated factory buildings and motley other disused structures.

Farley's frustration with Bourov was transferred to scenery:

"This place is the pits" he observed, casting his eyes over the forlorn surroundings. "It looks as if no one has spent money here in years. No wonder Hancock is facing problems with his business."

Further down the road he pulled the Ford through open gates that led into the builders' merchants yard of Lawsons, a well-known nationwide chain. He parked just to the side of the main entrance.

Around the front of the yard was every conceivable variety of pitch fork truck, dumper, JCBs, mobile generators, hydraulic cranes, and pneumatic drills. At the back of the yard was a substantial corrugated iron shelter held up by vertical metal pillars. Inside, beyond the open roll-down doors, were housed stacks of palleted roof tiles, breeze blocks, plastic piping, porcelain sanitary ware, window frames and wooden roof trusses.

Hancock appeared from out of a makeshift prefabricated office. He was probably in his late fifties with salt and pepper hair, oiled and brushed back from his forehead. Under an unbuttoned sheepskin jacket he wore a black and white chequered woollen shirt, open at the collar. A thick gold chain hung around his neck, and an undergrowth of tangled chest hair protruded above the open shirt.

He shook hands with the new arrivals, his vice-like grip probably an offensive tactic in advance of any commercial negotiations. Farley intuited at once that his visit was pointless. The man's eyes wore an aspect of wafer-thin sociability, behind which was cold self interest.

A desultory exchange of views on the subject of Farley's supplying roof trusses ensued; Hancock going through the motions of understanding Farley's problems. The conversation ground to its inevitable conclusion within minutes, notwithstanding Elvin's intervention with an impassioned plea to his old work colleague to be patient and not terminate the contract.

Having won this important battle, Hancock played ball when Farley raised with him the difficulties he was experiencing with Morley, Hancock's brother in law. With no guarantees, Hancock promised to talk to him by 'phone.

There was little more to be said. Farley knew he was leaving empty-handed. He stumbled through some empty words of thanks. Hancock's rejoining platitude fell on deaf ears. Hancock stuffed his bare hands into the pockets of his sheepskin coat, wheeled away from them and headed for his office. Farley and Elvin walked back to the Ford truck in silence. Elvin could tell that Farley's temper was simmering. Farley opened the driver's door and climbed up. As Elvin entered the other side onto the passenger's seat, Farley hammered the steering wheel in exasperation with the palm of his hand.

"Damn it !" he exclaimed.

He fired up the engine, thrust the gear stick into gear, and burned rubber off the Ford's tyres as his foot hit the accelerator and the vehicle rocketed away towards the yard exit. Turning out of the yard onto the feeder lane leading back to the A137, he settled the vehicle to a reasonable speed. He was still angry and frustrated, but not to the measure that he wanted to risk other drivers.

Elvin, still silent, pretended to be content watching the scenes outside pass by. Discreetly, he cast a glance now and then at Farley, trying to gauge if he had calmed down. After about five minutes, Farley spontaneously opened up.

"What else to expect ?" he rationalised. "Hancock's also not a free agent is he ? Like he said, it's the firm's head office that's dictating buying policies. They analyse the sales. They decide what's hot and what's not. Relationships and sentiment are out the window. It's the numbers that count."

"That appears to be it" Elvin consoled, lamely. He was feeling sympathy for Farley. He himself had been unable to leverage his old friendship with Hancock to convince him to maintain the business arrangements with Farley. What he had accomplished, he hoped, was to help Farley deal with the brother-in-law.

"There could at least be something positive coming out of that visit" Elvin ventured. "Mark did agree to have a word with Morley about the price increases on your equipment. I think that might bear fruit."

"You laid it on nicely there Elvin. Thanks." Farley said, referring to the subtle way Elvin had steadily ratcheted up Hancock's guilt feelings. "Let's wait and see though. Morley is in a strong position, 'cos what he's saying about the market is pretty much so."

They lapsed into silence again, each mentally absorbed in their respective worlds of worry. They were headed back along the A137, had passed the railway station and were in the outskirts of Manningtree. Elvin had asked Farley to drop him off at The White Horse in the centre of town. He was meeting an acquaintance there for a drink and bar meal at six o'clock. Farley himself had to be at Portman Road in Ipswich by six thirty. He and Craig Reddy would drink a pint before watching the evening home game against Burnley at seven thirty. Time was tight to catch the train leaving at twelve past the hour.

In the last couple of minutes, Elvin had taken up the conversation relating episodes of his past. This was highly unusual. Farley knew him more as someone who clammed up.

 "You learn to take the rough with the smooth, Simon. If you don't adapt you're dead." Elvin averred.

"I didn't know you were a Darwinian Elvin ?" Simon said, ironically.

"I didn't attend enough school to know what Darwin said" Elvin replied dismissively. "What I do know is that my old boy had to change his life to survive. I've had to do the same."

"Really ? I know you worked with Hancock before you started at Dears' brickworks. That's about it."

"Yeah, well you don't know the half of it. I only moved to Ipswich in nineteen seventy. I was twenty two then and both my folks were dead. I found work at Lawsons', the building materials firm ?"

Farley acknowledged this by nodding his head, eyes fixed on the road. He thought it best to say nothing. Elvin talking about his past was unheard of.

"That's when I teamed up with Mark. But I didn't like the work much. Through local contacts I got the kiln manager's job at Dears' in seventy two. In those days there was a boom on in house building. They had plenty of work. Although they always stayed in the quality end of the market. I've been lucky, thirty plus years with the same job. After a while the owners simply left me to my own devices running the kiln operations. Pretty much my own boss I've been."

"So where did you pick up the skills to do the brick making Elvin ?" Farley asked.

157

"That's where my old man come into it you see ? When I was a kid we lived up near Peterborough and my dad worked for the London Brick Company. He got me an apprenticeship there when I left school at fifteen."

Farley was driving down Manningtree High Street. He slowed the vehicle as the road narrowed. The White Horse Hotel was just half a kilometre away.

"Go on" he encouraged, realising that Elvin was almost at his journey's end.

Elvin told him.

Farley was astonished by what he heard, but had no time to discuss it. He decelerated the vehicle to a halt outside the White Horse. They shook hands and Elvin climbed out. Fearing that he may be late for the departing train to Ipswich, Farley executed a U turn that exasperated oncoming motorists, and left in the direction of the railway station.

Elvin's revelation had left him marvelling at peoples' many identities.

Chapter Sixteen

17.45   Tuesday 17th March 2009.   Reddy's Apartment, Ipswich Marina, Ipswich

The CD player was still switched on but the music had stopped a long time ago. Reddy had chosen to play Miles Davis' classic album "Kind of Blue"; a reissue from Columbia that included a first release of an alternate 'Flamenco Sketches'. The musical selection was his antidote to the seething bad mood he had had on returning to his apartment around lunchtime.

Having left police headquarters and chosen to walk back to his apartment, he had been hit by the equivalent of an Exocet missile when he accepted a 'caller identity withheld' call on his mobile phone. He was doubly unprepared for the resultant conversation. First, because the unknown caller was Samantha Cavendish. Second, he had carelessly not developed a well defined script in advance of this inevitable conversation. She had given him a deadline of Monday to give her his decision; a deadline which he had overlooked while in London most of yesterday.

He replayed their conversation in his head several times once back at his apartment. Being suspended from work encumbered him with a black humour. Irritably toying with the possible consequences of his new status only worsened things.

To calm himself sufficiently to be able to do some work, Reddy deliberately chose the soothing balm of extemporised dreamland that was the music on "Kind of Blue". The CD's cover notes asked: *"Don't we all enjoy a taste of heaven now and then* ?". Heaven's therapy effect was exactly what Reddy needed to focus his thoughts on the task before him. Namely, to write an article for The Messenger about the Audit Commission exposé of local government poor spending decisions.

Initially he had gotten off to a slow start, struggling to build the narrative and highlight the arguments. But eventually the text took shape into a work which, if not of inspiration, crossed his own quality threshold. It was now just past five forty five and he had a draft article ready to send to his Messenger journalist friend Peter Houseman.

That left him with about ten minutes before having to leave the apartment to meet Simon Farley. They had agreed to attend Town's evening match at Portman Road against Burnley.

Reddy opened his email inbox. He had not read it since yesterday evening. Amongst the list of unread messages he spotted one received early this morning from Stanislav Cerny. He opened it. Stan was replying to Reddy's request made at the Banking Conference yesterday. He offered the name and contact details of one of his Czech colleagues who worked on the Bank's trading desk. The email explained that this person - Radek Husarik - was already briefed by Stan what Reddy's requirement was. Husarik had promised to run a search the same day. Reddy should try calling him, the email suggested, by close of business Tuesday to see what he had unearthed.

Unsure of Bank trading desks' working hours, Reddy took the 'carpe diem' route, immediately picking up the cordless phone and dialling Husarik's mobile number. It rang four times before someone answered.

"Husarik" a voice said, in a hushed tone.

"Hello. Radek Husarik ? This is Craig Reddy calling. I'm a friend of Stanislav Cerny ? "

"Yes, I recognise your name."

"He suggested I give you a call this afternoon. Is this convenient ?"

"Not really to be honest. I can't give you more than a couple of minutes. I'm still on the trading desk. We're not supposed to receive private calls while trading."

Reddy did not offer to call back later. He was determined to have whatever new information was to be had.

Husarik had also decided the best policy was to give this guy what he had: "I looked earlier today at the recent share buying of this stock you're interested in. Redwood Country Homes right ?"

"Correct. It's in the FTSE 250."

"On the trading desk we have access to premium services. I can see details of all the share transactions. Buyers, sellers, quantities, and so on. What I can't see is the identity of the buyer, only which institutions and brokers are transacting. I ran a sort on the larger transactions over the past three months. What I've managed to identify is that there has been a regular buyer placing orders for standard quantities using the same broker."

Reddy listened attentively; impressed with Husarik's thoroughness.

"As it happens I know a guy at that broker so I phoned them up."

"And ?" Reddy encouraged, sensing that he was close to a breakthrough.

"After some wrangling he divulged that the buyer was a Panamanian nominee company. Which means, of course, that the real owners are hidden from view" Husarik concluded.

Reddy felt deflated. This result brought he back to the beginning.

"I went a step further"

"You see, our Bank has a Latin American markets desk. They're located here in the same office as me. All the guys speak Spanish and trade to local Latin time, so they don't come in to work until after lunch. Anyway, I've spoken with a mate who works on the desk. He's promised to speak later to our local office in Panama City to see if they can take it further."

"Should I be hopeful, do you think ?" Reddy had no clue what the chances were.

"Don't hold your breath. Unless my mate here can call in a few favours, this may take time. Panama right ? Latino culture. Anyway, can I reach you on this number, if something comes up ?"

Reddy gave him his mobile phone number, asking him to repeat it to be sure. He thanked Husarik profusely and then closed the call.

Noticing that the stereo system was still on, Reddy went over, took out the Miles Davis CD and turned it off. It was now past six o'clock. He switched on the television to see if he might catch the summary of the national news headlines. He was not a news junkie but could tolerate small doses of the private satellite channel.

He returned to his email inbox. There still were some unread messages. Keeping with his own priorities, he first opened a new email and attached a file containing the draft of his exposé article on local government financial mismanagement. He addressed it to Peter

Houseman. In his message he asked Houseman to read the file. Recalling Havering's deadline of the coming week end, he added that publication Saturday night/Sunday morning was his goal.

There were several more still unread messages. Two caught his eye as worth reading now. One was from his 'mole' at the FSA, Natasha. She had sent it from her private email address. She proposed to meet him in London tomorrow after work at four thirty o'clock outside Foyles' Bookshop. Enigmatically, the message said it was "important" and that he "wouldn't be disappointed". Reddy's male instinct spontaneously flagged the possible 'double entendre'. His rational self overrode it. Natasha, he knew, was signalling the availability of new information relevant to his dossier on the Ipswich & Blackwater Bank. Reddy quickly constructed an affirmative reply, asking her to send him a text message to his mobile if her circumstances changed.

The other email was from Charlie Hunt, an IT guy at the Daily Courier. Reddy only knew him because they had played five a side football together in the past. Hunt requested him to return his laptop computer for software upgrades and maintenance. He explained that Reddy had been overlooked in a circular email released at the start of the week and please could he return the machine before Friday.

The email's content surprised Reddy. He pondered what this might be about. However, he reached no conclusion as his attention was drawn to images appearing on the television. A photogenic female newsreader – already on the way to becoming a national 'celebrity' - was speaking to camera. Reddy leapt around the table, dexterously grabbed the remote device and raised the audio volume.

The newsreader was saying:

"......has resigned from the government earlier today. In a written statement to the press he said he had tendered his resignation to the Prime Minister because of irreconcilable differences of view on key policy questions. Here now, live from Westminster is our correspondent, Corrie McFadden. Corrie, the government must be embarrassed by this unexpected departure by Lord Preston ?"

Reddy recovered his composure from his initial reaction which was disbelief. He looked at his watch. He absolutely had to leave. Against his own will to stay he put on his shoes, gathered his coat and Town scarf, switched off the tv and went to the front door. Locking it behind him as he left, Reddy headed for the lift to keep his appointment with Farley to watch Town.

His mind was still focused though on the recent news of Lord Preston's sudden resignation. Reddy was bewildered by it. The lift came to a jolting stop at the ground floor, the doors automatically opening. As they did so, so to did an idea in Reddy's mind. Perhaps there was a connection between Preston's "irreconcilable" differences with the Prime Minister and Natasha's important new information about the Ipswich & Blackwater ?

Tuesday 17th March 21.10 pm

Outside Ipswich Town Football Club stadium, Portman Road, Ipswich

Farley and Reddy were both well wrapped up with warm outer clothing and sporting Ipswich Town scarves. They had joined the early leavers from the stadium to get a head start to the pub just around the corner. Exiting through the open gates onto the street, they heard the referee's final whistle bringing to an end Town's match against Burnley. The applause and shouts from the crowd rose into the cold night air.

They set off side by side across the street intending to cut through the car park opposite. More and more fans were pouring out of the stadium causing a wave of congestion for pedestrians and vehicles alike.

"Entertaining game. Shame that we didn't get three points though" Reddy commented.

"Right. I thought once Dos Santos got the equaliser we would be home and dry. It wasn't as if we didn't have the chances." Farley's tone was one of exasperation.

"Civelli should definitely have scored" Reddy asserted. "He was clean through. Truth be told though, both sides were saved by their 'keepers tonight. I thought Richard Wright was outstanding for us."

"Two home points dropped" Farley mourned. "We're definitely out of the running for the play-offs."

Reddy concurred: "When your goalscorer and best player is a loanee, no surprise. Even before tonight, I don't think there were that many

163

Town supporters who still believed in getting to the Premiership this season."

Reddy felt his mobile phone vibrating. Extracting the device from the inner pocket of his coat, he saw that a text message had arrived. It was from Husarik:

"*Dead end. Panama company registered by law firm: Hernandez y Ramirez. Nominee director is Ramirez. No name 4 beneficial owner.*"

Reddy tapped out "thanks", sent the message and replaced the phone in his pocket. He could do nothing now about Husarik's negative news; it was another roadblock to the investigation. He determined to negotiate his way around it.

They returned to their conversation about the match but it had petered out by the time they reached the pub. Two brawny security staff manned the door, checking that only Town supporters entered. Farley and Reddy were recognised as regulars and passed inside without ado. The main bar was thickly populated with bibulous drinkers.

Reddy bought two pints of Abbot ale at the bar, returning with them to where Farley was seated. He had found two high stools at a counter that ran along the length of the bar's outer wall and below the windows affording a view onto the lighted street outside.

With the interruption of Reddy's waiting at the bar to be served, Farley's thoughts had reverted to his lack of success earlier in the day with Hancock. He now recounted his woes to Reddy as they sipped their beers.

"So how do you see things from here Simon ?" Reddy asked, once Farley's story was told.

"No light at the end of the tunnel. I've got the final shipment of roof trusses due at the Docks tomorrow evening. That's another five thousand units on top of the thousand or more that are still stored in the warehouse. At cost price that's something like a hundred and twenty thousand pounds of stock which I can't shift. Plus the monthly storage costs. I'm in debt with the bank to the tune of nearly a hundred and fifty thousand, what with late payers and what have you."

"Hell's teeth !" Reddy exclaimed. "That's serious money."

"You don't have to tell me" Farley groaned. "I may need to sell the boat to repay the loan to Bank. I reckon I could get about ninety to a hundred for it."

"Who's the bank ?" Reddy asked, shocked at his friend's level of indebtedness.

"The Ipswich and Blackwater."

The name hit Reddy like a stone. He had not revealed to Farley the nature of his current investigative dossier. Maybe he should.

Chapter Seventeen

03.15 Wednesday 18th March 2009. Home of Mrs Cartwright, a suburban street, Ipswich.

At this hour of the morning there was no traffic on the residential suburban street. Pedestrian pavements either side of the road lay empty. The branches of cherry blossom trees lining the street, twitched and shuddered in the cold morning breeze. Overhead street lights bathed the road's curb sides in oval-shaped pools of dim light. Above them, the night sky was carbon black.

He parked the Ford Focus in an empty space about forty yards away from the house on the opposite side of the road. He cut the ignition and turned off the lights. Then he sat unmoving. Watching and listening. Like a cat, patiently awaiting the appearance of its prey.

Careful concealment was the guiding principle of his plan of action. Of course, Russell Westlake had been the catalyst. Westlake had required him to do this. But it was not for Westlake that he was here now. He was working on his own volition. The motives were his own; so too the iron determination and meticulous planning. The confidence he possessed arose from an awareness that he controlled the operation.

He had taken Monday and Tuesday off work to prepare. There had been plenty to do. First, he had hired the Ford Focus. Then he had driven to meet Westlake at the agreed pub car park outside Ipswich. Westlake gave him the key to the safe. Plus an assurance that the house would be empty and the alarm off. Mrs Cartwright was staying with her mother. Westlake designated the same car park for a follow-up rendez-vous at lunchtime on Wednesday. Then they had separated.

Next, he reconnoitred the residential area surrounding Cartwright's property. He drove around, memorising any obstacles that could impinge on the success of the operation. After that, he parked the rental car in a neighbouring street and walked back and past the house. As he did so, he captured mental images of the lay out: the low brick wall and small front garden; the bitumen-covered front drive leading down from the garage at the left of the house to the street; a wooden front door, slightly hidden from view by an external porch and a couple of miniature conifers in earthenware pots; protruding bay windows on either side of the porch; an alarm system attached to the house wall at first floor level; and the narrow paved path off to the right, leading to the back of the property via a locked wrought iron gate.

Later, back in his one bedroom apartment house in Colchester, he tooled up and selected the right clothing for the night's operation. Having done those tasks he placed a brief phone call through to his buyer. Then he ate a light meal and relaxed in front of the television awaiting the small hours.

Now seated motionless in the Ford Focus in view of the house, his eyes were fully accustomed to the varying shades of darkness along the street. There were no lights on in any of the houses near the Cartwright property. It too was in darkness. The street lamps' illuminations were sufficient to pick out movement within their limited range. But there was none.

He had made a calculation that the entire operation from leaving the vehicle to returning should take no more than fifteen minutes. He checked his watch. Three fifteen. There was no more time to lose. If anyone had heard or seen the arrival of the car, then they might wonder why the driver would sit without alighting.

From the passenger's seat he picked up the black peaked cap he had chosen to hide his face and put it on. The rest of his clothing was plain, selected to avoid the attentions of even the most observant. His tools – a key, a pencil torch, and some short lengths of thin wire – fitted unobtrusively into his inner coat pockets.

He slid on a pair of supple black leather gloves. Silently, he exited the car. Closing the driver's door gently, he locked it manually. As if with every right to do so, he walked confidently towards the Cartwright house. There was no gate at the entrance to the drive. He continued without hesitation right up into the front porch. He withdrew one of the pre-formed short wires from his coat's inner pocket. Placing it into the door lock, he dexterously performed the procedure that threw the lock open. Replacing the wire in the coat pocket, he opened the front door and glided quietly through. Once inside, he closed the front door behind him soundlessly. He had taken less than ten seconds to enter from the porch.

Motionless, with his back against the door, he breathed slowly and listened. His heartbeat was normal. Following Westlake's assurance that the house was unoccupied and unalarmed, entering by the front door was a risk he had accepted to take. Nonetheless, he wanted to reassure himself.

No lights were on anywhere. The only luminosity came through a glass-paned wooden door to his immediate right which gave onto the living room. Directly ahead, a corridor led to another door, which accessed the kitchen. Half way down the corridor on the left was a carpeted staircase rising to the first floor.

At his meeting in the car park with Westlake, he had questioned him about the lay-out of the house. Knowing exactly where to locate the safe would save precious time. Knowing the disposition of the different rooms might add to his security. Cartwright's study, Westlake had said, was on the ground floor at the back of the house, only accessible via a door in the kitchen.

A repetitive sound emanated from the living room off to his right. Rather than investigate it, he remained still. Concentrating exclusively on the sound, he recognised that it was the regular swish of the second hand of a clock, probably located on a table or mantelpiece somewhere inside the room.

Satisfied about his security and where he needed to go, he moved cautiously down the corridor. At the far end, while keeping his balance, he bent his head to one side and stole a glance through the open door into the kitchen.

Venetian blinds were drawn closed across the kitchen windows. Outside was the back garden, pitch dark. With one finger he put light pressure on the kitchen door until it opened sufficiently to allow him to enter. He made out the fixtures and fittings off to his left and heard a steady low hum coming from the refrigerator. In front of him was a round pinewood table around which four pinewood chairs were assembled. The door to Cartwright's study was hidden to the right behind the door through which he had come.

The door opened without sound, and he entered Thomas Cartwright's study. It was not difficult to find the safe. It was not secreted behind a wall-hung painting in a discreetly concealed wall cavity, or accessed by an electric switch under a desk, like in some movies he had seen. Mundanely, just as Westlake had described, it sat on the bottom shelf of a fitted bookcase positioned snugly into the corner of the far wall. The bookcase was stocked with box files, books and CDs. The metal safe was visible and not fastened to the wall. Thomas Cartwright, being the only person in the household who had a key and this study being his space, presumably believed that a theft was all but impossible.

Lifting the key from his coat's inner pocket, he held its' head firmly between thumb and index finger. Guiding it into the safe's lock he applied only the lightest of pressure to turn it. There was a light click inside the lock mechanism as the key turned evenly and then easily as the lock unlocked. The tools he had brought along, in case this given key failed to open the safe, would remain unused. Leaving the key in the lock, he pulled back the thick door to a fully opened position.

The room being dark, when he bent down and looked inside the safe he could not fathom if there was anything inside. With a shock, the idea flashed through his mind that the safe was empty. His instincts warned that he had been set up. Deterring incipient panic, he calmly put a gloved hand inside the safe's interior to feel for possible contents. Immediately he found a black velvet bag lying at the base of the safe. He extracted it. It was not at all heavy, maybe a couple of hundred grams. The bag was closed tight at the top by black cord stitched into the material.

Belatedly, he remembered that he had with him a pencil-thin plastic torch in the outer coat pocket. Annoyed with his memory lapse, he withdrew it and switched it on. Holding both the bag and torch, he moved to a desk in front of the study's only window. Venetian blinds again blocked out the outside world.

He put the torch down on the desk. Taking the top of the bag between the fingers of both hands he gently pulled it open and placed it onto a rectangular leather cover that lay in the middle of the table top. Slowly and carefully he tipped up the bag and its contents tumbled out. He took up the torch and directed the beam at the contents. In all there were about forty cut diamonds, reflecting and sparkling brilliantly in the beam's narrow light.

Inwardly exultant at his find, he nevertheless maintained the calm meticulousness of a professional. He returned to the opened safe, closed the door and re-locked it, withdrawing the key. Back at the table, he collected up the precious gems and gently let them fall back into the velvet bag. Pulling tight the black cords, he glided the bag into his coat inner pocket. He retrieved the torch and cut off the light. The door leading to the kitchen was ajar. He started to open it but then froze. There was a sound from the kitchen. Then silence. He waited, all his nerve ends like antennae listening for movement.

Finally, he saw the black object at the far end of the kitchen on the floor. Searching vainly for food in a bowl on the floor was a black cat, its tail raised in the air. In the dim light, he now identified the cat flap in the external door that opened to the garden. The animal could come and go as it pleased. Aware now of his presence, it cautiously padded in his direction and brushed the side of its body against his legs. It purred softly, pleased to find human company that might yield some food from somewhere.

Unimpressed by the cat, but relieved to have identified the cause of the noise, he left it to its own devices and retreated quickly out of the kitchen and back down the corridor to the front door. He manipulated the door latch so that it would close and lock on his departure. Before opening it to leave, he peered out of a narrow window to the right. Outside there was no sign of traffic or people. The only movement was the irregular swaying of the branches of the cherry blossom trees.

With his head angled down as a precaution, he opened the front door and stepped into the outside porch. The door locked behind him with the minutest of clicks. Then he was swiftly away down the drive and headed for the Ford Focus.

Back in the car, he attached his seatbelt. He glanced at his watch. It was three thirty three. The work had been done in eighteen minutes, three more than he had estimated.

He switched on the car's ignition and lights and pulled away into the road, intent on putting distance between himself and the locus of his housebreaking. The last part of his mission, Bourov told himself, still had to be accomplished.

Chapter Eighteen

08.25 Wednesday 18th March 2009. Ipswich station, Ipswich.

It was overcast, grey and drizzling rain. 'Another day in paradise'
Reddy reminded himself sardonically as he ran through the entrance to
Ipswich station. He fed his ticket through the machine at the barrier
and bounded onto the platform as the last commuter passengers were
climbing aboard the 8.26 train for London.

The squash match he had scheduled with Pandit Singh for 9.50 was at
a sports centre near Liverpool Street station. Assuming the train
arrived punctually, he would have ten minutes to dash there and get
changed ready for the game.

Carrying his briefcase and shouldering a blue sports bag, Reddy
struggled down the aisle of the first carriage. It was crowded and he
had to be careful to avoid protruding legs and cases still not properly
stowed. Having failed to find a seat, he decided to keep moving down
the carriages to the refreshments bar. A strong black coffee with a
caffeine kick might lift his spirits. He suspected too that standing might
be his sole option this morning. If so, then the up side of the
refreshments bar might be an absence of people making annoying,
unending calls on their mobile phones. He was not a fan of mobile
device owners imposing their supposedly private conversations on long
suffering fellow passengers. Technical innovations bring with them
ambiguous social progress, he mused.

After having struggled through two more teeming carriages he reached
the refreshments bar. Initially it was busy with customers, but most
departed back to their carriage seats. Eventually he succeeded to
purchase a cup of the smallest available size of coffee, misnamed
'standard' and containing coffee sufficient for three normal adults. A
standing space next to the train window was available together with a
ledge of table affixed below the window. Reddy encamped himself.

Earlier, rushing out of his apartment building for the bus station, he
had had the perspicacity to retrieve the morning's local newspaper
already delivered to his letter box in the ground floor entrance. He now
extracted it from his briefcase where he had inserted it beside his thin
laptop. It was a tabloid-size paper not a broadsheet, so he could just
lay it out on the high table where he was leaning.

Years of routine dictated that first he turned to the sport pages to read the match summary and commentaries of last night's Ipswich Town game. That Simon Farley and he had watched it, detracted nothing from the experience of reading the journalists' reports and interviews with the managers.

Reddy took a final glance at the photo capturing Dos Santos' scoring Town's solitary goal, then closed the sports page. He knew that Town, with only fifty five points and seven more matches left, wouldn't make the play offs. He also knew that that would still not prevent him from watching their next match at home on Saturday. He was an irrational fool, he told himself.

As that thought unpalatably matured, the train began to decelerate. Ahead was Manningtree, the only station stop of the entire journey for this particular train. Hence its' popularity with Ipswich-based commuters. If Carl Giles, the famous Ipswich cartoonist, had still been alive, wouldn't his artistry gleefully have run amok with the scenes of mayhem aboard this London-bound train ?

He looked absently out the window at the passing scenes. At this moment, the train was passing through an especially attractive area with stunning views out over the riverbanks of the Deben, and across the river estuary. The beauty of the whole took Reddy by surprise. But then, no sooner than he had taken an active interest, the landscape changed again. Within half a kilometre, the train was traversing a desolate zone of dilapidated and largely unused industrial buildings on the landward side. The juxtaposition couldn't have been more stark. It shocked him to think how quickly the artefacts of human industry can degenerate into ruins. Resignedly, Reddy put the thought aside and returned his attention to the local newspaper.

On the bottom of the front page, he found what he was looking for: an article titled 'Planning refused for new housing development'. It was a few lines only but continued on page five. Reddy read avidly and turned to page five. Next to the continued article there was a photo of some enclosed fields, in the foreground of which were two elderly men wrapped in thick coats. A caption below the photo described the men respectively as chairman of the Blackwater Planning Committee, and the Tory MP for Blackwater & Deben.

A key passage read:

> "The chairman emphasised that the Planning Committee's
> decision was final. He foresaw no possibility of the matter being

revisited. The necessary conditions were not present. He emphasised that the decision was not a vote against private sector developers, as some commentators were trying to say. However, it was a vote for common sense in light of the economic situation.

Mr. Hayward, speaking on behalf of the campaigners opposing the housing development, told the press: "We were never in agreement with the size of the development, nor its location. This is a great day for our campaign. With this decision we have also saved Loxwood Park, part of which would have been engulfed by the proposed new development."

Reddy paused to think. What impact did the planning decision have on the Ipswich and Blackwater and on RCH ? Running a quick mental calculation for RCH's 40 per cent share of the four thousand houses, at a conservative average sale price of a quarter million pounds per house, Reddy's math yielded a figure of four hundred million sterling in lost revenues. He hadn't the RCH annual accounts data with him, but from memory he knew that they had sold just over three thousand six hundred houses in 2008. So the 'lost' development at Loxwood was equivalent to nearly half of that year's sales.

But then, he asked himself, wasn't that a blessing in disguise ? With the drop in demand for new housing, RCH had been cutting back production anyway. This decision wouldn't hurt, it was surely a reprieve ? Then the penny dropped and he remembered the Holy Grail of the industry: land banking ! He had almost let slip the basic economics of the entire private house building industry: buy cheap land and reap the development value over the time. The probable pain for RCH and the Ipswich and Blackwater was that the land now had virtually no development value! Which raised the question: what land had been actually bought with the prospect of development gain? Or, another possibility, what land had not been bought but was nevertheless included in the scope of the original application based on 'promises' of one kind or another to their owners ?

Reddy now wondered if the death of James McAuley was indeed a 'coincidence'. Could it not be directly linked to RCH's interest in the Loxwood development ? He resolved at once that he should phone both RCH to request an interview Russell Westlake, and his friend Edmund Burleigh to ask about possible land transactions around Loxwood.

He recalled last night's disturbing conversation in the pub with Simon Farley. His friend had described to him the extent of his debts, capping the story with the fact that it was the Ipswich & Blackwater Bank that had extended him the original loan. There appeared to be no end to the Bank's entanglement in the region's economy. First, making loans for large house builders like RCH to acquire land. Now, it was clear that the bank had also entered into the market of loans for small businesses, which was news to Reddy.

As the train decelerated as it headed into Liverpool Street station, Reddy decided to raise the question of banks' loans diversification and its probable consequences for solvency with Professor Bernstein at their lunchtime meeting today.

Fortunately, the train's arrival had been punctual. Reddy marched as quickly as he could, avoiding the mazy criss-crossing of people, out of the station. He went towards Bishopsgate and the sports centre.

Entering the centre's reception he signed in. The young woman at the desk who attended to him exuded an aura of health and toned fitness; presumably a mandatory attribute for the job. She was dressed sportily in the club's signature orange T-shirt, blue track suit trousers and white trainers. When Reddy explained to her that he had a scheduled game of squash for 10.00am, she informed him that his game partner Mr. Singh had already arrived, paid for the court and headed off to change, taking with him the key to the court. All that was left to do for Reddy was to rent his squash racquet, which he did, and accept a key for the clothes' locker.

Leaving reception, he pushed through double swing doors into the huge hall that comprised the main gym. Its' ceiling was two floors high. This, in conjunction with the huge plate glass windows that ran across the entire length of one of the upper storey walls, generated the effect of airiness, light and space. The ground floor was populated with every conceivable type of training machine, forcing Reddy to marvel at the ingenuity. The arrayed moulded metal machines looked like a modern Heath Robinson creation. He himself hadn't a clue how to use more than a few of them, his regulars.

Off centre from the middle of this huge gym, a wide wooden-stepped staircase rose up in an arc shape to a mezzanine level. This being the route to the changing rooms and thence to the squash courts, Reddy climbed. At the top, he looked down to the ground floor below and watched for a moment the seekers of sculpted bodies avidly conducting repetitions of their selected exercises. Was it inane or commendable determination ? He wasn't sure.

The mens' changing rooms were off to the left. Reddy headed there, walking past an open floor used for dance movements and aerobics. Pushing open the door, he was confronted by a wall of humid heat. Its' source was the showers located beyond the far side of the changing room. Warm vapour clouds wafted. In the middle of the changing room stood rows of grey metal clothes lockers. Around the four walls were wooden benches on which at head height metal hooks were affixed. Here and there young men were in the process of dressing and undressing, or drying themselves down.

Reddy quickly cast around looking for his playing partner but he was nowhere to be seen. So he found a space on one of the benches, deposited his sports bag and briefcase and took off his overcoat. He stepped across to a large mirror further along the wall to examine his eye in which he felt some grit. Another person also stood there. When Reddy looked into the mirror the other person's face was that of Oliver Carrington. Smiling and looking back at Reddy, he was putting the finishing touches to the knot in his silk tie.

"Morning Reddy. What time of day do you call this then? Nothing better to do I suppose, eh ?" Carrington goaded.

Reddy understood that Carrington knew about his suspension from the Courier. The pleasure that gave him would be immense. So Reddy chose to rise to the bait. What was there to lose with this cockroach ?

"Part time job yourself too isn't it, if you've time to be here ? What's it like being Samantha's 'gofer' ? I would have thought anyone from Oxford with some balls would find a real job".

If the insult struck home, it didn't register on Carrington's face.

"Reddy, pack it in old chap will you? Stop being a loser. Rebellion will get you precisely nowhere. I advised you in the office last Friday to 'get with the programme'. But look where you are now because of your obstinacy and stupidity ? One step away from the rubbish heap".

"Thanks for the tender concern" Reddy shot back, "I can do without it thanks."

Carrington took no notice. He applied more barbs:

"You know, Reddy, you're your own health risk. I mean, you're reckless. What on earth got into your head to think that you could go to that Banking Conference on Monday in defiance of Samantha ? No wonder you're suspended. Serves you right".

"I'll keep doing what I consider to be right and necessary Carrington. I take my work seriously, not like some at the Courier. I'm not trading off my investigative work for some shabby smaltzing with CEO celebrities."

"Reddy, the day that you change your mind, let know. I can you get back "on track" at the Courier".

Carrington turned, strode back to the wooden bench where his bag lay, grabbed the leather handles and went to the exit door. Pulling it open to leave, he looked over his shoulder and back at Reddy:

"By the way, the IT guys apparently want you laptop back. Thought I'd remind you. Just as a mark of friendship, right ?"

Then he vanished through the doorway.

Inwardly seething, Reddy returned to his place and checked his watch. He was five minutes late already for his squash match with Pandit Singh. He hastened to get changed into his sports gear, simultaneously striving to calm his anger. This didn't work. A voice in his mind told him that the Carringtons of this world succeed.

Reddy picked up the rented squash racquet and exited the changing rooms. He again passed the open area devoted to aerobics, on the way to the squash courts at the other side of the building. As a consequence of his fractious exchanges with Carrington, Reddy no longer felt much appetite for playing squash.

He found Pandit Singh on court four, patiently practicing alone. They had played together before a couple of times and Reddy had been comprehensively defeated. What compensated for the one-sidedness of their games was the friendship and good spirit in which they were played. They exchanged cursory pleasantries, Reddy apologising for his lateness. Then they played, without Reddy hardly being warmed up.

After twenty minutes Reddy had lost three games to love. Not only that, his white sports shirt was saturated in perspiration and his face only a couple of shades shy of beetroot. As a filler for the remaining available court time, they played a relaxed second game. Singh eased off the tempo considerably this time around and Reddy won a few points here and there, enough to save face.

Following the second match, Pandit offered Reddy some helpful advice about his positioning for dealing with shots at the back corner of the court. Then they returned to the changing rooms, showered and dressed and went down to reception to return the squash court key.

Reddy invited Singh to join him for a drink at the gym's health-conscious café. Singh's original motive for arranging the match had been to learn more about Reddy's problems at the Daily Courier. That desire to know was doubtless redoubled now that Reddy had been suspended. He accepted the invitation.

Having been served soft drinks at the counter they found an empty table and bench seat in a corner of the café. Reddy was about to summarise for Singh's benefit the story of his investigation into the Ipswich and Blackwater Bank, when a recollection came to him about his laptop.

"Pandit, listen, before I give you the heads up on my investigation; I've a favour to ask. As you're off next to the Courier's offices could I request that you take my laptop with you and hand it in to Charlie Hunt in IT Operations ? I got a mail from him saying they need to do some maintenance or software upgrades on it. It's overdue apparently; everyone else has had theirs' done."

Singh raised his dark eyebrows in a sign of surprise. "Well if that's so, they haven't upgraded mine either so far as I know, unless it was some surreptitious online job while connected to the office network. Lets face it, IT guys are a law unto themselves; I think they genuinely wish that there was no such thing as 'users'. Anyhow, no problem, I'll take it. Charlie Hunt you say ?

Reddy carefully withdrew his laptop from his briefcase and handed it over to Singh who found space for it in his sports bag.

He now proceeded with a verbal summary of his investigation. It was a useful exercise even for himself, providing an opportunity to reassure himself that he was in command of the warp and weave of the argument. Singh remained silent throughout, listening attentively. When Reddy had wrapped up his description, he spoke:

"Interesting, Craig, interesting. If you can dig further and confirm your hypotheses about the bank's insolvency that would be a 'scoop' for you, certainly. Time probably isn't on your side though. You need to publish your investigation sooner rather than later if you want to avoid being overrun by events. The other aspect of the investigation – the links between the bank, Redwoods the housing developer, and the suicides of Cartwright and McAuley - sounds pretty speculative at the moment. If the police have their own investigation open, as you said, then perhaps it might be wiser to leave that to them ? You're not a crime reporter after all and if there are drug-related activities involved, putting your nose too closely into such things might expose you to serious risks. Drug barons are known to be violent."

"You may be right Pandit. The police investigation is focused on potential criminality arising from the drugs and diamond finds. They're not fundamentally equipped to look at the financial aspects of the affair. So I intend to keep going on that track. On your first point, you're spot on. Time is of the essence and that is why I need your help. I want to find out about a couple of things having an overseas dimension that may be important to the investigation."

"Fine, by me Craig. If I can help, I will. It'll just have to be discreet though, given your suspension. What are you looking for ?"

"First, I've got a nominee company registered in Panama that's a significant shareholder of Redwood Country Homes. It's been increasing its' shareholding in recent months as the share price declined. My problem is that the beneficial owner is hidden. I'd like to know who it is. That knowledge could be vital in understanding what is going on behind the scenes between RCH and the Ipswich & Blackwater. Second, I'd like to learn something about the building construction industry in Bulgaria. Especially, in the holiday area around the Black Sea. Who's active there and so on ? As I told you, both RCH and Cartwright have been investing out there".

"And you think that because I work on the Courier's Foreign Desk, I can provide you some local informants?"

"That's the long and the short of it, yes Pandit" Reddy beamed, expectantly.

Singh was already fumbling in his jacket pocket for his Blackberry device. He extracted it and tapped some keys.

"Here we are: the Courier's Sofia-based correspondent, Sarah Davidson" and he showed Reddy the number on the screen.

Reddy retrieved a biro from his own jacket and noted the number down on the drinks receipt slip laying on the table. He decided to try calling her once Pandit departed.

"Sarah's been out there a couple of years and has a great address book. Not sure about her knowledge of the Black Sea area though. Her work is predominantly in Sofia. Anyway, say my name and she'll be sure to help. No way she'll be aware of your suspension. Now on the Panama question, that's tricky because we don't have anyone there on a permanent basis. What there is, is our Central America correspondent based in Costa Rica. Don't know him though and he's not here on my Blackberry. Leave it with me though and I'll find out his contact details".

He put down the device next to his jacket and drank the remains of his chilled drink. He checked the time on his watch. Eleven twenty.

"I'm going to have to run, Craig. I have a conference call at the office for 12.30. Before I go though, just tell me. Is this suspension serious ? Where are the management headed with this, do you think? We don't want to lose you, you know".

Reddy was touched by Pandit's tone of sympathy and concern. It demonstrated that there was at least some current of support for his style of journalism at the Courier. Still, his differences with his boss Samantha wasn't a topic he wanted to expand upon now.

"Pandit, the management say there will be an internal inquiry run by HR. I don't know if they are intent on hounding me out. I'll wait and see how this enquiry unfolds before rushing to conclusions".

Singh nodded, in acknowledgement of the measured reply. He had been long enough at the Courier himself to appreciate the importance of having attuned political antennae. Moreover, he respected Reddy too much to pressure him on what was a tender subject.

"I understand" he said, "Just be aware that you're not alone. I'll get back to you regarding the Panama contact. Must rush now, thanks for the game!"

With that, he grabbed his bag and jacket and left for the Courier's office at Canary Wharf.

Reddy still had an hour available to reach Tottenham Court Road for his meeting with Professor Bernstein. Time enough to place a couple of calls. First he phoned Edmund Burleigh. He told him that he was suspended from the Courier. Burleigh was stupefied and offered gracious words of support. Reddy then explained that he had an agreement with Peter Houseman of the Messenger to publish anonymously in their Sunday edition the article based on Havering's information. Although Havering had provided Reddy with his business card, Reddy was reluctant to call him directly. There were too many details that he didn't want to discuss at this time; plus his instinct advised that it might be best not to be too influenced by this man while still working on the article. He quickly obtained Burleigh's acquiescence to convey to Havering the news of the article's imminent publication, a result that would fulfil Reddy's promise to the man. They commiserated briefly on the inadequate result of the previous evening's match at Portman Road, agreed to meet up again soon and terminated their exchanges.

Reddy picked up the receipt slip on which he had written the phone number of Sarah Davidson. He entered the name and number into his mobile phone's memory. Then he dialled the number. As the ringing commenced, he happened to look askance and saw Singh's Blackberry device still laying on the bench seat. In his haste to depart, Singh had failed to see it. Reddy retrieved it with his spare hand and put it into his briefcase. In his right ear, he heard the ringing stop and a female voice was online:

"Hello, Sarah Davidson"

"Good morning, Craig Reddy. I'm a journalist at the Courier. We don't know one another but Pandit Singh gave me your contact details".

"Yes, I recognise your name. I think I've read Courier articles of yours in the past. What is it that you want Craig ?"

"I'm conducting an investigation into a bank here in the UK, Sarah. I think it may be on the verge of insolvency. Its' CEO committed suicide last week end. He was also mixed up in property development in Eastern Europe, including Bulgaria."

"Which is why you want to talk to me?" Davidson queried.

"Yes, to an extent. Listen, my focus is what he was up to here. Nevertheless, there is a question mark whether it was really suicide or not. Even if it was, I'm left wondering whether his death may be linked to some unsavoury business activities and relationships abroad. Rumour has it that Bulgaria has its fair share of mafia ?"

He heard a wicked laugh at the other end of the line.

"They call themselves 'entrepreneurs' these days" Davidson remarked acerbically. "They had to clean up their act because the country joined the euro in 2007. Brussels put pressure on the government in Sofia."

"So the criminality and mafia control has been addressed ? They're no longer a force ?" Reddy asked, somewhat credulously.

Again the devillish laugh from Davidson.

"You clearly don't know Bulgaria and the Bulgarians, Craig. Let's say, there's been some sanitising. The 'X' rated material like daylight killings here in the capital are largely a thing of the past. Settling of accounts between gangs still goes on of course. However, most of the big bosses are too busy making serious money and switching to legitimate business."

"And that would include down on the Black Sea coast ? I understand that there is a lot of resort development going on down there? British expats and others soaking up the sun and cheap liquor ?"

"Sure, that's the package for the expats, but they're suckers. Just a source of consumer demand. For the local 'entrepreneurs' there's a different side. Drugs, prostitution, money laundering, tax avoidance using property companies. You name it. And while it goes on down there, the Sofia based politicians turn a blind eye. Or even better, quietly take a slice of the pie."

"I see." Reddy was quickly accustoming himself to the picture. Davidson had her fingers on the pulse. "So tell me Sarah, do you know any of these entrepreneurs ? If so,
are any of them likely to be operating outside of the country ?"

"Craig, I intend to leave Bulgaria alive, not horizontal, thanks. I have my sources, but as a journalist, being too close to an entrepreneur could massively shorten your life span."

"Understood."

"But to answer your question. Yes, several of them are working internationally these days on one thing and another. Although, they're not as footloose as the Russian oligarchs. Most tend to stay at home here. Anyone in particular that you are interested in ?"

"I don't have a name Sarah, no. I may do so soon though. As I said, Cartwright definitely was in business on the Black Sea in Bulgaria. No way could he have done that without substantial local support."

"True enough. Down there you would need to speak Bulgarian to be effective in business. Even then, you wouldn't get far unless you had the right protection and sponsorship from a recognised 'entrepreneur'."

"Just like here in the UK then ?" Reddy suggested, provocatively. "Having the right connections and access to decision makers in positions of power are pretty much the preconditions to accomplishing anything in the business world. If a Bulgarian 'entrepreneur' wanted to clean up his business and enter the UK market, he'd need friends in the right places wouldn't he ? "

"I'll pass on that Craig. When you've got a name, let me know. I'll probably be able to give you the background on him."

Chapter Nineteen

09.50 Wednesday 18th March 2009. South west of Ipswich, A12 direction Colchester

Rain had been pouring down incessantly since they had left Police headquarters in an unmarked police car. DI Wright and DS Adam were headed for an appointment with Russell Westlake at his company's main office located outside the village of Holton, south west of Ipswich. DS Adam was at the wheel. The intensity of the falling rain had obliged him to turn up the velocity of the windscreen wipers to maximum and also switch on the vehicle's headlamps. The A12 was a busy road at the best of times. Heavy rains, and heavy goods vehicles washing waves of water off the road's surface, made today's experience an even more testing one.

The two police officers had already discussed their strategy for interviewing Westlake. Now their conversation had progressed to their plans for after that. They had decided to make another unannounced arrival at the headquarters of the Ipswich & Blackwater Bank. On this occasion, their target was Harry Keogh, the bank's head of security.

"So my hunch was pretty much correct" DS Adam confirmed. "His police file states that he took early retirement three years ago."

"Which was in effect the official story for public consumption, right ?" DI Wright said, encouraging her colleague to complete the story. She was happy to be driven this morning. It freed up her thoughts for the two tricky encounters they had before them.

"Correct. Colleagues in the Force are unaware of the facts. I had this information released to me on an exceptional 'need to know' basis only, after your intervention."

"HR backed down once I said that the Chief was supporting me. Our investigation takes priority." Wright commented

"Useless gatekeepers" Adam averred, dismissing HR. "Anyway, it transpires that Keogh was a bent cop. At least, towards the end of his term. There was evidence he was conveying sensitive information about open investigations to third parties of a criminal disposition."

"But not enough to really nail him ?"

"No documentary evidence of any payments having been made. No 'in flagrante delicto' meetings with criminals caught on video. But plenty of circumstantial evidence. Enough to convince Haddock and the Chief Constable that Keogh's policing days were over."

"Haddock made the final decision then ?"

"That's how I was led to understand it, yes. Keogh was accompanied up to his office one day by the head of HR, supposedly for a routine performance review. By meeting's end he had signed off on his early retirement and was gone."

"So now Keogh is back on the radar as the probable source of the leak to the local press ? Recidivist behaviour and all that?"

"Is how I see" Adam affirmed.

Wright's prudential policing ethos considered that they should cover all angles; yet her instincts were in alignment with Adam's on this. The manner in which she had been stone-walled by the journalist at the local paper had been decisive. She had called him up after learning his identity from the Editor. He confirmed that he had penned the article about the diamond find at the Ipswich and Blackwater, but was adamant that he would not reveal his source.

"OK. In that case, we play hard ball with Keogh" she said.

"May I have the pleasure?" Adam smiled at the windscreen ahead, concentrating on the traffic.

"Be my guest" Wright acceded. After a moment's silence though she added: "But keep it within bounds. Let's not forget what the prize could be here."

"I understand, Paulie. We aim to win an informer. Who better to yield up the inside secrets at the Bank than the head of security?"

Indicating the road sign up ahead, Wright said: "I think this is the exit here."

Neither of them had ever visited Holton St. Mary. Redwood Country Homes' office was located just outside the village in the direction of the golf course, according to Westlake's personal assistant who had explained directions to Wright over the phone. DS Adam pressed the lever at the side of the steering wheel indicating to leave the A12.

Within a few minutes, after driving along a winding country road, they passed through the quiet village of Holton.

"Constable Country" Wright said, a propos of nothing.

"To the Manor born? " Adam suggested, maxing out on his Scottish accent to insinuate undertones of class warfare. He laughed contentedly at himself.

Out of the village, they followed the road signs for the golf course. They found the turn off to RCH easily enough a couple of miles further along. Two hundred metres driving down a pale concrete lane brought them to the site. Adam drove through the open wooden gates onto a wide gravel parking area, halting besides a black Mercedes. In the centre of the parking area was a circle of well-tended grass. Around the perimeter was a low black link chain held in position by regularly spaced vertical wooden stays. A white flagpole rose up from the centre of the circle and at its' pinnacle flew a flag bearing the logo of RCH.

The RCH offices were housed in an enormous converted barn with black painted wooden beams and pale red roof tiles that had been cleaned and re-laid. The site as a whole was enclosed by high conifer hedges kept meticulously well-trimmed.

No one was in sight as the two officers alighted from their car, so they headed directly for the main entrance in front of them. Inside, they entered into a large airy room with a modern feel to it. Neither hallway nor reception room, its exact function was unclear although there was a polished round wooden table to one side of the room on which illustrated housing and interior decoration magazines were on display.

Natural light entered through a glass sky light in the ceiling. All the walls were white, reflecting the light from above. On the walls hung framed aerial photo shots of residential housing developments, architects' scaled drawings of example model houses, and occasional abstract paintings whose colours enhanced the general sense of modernity. Wright spotted a Kandinsky that was one of her favourites.

Russell Westlake was alone in his office, standing behind his desk, listening to the voice on the other end of the phone line.

"So where is he then? He's not answering his phone"

It was Angelov, calling from his hotel in London. Initially, Russell Westlake hadn't wanted to take the call when his personal assistant called through to his office. With the police due in a few minutes, it was inopportune. More than that, it had him off balance. He hadn't known that Angelov had arrived in the UK. Although, given the death of Cartwright, he had expected a visit sooner or later. So at the last moment, he had changed his decision. 'Risk on' he said to himself. It was best to find out what Angelov wanted rather than procrastinate.

"Radomir, my friend" Westlake began, soothingly "I'd like to help you but I'm not Bourov's keeper. You agreed that he should switch over from working on my sites to the one at the London Olympics Village. He's been down there now for the best part of two months. I hardly see him."

"Has he changed his number ?"

"Not that I know."

"OK."

There was a silence on the line. Westlake chose to let it linger. Then Angelov changed tack:

"Listen Westlake, you and I need to meet. Cartwright's death complicates things. When can we talk?" Westlake picked up on the menacing insistence in Angelov's voice.

"That's a welcome proposal Radomir. When and where would you suggest ?" Westlake asked, maintaining his accommodative posture.

"Probably Friday. Up there in Ipswich, after I've completed my business here in London".

"Cartwright's funeral is scheduled for Friday morning, Radomir. I'll be going. How about yourself?"

"No. Not invited. Anyway, best that I stay in the background."

Westlake diplomatically agreed. He had Angelov accept to be passed back to his personal assistant in order make an appointment. Keeping the relationship on a professional basis with a planned formal meeting struck him as the smart approach.

He put down the phone and looked out the large French windows onto the garden. Alone, Westlake amused himself with the thought of how much information he had just withheld from Angelov. For one thing, Angelov had no clue about his using Bourov to reclaim the diamonds. For another, if the Bulgarian had known of Westlake's impending meeting with the police to discuss Cartwright, how would he have responded ?

09.58 Wednesday 18th March 2009. Redwood Country Homes HQ, Holton nearr Ipswich

A bell rung briefly as DI Wright and DS Adam opened and entered through the RCH office building front door. An attractive young woman entered through a door from the opposite side of the room. She wore a white cotton blouse with high collar, a tight-fitting sky blue woollen skirt ending above the knee, and matching coloured high heel shoes. Her hair, tied back behind her head in a pony tail, was blonde but not naturally so.

Welcoming them, she introduced herself as 'Sally' and led them through to the room from which she had come. It was her office; spacious and full of natural light. Two large French windows filled much of the office's outer wall affording a splendid view across the manicured lawn and rockery garden outside. Her desk occupied the area immediately in front of the windows.

She invited them to be seated, gesturing towards low armchairs available in the far corner of the office, circled around a coffee table. Both officers sat.

"Mr. Westlake is expecting you" she affirmed in response to DI Wright's introductions and request to see him. "Let me first check if he is ready." She disappeared through an unmarked door off to her left.

To pass the time, DI Wright picked up a brochure from the coffee table next to her. It was glossy marketing literature extolling the virtues of RCH's houses, with careful montages of happy young couples blissfully peering into tailor-made kitchens or relaxing at full length on modern settees and armchairs. Children were curiously absent from any of the photos.

DS Adam, untempted by the literature on offer, arose from his armchair and ambled aimlessly over to the large double French windows. He stood there awhile with hands behind his back admiring the view. Then, noiselessly, he turned his body through 180 degrees so he was looking at the personal assistant's computer screen standing on the middle of her desk.

The software onscreen showed a calendar for the current week. DS Adam's eyesight was fine. From where he was standing he could read the text with appointments marked for each day of the week. His eyes read Wednesday's appointments. Sure enough their names were there. For Thursday there were other names, but none that resonated with him. For Friday though, his attention was drawn to "Mr. Angelov Office 16.00" typed into the space in the calendar for the afternoon.

The door from the other office was opening. DS Adam memorised the name as he swung back again to admire the external scene. Sally appeared in the door frame wearing an appealing smile.

"Mr. Westlake is ready to see you now. Please come this way."

Russell Westlake was standing up in the middle of his office, waiting for them. He was dressed smart casual in well-fitting sand coloured wollen slacks, a dark blue jacket from Marco Polo over a white cotton shirt whose doubled sleeve cuffs were perfectly exposed below the ends of his jacket sleeves. The lack of any tie served notice that 'smart casual' was his office regimen.

DI Wright couldn't help but be taken by the man. With his good looks, elegant style, and obvious business power, he was highly eligible. While the accomplished manner in which he dealt with the introductions and engaged her in smooth pleasantries while holding very direct eye contact, suggested that he had charm in spades. At least, she warned herself, for women that he fancied. He had encouraged them to take seats, and the conversation arrived at a natural hiatus allowing them to get to the subject in hand.

"How can I be of assistance DI Wright?" Westlake enquired civilly.

"We are investigating the suicide of Thomas Cartwright, whom you knew sir. We identified your phone number stored on his mobile phone. It appears you exchanged calls with him frequently. Did you know Thomas Cartwright well?"

"Yes. There's been a business relationship between his bank and RCH for nearly three years. In that time, I've had plenty of dealings with him."

"When you say you knew him, you mean only professionally?"

"Not entirely, no. Over time we became friendly. I met his wife too, Elaine. Thomas and I occasionally spent time together socially. We both enjoyed bike racing.

"Did you have any sign or suspicion that Mr. Cartwright was a suicide risk ?"

"Absolutely not. The whole thing is tragic. His wife is distraught you know. They had no kids but they were a solid couple. I mean, they weren't about to separate or divorce. When someone you think you know commits suicide like he has done, it's an almighty shock."

He looked carefully at DI Wright: "Inspector, we think we know people and then discover that we don't. Isn't that so?"

DI Wright chose to forebear speculation of this nature:

"Sir, our forensics people found cocaine in Cartwright's Audi after his suicide. Are you aware that he was a user?"

Without hesitation Westlake replied: "That really does surprise me ! No, I never saw Thomas take drugs of any kind. He never spoke about them either. Inspector, he liked sport and kept himself fit. He played golf. I don't see that taking cocaine would be consistent with the lifestyle he led."

"Be that as it may sir, the fact is that traces of cocaine were also found in his bloodstream."

"I see." Westlake stopped, stood up, and walked to his desk. He turned around to face them arms folded in a defensive posture, perhaps reflecting on surprise news.

"Your thoughts on that sir, please ?" DI Wright pressed the advantage.

"Maybe he was stressed about something and started taking cocaine as a kind of crutch ?" Westlake suggested lamely. "I really don't know. Its news to me, it really is. I mean, I was not aware that he might be stressed enough to start taking drugs."

"Maybe it wasn't stress, sir" DS Adam interjected 'Cocaine is a stimulant. Many people take it as a leisure drug. For fun. Was Mr. Cartwright a fun-loving person in your opinion?"

The tenseness that appeared in Westlake's face suggested to DI Wright that he had taken an immediate dislike to DS Adam.

"Certainly not in the sense that you imply, Sergeant . Thomas had a sense of humour but he wasn't a party-goer."

DI Wright said: "So, in summary Mr. Westlake, you did not have any knowledge of Mr. Cartwrght's drug habit, nor did you have any suspicion that he might be suicidal?"

"Correct, Inspector. I'm sorry but I can't reveal anything on that score."

"Then let me return sir if you'll allow me, to the business relationship. Will the death of Mr Cartwright damage you or your company in any way?"

"There will definitely be a loss in human terms. As you know, Thomas was the CEO of the Ipswich & Blackwater. Knowing him on a personal level was a big plus for me and RCH. There was mutual trust. On the other hand, I do know the Bank's Finance Director too. It was she who negotiated much of the details of RCH's loans with the Ipswich & Blackwater."

From the table top before them, DI Wright picked up a folded copy of that day's Financial Times newspaper.

"These are tough times though aren't they, sir ?

DI Wright wore a doleful expression, as she cast her gaze over the paper's headlines.

"Meaning, what precisely?"

"Well, what with the stock market crashing, sir. I'm no expert on shares, but if companies' shares prices get hit doesn't that mean there's less money around to invest? "

With her free hand, DI Wright pointed to a page she had opened detailing all FTSE companies' stock prices.

"I see RCH are listed in the Footsie sir. Here" she pointed again. "The RCH share price twelve month high was £ 1,45 and twelve month low £ 0,52 . Yesterday's price was just off that 12 month low sir. A sixty per cent drop in share price must make getting funding difficult ?"

"I see what you mean, Inspector." Westlake saw that patience was needed to fend off questions from the financially illiterate. "Let me explain. RCH is able to adapt to changes in economic circumstances. We run a tight ship here with effective cost controls. Financial management is good. We do not get over-extended like many of our competitors. All our loans are carefully managed. Plus, we have positive cash flow and good assets."

"That's very reassuring for you sir, thank you."

DS Adam entered the discussion. "Do you play football, sir?"

"No. I only follow the results. Why?" Westlake looked puzzled.

DI Wright too was mystified by her colleague's chosen line of questioning.

"You'll have heard of Berbatov, won't you?" DS Adam continued.

"Yes, I know he plays for Manchester United. So what's this got to do with our discussion Sergeant ."

"A family name with an 'ov' ending and you know you're dealing with Eastern Europe or Russia don't you sir? Do you happen to know which country Berbatov's from?"

"Berbatov is a Bulgarian."

"Do you know Bulgaria at all, sir? Have you perhaps visited there?"

"Why didn't you ask? Yes, we have business on the Black Sea."

"Do you go there often?"

"Enough to keep an eye on our investments. The Black Sea region offers attractive opportunities for residential housing development. Many UK folk are looking for a low cost expatriate lifestyle in a warmer climate. Redwoods actively invests out there to meet that demand."

"It helps mitigate the housing recession here?"

"To an extent, yes . Although its still a relatively small segment of our business."

"I see. All this flexibility in the market is great for businesses then. Of course us poor consumers, if we don't' pay the mortgage the bank takes our house away. Tell me sir, what would happen to RCH if you couldn't pay your debts?"

"That's speculation. As I said just now, our loans are prudentially managed. We are not over-leveraged."

"Isn't that just your assumptions though sir? What happens when your assumptions are wrong ?"

"Of course it's based on assumptions Sergeant. That's what you have to work with in planning a business. That, and risk taking. But both assumptions and risk taking are grounded in analysis and experience, not plucked out of thin air."

"I understand you. But I remember my father twenty years ago. His business went bankrupt inside six months of the government jettisoning our being in the European monetary system. They called it "the snake". Very appropriate, I'd say."

"Perhaps, but what's your point?"

"Suppose your assumptions haven't planned for the financial equivalent of a tsunami. What happens to your business sir?"

"If you are implying Sergeant that the stock market crisis is RCH's tsunami then you are much mistaken. It is our opportunity."

"So the decision this week of the Blackwater and Deben District Council not to grant planning permission for the new housing development, doesn't knock RCH's assumptions at all?"

Westlake raised a wry smile. "Now I see where you are headed ! We never assume that all our leads come to fruition. The Council's decision is a setback, no getting away from it. But as I said, at RCH we adapt. We're resilient. Maybe we've got Scottish genes in us, Sergeant".

DS Adam ignored the sarcasm.

"Its *Detective* Sergeant, sir. Tell me, are you aware of the suicide of Mr. James McAuley last week end?"

Even Westlake the risk addict was taken aback by the lightning switch of direction in Adam's questioning. He began to fear that this meeting was going on for too long.

"Of course, I also knew James. He was connected with the bid to get the Loxwood housing development scheme implemented. Another utterly tragic event."

"Two friends' deaths in the space of one day. That's extraordinary isn't it sir ? You must be suffering tremendously" DS Adam's tone of delivery suggested, charmlessly, that he surmised the contrary.

"You know, I'm sure Detective, that trauma takes time to surface. I am a businessman with much responsibility and little time. We all grieve in our own way though. Believe me."

DI Wright intervened: "Indeed. Let's leave the topic of Mr McAuley's death for today Mr. Westlake. We won't detain you with further questions. Many thanks for your cooperation."

She stood up slowly to her full height, indicating that the interview was concluded. Westlake visibly relaxed. He said:

"I hope you are able to conclude your investigation soon Inspector. Thomas Cartwright's suicide is a great sadness felt by his friends. That includes me. I sense that it will remain shrouded in mystery, but not because of any criminal reason. Ultimately we never know ourselves or others."

"You may be right Mr Westlake. My experience as an officer is much more prosaic. When people die there are reasons for it."

Westlake kept silent, choosing instead to open his office door so they could depart, requesting Sally in the adjacent office to usher the two detectives out of the building.

Within ten minutes of the police officers' leaving, Westlake too was on his way out. He had an appointment to keep with Bourov, one that only he knew about. He tried to phone Bourov on his mobile but it was switched off. So be it, he would go to the appointed rendez vous anyway. As he stepped through Sally's office on the way out to his car she said:

"A journalist has called wanting to interview you. He's interested in Redwoods and the conditions in the housing market. I said I'd get back to him, as I wasn't sure if you'd want to talk to him."

"Who is he ? Who does he work for, did he say ?"

"Reddy. Craig Reddy. He works for the Courier ?"

Westlake nodded. "Call him back and offer him 30 minutes. Tomorrow morning. Sally, I'm off out for about an hour and a half. You can reach me on my mobile phone"

Sally smiled, wise enough not to ask where he was going or what he was doing. Now she'd have freedom to call her best girl friend for a long chat.

12.10 Wednesday 18th March 2009. Street outside Ipswich & Blackwater Bank HQ, north west suburbs of Ipswich

The drive back into the outskirts of Ipswich only took them about twenty minutes. The terrible weather and heavy traffic had both cleared since their earlier voyage down the A12 to Holton. During their conversation together on the way over to the Ipswich & Blackwater's head office, Wright and Adam shared views on Russell Westlake. They were wrapping up their collective thoughts when DS Adam disclosed with controlled mirth:

"It's interesting being nosy what people do on their computers isn't it ?"

"Why ? What have you seen ?" Wright asked, curiosity piqued.

"While Westlake's personal assistant was out of the room, I took a look at her computer screen. It showed Westlake's calendar of appointments for the week. One stood out to me in particular, Paulie. He's scheduled to meet a Mr. Angelov on Friday."

It dawned on Wright what DS Adam had been up to earlier when asking Westlake about surnames ending in 'ov.' Although driving, she gave him a quick glance and grin:

"The Bulgarian connection ! Mr. Angelov is probably a Bulgarian. DS Adam, your investigative skills are not by the book, but great work ! We now have Cartwright dead with a map of Sofia in his car, Westlake's company taking loans from Cartwright's bank, and also doing business on the Bulgarian Black Sea. Now a Bulgarian is in the UK with a business appointment to meet with Westlake. Is that all pure circumstance ?"

"I doubt it. My question is, Paulie: who is Mr. Angelov ?"

"And why has he come to the UK now to talk to Westlake ? And did he know Cartwright ?" DI Wright added.

They had arrived at their destination. Wright drew the patrol car to a halt immediately outside the building housing the Ipswich & Blackwater. It was pre-arranged between them that DS Adam would go alone to bring out Keogh; Wright keeping the car ready and occupied as it was on a double yellow line.

At the ground floor reception, DS Adam nodded solemnly at the young woman at the desk, at the same instant holding up his ID in the palm of his hand. She recognised him from the previous visit. This time her incipient smile drained away when she saw his stern demeanour.
He told her to find Mr. Keogh the head of security on the phone and then pass him the phone. She complied.

"Keogh, security. Hello ?"

"Mr. Keogh, DS Adam Ipswich police. We met last Monday here, together with my colleague DI Wright ? I'm sure you remember. I'd like to talk to you please"

Affability personified, Keogh replied: "Yes of course. Unscheduled again ? Never mind. Pass me back to the reception desk and I'll instruct them to give you a pass."

"That won't be necessary, thanks. I would appreciate it rather if you yourself could take some time out ? Just to join me and my colleague for a private chat off site. I've got a car waiting outside. It shouldn't take more than half an hour."

A moment's silence followed. Adam surmised Keogh was fast forwarding through his options.

"Yes, no problem" came back the forced reply. "Give me five minutes and I'll be down."

DS Adam handed the phone receiver back to the receptionist, this time coupled with a warm smile. "He's coming down" he said, to restore her confidence. She returned a half-formed smile, sat back down in her seat, and resumed her thankless routines.

DS Adam wandered to the other side of the reception area affording him a direct view of the opening and closing lift doors, so as to intercept Keogh the moment he appeared. The plan Adam and Wright had hatched entailed heading off in the car with Keogh to a nearby public park. There, they would park in the car park but remain in the vehicle, with Keogh in the back seat. The closed space was expected to create a more immediate sense of intimidation. Adam would turn on him from the front passenger's seat with an aggressive line of questioning designed to break quickly his resistance. If that worked, then they could ease up on him, so long as he agreed to talk openly about the Bank. Adam, as agreed, was to take the lead role. He decided to bring his rugby experience into play. As a forward, physical aggression in the scrum was important. Equally critical though was the use of the eyes when facing up to opponents. You put fear into them before the physical battle is waged. An opponent suffering fear, was an opponent more prone to defeat.

Adam was still rehearsing how this plan should play out when Keogh appeared coming out from the far right lift. As before, he was finely dressed in his pin stripe suit and tie, over which he wore a navy blue cashmere coat. DS Adam conceded to himself that Keogh played a good game. Whether the power dressing was to portray just a professional image or to instill a sense of authority, it seemed to work. Keogh looked the real deal.

Without ado, Keogh acceded to Adam's request to join them for a short ride. They left the building together and climbed into the waiting car outside in front of the exit. DI Wright gave a cursory greeting and then drove the car out into the traffic, headed for the park.

The ride took no more than three minutes. The park was almost devoid of people due to the weather. Although it was no longer raining, the wetness on park benches and underfoot deterred office workers and shoppers. Today, they preferred the warm and dry of the nearby commercial centre.

The car park where Wright pulled the car to a halt was also largely empty. She parked at the front, where there was a view across the park's undulating grass and evergreen bushes to a pond some fifty metres away. A few mallard ducks sat stoically near the pond's edge, undeterred. The sounds of street traffic from the main road behind them were muffled. It was a quiet, lonely spot.

Cutting the ignition, the three people found themselves intimately together in an enveloping silence. Their collective body heat caused the car's windows to start steaming up. Keogh, who had long legs, found limited space in which to place them and so sat uncomfortably with knees at a high angle. DS Adam, by turning his body around in the front passenger's seat and placing an arm across the back, could look directly at Keogh. He was seated at a slightly higher level than Keogh, affording him the advantage of being able to look down at the man. He stared rigidly and impassively at Keogh, waiting until the security head gave him his undivided attention.

"Why did you do it, Mr Keogh ?"

"Why did I do what, Detective ?"

"You leaked the news to the press about the diamonds we found at the Bank."

"That's not true."

"Mr. Keogh, I do not have time to be messed around by you. DI Wright here is leading an important investigation into the death of your former boss. We have evidence that his suicide is linked to circumstances which may have criminal ramifications. I warn you it is not in your interest to lie to the police or obstruct our inquiries."

"You asked that the discovery be kept under wraps. Other than informing Mrs. Donoghue, on a need to know basis, I have kept to your instruction."

"That is a lie, Mr. Keogh and you know it."

"Detective, that is an unsubstantiated allegation."

"It is fact. You have form, Mr. Keogh. You need money. You always took money in the past, didn't you ?"

"What the hell are you talking about ?"

"Yes, you do. You were a bent cop. I know. I've seen your files. I mean, the real story, not the cover up Mr Keogh. You were pushed out of the force because you were bent. They granted you leniency by allowing you to retire rather than be dismissed. A case of misplaced faith. Now you're still at it. Taking money for information. Breaching loyalty. Exploiting your position."

Keogh's facial expression, which had initially shown defiance, rapidly crumbled into dumbfoundedness as Adam destroyed the fable of his integrity. He sat with his hands locked together in silence. He tried to weigh his options. But with DS Adam's face invasively only two foot from his own, there was no place to hide. No time to dissimulate or conjure. With a deep breath and a heave of his shoulders, Keogh looked back into DS Adam's unrelentingly stern face. There was resignation in his voice when he spoke:

"The past can't be changed Detective. Don't think that because you've had access to those police files you know the truth. You don't. You know only the version they want you to know."

"I'm not interested in your justifications Mr. Keogh, only the facts. Let me ask you: do you admit to releasing the information about the diamonds to the press ? Make that a simple 'yes' or 'no', please"

Keogh hesitated, casting his eyes away from Adam's gaze. However, the car's windows were too steamed up for his eyes to alight on anything outside to hold his attention.

"Yes" he said, still with his eyes averted.

DI Wright had been silent, intently following proceedings. Her colleague's direct, abrasive technique had won them the desired breakthrough. Keogh's defences were decisively breached. He should now be theirs'. She judged it was time to see.

"Mr. Keogh" she began, calm authority in her tone, "thank you for your admission. It's for the best, as I'm sure you know." She paused a couple of seconds to let that sink in, before continuing:

"We could take a lenient view on this. Or else we can wield the big stick. If we go public, you in all probability lose your job."

She left those propositions hanging in the air. Keogh was after all a former policeman, he could decipher for himself where the conversation was headed. Perhaps she was mistaken, but as she watched carefully his reactions, she thought she caught the flicker of a smile in his eyes.

As soon as DI Wright had taken over the reins of control from the other detective, Keogh sensed that the tone and direction of their meeting would change. His experiences as a policeman kicked into play. He now saw their game; knew their goals. The panic that had affected him a few moments ago, faded. He had no problem with trading information; especially if this would get him off the hook. More than this, he believed he could leverage this role to curry favour with the two officers. After all, they were low paid cops and could sympathise with his predicament of money problems.

Keogh began tentatively, not looking at her: "I think I understand you Detective."

Both Wright and Adam remained silent.

"You are expecting me to cooperate with your investigation ?"

"Nothing less is expected from any member of the public Mr Keogh. But in your case, it is much more. If you want us to adopt a lenient approach, then we urgently need high quality information on the behind the scenes activities at the Bank."

"I see."

Keogh did see indeed. There was no question here of claiming confidentiality under his employment contract with the bank. That stance was rendered obsolete by his self-induced predicament with the police.

"And now is a good moment to start, Mr Keogh" DS Adam interjected, with a rapier-like thrust."

Chapter Twenty

As he reached the end of Stephen's Street, Reddy looked across the road at the faded red brick building facing him in Gresse Street. It stood only four storeys high, lined across its façade with old metal-framed windows on each floor and with black iron railings at ground level.

Unprepossessing, it spoke of an early post World War II era of solid aspirations but most means. Strangely out of kilter with the glitz and modernity of the office blocks and shops recently built on the corner of Stephen's Street and Tottenham Court Road, Gresse Street was a decaying backwater alongside which this building might as well have been a disused cotton factory rather than the home of a prestigious College, part of the University of London.

A large removals lorry was parked outside the main entrance to the building. As Reddy approached, the main doors were held open by a portly security guard. Two young men dressed in old jeans and matching denim jackets came out tentatively carrying a grey filing cabinet. They then started descending the entrance steps to street level.

Reddy stepped aside to let them pass then skipped up the steps. He fixed the attention of the security guard with his eyes, who in turn gave him an appraising stare.

"I have an appointment with Professor Bernstein for 12.30. Could you let him know I am here please ?"

"Certainly sir. Your name is....?"

Before Reddy could reply there was a commotion across the reception area as the lift doors opened and a tall man in grey trousers and navy blue pullover backed out followed by two removals men carrying heavy cardboard boxes filled with books. Their noise and movement distracted both Reddy and the security guard, who looked across at them.

The security guard was the first to react. "Professor, this gentlemen has arrived to see you."

Agilely for a man in his seventies, Bernstein pirouetted round to face first the security guard, then Reddy. A look of bewilderment momentarily etched itself on his face, until he removed his spectacles.

"Craig Reddy. Daily Courier ?" Reddy offered. "We met briefly at the Banking Conference last Monday ?"

Bernstein, now stock still, arched a bushy white eyebrow above his right eye and gave Reddy his full attention. Recognition then flowed across his wrinkled face. Spectacles in his left hand, he pointed them at Reddy in acknowledgement.

"Yes, of course. Delighted to see you Mr. Reddy. Of course, I was expecting you. Well then, let's not mess around here. Complete chaos here, as you can see. The whole Department has upped and left already. I'm the last one still clearing things out. Utterly stranded."

He looked around the entrance area quizzically, as if expecting one of the removals men or the security guard to endorse his view. But there was no vindicating response.

"Let's go and get some lunch around the corner."

Spritely and lithe for his age, Bernstein danced towards the exit with evident relish at the prospect of food. Reddy caught a mental image of him as if in a cartoon, where two or three lines drawn in empty space by the cartoonist mark the place where the person last was. He unmoored himself and went out through the swing doors in the Professor's wake.

They were seated at a small table in a corner at the back of "Da Jessica's" Italian restaurant, down a side street behind Charlotte Street. The restaurant had been Bernstein's choice. By the way that they were warmly greeted and served by the Sardinian owner and his family, it was obvious to Reddy that Bernstein was an honoured regular guest.

They had finished their food which, Reddy reflected, had been simply prepared but excellent to the palate. Bernstein's age was no impediment to his appetite, as he had demolished a wonderful looking risotto "Da Jessica". His empty plate produced an effusion of affective Italian for him from the owner's wife when she came to collect.

Reddy's own spaghetti putanesca had also hit the spot. They had ordered two espressos which they were now awaiting.

During the meal, they had quickly warmed to one another. However Reddy selected to venture indirectly towards the questions and issues that he wanted the Professor's advice on, preferring first to let the conversation drift desultorily around the Professor's past.

Bernstein recounted that his father had been born in Vienna in 1906. There he had studied economics at the University with Professor von Mises who was one of the fathers of the so-called "Austrian School" of economics. The Bernstein family left Vienna in 1937 for England, to escape Nazism. Bernstein himself, born in 1935, had studied economics at the London School of Economics in the mid 1950s under Professor von Hayek. Hayek, a close friend of von Mises, had been the catalyst for Bernstein's own choice of an academic career in economics. Now seventy four years old, Bernstein was Emeritus Professor of Banking & Finance at London University. He had stopped teaching duties over 10 years ago.

"That's interesting" Reddy interposed, seeing an opening to navigate Bernstein into his port of interest. "Why is it then that no one has heard of von Mises ? I have no memory of having had to read his work when I was studying undergraduate economics at the LSE back in the late '80s. von Hayek was essential for monetary economics. But von Mises, no.

"Quite so, Craig, quite so."

They had agreed on arrival at the restaurant to use first name terms. Bernstein was erudite but not one to stand on ceremony. He sighed and took a deep breath.

"You know, if there is one thing that you learn in professional academia, certainly in the social sciences at least, it is that the search for scientific truths is entirely secondary to the preservation of the prevailing orthodoxy."

Reddy smiled. "Does that mean that von Mises and you other Austrian economists are just bitter and twisted ? Jettisoned and ignored by the mainstream ?" he asked, putting up a straw man to see how Bernstein would react.

"Bitter and twisted, no. In the context of where we are with this current crisis I think the understanding offered by an Austrian approach is coming into its own again. But yes, Austrian economics undoubtedly has been ignored by academic economics.

"And the reason for that being...?" Reddy pressed.

"Reasons", Bernstein corrected. "First, all Mises' important work was published in German and mostly not translated into English until the 1950s by which time it was too late and simply ignored."

"And why was that ?" Reddy inquired.

"Because of Keynes. Keynes is reason number two. He grabbed the policy high ground with his publication of the General Theory in 1936. It claimed to explain the Depression of the 1930s. Economists, policy-makers and politicians of all hues jumped on the bandwagon. 'Keynesianism' was born and became the orthodoxy. Government interventionism – starting with Roosevelt's New Deal in the '30s and since then during the whole post war era in the Western world - has been built around the idea that government can achieve full employment through influencing the level of effective demand. That was the crux of Keynes' policy argument."

"Game, set and match to the Keynesians then ?" Reddy served back provocatively.

Bernstein fingered the glass in his hand for a moment looking contemplatively at the bubbles rising in the mineral water. He returned:

"Not so. It's true Keynesian thinking has crowded out alternative explanations and approaches. The orthodoxy was challenged briefly during the Thatcher era, when von Hayek's monetarist theories came on the political radar, with their prescriptions for solving rampant inflation. However, with the current financial crisis, I see and hear more of the Austrian approach coming to the surface, especially in the USA."

"That approach consists essentially in what ?"

"First and foremost, praexology."

"For heaven's sake what does that mean in layman's terms ?"

"It's not very felicitous is it ?" Bernstein conceded. "What it means" he continued "is purposeful human action. Mises' magnum opus is indeed titled just that: "Human Action". He took the early achievements of the classical political economists, plus the subjective value theories of his teacher in Vienna Carl Menger, and elaborated a theory of human action."

Bernstein glanced apprehensively at Reddy; sensing that his listener thought he was being led off into the abyss.

"Craig, let me give you an example that Mises himself liked to use when teaching students. He asked them to think about ways of understanding human behaviour at Grand Central Station during the rush hour. The empirical behaviourist would simply observe people rushing back and forth aimlessly at certain predictable times of day. Whereas a theorist of human action, starting with the truth that all human action is purposive, would understand that the purpose is to get from home to work in the morning by catching the train, and do the same in the opposite direction in the evening. Obviously the latter discovers and knows more about human behaviour.

Mises' fundamental position was to take as an axiomatic truth that people consciously pursue purposeful actions which provides definite knowledge; knowledge which is always valid as far as human beings are concerned. This provides the base for a coherent framework to analyse the state of an economy."

Reddy liked the practical example. He was sympathetic too to the idea that some basic deductions could provide the building blocks of a theory. Unfortunately, a slowing post-prandial metabolism was threatening to overwhelm his alertness. Heaving his mind back from the brink, he determined to detonate the conversation back into a more calibrated orbit.

"Fine, Immanuel. I'll leave that as read for now if you don't mind. Tell me please, how this all brings us to the epicentre of the current financial crisis ? That's what your paper was about; the one you presented at the Conference this week ?" he encouraged.

If Bernstein was dismayed by Reddy's flight from theory to pragmatism, his face failed to betray it. He had learned to be both a patient and a resilient man. He smiled sagely at Reddy. His eyes glistened like the Ancient Mariner's.

"Yes, indeed. Of course, the people organising these Conferences haven't got a clue what my theoretical orientations are. Neither do they care. I suppose the reason I was invited to speak was because my academic specialism in Banking & Finance appealed, given the title of the Conference", he suggested diffidently. "I think I came onto their radar because of the recent journalistic piece that I wrote for your competitors at the FT. Notoriety breeds success does it not ?" he added mischievously.

Reddy wracked his brains for a memory of the notorious article in question. He had little time for the FT these days; they were orthodoxy personified. However he guessed that it was probably similar to what Bernstein had presented at the Conference. He said:

"Was that the one on systemic risk in the banking system ? You were criticising commentators' proposals for ways out of the financial crisis, if my memory serves ?"

Mama Jessica arrived at their table. With a maternal smile she served them with the two espressos they had ordered to complete their meal. Sensing that the two men were deep in conversation, and knowing from feminine conviction that that could be of no practical consequence whatsoever, she retreated to the kitchen.

Bernstein adjusted his position in his seat and straightened his back, as if threatening to launch into a major speech. Instead, he delicately steepled the fingers of his left hand over the small espresso cup, and looked across at Reddy with his right eyebrow again arched in characteristic fashion. Reddy wondered if he had caught the affliction from Patrick Moore the astronomer.

"Craig, I think everyone sees what they want to see. And most of that is superficial and emotional. Amongst the public there is anger against the bankers for being greedy and negligent. There is disaffection with the politicians for taking toxic bank liabilities onto the taxpayers' shoulders. Confusion amongst professionals and investors about the risks surrounding derivatives products such as CDOs. Interventionism from the policy makers saying banking is too de-regulated. Conflicts between governments pointing their recriminating fingers at each other's fiscal policies. Acrimony from the private sector against central banks, saying they have fuelled the crisis through cheap credit. You name it. A veritable pot pourri."

Reddy was aware of all these positions. Who wasn't ? Since the Lehman Brothers' collapse in the US and the UK government's nationalisations of Northern Rock, Royal Bank of Scotland and others, there were thousands of column inches written daily about the financial crisis in the written media. Never mind the endless entertainment on the business news tv channels, hosted by testosterone fuelled anchors grilling insiders from the City of London or the trading floors at the NYSE.

"So are you saying that none of that is on the mark ? The fundamentals have been missed ?"

Bernstein deliberately withdrew his now warmed fingers from over his cup and pointed the index finger at Reddy.

"Precisely".

He fired an imaginary shot across the table, held up the finger vertically and blew on it, as if having disposed of some villainous outlaw in a spaghetti Western.

Reddy was curious. This is where he wanted to get to with Bernstein. Pick his brains to help him delve into the heart of this darkness that was his own investigative efforts into the affairs and ramifications of the Ipswich & Blackwater. Bernstein continued:

"What is not being addressed is the structural reality of the modern banking system. That is, what is called 'fractional reserve banking'."

Reddy's spirits started sinking again. The mental alertness gained from the hot peppers in the putanesca sauce was in danger of losing out to the soporific effect of spaghetti settling in his stomach. He took up his espresso cup and knocked back the contents in one gulp, hoping for a caffeine hit to the bloodstream.

Bernstein had stopped talking. He studied Reddy, waiting patiently to re-engage his undivided attention.

"Educate me." Reddy rejoined in an even voice. "But please keep it simple."

"Simple it is Craig" Bernstein shot back, as if responding to commands from the bridge on a ship. He smiled benignly.

"The bottom line is this. Some people understand that Central Banks can print money and that if they do so excessively this can lead to inflation or even hyperinflation. What almost nobody understands, other than the 'insiders', is that all banks in a fractional reserve banking system can create money."

The benign smile had transformed itself into a Cheshire cat's grin from ear to ear. Reddy suspected Bernstein was entertaining himself royally at his expense. Reddy was not to be played with. This was nonsense. He challenged:

"How do you arrive at that idea ? Money creation is legally restricted to national or supranational central banks like the European Central Bank. Anything else is illegal. Banks can only create credit backed by deposits and shareholders' capital."

"Ah, Craig ! Like almost everyone you too are behind the curve. You see, the fact is that banks no longer labour under those constraints. Let me give you the history. The origin of the problem was back in 1848 when the legal system intervened decisively in the evolution of deposit banking to allow money creation. The House of Lords found in favour of Foley versus Hill saying that once a money deposit is made to a deposit bank, the money is to all intents and purposes is at the bank's disposal to decide what to do with. Incredible; but there you have it. The inherently fraudulent nature of fractional reserve banking was born in that decision. Deposit banking becoming loan banking, lending out money or money certificates that it did not own - effectively, money creation - with a view to making profits through interest. Banks' money reserves available to pay their depositors on demand were only a fraction of the liabilities. The whole is inherently unstable because of the mismatch of maturities between immediate redemptions to depositors and long term repayment maturities by borrowers."

"OK. But why is that so important or relevant today ?" Reddy inquired.

"Because the business cycle booms and busts that have occurred over the past centuries have all been built on the inflationary expansion and subsequent deflationary contraction of bank credit. It was Mises who first developed a theory of the business cycle to explain that. The latest mess that the US and other Western banking systems have gotten themselves into is the latest, and worst, manifestation of that."

"That's all well and good" Reddy interjected, "but in practice bank's lending and investment activities are governed by regulations like the Basel II rules and so on. Banks don't have carte blanche."

"Banking regulation is indeed with us. But it is always fighting the last crisis, and never ahead of the curve. Added to that, there is 'capture' of the regulators through the reality of the revolving door: most of the people working in the regulatory authorities either have come from the same institutions they are supposed to independently regulate, or are expecting later to develop their careers there. So the likelihood of sustaining robustly enforced regulation is permanently counteracted by "institutional capture". But those regulatory problems pale into lesser significance compared to the policies of western governments and their central banks. They are today's central planners. And their addiction to Keynesian policies pours more fuel on the fire.

Craig, Governments have been addicted to deficit spending for decades and the addiction is now becoming chronic. Public sector debts as a proportion of GDP are rising towards uncontrollable levels. Here in the UK, the government is spending annually £150 billion more than the revenues it raises through taxes. Funding the gap through selling debt is all well and good but it does damage to the economy. More and more scarce government revenues are diverted simply to paying debt interest. When the markets wake up in the near future and perceive the risk of government insolvencies, yields on government bonds will go through the roof."

"Of course, the Federal Reserve and the Bank of England are already starting to print money in order to buy up their respective Governments' bonds. That's so called 'debt monetisation' and it's no panacea. It will not resolve the crisis, only delay its resolution and exacerbate it meantime."

"Why so ? Reddy queried. "Because you are anti-Keynesian and do not believe they can reflate the economy through deficit spending ?"

"Craig, simply put: you cannot solve a debt crisis which is structural in nature by throwing more debt at it. If the problem is structural, problem resolution must involve structural change. The current US administration is about to introduce a Keynesian style stimulus package. We'll no doubt hear more about it at this forthcoming G20 Summit here in the UK. But it will accomplish very little, mark my words."

"Well, let's wait and see. But what does structural change mean in practice ?" Craig pressed.

"Look what has happened in the US where the scale of the problem is most evident. Since President Nixon took the US dollar off the gold standard in 1971, money creation through the mechanisms of fractional reserve banking has generated exponential debts. You know, in the USA total credit market debt has been doubling every 9 or so years since then ? Its estimated to be around 50 trillion US dollars today whereas it was a mere one trillion in 1971. A doubling rate that remains constant produces an exponential curve. The banking system is dependent on this exponential credit growth. Money is simply loaned into existence and becomes debt. It is the other side of the credit coin. To survive in this exponential manner, the US system requires credit doubling over the next decade too. That doubling, if it were to occur, would take the US total debt from $52 to over $100 trillion before 2020. It would mean creating close to $5 trillion of new credit each year in the US alone. I'ts not going to happen Craig. I think that many countries in the Western world – including the UK - are living on borrowed time."

"So why do you not support the calls for reform of the banks. Isn't it sensible to look at increasing capital ratios for instance ? And what about the proposals to separate out the retail business of banking from the "casino" activities of the investment banks. Wouldn't that be sensible as well ?"

"My honest opinion ? 'Fiddling while Rome burns'. 'Arranging deck chairs on the Titanic'. Of course, such reforms might have some impact Craig. But it would be no more than papering over the cracks. Don't get me wrong. At the margin some of these proposed reforms might have positive effects. But regulatory change is slow, replete with huge political compromises and usually it has limited jurisdiction. Whereas the financial system is global and so too is fractional reserve banking. Once the debt is out there in the system, globalised banks can move the money more or less wherever and whenever they like."

"So how do you explain the fact that the banks were accused recently of the opposite: hoarding ? The inter-bank lending market almost dried up a few months back."

"Well of course !" Bernstein ejaculated, his left hand now wheeling around beside him. "That was simply a manifestation of fear after the onset of the banking crisis and collapse of Lehmans'. Each bank tried to protect its capital because of the risk that its erstwhile banking brothers were concealing huge solvency problems from non-performing lending or speculative losses in derivatives."

"So what results are you expecting from stimulus and central bank money expansion ?" Reddy asked.

"One of two alternatives. Central banks may continue to massively expand credit to commercial banks. If they do, this will cause price increases and asset bubbles in stocks and commodities. If that goes on unchecked then watch out for rapidly rising inflation, a crash in stocks, followed by a collapse of the money and credit system. Worse than the one we've just witnessed these last months. The other possibility is that central banks and governments stop before this point is reached. They pull back from further credit expansion. Even this however will bring about another crisis, with sovereign government bankruptcies and bank failures. The depression follows in both instances. Believe me Craig, there is insolvency coming. Both to governments and the global banking system. In my view, it will be solved only by another great Depression which will wipe out much of the debt. In the aftermath, we may then at last see radical change in the rules of how money is created and debt managed."

"That's a hugely pessimistic scenario, Immanuel. No wonder it's a hard sell. Is there anyone who wants to hear the message ?"

"Very few to be honest. Hardly anyone sees that today the core problem to resolve is governments' monopoly of money. Mises observed, it's the plaything of political decision making. With irredeemable paper money it is the political elite, not market forces, which determine the purchasing power of the means of exchange. Don't forget either that the collusion between government and central Banks to ensure that interest rates remain low also exacerbates the crisis in banking. It forces banks to look to ever riskier lending in order to make money. Persistently low interest rates perpetuated by the policy of the central bank insidiously benefits governments hooked on debt. At the same time, it's having malignant impacts in the broad economy by encouraging investments projects which otherwise would not materialise. At the same time, it drives a redistribution of wealth and income towards the banking sector. "

Reddy felt overwhelmed by this new world view that Bernstein had exposed him to. He sensed that it was powerful as a way of explaining the unfolding global crisis. He could see too that the microcosm of failings and symptoms he had identified so far in his investigation of the Ipswich and Blackwater, would benefit from being set on a broader explanatory canvas. He took a chance and asked:

"Tell me, Immanuel. You know I'm presently investigating the Ipswich and Blackwater Bank's possible insolvency."

"Indeed. You mentioned that to me at the Conference on Monday. How is it progressing ?"

"Well, I've got an agreement to publish some of the findings in the Messenger. In two parts, one on Thursday tomorrow and a follow up next Monday. I'll be completing the first tonight. The second I still haven't begun. It is to deal with the wider context. Would you perhaps be interested to help me ?"

"Well of course. Absolutely. If you're in sympathy with the things I've been telling you about. It's never a bad time to educate the public on the truths that have been hidden from them !"

16.15 Wednesday 18th March 2009. Fowles Bookshop, Gower Street, central London

As Reddy stepped out of Goodge Street underground station, he saw there had recently been a localised rain shower. The surface of the pavements and road in Tottenham Court Road were both shiny and slippery. The rain had stopped however and a few blue patches of sky were visible.

He jay walked across the road, avoiding the slow moving heavy traffic, and went down Chenies street to Fowles' bookshop for his meeting with Natasha. He felt a rising sense of excitement, uncertain what new revelations she might have for him. At the back of his mind too, there was that unasked question about her motivation for doing this. Prudence told him that the question needed to be put. Reddy knew that Natasha's father had been a Russian diplomat on active service in London when Gorbachev had introduced Perestroika in the 1980s. He had exploited the opening to defect. Natasha had been born in Moscow but had lived nearly her whole life in London. Reddy guessed she was about twenty seven or eight.

He was still ten minutes early for their meeting, which Natasha had suggested occur inside the bookshop at the subject section for Feminist Studies. Reddy, unsure of her personal views, had been taken aback with the reason given in her text message "…..because there'll be no one there."

He was standing outside the bookshop on the inner section of the broad pedestrian pavement. A perpetual flow of young people passed before him, many of them students at the University of London. In the main they appeared wilfully idiosyncratic in their choice of apparel and other decorations. Even though the weather was inclement, that did

211

not inhibit their taste for the bizarre. 'Making a statement' these days translated into outlandish hair colourations, piercing of noses and lips, and abundant tattoos. Reddy felt old; or at least, alienated from this generation of youngsters. Was this emphasis on incongruous appearance some type of post modernist tribalism ? He didn't know and didn't understand, but did it explain why the 'Feminist Studies' section of the bookshop is, if Natasha's observation is accurate, devoid of readers ?

He elected to wait a while outside in order to check his mobile phone for messages. If she was delayed, he had asked her to let him know. Looking into his briefcase for his mobile phone, he came across another device. It was Pandit Singh's Blackberry. He made a mental note later to email Pandit that his smart phone was safe.

Retrieving his own phone from the briefcase, he checked for messages. There was none from Natasha. However, Mina Patel had diligently unearthed a mobile phone number for Elaine Cartwright. Reddy fired off a text reply thanking her then placed a call immediately to Cartwright. The ring tone persisted for five rings before the call was accepted. There was silence at the other end of the line.

Reddy asked: "Hello. Is that Mrs. Cartwright ?"

There were a few seconds hesitation before a reply was forthcoming.

"Yes. Who is calling please ?" The voice was faint, tremulous.

"Mrs. Cartwright, sorry to disturb you. My name is Craig Reddy. I'm a journalist at the Daily Courier and...."

"I don't want to speak to the press"

"Mrs. Cartwright, I understand. If you would please just give me a few moments to explain ?" Reddy applied his best diplomatic tone.

"You're completely untrustworthy the lot of you. I want my privacy. My husband has died last week end. I want privacy" Mrs Cartwright's voice was strained.

"Mrs. Cartwright, I'm absolutely not interested in any sensationalism or personal disclosures. I fully respect your need for privacy. May I offer my condolences regarding your husband ? I interviewed him a few days before he died. We talked about the Ipswich and Blackwater Bank and his role there. He was most helpful to me."

212

Reddy stopped. Better to let that information sink in and take seed. There was again silence on the other end. Eventually Mrs Cartwright asked:

"What do you want ? I don't wish to spend time on the phone now. I'm with my parents."

"I appreciate that Mrs Cartwright. I don't want to disturb. Would it be possible that we meet up somewhere in Ipswich tomorrow ? Could you perhaps find time to talk to me ?"

"About what ?"

"Your husband's interview with me left a few areas of conversation unfinished. I'd wanted to have a follow up meeting with him but of course that wasn't possible."

"I'm not the one to ask questions about his work."

"I think you might be able to help Mrs Cartwright. He told me he went on trips abroad to look after the CEGB's activities in eastern Europe ? Sometimes he took you with him to Vienna ?"

"That's true. Once or twice I went with him. It's a lovely city for the arts and culture. I still don't see what I can tell you that's relevant."

"Mrs. Cartwright, please trust me. I promise that my interest is only in the business side of the bank and the CEGB. Could you possibly meet me please ?"

Against the odds, Elaine Cartwright conceded:

"Alright. Tomorrow some place in the centre of town. On condition though that you publish nothing I say unless I agree beforehand."

"You can trust me on that Mrs Cartwright. Where would you like to meet ?"

"Next to Granny" came the reply.

"Sorry, where ?"

"The statue of Carl Giles' character Granny. Its at the top end of Princes' Street opposite the local newspaper offices ?"

"Of course, I know it. We can find a café nearby to sit and talk. What time would suit ?"

"Say midday"

The conversation over, Reddy turned and entered the bookshop. From the large directory list of book subjects affixed to a wall inside the entrance, he identified the floor where Feminist Studies books were kept and climbed the stairs. He found the section without difficulty, but there was no Natasha, but a couple of middle aged female browsers. With a wry smile, Reddy suspected that with perverse logic she had deliberately led him here as a stratagem to entice him to peruse the book titles in Feminist Studies, and perhaps but one.

Reddy was much too immersed in the prospect of discovering what new disclosures Natasha might have for him for his Ipswich and Blackwater dossier to give that thought further credence.

On the point of moving across to an adjacent book section to avoid attracting attention to himself, Natasha arrived. She was radiant and slightly breathless having climbed the staircase rapidly. Her long black hair fell straight down the back of a pastel yellow raincoat which was unbuttoned at the front. Under the coat she wore an elegant one piece white dress held-in tightly at the waist by a yellow leather belt and buckle. She carried a Gucci handbag and her ear lobes sported tiny gold earrings.

She smiled at him as they shook hands briefly, her bright white teeth flashing.

"Glad to see you could make it" Reddy said, "It's a fair ride over from Canary Wharf at this hour."

"Hi Craig. Yes, it took a while and you suffer being crushed in the carriage by all those City types."

Natasha unexpectedly grasped his wrist. Moving closer to him she confided:

"Let's move over there, out of earshot".

His wrist still in her firm grip, they migrated to the other side of the room. Fixing him with an appealing look in the eyes, she insisted:

"Craig, you must first swear to me that you will never reveal your source. What I've got here is explosive. It's crying out to be published. You'll see what I mean when you read it. But you must never expose me."

Reddy was amazed by her fervent behaviour, unsure if it was a measure of the sensitivity of the information she was delivering him. The grip she had on his wrist tightened and he found himself staring into the depths of her irises as she gazed unwaveringly into his eyes, as if in supplication for her life.

"I swear" he whispered. Nervousness was overtaking him, driven by the unexpected intensity of Natasha's determination and the intimacy of their closeness.

"Good. Then let me first give you this" she said, withdrawing her hand and pointing discreetly at her Gucci bag.

Reddy recognised at once her desire to be unburdened of whatever document she had brought with her. He bent down and quickly opened up his briefcase. Natasha withdrew a USB flash disk from her Gucci bag and dropped it inside.

"From Russia with love" she said sotto voce, the smile now transforming into an amused grin. This is very 'cloak and dagger' isn't it ?".

"Well, you're being rightly careful to meet a long way from your workplace. In here, anyone can be innocently searching for a book to buy. But yes, it has a Deighton-esque feel to it" Reddy responded, closing his briefcase.

"A what feel to it ?" Natasha queried, suddenly bemused.

"Deighton-esque. Len Deighton. Don't you know him ? He wrote great spy novels during the Cold War era" Reddy explained.

"Were his books like the James Bond novels ? Deliberately 'cloak and dagger' but with a romantic style ? Where the Bond gets his girl ?"

"Rarely, no. Deighton had more rough edges, I'd say."

Reddy's comment left Natasha looking disappointed. To his surprise and astonishment she then responded:

"There you are. Reality is better than fiction, Craig. You should try it. "

The unadorned directness of this threw Reddy off balance. He felt confused, unsure what message Natasha was sending.

He bumbled something about being grateful to her for providing valuable information to him, but sensed that that was not where she had wanted the conversation to go. The moment was lost. After a couple more minutes of sterile talk she turned on her heels and was gone. Without even a departing smile.

Annoyed with himself for having fumbled his lines, Reddy re-ran their conversation in his head to fathom what he'd done wrong. Then he acted on his conclusion, heading immediately downstairs to the thriller-crime section of the bookshop. There, running a rule over the authors ranged in alphabetical order, he alighted on Len Deighton's books. He chose 'Berlin Game', went to the payment desk and bought it. If his conclusion was valid, then he no longer needed to ask Natasha about her motives.

The book and the USB both safely stored in his briefcase, and with a renewed sense of purpose, he left the bookshop and walked off back to Goodge Street underground, heading for the first train leaving Liverpool Street Station for Ipswich.

Chapter Twenty One

13.45 Wednesday 18th March 2009. Public Bar, The White Lion Hotel, Manningtree, Essex.

Mark Hancock pushed the empty dish away towards the centre of the table. The shepherds' pie had replenished his flagging energy. He wiped his lips with the paper serviette, without bothering first to unfold it.

"You can't beat home made pub food, Elvin. This fancy foreign stuff that's everywhere these days, it doesn't fill you up."

Elvin, who was still finishing his Ploughman's lunch, let Hancock's assertion fade. Although he too was partial to traditional English food, he thought better of telling his ex-colleague about his liking for muscles, a Belgian favourite.

The two men had met an hour ago for a pub lunch and drink. It was at Hancock's instigation. He had cancelled their meeting planned for yesterday evening at the last moment, but had called Elvin earlier this morning. He urgently needed to re-schedule because of the disturbing news he had to relay.

"These guys said they were from SOCA, is that right ?" Elvin asked, wanting to be sure to get the story right before having to explain it to Simon Farley.

"Yeah. It stands for Serious Organised Crime Agency. I'd never heard of them. Anyway, they showed me their IDs. Looked genuine enough. The guys were polite as hell but you could tell they were mean mothers. Plain clothes, but I swear they were ex Special Services or something. You wouldn't mess with them Elvin, that's for sure. And they specifically wanted me to confirm that I know Farley and do business with him. Of course, I co-operated with them. I had no choice. But as I see it, there's nothing to hide. Is what I told them too."

Hancock fiddled nervously with his gold neck chain.

"Sorry Elvin, but I'm going to have to rush. The yard is supposed to re-open at two o'clock. I wanted you to know about them though. It's better that you inform Farley, rather than me, don't you think ?"

Elvin looked across indulgently at Hancock and offered a warm smile. He said:

"Leave it with me, Mark. I'll give Simon a call and put him in the picture."

"Thanks. I hope for his sake that he's not in trouble. These SOCA officers are hard as nails. It's my call on the food by the way."

Hancock took an old wallet from inside the sheepskin coat lying beside him and put a twenty pound note on the table.

"That should cover it all. OK Elvin, bye for now. Let me know how things go with Farley."

He stood up and shook hands firmly with Elvin. Putting on his coat, he smiled briefly and departed through the far door out into the main street and to his parked car.

For a few moments Elvin sat back in his wooden chair and reflected. Down the years, since his move to operating the brickworks at Dears, Elvin and Hancock had maintained a casual friendship. He had observed a gradual hardening of Hancock's attitudes over that time as he dealt with the adversities of running the building materials yard. His unyielding behaviour yesterday when confronted with Simon Farley's problems was a case in point. The business was not his own; he was accountable to head office for sales and profits, hence had no place any more for 'gentlemens' agreements' or other variants of commercial lassitude. Yet the gregarious side of Hancock's personality, although hardened, had not entirely ossified. Elvin understood that today his friend had tried to make amends for his obduracy with Farley yesterday.

The public bar's lunchtime clientele had thinned out, but the pub was open all day today and Elvin saw no reason to hurry. With measured ease he heaved his bulky frame up from the seat and went to the bar to order a black coffee. Waiting for the drink, he leaned his elbows on the bar to take some weight off his feet and gazed around.

The interior was dominated by original old oak beams exposed in a low ceiling and along the walls. Furnishings and fittings were all hardwoods. A few cushions on benches and chairs here and there added a modicum of comfort. There was nothing garish, modern or loud. The public bar had an air of unpretentious hardy homeliness about it. The kind of establishment likely to attract people like himself who preferred old fashioned peace and quiet when having a drink and conversation with others.

The owner's wife, a women in her forties jauntily made up and wearing her faux blonde hair high on her head, returned with a piping hot cup of coffee. She looked like a character out of East Enders. The coffee she brought to him was filled to the brim. It was a small gesture that she cared for her regular customers. He paid her for the earlier meals and drinks, then retraced his steps carrying the cup and saucer before him, mindful to avoid spilling the contents. Having first settled the coffee cup on the table, he sat down.

Unobtrusively, he spied upon the few remaining customers in the room. Some locals, who sat at high stools ranged at the bar, had acknowledged Elvin when he arrived an hour or so ago. They were now deep in conversation, probably about the days' horse racing. When Elvin had gone to the bar, they hadn't paused for breath to speak to him, a copy of the 'Racing Times' folded on the bar counter next to one of the punters. Over the other side of the L-shaped bar there were two elderly men standing around an equally elderly lady in a wheel chair. The men both wore corduroy trousers and old tweed jackets and held pint glasses of beer. Their physical similarities suggested to Elvin that they were brothers. They listened solicitously to the lady who appeared to be dominating proceedings with a long account of something that had caused her irritation, her voice sometimes audible when reaching its' highest decibels. Elvin wondered how much longer the much powdered dame would drone on for, and whether the solicitousness of her interlocutors was genuine chivalry or pretence. He amused himself with the idea that he could measure between the two behaviours by how quickly the gentlemen supped their beers with a view to breaking the monologue by ordering more drinks.

Elvin took a sip of his coffee. It was only then, replacing the cup gently in its' saucer, that he heard the conversation taking place behind his right shoulder. He cast a surreptitious glance around. A couple of men had taken up residence at a table near the window, presumably while he had been at the bar. They had bought soft drinks and had been given knives and forks wrapped in paper serviettes, a sign that they had ordered pub lunches.

Neither of the two men had paid any attention to Elvin. He turned his back to them again. Straining his ears, he sat spellbound trying his hardest to catch a few of the words that made up their conversation. It was definitely for private consumption and assumed that no one in the pub would understand them.

It came in snippets. The main speaker was facing in Elvin's direction, albeit towards his back. When he raised his head, the words he spoke carried to Elvin. When he sat back or moved head to head with his partner, the words got lost in the barrier that was the other man's body.

"........ took delivery of the diamonds this mor......went smoothly.....at the A12 service station near......."

The other man asked a question, inaudible for Elvin. The first then continued:

"....... from east europe....not sure where.......spoke Eng......"

Another inaudible question. Then:

"..........phoned me Sunday..........knew my num.......

........calm guy......obviously a pro........

..........i reckoned the value at..............was happy with half that.........

.......paid him cash........over in five minutes..........."

Another inaudible question. Then:

".......sure they're genuine......

.......your job now......down to Harwich and get them back to ......"

Suddenly there was silence. The two abruptly halted their exchanges. Elvin saw why. A serially-tatooed young woman in faded blue jeans and orange T-shirt sporting the name 'Coldplay' approached carrying two dishes of hot food. Stopping in front of the two men's table she asked them to confirm their orders and then placed the dishes down before them, returning languidly from whence she came. The arrival on their table of the food terminated further discussion as the two turned their attention to eating with evident relish.

Throughout, the two had been resolutely oblivious of Elvin's presence. They had spoken to one another in Flemish, assuming their words couldn't be heard or understood.

The two men had miscalculated. There was another Flemish Belgian in the pub, and he was sitting two metres away from them. Elvin, who had been born in Bruges in 1948 and named Eddy van Kuyt, had understood them.

His coffee finished, Elvin rose pensively from his chair, gathered his shabby donkey jacket, and left the pub unnoticed.

Chapter Twenty Two

18.20 Wednesday 18th March 2009. Bar, Excelsior Hotel, Curzon St, Mayfair, London

Angelov loved London. Or rather, he loved those parts of central London that enabled him to work hard and play hard. London provided a stage on which Angelov dreamed to become a major player. He was determined to show it was not just the Russian oligarchs who could migrate to London, win coveted friends in high places and gain access to the bastions of City of London finance.

Angelov's ambitions and plans foresaw him becoming a powerful and respected player on the London business scene. The unexpected and untimely demise of Thomas Cartwright was a set back; but not a decisive rupture for Angelov's business strategy to strengthen and expand his 'legitimate' entrepreneurial activities outside Bulgaria. He had developed a 'Plan B' in his head while flying to Heathrow. Depending upon the way events unfolded, he intended to use this Plan B to pursue his interests further.

However, since arriving in London the previous day, Angelov had had a torrid time. Circumstances seemed to derail his every move. Even the trivial details weren't running smoothly. The five star hotel in Mayfair at which he had made a reservation had mistakenly double-booked his room. He was obliged to wait half an hour in the coffee lounge while housekeeping prepared another room. That delay did nothing to improve his mood.

Then there was the matter of Bourov; also, in its' way, a matter of 'housekeeping'. In Angelov's view, Bourov owed him unconditional allegiance. Without his tutelage, Bourov was a non-entity. It was Angelov who had trained him in the art of mafia survival in Bulgaria and provided him with a job. It was Angelov who had encouraged and paid for him to learn English. It was Angelov who had set him up in the UK working for Russell Westlake's Redwood Country Homes. It was Angelov who planned his future in the UK, even if Bourov himself remained in the dark about it. In short, Angelov owned Bourov body and soul.

So far as Angelov could understand, Bourov had now gone absent without leave. He had turned off his mobile device and was uncontactable. Russell Westlake had confirmed earlier on the phone that Bourov's whereabouts were unknown to him. There might be extenuating circumstances for this, but Angelov's instincts signalled this was not the case. His continued survival as a Bulgarian entrepreneur was conditional, in part, upon his ability to identify disloyalty and treachery. And then neutralise it. That was the course of action he had determined upon.

That morning he had instructed his two guards Vladimir and Igor to hire a car, go to Colchester, and visit Bourov's rented apartment. They had done so, and had arrived there around 13.15. They broke in with the usual pros' tools, then Vladimir phoned Angelov.

"Boss, there's no sign of Bourov. But it looks to me like the apartment is still occupied. There's still fresh food in the fridge. The garbage bin contains rubbish that's not yet putrid. Little signs like that."

"OK. In that case, the likelihood of Bourov returning soon is high. I want you to leave the apartment as it is. Get out and lock the door behind you. Make yourselves scarce, but stake it out. If Bourov returns, I want him held captive in his apartment. Use whatever measures necessary and keep him quiet. Just don't kill him. Understood ?"

"Yes, boss. Leave it to us."

"Call me again as soon as you've got him. I intend to interrogate him personally. Stay there all night if need be. He's sure to return."

Their phone conversation terminated and Angelov mused on Bourov's fate. Uncertainty surrounding his case would be resolved one way or the other. Nevertheless, it niggled Angelov enough to add to his sense of operational disequilibrium.

Further bad news struck soon after. Angelov had thought he had engineered a meeting with Sir Peter Westlake at the Excelsior Hotel for 18.30 . That at least was the information he had from Sir Peter's personal assistant yesterday. Yet in a further call from her today around 14.00, she apologised and explained that Sir Peter was tied up due to unforeseen circumstances. She proposed to re-schedule, for Friday breakfast at the Excelsior at 7.00am. Angelov had had no choice but to accept, but it was another obstacle in his path.

He was now seated in the Excelsior hotel's main bar. It was empty but for two men in suits sitting together on high chairs at the bar drinking cocktails. They had their backs to Angelov so he could not see their faces, nevertheless from the fragments of conversation that reached him, he knew they were speaking a Slavic language.

Angelov himself had only a half filled bottle of Scottish Highlands mineral water and a glass tumbler as company. He had been here already nearly an hour, having grown tired of his hotel room. Lounging in a deep low armchair, he had a view across the lounge bar and out to the reception area. Observing the comings and goings of well-heeled cosmopolitan visitors provided a source of some amusement to lighten his mood, in the interludes between his careful analysis of how best to proceed with his business interests.

He was awaiting the arrival of Mary Donoghue, the Ipswich and Blackwater's chief finance officer. After the disappointment of having his meeting with Sir Peter Westlake postponed, Angelov desperately wanted to avoid an evening alone in London. He knew where to go in this city to have an 'escort' for the evening, but that was not his style. While pondering his options what to do for female company, Donoghue had unexpectedly phoned his mobile.

After the usual introductions she told him:

"I'm now acting CEO of the Ipswich and Blackwater, following Thomas' death. Russell Westlake phoned me yesterday. He said you'd arrived in the UK and are staying in London?"

"That's right. In Mayfair at the Excelsior." Angelov was keen to impress the five star quality of his credentials in London.

"I thought that probably you'd want to discuss the new situation ? There's a lot at stake." Donoghue used her lilting accent and guileful style to tempt Angelov's thoughts to where she wanted them.

Angelov, recalling the meeting scheduled for Friday afternoon with Russell Westlake at the RCH offices near Ipswich, immediately seized on the opportunity:

"Absolutely, yes. I want to talk to you. Are you available Friday, I'll be visiting Westlake that afternoon. Perhaps afterwards, around six o'clock ?"

"We can do better than that, if you like. I'm in London now. I was summoned down here by the CEGB top brass for an urgent meeting. They're nervous about a few things at the Ipswich and Blackwater because of Thomas' death. Plus they're testing me. They're unsure whether to trust a woman as the permanent CEO of the bank. I've just spent the last two and a half hours being subjected to an unofficial job interview by a bunch of late middle-aged male chauvinist under-achievers. I could do with a drink ! Why don't you invite me ?" she asked, in a manner that no alpha male could fail to accept.

They'd had that conversation about half an hour ago. She'd told him to expect her at the Excelsior for about 18.30. He was thinking about where they might go to eat after an initial drink at the hotel when his mobile phone rang. It was Vladimir.

"Boss, Vladimir. We've got him."

"Bourov ? Where ?" Angelov had difficulty camouflaging his intense interest.

"At his apartment. He came back about twenty minutes ago. We went straight in after him."

"So what condition is he in ? How have you restrained him ?"

"Boss, we had to do a little physical damage to knock him out. We've tied him up and Igor gave him some drugs to sedate him. He's out for the count. Won't disturb anyone till tomorrow I'd say."

"Good. Listen. Stay there with him. Avoid disturbing the neighbours. Keep inside the apartment as much as you can. I'm going to get a train up there tomorrow morning.

"OK, boss. No problem. We've got the situation under control."

"Anything else I should know about ? What he said ?"

"Not what he said, boss, but what he had. Probably better not to talk on the phone though ?"

"I don't think the English speak Bulgarian. Give me a heads' up."

"Money, boss. A lot."

This was not a reply that Angelov had expected. His natural reaction was to ask how much. His instinct for self preservation warned him that, even in Bulgarian, this might not be a conversation to pursue over the telephone.

"Vladimir, keep it and him safe. Let's leave it like that for now. I'll call you tomorrow morning with my arrival time. You can collect me at the station."

Angelov cut the call. Immediately his thoughts returned to Bourov and his probable treachery. How could he be in possession of a lot of money ? Had he done some freelance thieving ? Was he working for someone else or alone ? Angelov knew that he had to get answers to these questions fast. He also had to decide Bourov's fate.

Angelov noticed that the two men at the bar who he had overheard earlier, were departing. As they left for the lounge bar exit, he observed them. Perhaps he was wrong, but he thought he knew one of them, a Serb who had made millions in his home country and who now invested much of it in the UK. Angelov felt a momentary twitch of annoyance, recognising that his strategy to 'go legitimate' outside of his homeland was pioneering only for a Bulgarian. Others from Russia, the Balkans and elsewhere had already trodden the path. The wealthy Serb and partner disappeared through the open door.

Casually watching them go, Angelov then observed Mary Donoghue's arrival in the lobby outside. She wore a red raincoat, red tailored suit and matching shoes. Together with her natural red hair, the combined impact was vivid and immediate. Her movements were quick and decisive. After a cursory scan of the reception she turned on her heels and came expectantly towards the lounge bar door.

Angelov stood up from his armchair and gave her a discreet wave to attract her attention. She acknowledged him at once and came over. Angelov remained standing with a welcoming smile, at the same time assessing her. He liked what he saw. A distinctive woman with a freckled face, emerald green eyes and firm cheek bones. He assumed that she was in her early thirties. Although dressed as a professional, her personality and femininity were not eclipsed. There was almost a magnetic effect in her animated movements.

They had met one another before on a few occasions, mostly at the Ipswich and Blackwater's head office in Ipswich, and then usually with Russell Westlake present. Angelov knew from those encounters that Donoghue had a formidable financial brain. She it was who settled the finer points of the loan deals that the Ipswich and Blackwater made with Redwood Country Homes. Angelov, with no formal training in finance, had benefited from exposure to these meetings, absorbing valuable information about UK bank loan contracts.

Tending her hand in greeting, Donoghue smiled: "Hello, a pleasure to see you here in London, Radomir ".

"My pleasure it is too Mary. An unexpected one too."

They shook hands, looking one another in the eyes. The grip she offered him was light and her skin soft. The greenness in her eyes fascinated him, an attribute rarely found in Slavic womens' eyes. To avoid being mesmerised by them, he invited her to sit in the armchair opposite. She took off her coat, and sat carefully, crossing her legs but allowing her skirt to rise up her thigh.

A waiter approached and they ordered drinks.

This was the first time the two had met outside of a formal business environment. Angelov could not fail to be attracted and fascinated by the woman. While flying to London on Tuesday, he had considered that, with Cartwright gone, there could be opportunities to use Donoghue as a valuable ally for his business. Looking at her before him now, he was having to recalibrate his thinking. Out of her office environment, this woman presented herself on a different plane. Her calculated self-invitation to meet him when they had spoken on the phone was not an aberration. Angelov had the impression that she was keen to have a lively discussion, and not just or even mainly about business. Perhaps their relationship was to evolve further and faster than he had assumed. He determined to keep the formalities short, finish their drinks quickly and then take her out for dinner.

The waiter returned from the bar with their drinks on a silver plate tray. Angelov judged from his looks and accent that he was Spanish. In his short time in central London, it seemed to Angelov as if everyone and his dog had washed up on England's shores to find work.

There were a couple of things he needed urgently to know from Donoghue. He decided to broach them with her at once.

"If I understood from your comment on the phone, you're tired of discussing business ? At least for today after your talks with the CEGB bosses ?" he enquired with kindly consideration.

Unexpectedly, she laughed outright, and responded with an amused irreverence:

"Let the devil take the hindmost ! They're a bunch of tossers. Addled on malt whiskey and suffering incipient senile decay."

"My English doesn't stretch to some of that, Mary" Angelov said, "but I think I understand. You're not too impressed with your bosses, right ?"

"Understatement Radomir ! They appoint me immediately as acting CEO in the aftermath of Thomas' suicide. You know, like stability and continuity on the ground ? Next thing you know, I am summoned to London to meet the chairman and Group CFO. They were stressed out on rumours that the bank is insolvent. Already trying to cover their arses, in case things are not stable."

"So you would be what you call the 'scapegoat' ?" Angelov suggested, using the word tentatively.

Donoghue spontaneously clapped her hands: "Radomir, no problems with your English at all ! Yes, indeed, scapegoat. Or, as the Americans say, 'the fall guy'."

A muffled ringing sound announced a caller on Donoghue's mobile phone, which prevented Angelov from pursuing the conversation. She pulled out the device from her suit pocket and took the call. As she listened to the caller, Angelov observed her closely. Her demeanour transformed from relaxed sociability to steely determination. Rising from her seat she said:

"Excuse me, Radomir. I need to talk privately for a moment. It's one of my key traders from the bank. I need to sort out one or two issues. Just a couple of minutes."

She smiled reassuringly at him and then retreated to the far side of the bar to an empty couch, out of Angelov's hearing but not his sight. As she sat sideways on to his field of vision, he could continue discreetly to observe her behaviour. She was animated and moved her free hand with a pointed forefinger to help make her arguments. It was clear to Angelov, watching her mouth, that she was dominating and directing the conversation. Whoever was on the other end of the line was being given their marching orders in no uncertain terms. The woman, he concluded, had balls. Whether or not she was in control though, he was not sure. Perhaps her animation and dictatorial manner betrayed instead an executive desperately fighting for their corporate life ?

Eventually, Donoghue closed the call. By the time she had returned to take a seat with Angelov, she had regained her composure. Whatever it was that she had had to deal with, was buried from view.

Angelov posed the first question he needed an answer to: "Are you really in danger of losing your job Mary ?"

"To be honest, right now I don't know. These guys played their cards close to their chests. They gave nothing away about what they planned to do. It was more an Inquisition about what I knew of the financial health of the bank and whether Thomas had been up to anything untoward."

"Untoward ?"

"Illegal or at least, not entirely professional" she translated. "As I say, they're worried. I believe that there are certain events in Dublin that have unhinged them too. One of their directors hasn't been behaving himself. Thomas' death coming hard on the heels of that has raised the tension a few notches. You know the chairman, Declan Moroney, looked like he wasn't far off a heart attack at one stage" she laughed and took an avid drink of her cocktail. "Cheers !"

Angelov replicated her call, sipping somewhat more cautiously at his spritzer. He wanted to be entertained but not drunk. The news that the CEGB's top executives were concerned about the health of the Ipswich and Blackwater was disconcerting. It was not something he had countenanced. He decided not to pursue the subject now, but logged it for later.

"Mary, it is important to me that you keep your job. Especially with Thomas no longer running the bank, I need someone there I know and trust. Do you intend to stay, if you can?"

"Of course, if I can. It's just that my intuition says that the CEGB are going to appoint someone from outside over my head. If they do, it will remain to be seen if I can hang on to the CFO job. You know, when a new CEO comes in it's usually with a free hand to name his own team. I could be toast in very short order."

"I see. Well, you know, I'll be in Ipswich on Friday to talk to Russell about the RCH and Bulgarian businesses. Maybe we meet up again then and talk about the Ipswich's loans? That will free up this evening for dinner instead ?"

"That sounds fine. By the way, how are things between you two ?" she asked , disarmingly.

Angelov was thrown off-balance by the question. It was apparently posed in innocence, but unexpected.

"We're doing ok, I guess" he said, hedging.

He had not yet taken stock sufficiently of Donoghue's motives and trustworthiness to disclose to her his 'Plan B' strategy. That was to take full control of RCH by offering Sir Peter Westlake to buy out all of Dominion's remaining shareholding, without Russell Westlake's knowledge. He would benefit from knowing in advance what Donoghue and the bank would think about this move. However, caution told him that he first get inside Donoghue's head and understand her motives. His second question aimed to open up this avenue:

"Never mind us. What about you and Thomas. You worked three years together on a daily basis. It must have been a great shock to you. Was it definitely suicide ?"

"I never thought he would do anything like that. He handled work stress well. I only dealt with the Ipswich and Blackwater side of his business. He had the other CEGB responsibilities as well in Vienna ? I don't know much about those. But he was stable mentally. You know, the police are still making enquiries into his death ? Chasing shadows if you ask me."

Angelov discerned Donoghue's swift eye movements. They darted around looking for a home. He wondered whether she was being honest. He asked again:

"So it was a shock ? You thought you knew him well, but not well enough ?"

Donoghue's eyes ceased their dancing and focused solely on Angelov's face. She unfolded her legs and sat forward in her armchair, intent on securing his total attention. She said:

"Radomir, Thomas and I were lovers."

Chapter Twenty Three

21.35 Wednesday 18th March 2009. Reddy's Apartment, Ipswich Marina, Ipswich

Reddy was in his spare bedroom that served as his home office. He had completed the draft of his article and emailed it before nine o'clock to Peter Houseman, asking Houseman to call him back as soon as he had read it. If the article was to make the Messenger's morning edition tomorrow, then there may still be modifications to make based on Housemans' feedback. Awaiting that call, he selected Van Morrison's 'Astral Weeks' from his music collection to provide background musical *ambiance* and tried to relax.

The computer on his writing desk was still on. Its' screen had gone black, in sleep mode. Reddy kicked off his shoes and took up a comfortable lounging position on the settee that doubled as a folding bed. Around him on the floor and stacked on the writing desk were documents and papers that made up his dossier of information on the Ipswich and Blackwater Bank.

He chose not to switch on the room's main ceiling lamp. Instead, he took the angle poise light off his desk, plugged it into a wall socket besides the settee and balanced it so that the light beam angled over his shoulder and down into his lap where he continued to pore over his draft article, looking for possible ways to improve it.

He had returned to Ipswich by train from London and arrived back in his apartment by 19.30. During the train journey he had read the sensitive information furnished him by Natasha and thought about how to incorporate it into the draft file that he had already worked on previously.

The new information furnished on Natasha's flash disk revealed explosive evidence that Mary Donoghue was hiding a gaping hole in the IB&B's balance sheet resulting from both trading losses on the proprietary trading desk and losses from loans to CPI Gmbh, the Austrian company run by Thomas Cartwright.

Natasha herself had done the calculations based on confidential material available to her, estimating the losses at between £ 1.2 and £2 billion. Reddy now appreciated why she had behaved so intensely when they had met at the bookshop earlier in the day. The consequences of such losses for the IB&B's solvency, given its other known financial difficulties, were ominous.

The phone was ringing in the lounge. Expecting that it might be Peter Houseman calling, Reddy pulled his weary body upright and darted out of the room through to the lounge. He grabbed the cordless receiver but the ring tone had stopped. Fortunately, the caller had left the calling number available and Reddy retrieved it from memory. Sure enough, he saw it was Houseman's number. He dialled back. A voice answered after only two rings.

"Good evening Craig. I thought maybe you'd already gone to the pub, having worked so hard" Houseman suggested, with a hint of mirth in his voice.

"No way, Peter. I've had a long day and tomorrow morning I've an appointment too. But after having put together the article for The Messenger, I'm keen to make sure that you're ok with it. Have you read it ?"

"Sure. Look, I think its good and I've already convinced Arthur Givens to hold space for it for tomorrow's newspaper. He's also had a look and told me it's important enough to merit an Editorial."

"That would be fantastic. Please convey my thanks to Arthur for giving it prominence."

"Yeah, well you can thank me too Craig because its muggins here who has been tasked with putting together the Editorial's text."

Reddy decided flattery was called for: "Meat and drink for a man of your manifest qualities Peter."

"Maybe. Anyway, first things first. If we're running this article on the IB&B, it means that your other work leaking the failures of local government finance – the findings of the Audit commission Report – will have to be put on the back burner. Is that ok with you ?"

"With me yes. With the people who want it publicised, is another matter. But it's my problem to solve. Leave it to me."

"Good. Now, I need to make sure that we have the message right in the Editorial. I understand that you're using your detailed knowledge of the Ipswich and Blackwater's situation to highlight the risk of a possible insolvency. Isn't that so ? And you see the bank's predicament as an object lesson for all that's still wrong with the UK's banking industry as a whole ?"

"Yes, that's right. Although I don't want to be sensationalist. Judgement on whether a bank is insolvent or not will ultimately be taken by the markets or by the authorities stepping in. As for the Ipswich and Blackwater, the bank is having aggravated illiquidity issues. The insolvency question is out there too and my latest material – the stuff about the gaping hole in the balance sheet – underlines that."

"OK, I got that, but let's not get bogged down in the accounting arcanery. What I need to agree with you now Craig are the two or three key messages that I can carry into the Editorial. That's where the newspaper sells itself. Arthur and I agreed to put a line in the sand that says 'enough of bank bail outs' and 'stop socialising private debt'. We think that those are clarion calls the public understands and wants to have voiced to the politicians."

"Those make sense, Peter. Certainly, they can tie–in well to the article. However, please don't underestimate this hot news about the trading losses by the bank's proprietary trading desk. My sources indicate that loss contributes at least £ 1.2 billion of the overall loss. I think that is something the public needs to know about."

"Sure, but is it just a 'rogue trader' story like that French guy Kerviel last year at Societé Generale or is it rather pervasive ? You know, part of the culture of the bank ? The distinction is important. It impacts how to present the story. Can we go with a 'casino bank' critique of the IB&B. "

In his own mind, Reddy tended to agree with Houseman's comment. However, he did not want to reveal to him that, as a part of the new material provided him by Natasha, was the name of her 'mole' inside the IB&B who had compiled and sent her most of the incriminating material. It was imperative that Reddy meet and talk to this person to establish his bona fides before exposing in greater detail the nature of the goings on at the bank. He decided to back pedal with Houseman:

"Look, right now I don't have a definitive answer to that question. I need more time to investigate. Bear in mind that we agreed to two articles being written. I promise to address that in the second article for Tuesday next week."

"OK Craig, I 'll hold you to that. So coming back to this article. There are general lines of argument about the IB&B's predicament that replicate to the banking industry as a whole, right ?"

"Absolutely. I think that the key messages are one, overly risky business models; two, overextended leverage; three, chicanery amongst top bankers in massaging the accounts. You could add a fourth, over reliance for profits on poorly understood derivatives products.

"What about the "too big to fail" argument Craig ? The Ipswich and Blackwater is only the 6th largest bank in the UK. However the way you weave the CEGB into the story I understand you want to show the interconnectedness effects of the banking industry. Systemic risks, is that so ?"

"The CEGB is far bigger than the Ipswich, Peter that's for sure. They've a huge footprint in central and eastern Europe. That's blowing up on them as property markets there come off the boil. As regards their connection with the Ipswich and Blackwater, bear in mind that they do not have full control. They're the largest single shareholder but that stake is only 25 per cent. The particularity of their control is that they've had their man as CEO for the last several years."

"Thomas Cartwright ? The guy who committed suicide last week end ?"

"Correct. It's his business strategy that has been driving growth at the Ipswich. Now he's dead and the chickens are coming home to roost. I don't think that the top executives of the CEGB in Dublin had a firm hand on how he expanded the bank's loans business or its proprietary trading. As shareholders, they were only too happy to see the expansion of assets, profits and the share price."

"Yes , your article provides evidence that the bubble has burst. Which reminds me, are we on solid ground in terms of the information we're publishing here ? Is there anything that you've written that might betray confidential sources ?"

"It's as I told you before Peter when we talked at the Conference. I'll protect my sources. I'm confident that the information in the article is accurate."

"Understood. Then let's do the following. I'll email you my comments on your article. There are just a few suggested changes. Send the new version back to me within the hour. Meantime, I'm going to write an

Editorial. I'll mail it to Arthur and yourself. Any comments you have, send them to Arthur. He'll be responsible for final copy. Twenty three hundred deadline. Agree ?"

"Consider it done."

Chapter Twenty Four

05.50 Thursday 19th March 2009. Outside Ipswich Docks, Ipswich

The sky was pitch black, bearing heavy clouds from out across the North Sea. A chill wind whipped across the darkened waterfront. Sail boats moored at the jetty opposite bobbed about on the choppy waters, the cordage along their masts snapping and cracking in the wind. A few gulls were airborne in search of food, but first light was still half an hour off. The only light came from the Docks in the distance, where high powered lamps beamed light all night long onto the loading quays. Two massive cranes, both painted light blue, lay idle pointing up into the night sky like oversized anti aircraft guns. A cargo ship, moored alongside the quay, awaited the morning shift for its next cargo to be loaded before sailing.

SOCA Officer Peter Lean was kitted out in full operations gear. He was responsible for the operational aspects of the mission and was now verifying that all the planned logistics and assets were in place and mission-ready. Lean, an ex-Army combatant with operations experience in West Africa and Iraq, had joined SOCA in 2007 on retirement from the Armed Forces at the age of forty. His war zone experiences and Army training equipped him more than adequately for this morning's action.

He had planned for the worst, with all the officers heavily armed and prepared for armed violence and a possible break-out attempt. However, he had satisfied himself that the operational set up was rigorous and that any such violence could be contained and quickly and effectively quelled.

The mission's target was a warehouse on the waterfront, situated immediately outside of the Docks. The sole access road ran directly along the waterfront for about a hundred metres and then turned right into a long straight side road, on one side of which was a block of residential apartments and on the other, the high external brick walls of the warehouse itself. One way in and out.

The streets were desolate but for a few parked cars.

Lean had an unmarked Audi parked on the landward side of the road just before the right turning into the side road. From the car there was a clear view down towards both the Docks exit and the warehouse exit. Including Lean himself who sat in the front passenger's seat, there were four occupants. The driver and another colleague in the back seat were armed officers, both wearing operations kit like Lean. The other individual in the back seat was Commander Dullingham, responsible for the intelligence on which the mission had been approved. Dullingham was armed only with a hand gun worn in a shoulder holster under a knee length black overcoat.

Out of sight down the side road, was one other unmarked vehicle – a white Range Rover - in which were two trained sniffer dogs with their handlers, together with two more armed SOCA officers. Lean was in radio communication with them.

The warehouse itself had been under observation for several weeks by the SOCA intelligence services, under Dullingham's guidance. Dullingham it was who had marshalled the intelligence that quantities of cocaine were being brought off certain ships arriving from Antwerp, hidden in wooden roof trusses. The roof trusses were unloaded in bulk in the Docks, checked by the warehouse administration and customs, and then transferred out of the Docks to the nearby warehouse to be stocked temporarily pending collection or dispatch.

This particular exit from the Docks was not the main one. Port Authority security was permanently present checking documents of all lorries leaving and arriving, but there was rarely any customs search. The majority of merchandise leaving the Docks at this exit was destined directly for the adjacent warehouse.

According to Dullingham's intelligence, there was no insider collaboration in this illegal trade either on the Docks side or from the management of the warehouse. The people in the UK organising the shipments ostensibly had legitimate business interests and no criminal records. On the Antwerp side, the suppliers of the drugs were known and had a logistics network that stretched across the continent.

Dullingham was experiencing a rising sense of excitement. As expected based on intelligence received, a ship from Antwerp had arrived and docked yesterday evening. It was the one that was still in the Docks this morning and just visible to the four occupants of the first car. Its' cargo had been unloaded from the hold, passed customs, and transported to the warehouse last night before it shut. Amongst the merchandise had been a consignment of wooden roof trusses. Dullingham's confidence level for the mission was now sky high. According to a member of his intelligence team who had chatted casually to one of the warehouse office staff, a lorry was scheduled to arrive first thing after opening time to collect a first load of the roof trusses, and presumably too the drugs.

There was silence in Lean's car. He preferred it that way. Needless banter could endanger. Lean relied on clear and simple procedures, initialised by known and understood instructions. The operational necessities of a mission required nothing less. He had set up his mission assets to ensure success. Whether or not drugs were found was not his primary concern. Although if they were, then the apprehension of those responsible with a minimum of risk and collateral damage was. It was Dullingham, not Lean, whose reputation was on the line here if the raid failed to discover anything.

The plan agreed was to move on the warehouse just after 6.00am, when it opened up for business. Dullingham had convinced Lean not to move before the arrival of the expected lorry. If none came within thirty minutes, then they would go into the warehouse anyway.

Only one vehicle entrance – blocked by a wide red metal gate – existed, permitting access to a large open yard. The gate's movement was controlled by security staff who sat in a small brick office to one side. The yard provided space for arriving trucks and lorries, as well as for palletised stocks of building materials wrapped tight in industrial strength plastics. A number of heavy duty fork lift trucks were parked together along one of the outer walls.   Behind it, the main warehouse structure rose up high, capped by a corrugated iron roof and enclosed by vertical timber-slatted walls.

A crackle of sound emitted from Lean's miniature short wave receiver attached to his jacket.

"Car approaching down side street" said the speaker, the driver of the Range Rover.

A metal blue Toyota passed down the side street and turned right, in the opposite direction to the Docks and warehouse. Lean cast a look into the Audi's outside rear view mirror and saw the Toyota's tail lights. The vehicle pulled up and parked in a space in front of the residential block. Two men got out. They were some fifty metres down the road from where the Audi was stationed. Instead of disappearing into the residential building as Lean hoped they would, the two men set off on foot at a rapid pace towards the Docks.

Lean watched them intently as they approached. They wore jeans, thick weatherproof jackets and woollen hats and seemed in a hurry.

238

With heads down and shoulders hunched up against the chill wind, they marched passed the Audi on the other side of the street. Neither of them was observant enough to notice the Audi and its occupants. They crossed the road a little further up and came to a halt at the access gate to the warehouse. After a few seconds delay, the gate opened automatically and the two vanished inside. The gate closed after them.

"First of the employees arriving ?" Dullingham suggested.

Lean said nothing.

His short wave receiver crackled again.

"Lorry approaching down side street" said the driver of the Range Rover.

A large, dirty truck passed the parked Range Rover and decelerated to a stop at the T-junction accessing the waterfront road. It indicated, and turned left towards the Docks' entrance.

Lean again cast a look into the Audi's outside rear view mirror. He caught sight of the truck, headlamps lit. He inclined his head to the driver and nodded in affirmation.

"Let's move" Lean instructed into the microphone.

The driver of the Range Rover started its engine and pulled out. At the T-junction he too turned towards the warehouse and followed the truck. There was no traffic at all and no pedestrians about. The street was deserted.

Lean remained silent and calm. As the truck came past the Audi, he looked up and across in front of his own driver at the cabin of the truck. So far as he could tell in the instant that it passed, there was only one occupant, the truck driver, a man with shaggy blond hair.

The Range Rover had accelerated and now sped past the car containing Lean and the others. The driver of Lean's car turned on the ignition and was pulling the Audi out into the wake of the Range Rover.

Ahead of them the truck had reached the warehouse's red metal gates. One of the two security guards manning the gate stepped out of the small brick outpost, waved acknowledgement to the truck and jotted down the vehicle's registration number on a hand-held board. The gates slipped rapidly open with a creaking noise and the truck started inside to the yard.

The two SOCA vehicles reached the warehouse main gate within five seconds, stopping next to one another across the threshold of the entrance, preventing the gates from closing. Their car doors opened simultaneously. From the Range Rover, the two armed officers stood behind their respective doors with automatic rifles poised in their arms. From the Audi, the armed officer in the back of the vehicle did likewise.

Lean, with an agile leap, was out and bounded the short distance to the guards' hut. He brandished his SOCA ID at them. Addressing the nearest of the two men, who had assumed an expression of unfeigned alarm he shouted:

"We are police and armed. This is an authorised raid on this premises. No one is to leave until we have finished a search."

Whatever the security guards' training was, it was to no avail. They stood frozen on the spot, aghast. Lean wheeled around and waved vigorously to the driver of the Range Rover to proceed into the yard. The two armed officers closed the car doors and the vehicle rode quickly across the yard's open ground to park close to the high open doors that gave access into the interior of the warehouse. The officers ran on behind, still carrying their weapons. They gained the threshold to the warehouse, took up protective positions either side of the entrance and peered inside.

The Audi remained where it was, blocking any exit by another vehicle. The armed officer meantime had run across the yard to the parked dirty truck, its' occupant at that moment descending from the cabin. He found himself face to face with an armed man. Without even being asked he raised his hands as a sign of surrender.

Dullington too had left the vehicle, walking calmly over to join Lean. It was still Lean's show. Once the premises was secured to his satisfaction, the search could commence.
"Who's in charge here ?" Lean asked the taller of the two guards.

"The warehouse manager, Charlie"

"Where is he ?"

"Just arrived. Probably in the office."

"Which is where ?"

Tall guard pointed towards the warehouse interior. "In there, on the other side of the warehouse." He shrugged his shoulders, in despair.

"You two, join us please inside" Lean instructed the guards.

Tall guard and his colleague meekly did as they were bidden.

As Lean and Dullingham arrived inside the warehouse, one of the two armed officers emerged bringing with him two men, the same ones as Lean had seen a few minutes earlier walking past the Audi. Lean imposed his authority immediately:

"Which of you is Charlie, the manager ? I am Officer Lean and responsible for this raid. My team are going to secure this premises. My colleague here, is then going to conduct a search."

One of the men, thick set and with owl like round eyes peering from thick dark eyebrows, said:

"I'm Charlie. Charlie Morgan. Warehouse manager. Where's your ID please ?" His accent and name revealed him as a Welshman. Unlike the security guards, he showed no signs of being intimidated or willing to be browbeaten.

Lean, still holding his ID in his hand, showed it peremptorily to Morgan. He wanted urgently to assure the safety of the premises. Without waiting for Morgan's assent, he turned to the two armed officers who had entered the warehouse.

"Run a thorough check. Go to it."

Behind Morgan and his colleague, there were regularly spaced rows of robust metal shelves towering up to a height of perhaps four metres. They were for the most part laden with palletised packs of building materials of various kinds. Visibility for anyone standing at the warehouse's entrance was severely constrained.

The two officers, their weapons still in evidence, moved briskly forwards down the main access alley splitting the warehouse into two halves. At each new row of shelves they took time to observe carefully for any trace of personnel or movement.

"Officer, I don't know what you're looking for but we have nothing to hide here" Morgan stated, with confidence. "May I suggest that you come down to my office and we talk about this ?"

Lean was not to be distracted, but he did want to run the rule over the other end of the warehouse which housed the administration office. He looked at Dullingham.

"I'd get those dogs busy. The quicker you have the search done the better. I'll complete the security check."

Dullingham assented calmly without a word and turned away to instruct the dog handlers to get started. As an afterthought, he swung back towards Lean and the two warehousemen.

"Mr. Morgan, please show my men where you store the roof trusses."

A light of recognition switched on in Morgan's owl eyes, but to Dullingham he made no comment.

"Colin, do as the man says" he said to the man standing next to him.

Lean and Morgan parted in the direction of the administration office at the far side of the warehouse. The man called Colin teamed up with one of the dog handlers and they disappeared down one of the rows stacked with goods.

Dullingham glanced at his watch. It was 6.06 am. For the moment, he left the matter of the roof trusses to the dogs. They were best placed to discover the cocaine. He retraced his steps outside into the yard. Dawn had not arrived but the yard was now lit by a powerful floodlight positioned high up on a metal pylon in the yard's far corner. Either someone had switched it on, or it had been timed automatically to synchronise with the warehouse's opening hour.

Dullingham walked over to the large truck that had driven in before the raid had commenced. His officer was standing alert, automatic weapon in hand, guarding the truck's driver.

The man looked like he was about forty, and wore an old fur-lined bomber jacket, which fitted tightly over his muscular shoulders. He had long shaggy blond hair and strong blue eyes. His face betrayed fatigue . It was evident that the man earned his living from manual work; yet there was a sharp intelligence lurking in those blue eyes. Dullingham was sure he knew who this person was. He confirmed that to himself by reading the company name written on the truck's side panels, 'Farley Construction Services'.

Dullingham ignored the driver and questioned his officer: "Weapons ?"

"None, sir."

He then turned towards the driver.

"Mr. Simon Farley ? Good morning" Dullingham said congenially, endeavouring to assuage the man's fear, the more so to get him to talk openly.

Farley, who now had his hands in his jacket pockets for warmth, looked quizzically at his interlocutor. The man looked like a Detective. He was tall, thin and angular. He wore a black overcoat, black jeans and black leather gloves. If he carried any weapon it was not visible. His eyes protruded slightly and his long nose had a kink in it as if it had been broken at some point in the past. To Farley, his demeanour signalled supercilious arrogance. He didn't like him.

"Morning. How do you know my name ? What's this about ? Are you police or what ?"

"That's a lot of questions, Mr. Farley. I am Commander Dullingham from SOCA and this is an authorised raid in search of drugs."

Farley was confused and still very wary of the proximity of the armed officer. He asked:

"SOCA ? What's that ?"

"The Serious Organised Crime Agency. A special police force Mr Farley. Amongst other things tasked with combating illegal commerce in class 'A' drugs, like cocaine."

"And what's that got to do with me ? I'm here to collect some supplies. Roof trusses."

"Precisely, that is my understanding" Dullingham smiled openly at Farley, failing to hide his conceit.

"Listen, I don't take drugs and I don't sell drugs. If you think I've got cocaine stashed here, then you're mightily mistaken" Farley pleaded, with verve.

Dullingham wasn't naïve. He had no expectation of a Damascene conversion and spontaneous confession. Nevertheless, he was momentarily taken aback by Farley's forthrightness.

"If true, that's very wise of you Farley. Drugs ruin so many lives" Dullingham intoned. "However, our information is different. You might consider co-operating with us now by assisting the search or at least telling me what your role is in this. It would benefit you later, believe me."

Farley shifted his feet uncomfortably. It was cold, the east wind was unremitting, and his tiredness made him irritable. Had he found Dullingham reasonable, he might have tried to co-operate. But he distrusted the man already and sensed that the longer he was in his company the more likely it was that he would loath him. He decided to adopt a diffident stance.

"Listen, there's nothing for me to tell. I'm innocent. Go ahead with your search. Do whatever you have to do. Just do it quickly. I've got a business to run. I need to collect and go."

"Understood Farley. You are going to be in for a long hard morning. Follow me please."

Dullingham signalled for the armed officer to take a position behind Farley and he led them in the direction of the warehouse interior to join the dogs and dog handlers who had migrated far across the warehouse to the stock of roof trusses. Dullingham, with relish, walked with a bounce in his step.

Chapter Twenty Five

09.15 Thursday 19th March 2009. Reddy's Apartment, Ipswich Marina, Ipswich

Reddy was feeling pleased with himself. He had awoken early at six forty in time to catch the tail end of the television programme reviewing the main news articles in the morning's press. Among the articles highlighted, the programme's guest journalist had drawn attention to his article in the Messenger about the Ipswich and Blackwater Bank, as well as to an accompanying Editorial questioning the government's approach to the handling of the banking sector crisis.

Buoyed by this early success Reddy turned off the television. He showered and dressed. Then he went into his study and put on a CD of Pavarotti arias. Next proceeding into the kitchen, he ignored the pile of dirty plates in the sink. Instead, he put fresh Arabica coffee into the coffee machine and prepared toast covered with his favourite Tiptree marmalade. Waiting for the coffee to percolate, his eyes fell again on the sink full of unwashed dishes. The nagging thought returned about the lack of a dishwasher in his kitchen. High on self-satisfaction, he pushed it aside with the conviction that washing dishes manually was an edifying manual discipline; even if one observed mainly in the breach.

By the time he returned to the living room with his breakfast to enjoy a few minutes relaxation, Pavarotti was singing 'Nessun Dorma'. That had the effect of further uplifting his already lofty spirits. He lounged down into the modest comfort of his Scandinavian sofa. Noting the time from his wrist watch, he realised that he would have to leave within thirty minutes to drive to his ten thirty appointment with Russell Westlake.

As he enjoyed his coffee, he became captivated by the colourful scene of the Marina outside his windows. As ever, yachts were moored, sails furled. There were a multitude of small cotton wool clouds drifting westwards across the sky. Occasionally one would obscure the sun for a few moments and the bright colours of the Marina scene would collectively ebb several grades until the cloud passed by. The morning's mild winds evidently didn't impress the ever-present seagulls, most of whom remained grounded rather than trying to glide on the frail air currents.

Reddy's captivation with the outside view was distracted by a ringing sound behind him. Out in the entrance hall, the intercom bell for the apartment building main door was ringing. Not expecting any visitor, Reddy suspected it was the postman. Oftentimes in the morning he would ring any bell randomly in order to have the main door opened so he could deliver the mornings' mail to the mailboxes installed in the building's ground floor entrance. The bell kept ringing insistently. Frustrated at the unwanted disturbance, Reddy quit the sofa and padded out into the hall to activate the intercom.

He pressed the speak button: "Hello, who's there ?"

"It's me, Simon."

Farley's familiar voice sounded excitable.

"OK. Come on up. The door's open."

Reddy pressed the second button on the intercom which opened the ground floor front door, then unlocked his apartment's main door and left it ajar so Farley could enter directly. He went into the kitchen and poured a cup of coffee for his surprise visitor and then waited for him on the threshold of the kitchen, leaning against the door frame.

Within a couple of minutes he heard the door of the elevator down the corridor open and strident footsteps approach. A large-knuckled hand pushed the apartment door wide open and Simon Farley entered. He looked tired and stressed; his long blond hair was tousled and his demeanour was aggressive. Reddy rarely saw his friend in this kind of mood, yet knew him well enough to know that when he was like this then he was volatile. Rationality and calm good sense would be restored only after he had vented his anger.

"Damn them, the bastards !" Farley spat out. He gave Reddy an unseeing grimace and stormed straight past him in high dudgeon into the living room. Reddy was taken aback and worried what was the cause of his friend's squalid mood. He followed in his wake, carrying the proffered coffee cup that his friend had failed to see.

As Reddy entered the lounge, Farley turned around from in front of the floor to ceiling windows. His body was silhouetted against the sky outside and his arms were flailing about in his leather bomber jacket. It reminded Reddy of a younger Joe Cocker in concert. He was speaking at breakneck speed, however his words were being drowned by

Pavarotti, who was now singing 'Non ho colpa è mi condanna'. To prioritise Farley's tale of woe over Pavarotti's, Reddy put down the coffee cup on the nearest table, retreated into the study and turned off the music.

On his return to the lounge, Farley was still standing but now sipping the still hot coffee. His free hand no longer turned, but was safely pocketed in his trousers out of harm's way. Reddy chose to seize the moment's peace to find out what had happened to his friend:

"You look like someone gave you a bad start to the day. What's the matter ?"

"The bastards !" Farley repeated. He put down the coffee cup and became animated: "They're out to get me. I'm sure of it. It'll be a stitch up. They don't care I'm innocent." His blue eyes flared and Reddy surmised that he was scared.

"Hey, calm yourself. Who's 'out to get you', Simon ?"

"The bloody cops. Not even cops. Some heavy guys. Called themselves SOCA, whatever the hell that is. Toting automatic weapons ! Christ, is this the UK or some damn Police State or what ?"

"You've been held up by armed police ?" Reddy asked, incredulous and now genuinely alarmed.

"The hell knows who they were. Bottom line is they jumped me down at the docks this morning. Some kind of military operation at the warehouse. No sooner I arrive to load up some of my newly arrived roof trusses than they come down on me like the bloody SAS going after terrorists. Several guys all kitted up. First thing I knew after climbing out of my wagon was this dude in fatigues pointing a Kalashnikov or something at me. Shit, Craig, I thought they were going to shoot me !"

"Did they arrest you ?"

"They sure wanted to. Some cool looking guy with a giraffe face tried to spook me. Said they knew I was trafficking drugs. Cocaine. Ass holes ! Who did they think I am ? A drug smuggler ! Never taken drugs in my life. I told him. Bastard didn't listen did he ?"

"OK, Simon. But did they arrest you ?" Reddy repeated trying to stay calm. He wanted to decipher the facts. Only then would he be able to bring Farley down off his roller coaster emotional ride.

Farley was silent for a few moments. For the first time since his arrival, he looked at Reddy and actually saw him. He swept his hair back out of his face and then rubbed his bristly unshaven chin. With a slightly calmer voice he said:

"Well, they detained me while they did a search of the warehouse. Then they interrogated me. Finally let me go about eight twenty. I think they cautioned me or something. Took my name and address, phone number. Said they'd want to talk to me again."

"But they didn't find drugs and they didn't arrest you ? Is that right ? You weren't taken down to the police station and formally charged with any offence ?"

"That's more or less it. But, hell's teeth, they treated me like I was a god damned criminal. They were convinced they knew they'd find drugs there."

"But they didn't and you're innocent, right ?"

"That's the worrying part, Craig. They had sniffer dogs there and eventually the dogs found traces of something. The cops said they were taking it away for analysis. Said it was probably cocaine."

"So that's why they've cautioned you, but not arrested you. Was it really just traces that they found ?"

"What do I know ?" Farley said petulantly. "Perhaps it was a plant ? These drugs cops do that kind of thing don't they ? So long as they get a conviction, they don't care. I'm in the brown stuff here Craig. I'm innocent but these scum are intent on stitching me up. As soon as they get the analysis done they'll arrest me and claim that I've been drug smuggling. But it ain't me ! Its that bugger Westlake. I swear it !"

An electric shock passed through Reddy's brain on hearing this. Had Farley lost the plot totally here ? What was it that he knew ?

"You mean Russell Westlake ? The RCH boss ?" Reddy quizzed.

"Yup. He's the one." Farley fired back, adamant.

"Are you crazy ? Why would a guy like that get involved in cocaine smuggling ? He's got bigger fish to fry running a big company."

"His psychology is not my problem. I don't have to explain his motives" Farley fumed defiantly. "The fact is the traces of substance they found were around the storage spaces previously reserved for his consignments, not mine. That's what I told giraffe face, but he didn't listen."

"Simon, you need to cool down here. Making allegations like that against Westlake can land you in big trouble. Whatever you might think, I advise you to keep it to yourself. Wait until these police come up with the lab test results. In the mean time, we need to get you a good lawyer. That way you are represented and the police will have to behave themselves. By the way, did they knock you about at all ? Any bruises or evidence they over-reacted ?"

Farley's hyperactive emotions made for slow absorption of rational advice:

 "Westlake suddenly quit ordering roof trusses. Maybe he had knowledge of a police operation and was happy to le me be the fall guy. Any case, he's the type of guy that would take cocaine socially I reckon. Bit of a high flyer. Womaniser. Lives on the wild side with his fast bike and cars."

This was news to Reddy. He knew nothing of the private life of Russell Westlake. He wondered how accurate his friend's picture of the man was. It reminded him that he was running out of time to get out of the apartment precisely to drive over to the RCH offices to interview Westlake.

"Simon, this is a bizarre coincidence but as part of the investigation I'm working on at the moment, I've got an interest in RCH. They're a major borrower from the Ipswich and Blackwater Bank which is what my investigation has been targeting. I've an interview scheduled for ten thirty this morning with Russell Westlake to discuss his firm's relationship with the bank."

Farley paused and went silent. He took some moments to absorb what Reddy had revealed. His face darkened. Perplexed and uncertain he replied:

"Is that why you're trying to protect him ? I thought I could trust you with this ?   Now it appears you're teamed up with the enemy !"

"Cool down, Simon ! Nothing could be farther from the truth. My meeting with Westlake is purely on a professional basis. I've never met the man. What I can do though, if you want, is use the meeting as an opportunity to put a few pointed questions to him about his importing activities and also see his reaction to hearing that the police raided that warehouse this morning."

"I dunno. Maybe I should go there myself and wring his neck."

"That would certainly get you arrested Simon. You're not thinking straight. I suggest that you get yourself back to work and calm down. Then take a look at things with a lawyer. Have you got one ?"

"The only guy I know is the man you introduced me to in order to set up my company. Burleigh, right ? Has an office on Northgate Street, near the Library ?"

"Edmund Burleigh. He's a rock. Utterly reliable. But he doesn't do criminal law. Let me help you. I'm seeing Burleigh myself this afternoon, I can ask him to recommend a criminal lawyer in town to assist you."

His mind still not functioning lucidly, Farley reluctantly agreed. Their conversation drifted as Reddy started to prepare his departure, putting on his lace up shoes and disappearing into his study to collect papers and his briefcase. Farley was finishing his coffee when his mobile phone rang. He snatched it from the pocket of his bomber jacket. It was Elvin.

"Hi Elvin, how you doing ?" Farley enquired, mechanically.

"Good morning. Busy loading the kilns Simon. With the company closure not far off, we're committed to meeting all the existing orders before then. So I'll be working this week end to get over the back log. But I wanted to talk to you. To be honest with you, I need to apologise."

"Apologise ? What for ?"

"I should've phoned you yesterday, see. After I'd had a chat with Mark Hancock over lunch at the White Lion. He asked me to tell you about something what happened here."

Farley was bemused. The events of the morning hadn't left him with much spare mental energy to keep switching to unexpected subjects. After his last unproductive encounter with Hancock he doubted that anything positive was likely to have transpired from a pub conversation between him and Elvin. Glumly, he continued:

"Go on Elvin, I'm listening, chum."

"Well what it is, is that some plain clothes police officers paid Hancock a visit at his place out at Catterwale. They were asking him questions about his business relationship with you. Hancock had nothing to hide. He told them the basics of the trade you two were doing. Said everything was above board. Offered to show them the books and stuff because he thought they might be from HM Revenue. But they weren't interested. Said they were SOCA officers. Stands for Serious Organised Crime Agency ?"

A low whistle escaped involuntarily from Farley lips. The red mist descended on him again. This latest twist to his tortured morning reconfirmed his fiery contempt for his oppressors and conviction that they were conspiring to frame him. In a flash, he made up his mind that he had to talk directly to Hancock. He wanted to get to the bottom of what these SOCA guys were up to. He wanted to know whether it had been giraffe face himself. This was personal and Farley had the heart of a fighter.

Reddy reappeared in the living room, having put on his Burberrys' raincoat and collected his suitcase and keys.

"I'm going to have to get a move on to make this meeting Simon. What's with Elvin ?" he asked, curiosity getting the better of him.

Farley ignored his question, replying instead to Elvin who was still on the line:

"I'm coming over there Elvin. I need to talk to Hancock. I'll drop by in about an hour. I'll explain things to you later. Just to let you know though, these SOCA characters have already been visiting. I made their acquaintance early this morning. Tell Hancock please I'm on my way. Bye."

Having heard Farley's words, Reddy inquired tentatively: "Not going down to work at Stratford today ? Shouldn't you give Barry Moore a buzz ? Explain what's happened."

Acknowledging the good sense in Reddy's question, Farley's facial expression nevertheless was one of exasperation, as if the world's woes were falling down on his head.

"You're right."

He immediately tapped some buttons on his phone's touchpad, placing a call through to Moore. As he did so, Reddy used sign language to indicate to him that they should leave the apartment and head for the exit, as time was running out.

A few minutes later they were both standing outside in the apartment block's reserved car parking area. Most of the residents' vehicles were already departed. Farley's old truck looked slightly incongruous in this environment, parked in splendid isolation at the far end where the area's boundary was marked by a line of recently-planted short saplings. The two men were standing facing one another next to Reddy's black Mondeo. The air was still cool. No one else was in sight. Reddy had unlocked his car and already placed his briefcase on the back seat. He now agitatedly fingered his key ring, keen to be underway. Farley was no less agitated, regurgitating the latest news from Moore:

"......isn't working well either. He said we're now behind schedule with the cladding. Bourov still isn't back at work. Barry wasn't too impressed with my absence. I told him I'd try to get down there this afternoon though. At least he understands the shit I'm in. I told him about the warehouse raid."

"So Simon, do you want me to raise this subject with Westlake or not ? It's entirely up to you."

"Can't do any harm can it ? Put some pressure on the man. I should really call him myself but I've got no time now. I used to trust him, but I don't any more. But first I want to hear what Hancock has to say about these SOCA guys' visit. Then I think you're right, I need to talk to a lawyer. You think Burleigh can help ?"

Reddy gave him a reassuring smile and gently took hold of his arm in a gesture of solidarity.

"Leave it with me. I'll talk both to Westlake and to Edmund. I suggest we talk again this evening, OK ?"

Farley concurred with a nod of his head, his mind a flood of half-formed thoughts and energy sapping anxieties. He turned to go towards his truck, head down. But Reddy tightened his grip on his arm forcing him to halt and look up.

"Simon, we'll get this sorted out believe me. You've got friends to help. You're not alone on this."

Farley stroked his chin pensively with one hand. Slowly he turned his face back towards Reddy. A mischievous grin emerged and his blue eyes sparkled.

"Craig, I never accept defeat. Thanks for your support. Don't forget, there's Town's home game against Watford on Saturday to look forward to."

"It's a date" Reddy confirmed, heartened to see evidence of enthusiasm returning to Farley's behaviour. If he could still find reason to talk about Town then he hadn't let events overwhelm him.

Farley took Reddy's hand and shook it firmly. Then he turned and headed determinedly to his eponymous truck.

Reddy climbed into his Mondeo. He hoped that the drive down the A12 to Holton St Mary would be enough time for him to get his thoughts reoriented for his appointment with Russell Westlake. He felt guilty for not having given Farley more time. He hadn't even broached the subject of Farley's debts with the Ipswich and Blackwater Bank. He hadn't even......He abruptly re-opened his driver's side door and shouted at Farley's back:

"Simon !"

Farley, in the process of unlocking his own vehicle, half turned with a surprised look but said nothing.

"Simon, I forgot to say something important. Its about the Ipswich and Blackwater Bank."

Farley now turned fully to face the Mondeo from which Reddy was now hanging out of.

"What about it Craig ?"

"Listen, please take this as serious advice. The money you've saved with them ? I'd take it out. Today."

"What the hell for ?" Farley challenged, nonplussed.

"Because they could well be insolvent. I'm telling you this both as a friend and a professional. I think they're in trouble. And I don't want your situation to get any worse than it already seems to be."

"I'll think about it Craig. Let's talk again tonight."

Without waiting for any further response, Farley opened the door to his truck, hauled himself into the driver's seat and started the motor.

Seeing that his friend had no intention of pursuing the matter for the moment, Reddy closed his own car door, and quickly had the Mondeo moving out of the car parking ahead of the truck.

As he drove away, he wondered ominously whether his friend would be able to pull through the mire into which he had fallen.

10.10 Thursday 19th March 2009. Redwood Country Homes HQ, Holton St. Mary nr Ipswich

Sally, Russell Westlake's personal assistant, heard the roar of a motor bike arriving outside. It boomed defiance one last time and then the engine cut out. It was extremely rarely that her boss arrived at work on his Kawasaki 500cc. When he did, it meant that he was "on steroids" as she defined it to herself. It meant too that she would be walking on eggshells this morning, dealing with his behavioural foibles and potential follies. She had learnt that her best survival strategy in these circumstances was to try and understand what it was that was eating him; provide caring feminine support, and then stay well out of his way unless called upon to do something. Seated at her desk, she adopted a pose of calm industriousness.

Her office door opened and Westlake entered. He held a silver coloured crash helmet, into which he had stuffed large leather gloves, and still wore black waterproof leggings and jacket. The thrill of speeding down the highway had left a broad smile etched on his face, revealing a perfect array of white teeth.

"Good morning Sally" he said, lustily "Nothing better than a zippy bike ride to blow away the cobwebs ! Great sense of freedom. You should try it, you know. Happy to take you pillion if you like ?"

"Mr Westlake, good morning. Thanks for the invitation, but you know I'm content with my little Peugeot. It's comfortable, warm and dry. May I remind you that you have a visitor at ten thirty ? Mr. Reddy, a journalist from the Daily Courier ? "

"Why on earth did I agree to see him Sally ? What does he want, do you know ?" he asked testily.

Sally registered the quick-fire change in Westlake's temper, an early warning sign that the volcano was molten below the surface. She said:

"He's a financial journalist. Writes things about the City ? He told me he's running an investigation into the banks' lending practices. He's interested in Redwoods' experience of dealing with them. We agreed he could have thirty minutes, if you remember ?"

Westlake cast his eyes up to the heavens. Was he resigned to half an hour's pointless tedium, or might this be a chance to cement a useful relationship with someone in the national media ? Perhaps with an address book full of City contacts ? His rational mind advised him to stay alert. Opportunity was everywhere.

"Fine Sally. Buzz me when he arrives. Is that financial report still on my desk ?"

"Yes, but I placed it face down. Just a precaution" she said.

It suddenly dawned on her why her boss was in turbo-charged mood. Yesterday afternoon's meeting in his office with Terry Murray, the finance director, had been a particularly fiery affair. Murray had been ordered out, leaving wordlessly via Sally's office to nurse his wounds. She hadn't been able to hear the exchanges between them but this morning had taken a quick, furtive look at the report while Westlake's office was unoccupied. She didn't really understand it, but her take away was that there undoubtedly was bad news wrapped up in it.

Westlake said: "Sally, Terry Murray is *persona non grata*. For his own good, please don't let him near me today. Understood?"

She offered him a sublimely demure smile: "Absolutely !"

Momentarily disarmed by her feminine charm, Westlake departed silently into his neighbouring office. He stripped out of his biking clothes and hung them on a tall wooden coat hanger in the far corner of the room. Turning around to face the view through the outer windows, he also saw the report laying face down on his desk. It had been produced by Murray under his instructions and presented an analysis of RCH's debts, their payments schedules and the company's cash flow. In conclusion it summarised the steps that could be taken to address the mismatch between repayments obligations and current ability to pay. Westlake had read the document yesterday afternoon on his return from the failed meeting with Bourov at Alton Water.

In his mind's eye, he now recalled an episode from yesterday's meeting with Murray, seated submissively in front of his desk. Westlake had exploited the light coming through the huge French windows behind the desk by standing in front of them to create an imposing and massive silhouetted figure, breathing verbal fire.

"Tell me" he had insisted, menacingly "what do I pay you for ? Why is it me that has to raise a red flag ? If the numbers aren't adding up, it's your responsibility to bring that to my attention. Isn't it ?"

He had raised his voice a few decibels and his eyes flashed. Murray re-crossed his legs nervously, aware that he was damned if he replied and damned if he didn't. With the last ounces of his courage he summoned his defence:

"The regular monthly financial reports have been highlighting the deteriorating position for the last two or three months. It would have been red flagged by my department at the end of this month. It's not as if you didn't know these problems existed."

Impatient with Murray's apologetics and annoyed at his implied criticism, Westlake had 'You're fired !' on the tip of his tongue but held it back.

"Terry, I don't want interminable reports. I want actions. The trouble is I can't rely on you for that. I'll sort this shit out for myself. Meeting over. Now get out !"

Murray had stood up, avoiding eye contact with his boss, and retreated to Sally's office, his dignity in tatters.

That was yesterday. Now, there were only a few minutes available before his meeting with the journalist. Westlake used this lack of time to force himself to act. Yesterday evening had been the time to reflect on his options. But that contemplative approach had only succeeded in bringing him out in a cold sweat. He had even recalled his father's admonition about not becoming enslaved to creditors. Now, in contrast, he revelled in the highly charged excitement of *carpe diem* decision-making.

He reminisced a conversation he'd had a few years ago with his father, Sir Peter, when Redwoods was a start up. He'd given his son a wealth of useful business advice, including warning him of the dangers of over-leveraging the company with debt. "Your creditors are your friends when you're paying them on schedule. But they'll take your assets over when you don't." Westlake had long since put his father on "ignore", confident to do things his own way. Nevertheless, ruminating on Redwood's current financial predicament, he grudgingly acknowledged the prescience of his father's comment. The Ipswich & Blackwater had been his strongest card for inflating RCH's returns to equity; yet the uncertainty swirling around the relationship in the wake of Cartwright's untimely suicide could bring RCH down unless Westlake acted fast and effectively to stabilise things.

The bottom line was he needed to find a solution quickly to the hole in RCH's finances. It had total borrowings of £1,18 billion, of which two thirds were with the Ipswich and Blackwater. There were capital repayments of up to £260 million due in the next nine months. Cash flow from house sales was sufficient to fund annual interest payments of about £ 58 million, but not repayments of principal. Raising new money on the markets, either through a share issue or bonds would be too expensive. RCH's share price had dipped again on negative news of the refused planning permission for the Loxwood residential development. And there was no way Westlake would part with the firm's crown jewels, which was its huge land bank. That was its' only real assets and currently they would sell at heavily discounted prices because of the weakness in the housing market.

"Angelov or Donoghue, that is the question ?" he said to himself, with dramatic amusement. "Whether 'tis better to play with the one's money or the other's brains ?"

The question was purely rhetorical, because his mind was already made up. He picked up the phone:

"Sally, can you please get me Mary Donoghue on the line ?"

While he waited, he replayed the decision in his mind. Angelov was safe and useful while on his own patch. The two of them could continue to exploit opportunities on the Black Sea. But the Bourov experience underlined starkly that there was no way he could trust him or Angelov in the UK. That was an experiment gone awry ! What passed for legal in a Slavic milieu would not pass muster here. Even if Angelov had more money than sense, it was sense that Westlake required. Hence Donoghue. Westlake had had an immensely fruitful relationship with Cartwright which had enabled him to fund RCH's rapid expansion. With Cartwright dead, Donoghue was the natural successor. It was in Westlake's interest to get closer to her. As he had with Elaine Cartwright. His phone rang.

"I'm passing you to Mary Donoghue" Sally said.

"Mr. Westlake, top of the morning. How are you ?" came the lilting voice of Donoghue.

"Mary, I'm fine. And by the way, 'Russell' will do, OK ? I'd prefer we were both on first name terms ?"

"To be sure. I'm happy with that. Tell me, what is it that I can do to help ?"

"I was wondering" Westlake half-jested "whether I could already congratulate you on your promotion to CEO ? You are Thomas' natural successor after all. They've made you Acting CEO. Surely they'll consummate the deal ?"

"Ah ! That's premature at best Russell. The decision's dependent on the CEGB board back in Dublin. Poor Thomas ! You're aware it's his funeral tomorrow ?"

"I am and I'll be there to give support to Elaine."

"I'm pleased to hear it. You and Thomas were good friends. It wasn't just a business relationship was it ?"

"True enough. Thomas was a solid guy. He's a great loss. I hope that at the Bank you're coping ?"

"There are some challenges, let's say" Donoghue parried. "But tell me, is there any particular reason for the call ?"

"Yes Mary. I need to meet up with you please. I know you're in charge of things now and we've worked with you in the past. You know well the terms of our loan agreements, right ?"

"Pretty much so. I'd need to refresh myself on details if there's something specific. Is there ?" she inquired, rather too innocently.

"Well, rather than do this impromptu on the phone, can we fix an early date for a meeting ? Say next Monday ? I can come up to your HQ if that suits ?"

"Wait a second"

There was a brief silence on the line. Westlake visualised Donoghue turning the pages of a desk calendar.

"Monday afternoon. Two o'clock ? Does that work for you ?"

Westlake didn't care what else he might have committed to for that time, this was his number one priority:

"Done. I'll be there."

"Russell, what do I need to prepare ? What's the main topic for discussion ? The RCH loan portfolio ?"

"That" Westlake affirmed, "and us, Mary."

They ended the conversation there.

Westlake sat down in his brown leather swivel chair, leant the chair back and put both his feet up on the corner of his desk. The thought crossed his mind that while at the Ipswich and Blackwater next Monday, it would be a good moment to access his safe deposit box and extract the diamonds. Thinking of the diamonds at the bank made him also think of the diamonds lifted from Cartwright's house. On impulse, he picked up the phone and dialled Elaine Cartwright on her mobile keeping active the caller ID, to encourage her to answer. It rang several times before she answered.

"Hello, Russell."

"Elaine, how are you ? Still at your mother's place or did you return to the house already ?"

"I'm still with mum" she answered, her voice frail. "Can I go back ? I need to go. Thomas' funeral is Friday. You are coming, aren't you ?"

"Of course. I'll be there. I've got it noted for 10.00am at the non Conformist church in the cemetery."

"Russell ? Can I ask a favour ?"

"Will you come by the house beforehand to collect me and take me there ? I need some support."

"What about your parents, or your brother ? They'll be there surely ?"

"The folks are coming, Daryll's overseas and can't get back in time. Can you do this please ?"

Westlake was reluctant but in view of the situation hard placed to find a reason to refuse.

"OK, I'll drop by and collect you. Say, nine thirty?"

"Not later, thanks Russell."

"Now, get yourself back home. The job's been done last night. Everything should be as you left it."

She confirmed that she'd return but probably in the morning, and then he rung off.

Westlake had told her in broad terms what happened at her house while absent. She didn't know the precise contents of the safe but was aware it had something to do with the business between her husband and Westlake. She was aware too of Westlake's penchant for risk. It had an attraction for her, which Westlake had understood and exploited.

His phone rang. It was Sally.

"Mr Reddy has arrived. Shall I show him in ?"

After the briefest of knocks at the door, Sally entered bringing with her Craig Reddy. After making the formal introductions she beat a hasty retreat. The two men shook hands firmly. Reddy accepted Westlake's offer to take off his coat and be seated in one of the comfortably upholstered chairs placed in the middle of the office around a low rectangular table. Westlake hung up his guest's Burberry next to his own biking gear on the clothes' stand. Reddy noticed the clothing. On arrival in his Mondeo, he had parked outside near to a striking silver coloured Kawasaki 500cc. Putting two and two together, Reddy understood that Westlake was the owner. He recalled Simon Farley's angry words about Westlake's reckless character. Perhaps, he pondered, there was a grain of truth in that ?

Westlake was a believer in first impressions. His first impression of Reddy was ambiguity. The man dressed reasonably well, if a tad conservatively. He wore slate grey slacks and black belt, blue and white striped cotton shirt open at the collar, and a navy blue woollen jacket. The Burberry's coat Westlake had just hung up was a matching dark blue. What was ambiguous was the journalist's behaviour. His style appeared a little stiff. Was that just introversion or was the guy plain nervous ? It seemed most unlikely that a journalist from a national daily could be any kind of a shrinking violet. Journalists were a bunch of pimps, Westlake thought. Most of them had no morals. They pawned their integrity to the unrelenting quest for sensationalist column inches to sell their news rags. And, in Westlake's opinion, that included the ones like Reddy here, working for the broadsheets. Keeping his distaste disguised and his bafflement concealed, he started the meeting:

"So tell me Mr Reddy, what is the purpose of your visit ? I'm afraid I only have 30 minutes for you and my PA was short on details as to what we should be accomplishing here ?"

"Maybe I can summarise for you my interest in you and your company Mr Westlake ?" Reddy offered politely.

Westlake took a chair opposite Reddy and by way of acceding to Reddy's offer, made a brief accommodative wave of his hand towards the journalist.

"As you know, I work at the Daily Courier as a specialist for the business and finance section of the paper. In addition, I also undertake occasional investigative dossiers; stories that require longer term, and more in depth, analysis. I've been working on one for the past few weeks. Through my work on the paper I became involved in writing about the recent events in the UK banking industry ? I'm sure I don't need to remind you of the government bailouts of Lloyds' and Royal Bank of Scotland ? Well, most of the public have probably concluded that the crisis is now over. I'm not convinced. So much so that I've been on the look out for possible further failures. Largely by happenstance I've been investigating the Ipswich and Blackwater Bank. You see, although I work up in London I'm originally from around here. Looking for a local angle to analyse the banking crisis I began researching them. Well, to cut a long story short, it's culminated in my publishing a critical article about them in today's paper."

Reddy paused to gauge what impact his words had had. Westlake sat motionless and impassive, like a wild leopard confident of its' impending prey. With heavy irony he said:

"So you have brought me an article to read about the Ipswich and Blackwater Mr Reddy ? I don't read the Courier myself so I haven't seen it. Nevertheless you could have saved yourself the trouble. The Ipswich and Blackwater is a solid bank. My company has been a client of theirs for several years. We get along just fine."

Reddy grew uncomfortable. The meeting had gotten off on the wrong foot it seemed. Moreover, he himself still hadn't seen the article published in the Messenger. There had been no time for him to stop by at a newsagents on the way out from his apartment to RCH's offices to buy a copy. And how to correct and explain to Westlake that his article was not published in the Courier ? Reddy chose to avoid backstopping the misunderstandings and ploughed straight on:

"Mr Westlake, it's your relationship with the Bank as a borrower that's of interest. As I said, the local angle of this investigation is important. Redwoods has a strong presence in the Suffolk and Essex borders. I've done my homework on you. Even if you've cut back on house building due to current weak conditions, you're an important employer and supplier of new homes in the region. Yet your last accounts for 2008 show borrowings of over £1 billion and, unless I'm badly mistaken, the Ipswich and Blackwater is far and away your biggest creditor. Isn't that so ?"

Westlake was not amenable to the direction that Reddy was taking the conversation. The details of his finance director's report still nagged the back of his mind. He said:

"What's out in the public domain I wish neither to dispute nor deny. Our borrowing from the Ipswich and Blackwater is unexceptional. Well within prudential limits and not something our shareholders are criticising us for. Frankly, what you as a representative of the press may think is irrelevant compared to the interests of the shareholders."

Westlake's reply had advanced the conversation quicker than Reddy could have expected to a place he wanted to be: the Redwoods' shareholders.

"I'm well aware that the business community often hold members of my profession in low esteem Mr. Westlake. That's an occupational hazard. But since you mention your shareholders perhaps you could clarify for me who actually controls the company and what its' strategy is ? The reason I ask is because from your company's last report and accounts it appears there is no clear controlling stake. There's Dominion Properties' 5% holding, the Witley Trust with 10 % and then a mysterious nominee company based in Panama with 12 %. That doesn't look like a recipe for stable ownership ? As CEO, aren't you concerned by that ? Maybe you're vulnerable to a takeover , especially given the softness in your share price ?"

An amused smile wreathed Westlake's face. He steepled his fingers in front of him and cast a dismissive glance at this lion cub reporter who had apparently no idea of business practice, only a researcher's enslavement to the written word.

"Mr Reddy, as you are a financial journalist you know very well that I can't possibly comment or speculate on events that might move markets. However, let me tell you something. Redwoods is a highly successful developer. Our growth in the sector has been second to none over recent years. Our corporate culture is meritocratic and entrepreneurial. We value innovation, welcome competition, and respect our partnerships. Now, as regards ownership of this company. Redwoods' origins were a family affair. My father Sir Peter, was instrumental in helping me get the firm started. The legacy of that is still there today. Dominion Properties, as you may know, is run by my father and its' shareholding in Redwoods is friendly. The Witley Trust, also set up by my father, is equally so. The beneficiaries are my sister and I. Together those shareholdings are a sound bedrock for stability of ownership. Other institutional investors have backed us at our last AGM. I see no cause for concern."

"And the Panama-based company ? That is a friendly shareholder too or might it have predatory motives ? Do you have any idea who is the money behind it ?"

.

"I cannot say, and I do not speculate. I have a business to run in a difficult operating environment. That is sufficient to keep me fully occupied. If anyone attempts to take over this firm they would have to declare themselves. I'm sure you're aware of the Stock Exchange's rules for takeover ?"

"Does that 'difficult operating environment' for your business include difficulties in the relationship with the Ipswich and Blackwater ? Isn't Redwoods at risk to their aggressive commercial practices ?" Reddy ventured.

"What practices would they be ?" Westlake countered.

"Isn't it the case that Redwoods have been forced increasingly to concede more and more of their potential profits to the bank as a condition for continued lending on your development land acquisitions ?"

"I don't know where you come by that idea Mr Reddy. Anyway, in a low interest rate environment, banks' instincts are to look for new profits sources. That's called risk taking. Interest payments on loans to businesses aren't attractive enough for their shareholders. The Ipswich and Blackwater is no exception. The deals that Redwoods has engaged with them are innovative to a degree but fundamentally in the interests of both parties. It's a win-win in the longer term as our pipeline of development projects come on stream."

"I appreciate that. However, in this bearish market environment, can Redwoods survive the 'longer term' ? Indeed, if I'm right in my assessment of the Ipswich and Blackwater, can they survive either ?"

"Mr Reddy, I can only think that you must be an economist with all this doom and gloom analysis. It won't take you anywhere, believe me. I'm a realist and a pragmatist. If I see a problem I deal with it. The eventuality that the Ipswich and Blackwater is about to go bust is remote in my opinion. But even if it did, Redwoods would survive I can assure you. We do not live in hand to mouth dependency on our creditors." Westlake asserted, inwardly proud of his skills in subterfuge.

"You can secure easily other credit lines ?" Reddy persisted, sceptically. "Even in the context of your recent disappointment with the rejected planning application for the huge Loxwood Estate development ? Wasn't that to be Redwoods' flagship development for the next couple of years ?"

"It's a setback for sure. But Redwoods will never make the mistake of overly relying on one path for its' commercial evolution. We are constantly monitoring our strategic options. We are adept at adopting new lines of profitable activity. Now, I'm sorry, but time is running short. I don't know if you have obtained what you wanted from this interview Mr Reddy but I really need to bring this meeting to a close."

"I understand. May I raise one final matter ? You mention new lines of activity. One of those has been Redwoods' decision to go overseas to source its' demand for roof trusses. Isn't that so ?"

Westlake had already half risen from his chair in the expectation that he could quickly terminate the meeting. Yet this last question was an unexpected curved ball. He remained seated, but now on the edge of his chair. He clasped his hands across his knees. Looking at Reddy with studied irritation he said:

"It was so yes. But we've recently cancelled further orders. The downturn in the housing market has had a knock on effect to the volume of our output. Result: we don't see the value in importing roof trusses for the foreseeable future."

"I see. And you were only importing roof trusses ? Nothing else ?"

"Just roof trusses" Westlake confirmed, perhaps with too much emphasis. "Look, what is this about ? I can't imagine that you have the slightest interest in such matters. Or is there some agenda here that I'm missing ?"

Reddy could feel the irritation in Westlake's voice notch up another level. Was this the real Westlake shedding his outer skin ?

"Mr. Westlake, you do know Mr. Simon Farley, don't you ? He was a partner with you in the importing venture ? I know you know him. You see, he is an old personal friend of mine since schooldays."

"I don't deny it, of course not. But if this is a personal matter I'm afraid this is not the time to discuss it. If Mr. Farley has a problem with his side of the business that is his affair, not mine. In any case, it is not something I will talk about with you. I think we can conclude this interview immediately" he said, indignation now mixing with the irritation.

Westlake stood up. He walked over to the clothes stand, unhooked Reddy's coat and went to the door. He opened it and held out the coat for Reddy to take. Reddy arose slowly, deliberately taking his time. The cocktail of aggravation he achieved was to his liking. He approached

Westlake with a serene confidence. The two men were of similar height so that when he was close enough to receive his coat, their eyes locked like two bulls' horns.

"Good day, Mr. Reddy"

"We live in interesting times Mr. Westlake. Mr Farley informs me that the Serious Organised Crime Agency conducted a raid in the early hours of this morning on the warehouse where you both stored those roof trusses. Their sniffer dogs took away traces of a substance for lab analysis. According to Mr. Farley those traces were found in the area where your roof trusses were kept. Good luck and good day."

Reddy took the proferred coat and without hesitating to see Westlake's reaction departed through the door. He smiled politely at Westlake's PA, on the way out and disappeared to the main exit.

Westlake, momentarily speechless, stood still in the open doorway like a salt pillar at Gommorah. Sally's voice failed to register initially:

"Mr. Westlake, while you were busy DS Adam of the Ipswich police phoned. He's requesting another meeting for Friday, tomorrow. He asked that we call back with a confirmation this morning."

"Sally, I've a commitment to attend Thomas Cartwright's funeral on Friday. Call and propose Monday as my alternative proposal. Explain why."

He turned briskly on his heel, and vanished from the doorway, slamming the door.

Sally took note that the volcano was erupting.

Chapter Twenty Six

10.55 Thursday 19th March 2009. Police Headquarters, Civic Drive, Ipswich.

The atmosphere in Chief Inspector Haddock's office was electric. Seated one side of the metal table were SOCA officers Dullingham and Lean, on the other Haddock and DI Wright. Dullingham and Lean had spent the last twenty minutes outlining the raid conducted early that morning on the warehouse at Ipswich Docks.

Haddock and Wright had listened with a growing sense of anger and frustration. Lean had opened, explaining the logistics and operational details. Dullingham had concluded, focusing on the intelligence that SOCA had collated to justify the action. A silence descended on the room as the SOCA officers awaited deferentially for feedback.

Haddock asked: "Commander Dullingham, you were responsible for the decision that the available intelligence justified this raid ?"

"That is correct sir."

"The net result of the raid is no drugs discovered and no arrests made. Isn't that so ?"

"Yes sir. However, we aren't convinced........"

Haddock firmly cut him off:

"Adding insult to injury, this raid was conducted on Ipswich Police's territory with no advance warning. Your boss called the Chief Constable only after the raid got underway ?"

"Sir, there were sound reasons for that. We considered that......"

Again Haddock blocked any justifications:

"You failed to communicate and cooperate effectively with the local force."

"Your CC was understanding of our position sir. He......"

"The Chief Constable was presented with a 'fait accompli'. What else could he do ? He has to assure political cooperation with SOCA. At such short notice he had no effective power to demand that the raid be postponed. Isn't that so ?"

"I believe that would have been difficult sir, yes." Dullingham conceded, rubbing his nose.

Haddock leaned imposingly across the table towards Dullingham, and in a menacingly low voice continued:

"I am responsible for the Ipswich force's operations. We have investigations running here Commander which your raid could have interfered with. Potentially you put both us and yourselves at risk. Your people were armed and by your own admission you expected possible resistance. I do not accept SOCA's actions and will take this back to the Chief Constable. My position is this: there will be no repeats of this kind of action in our territory until or unless there is advance agreement. Is that clear ?"

"Utterly clear" Dullingham confirmed, diplomatically. "As I said at the start sir, our action was based on sound intelligence. We have reliable sources in Antwerp as well as local informants monitoring both the Felixstowe & Ipswich docks. SOCA's top priority as you know, is combatting illegal trade in Class A drugs. The raid this morning fits with that priority. "

The expression on Haddock's face was enough to brush aside Dullingham's feeble attempted advert. He undercut Dullingham with a terse riposte:

"What the politicians define as your goals is not my concern, Dullingham. Your intelligence sources clearly are not fit for purpose. Any further failures like this and I can see your career in SOCA will be short-lived. Consider yourself lucky that you don't work for me ! Now, before I dismiss this meeting, repeat the intelligence information you had as the basis for this flop."

Eyeing Dullingham's body language, DI Wright had the impression that he momentarily weighed up his chances of winning the argument with some invective. Instead, he opted for self-preservation by doing as he was told:

"Sir, we believe that cocaine was being imported regularly on a ship coming from Antwerp. It was hidden in hollowed out roof trusses.

The trusses were coming in by order of two companies: Farley Construction Services and Redwood Country Homes. Unfortunately, this morning's search with sniffer dogs has not discovered any product. Simon Farley, the owner of Farley Construction Services, was apprehended during the raid. He claimed his innocence. It is true that our dogs failed to identify any traces of the drug either on him or in his truck. However, in the warehouse where the roof trusses were usually stored, the dogs seem to have identified tiny traces of the drug but not in the roof trusses. We have sent the evidence to our labs for testing. Farley has not been cautioned not charged."

"So can I conclude that this is not only the end of the operation but the end of your enquiry Dullingham ?"

"No sir. We are keeping Farley under surveillance. It is our view that the SOCA operation may have been either compromised or too late. We aren't convinced that the absence of tradeable quantities of cocaine from today's raid is proof of innocence."

"That sounds to me like clutching at straws Dullingham. Face-saving spin. What facts have you got supporting that ?"

"Sir, one salient factor is that with the latest shipment of roof trusses, there was no participation from Redwoods. We suspect that means our intelligence was compromised. Redwoods has been a regular buyer of these trusses from the continent. It is suspicious that they stop now."

DI Wright spoke. "You're sure this is the first time they have not received a consignment ? Did this man Farley confirm that ?"

"We haven't interrogated Farley as regards his knowledge of the Redwoods' consignment."

"Why not ? Perhaps he has vital information ?" Wright persisted.

"Our view is to let Farley believe he – and Redwoods – are off the hook, Inspector. We will maintain our surveillance of Farley. He may lead us to Redwoods and then incriminate them both."

"Do you really assess that as a probable outcome ? Aren't there other feasible explanations for what's going on here ? I mean, there's an economic crisis on in the real world. Couldn't it be simply that Redwoods didn't need any more roof trusses this month ?"

"It's not impossible. However, we see it differently. Our intelligence has the CEO of Redwoods heavily involved in business on the continent with criminal commercial interests in Bulgaria. You may not be aware, but there are illegal drugs, immigration and money laundering activities prevalent in that country. There is also a known logistics trail to the UK through Antwerp. The port of Antwerp has been used as a conduit for some time. Our Europol colleagues are orchestrating an undercover operation there to find out how the smuggling at the port is concealed."

DI Wright enquired: "Tell me, does this Farley have a known criminal record ? Is he a local from this area ? It's not a name that resonates with me."

"No criminal history on file. Nevertheless, we know that his company has serious debt problems and that he's a close acquaintance of Mr Westlake, the Redwoods' CEO. We're persuaded that they're in partnership in this. Not having previous is not an argument, in my view, to assume innocence."

Haddock resumed control of the meeting:

"Gentlemen, I've heard enough. If SOCA is keeping this dossier open, then I shall insist to your bosses – through the Chief Constable - that there is an effective flow of information from you to DI Wright here. She is in charge of an investigation which has possible links to Westlake and I will not accept that her investigation is negatively impacted. This is the first and last time SOCA operate on my territory like cowboys. Is that understood Commander Dullingham ? Lean ?"

"Yes, sir. I will report back to our boss your requirement." Dullingham promised.

"Good; and while you're doing that, tell him I also expect to be copied on the full report that I am sure you will have to submit. I repeat, the full report, not a summary of sanitised highlights."

DI Wright left the meeting confused. It was unclear to her if the SOCA raid may have disrupted her own investigation into Cartwright's death and relationship to Westlake and RCH. Haddock's relentless demolition of Dullingham and the SOCA raid had plenty to do with his maintaining full control over the Ipswich force's jurisdiction. She admired his determination in that. He had at the same time unintentionally won her a little more time to conclude her enquiries, since she could claim that the investigation's complexity and scope had increased.

Desiring to get back to business, she called DS Adam on his mobile. He took her call, saying he was in the staff canteen having coffee. Wright took the stairs to the first floor to join him.

The staff canteen was devoid of people, other than DS Adam who occupied a table near to the drinks and snacks vending machines, off to the left side of the large room. As Wright approached the white formica-topped table at which he was seated, she perceived that Adam was immensely chuffed about something.

"Let me get you a coffee, Paulie. White no sugar, right ?"

Returning from the vending machine, he placed a white plastic cup before her.

"Compliments of the house. Instant, but at least it's hot."

Before Wright could muster an opening sentence about what had transpired with the SOCA officers in Haddock's office, Adam enthused:

"Listen, I've got fresh news. Interpol have come back to us this morning about that Panama-based nominee company. It turns out that the beneficial owner is called Angelov, a Bulgarian. You remember that was the name I saw on Russell Westlake's calendar when we visited ? Bingo !"

DI Wright registered Adam's news without demonstrable enthusiasm. Adam, still fired up with this success, failed to notice. He sallied on:

"Our Interpol contact called in a favour with the Panama City chief of police. It seems he knows the legal firm that handled the company's original registration. The legal firm provides the nominee director too. The way the Interpol guy told it, the director of the legal firm was 'incentivised' – that was the term he used - to yield up Angelov's name."

Adam's sequence of enthusiastic narrative dried up. In the silence, it dawned upon him that this latest news hadn't ignited the same enthusiasm from his boss.

Wright sighed and looked beyond him at the long rows of empty formica-topped tables. At the far end of the room in front of the kitchens, two canteen staff had begun delivering the containers of hot food to the long steel counter from which the daily meals were served. The canteen opened for lunch at mid-day, in about twenty minutes. There'd be queues of people arriving soon and their privacy would be destroyed. With an effort of will she returned her attention to DS Adam.

"Charlie, thanks for that. It may be important but we don't yet know. It's past the time where we can go on working with incidentals. Haddock's going to want tangible progress from this investigation by early next week. The way we're going we won't have it" she concluded despondently.

"Hey, what's been going on up in Haddock's office to eat you up ?" Adam asked, disquieted by her reaction. "I thought it was the SOCA guys who were being hauled over the coals, not you ?"

"That's right. Haddock read them the riot act. Denigrated their poor intelligence work and ridiculed the failure of the raid. He even threatened escalation to the Chief Constable. Said they would be in early retirement if ever SOCA undertook another operation here without first having his buy-in."

DS Adam grinned spontaneously. He was a signed up member of his bosses' fan club.
 "That's great. The boss sticks it to them when it counts. No retirement vibes from the man. What's not to be pleased about then ?"

"Charlie, I didn't say anything about it in the meeting because I don't want to mess up our chances of coming up with the goods here."

"But ?"

"But, this Dullingham, the one responsible for the intelligence behind the raid, he mentioned that their work with Europol on this has established links to criminal commercial activities in Bulgaria. They also...."

"Angelov ?"

"No names were offered, and I didn't ask because I want to avoid SOCA muscling in on our investigation. But, so far as we are concerned, potentially yes. Angelov."

DS Adams whistled through his teeth. He looked intently at Wright and was formulating a question when she continued:

"They also brought up the names of Russell Westlake and one Simon Farley. According to SOCA the two of them organised the import of cocaine in hollowed out roof trusses. Dullingham claimed that Westlake has backed out of the trade because he may have had advance knowledge of SOCA surveillance."

"Sounds far fetched to me."

"Agreed Charlie. Which is my main point. Let's go back to basics. Find motives amongst this morass of circumstantial events."

"Where do you want to start ?"

"Let's consider for instance that the drugs angle is a red herring. The SOCA raid was a failure. Was that just bad luck or symptomatic of their being off track ?"

"There are increasing quantities of cocaine out on our streets Paulie. Haddock was on our backs about it, remember ? Cartwright and McAuley both died with cocaine in their bloodstreams. Some one has to be importing and supplying it. Russell Westlake knew them both. We now know he knows Angelov. Who is Bulgarian. And – this is what I didn't yet tell you – the guy at Interpol who phoned me with the information about Angelov being the owner of the nominee company ? He volunteered too the fact that Angelov is on their files. He's a known player on the Bulgarian mafia scene. Result: marriage made in criminal heaven with Angelov tapping into the lucrative UK market leveraging a legitimate local businessman."

"Charlie, for me that doesn't stack up. Where's the motive for Westlake to risk his business success and lifestyle. Teaming up with a Bulgarian gangster ? You'd have to be crazy in his position to countenance such a move."

"That's a rational view, seen from the outside. But if you want to play the contrarian, then what about Westlake's personality ? He seems to have an appetite for risk. Could it be that he's simply tempted to take on risky propositions ?"

"Perhaps, but we'll need more than that type of speculation to convince Haddock."

"There's the diamonds, don't forget !"

"I won't Charlie. But let's first consider all that we've learnt from Harry Keogh"

Adam, proud of his role yesterday in getting Keogh to talk, launched into an impromptu   summary of the new information divulged by Keogh:

"We struck a rich seam with our Harry, didn't we ?" he began, with a broad grin. "The hot topic is his claim that Cartwright and Donoghue were having an affair. To be honest, I'm not surprised. When we first met her on Monday, my intuition said to me that might be the case. Remember the woman's vanity mirror which was found in Cartwright's Audi ? I think if we could get fingerprints lifted they'd be hers."

"If they were in an affair then she's lied to us. Which then raises another question: what else does she lie about or hide ?"

"You think she is in the know about what Cartwright may have been up to ?" Adam asked.

"Pillow talk ultimately involves the parties talking to one another about their secrets and ambitions, doesn't it ?" Wright said, disarmingly, giving Adam a piercing look.

"So there was potentially collusion and conspiracy ? Just with regards to Cartwright's private clients and the contents of their safe deposit boxes or something much bigger ?"

"That's what we have to discover Charlie. I don't want to be overly dramatic, but the fact that Cartwright is dead doesn't mean that his influence isn't still being felt. I suspect Donoghue is potentially a mine of information for what he was about."

"Maybe so" Adam replied indecisively, "However what I have difficulty with is, why Cartwright fell for her? She had been with him at headquarters for three years. Yet according to Keogh their relationship got started only a month or so before Christmas last year."

"Doesn't that suggest that one of the two was using the other and made a move to start the relationship for reasons not mainly to do with sex ?"

"We could have any number of hypotheses then, depending on who was the 'predator', the one who kicked off the relationship. If you look at it from Cartwright's point of view though, if he was simply leading a 'normal' life but bored or unhappy with married life, why take the risk of having an affair with someone at work ? Chances are it gets found out, and then information leaks back to the wife. Much better to find your lover away from work, if you want to 'play away' ?"

DI Wright grimaced ironically at her colleague: "For a single man Charlie you sound something of an expert on the strategies of infidelity. Anyway, Keogh told us that his assertion about their relationship could be backed up. He's got access to all the HQ security tapes and access times. The evidence is there when we need it, is what he said."

"I come back to my question. If Donoghue was the 'predator', not him, why wait over two years ? You know what ? I think we should bear in mind that Donoghue is one very smart cookie when it comes to finance, Paulie. The copy of her CV that Keogh has provided us ? She did advanced maths at university. At the CEBG in Dublin, before taking the CFO role at the Ipswich & Blackwater, she helped develop some of those clever financial derivatives products, whatever they are."

"If she was that good, why did Dublin let her go ? Why did she come over to sleepy Suffolk and join the Ipswich and Blackwater ?"

"Because the Ipswich was in a phase of rapid growth and Cartwright needed a trusted and capable finance specialist to manage the bank's expansion ? Something professional along those lines ?"

"Or, alternatively, Cartwright's extra curricular activities were weighing on him and Donoghue lent a hand to sort them out ? Don't forget the map of Sofia. Don't forget that Cartwright and Donoghue both had a business relationship with Russell Westlake. We have also Westlake implicated with Angelov, a Bulgarian businessman who according to Dullingham, is associated with mafia activity in his home country. Plus we have the phone numbers on Cartwright's phone which show that he was talking recently with a number in Bulgaria."

"The other piece of the jigsaw to factor-in is the private clients' safe deposit boxes and the diamonds. The list of client names that Keogh has furnished us with makes for interesting reading."

DI Wright asked: "You mean the fact that the diamonds were in a safe deposit box in the name of Westlake ? Yes, that is a surprise. There are some new questions that he's going to have to answer when we talk to him next."

"That's one thing, yes. But also important is that most of the occupied safes are in the names of people who seem to be of Irish background. You recall what Keogh told us ? He said he was often present when Cartwright's clients came to use the safe deposit boxes. Some were Irish folk; in his view, of dubious propriety. But he was told to mind his own business. Which is exactly what he did."

"Charlie, I want you please to have background checks run on the names of the people on that list. Find out if any have a criminal or possibly IRA history. In addition, let's request Mary Donoghue to pay us a visit here tomorrow for an interview. Tell her we would appreciate that it is here not at the bank."

"Will do. By the way, we still haven't spoken to Mrs Cartwright ? Our people don't get any reply on her home number and it seems no one has a mobile number for her."

"Disturbing. She doesn't work does she ?"

"Not so far as we know. I suggest we send a squad car around to the house ? Check up what's happened to her ?"

"Please, do it. While you're about it, we should get hold of Cartwright's passport once we contact his wife. He may have been living a different life on his trips abroad. If we want to see behind the enigma then we should study the trail of visits he has made."

Adam nodded. Wright glanced at her watch. It was nearly mid-day and one or two administration staff were already entering the canteen and forming a small huddle around the notice board to read the options on the daily menu.

"One final thing, Charlie" Wright said. "What about Reddy ?".

"Craig Reddy ? What about him ? He's a journalist. You suspect him being complicit in this ?"

"Maybe. Journalists are known to break the law too aren't they ?"

"True. Where do you see him involved ? I must be missing something" Adam confessed.

"Motive Charlie. What's his motive ?"

"As a journalist he's after copy. That's his bread and butter."

"Good. What sort of journalist is Craig Reddy ?"

"A big shot at a national daily ? Well known as a specialist on business and finance. How am I doing ?"

DI Wright could tell that Adam was beginning to flounder. She grinned and said:

"Maybe he's after more than just copy. I mean, why would a nationally known journalist who can find all the copy he wants by pitching up at corporate press events in London, invest scarce time and effort on an investigation into the Ipswich and Blackwater Bank ?"

"Because bank bashing has become a national pastime ?" Adam volunteered lazily.

"No. The Daily Courier doesn't do bank bashing; that's for the tabloids. No, what I think Mr. Reddy is after is a scoop. I think he's onto something big that's happening behind the scenes at the Ipswich and Blackwater."

"Other than the loss of their CEO, right ? And what would that be ?"

"How about financial crime, Charlie ? What if Cartwright and Donoghue were cooking the books for instance ?"

DS Adam puffed his cheeks expressively. He looked at his colleague with admiration. He himself hadn't given this idea any airtime. He said:

"That could be a smart call. We saw the queue of depositors outside the bank at the start of the week. I'd put that down though to customers' nervousness following the news of Cartwright's death. You're aiming though on another track. You think Cartwright may have been skimming ? In collusion with Donoghue ?"

"I don't know, it's speculation. And don't forget financial crime these days is more sophisticated than old fashioned fraud and embezzlement. Why even stop with financial crime ? How about incompetence and negligence ? Or flouting of bank policies on lending practices ? Who knows ? You and I are not finance wizards. But I'm convinced that Reddy has motive. I think that with us, he's been

277

economical with the truth and his investigation may have answers to some of our questions. Our mistake with Reddy was not to know the right questions to ask ! We need to get him back in here Charlie and grill him on what his investigation has uncovered. Can you call him and get him in here for tomorrow ?"

"Will do, no problem" Adam said enthusiastically.

DI Wright picked up her empty plastic cup, pushed back the moulded plastic chair and stood up.   Adam remained glued in his chair.

"OK, plenty of work to do. Are you coming ?" she asked

"Not yet. I thought I might grab a quick bite to eat. There's one of my favourite desserts on the menu."

DI Wright was a rare user of the canteen because of its reputation for stodgy food. She said: "Which is ?"

"Apple crumble and custard !"

Twenty Seven

09.45 Thursday 19th March 2009. First class carriage, 9.30am train to Colchester from Liverpool Street station

As the train passed through Stratford, Angelov had peered through the rain-spattered windows and caught sight of the London 2012 Olympics stadium site. The stadium was not yet under construction so far as he could tell, but there was already some preparatory activity. Seeing the site for the first time, he was enthused yet frustrated. He wanted some of that forthcoming commercial action, yet he still hadn't arranged a practical way to do so. Who said it was easy to do business with these English ? The door seemed shut in his face.

He had settled back in his comfortable first class seat, discomforted by his perceived exclusion. There was still another forty minutes to go before he would arrive at Colchester where he was to be picked up by Vladmir. Time enough to think more about his strategic plans and how people around him might fit into them. Or not, as the case may be.

The first class carriage was virtually empty, which was much to his liking. Before entering the train he had bought himself a coffee and three daily papers. The papers lay together stacked unopened on the table. The coffee cup was open, its contents already half consumed. The caffeine was beginning to have a positive influence, sharpening his thoughts.

Memories of yesterday evening's entertaining dinner with Mary Donoghue gradually flowed into his consciousness. He had chosen to indulge her by having dinner at Marco White's restaurant. They had spent over two hours there spoilt by delicious cuisine, fine wine and cosmopolitian *ambiance*. By the time she had taken a taxi to catch the 22.00 departing train for Ipswich from Liverpool Street station, Angelov's male intuition sensed that Donoghue was his for the taking. He had applied deftly his seductive skills and quiet masculine assurances to win her confidence, make her laugh and flatter her. Of course, she was far too intelligent to be taken in. Yet she fully understood and enjoyed the dance of dalliance and its' rituals. She was a player, he discovered; evidently relishing the role of *femme fatale*, momentarily betraying naked vulnerability only then to elide overt male advances. All of which had been erotically intoxicating for Angelov.

The more so, because of her extraordinary intelligence. Especially how she applied it to the world of finance. In his eyes, it made her more potent than many other women. They had talked about her position at the Bank, both pre- and post- Thomas Cartwright. She confirmed that it was her financial engineering knowledge that drove much of the Bank's growth in the last two or three years. She ran their proprietary trading desk and managed their borrowing in the wholesale markets. Angelov listened attentively, keen to learn and even keener to gain control.

Eventually, he had guided the conversation around to the Bank's financial dealings with Redwood Country Homes in hope that he might gain from her valuable insight that could help steer his own course of action. Whether or not it was the white wine that might have loosened her tongue he could not tell, but Donoghue displayed no reluctance to share her views on RCH's position. Indeed, the alacrity with which she set out her analysis had startled him:

"Look" she explained "there's a real possibility of obtaining control of RCH very cheaply. They've got total debts of over a billion pounds. Some £ 750 million of that they owe to us. Private sector housing building in this country is down big time because of the crisis. So their core business of house sales is down. Their share price is the cheapest it's been for ages. What they've got however is a great reserve of land to build on. That's their main asset. Trouble is though, they can't build it out aggressively until the economy gets back on its feet. Meantime, they've got their creditors to pay. The Ipswich and Blackwater is at the front of the queue. Thomas indulged Westlake in the past. The Bank certainly saw RCH as an attractive loanee with huge profits potential. That's all changed though. Not because of Thomas' death. Just business reality. The fall out of the financial crisis has been so bad – none of our scenarios predicted it – that we're going to have to come down hard on RCH and Westlake. Bottom line: we want our money back or we'll go after their assets."

Her delivery was silky smooth and he remembered her flaming red hair and matching red outfit, the combined effect of which left a powerful impression on him of an exceptional woman. One able to fight with ice-like coolness. One able to act with passionate ruthlessness.

In the cold light of day, Angelov now reflected more deeply on the matter. He had not been tempted to ask her outright whether she and the Bank would support him in an initiative to wrest control of RCH from Westlake. That would have been premature. Nevertheless, her evident willingness to signal to him that RCH was vulnerable and that she personally held no sentiment to preserve the status quo indicated to Angelov that the Bank deemed Westlake as not indispensable. Maybe – just maybe – it was personal too ? His intuition told him that, whereas Westlake and Cartwright had been firm partners, the same was not so between Westlake and Donoghue.

Angelov was convinced by Donoghue's analysis of RCH's vulnerability. He was less certain of her assertion to act now to take control. She had said that the Bank would force asset sales on RCH if they were unable to meet payment obligations. But then where would that leave Angelov if he took majority control ? In truth, he was unsure how to proceed. Partly because he did not yet have a UK registered company to act as purchaser, but also because he needed someone of Donoghue's ability with finance expertise and knowledge of the UK scene to assist him.

But could he trust her ? He had trusted Cartwright. Before he died, Cartwright had told him that Donoghue was only partly complicit in the central and eastern European activities run through CPI Gmbh in Austria. He had confirmed though that she was the 'financial architect' of the Ipswich and Blackwater Bank's successes in recent years. It was she too who was the link person bringing 'friends' for retirement into Bulgaria. Cartwright himself had had a free hand to run the central and east European operations. Was that because separation of knowledge between him and her was a means for mutual self protection or rather because Cartwright too had placed limits around the trust he held in her ?

Angelov finished his coffee, even though it was no longer hot. He looked out the window at the passing scenes. For the moment, it consisted mainly of enclosed agricultural land with hedgerows and occasional woodland copses. A verdant green was the predominant colour although the absence of sunlight muted its hue. Angelov was a creature of the urban world and didn't have time for things rural. Nevertheless, he couldn't help remark the difference between what he saw here and back in his home country. The fields were all immaculately tended, and obviously valuable. Every inch of the landscape was productively used. He was quietly impressed.

"So" he said to himself, and reverting to the matter at hand, "attention to detail is vital."

Where was he headed with this 'business strategy' that had been exercising him greatly these past weeks ? He was not making any material progress it seemed. Moreover, since his arrival in the UK, things had become more complicated. He let his head recline back into the seat's headrest, let his neck muscles relax, and closed his eyes the better to block extraneous distractions.

Detail might be important, he told himself, but getting the big picture right comes first from a strategic viewpoint. So what was that picture ? He ran a fast news reel through his mind capturing the big concerns. First, Bourov. He was unreliable and no longer a feasible option to use in Angelov's UK activities. Next, Redwoods. Was it really the right vehicle for him to pursue his ambitions in the UK construction sector ? Given what he had now learnt from Mary Donoghue, he was unsure if RCH was worth buying outright given its indebtedness.
Third, and here his intuition was speaking strongly to him, Angelov preferred to gain effective access to Westlake's father, Sir Peter. As head of Dominion Properties, he had far more strategic potential. But why would he partner with Angelov, a foreigner with no UK track record ?

A moment inspiration assailed him. For the first time he saw the route to accomplish that entré to Sir Peter's world. He should buy out the interests that were under Cartwright's control in Vienna !!!. That would provide him with tangible assets to trade with Sir Peter in order to convince him to bring Angelov onboard for joint bids for lucrative London Olympics construction projects. Buoyed with this idea, Angelov decided that it was probably his best course of action. He would call Donoghue and ask her for contacts at the CEGB to open negotiations on a takeover of the Vienna company.

Yet at the back of his mind, an annoying question remained. What to do about his RCH shares and his business relationship with Russell Westlake ? This question couldn't be ignored. He opened his eyes again and his brows furrowed. At every turn, there appeared to be an impediment to his progress. Angelov had a growing realisation that this business strategy game was more nuanced than he had originally assumed. He needed more time to think.

Angelov's eyes fell on the unopened daily newspapers laying on the table in front of him. He had bought the Financial Times, the Messenger and the Daily Courier. From natural curiosity, he first opened the FT and sought out the pages near the back detailing individual listed companies' shares prices. In the construction industry section he checked for RCH. The firm's closing share price yesterday was at £ 0.49, a new 12 month low. Then he looked for Dominion Properties. It too had a share price not far off its 12 month low. His curiosity made him look finally at the Ipswich and Blackwater's share price. It stood at £ 3.85, just off a 12 month low. Angelov was unnerved. He turned back to the front page, where he checked the summary information on the stock markets as a whole. Sure enough, the London, New York and Tokyo exchanges all uniformly revealed near rock bottom prices.

It gave Angelov pause for thought. What in hell's name was up ? Was capitalism – the system that he now wholeheartedly wanted to embrace - in some terminal decline ? He was aware of the sub prime crisis in the US and its' knock on influence to the US banks. What he hadn't fully understood was that *everything* was down. If that was the case, what was to stop the markets from totally imploding ? Was it wise to invest at all in such an environment? Did he want to lose all that he had accumulated due to ignorance of how these markets worked ? A chill ran down his back. He was, he conceded, on thin ice.

To avoid falling into a destructive bad mood occasioned by this impasse in his understanding, he exchanged the FT for the Messenger, with the intent to read some UK news. He glanced at the front page headlines. Then he turned the page. There was an Editorial, the title of which caught his attention. He read the piece:

Messenger Editorial

The next banking failure is out there

Since the financial markets crashed in 2008 on both sides of the Atlantic, western governments and central banks have sought to deal with the biggest set of deflationary events since the Great Depression of 1929-32. The UK government's response to the imminent failure of banks such as Northern Rock, Lloyds' and Royal Bank of Scotland was to nationalise them. This may have been expedient to stem potentially systemic risks and protect depositors, but it raised the spectre of moral hazard in the banking industry. That encourages, rather than restrains, high risk banking business models.

Today on page 12 of this newspaper, we publish Part 1 of Craig Reddy's investigation into a banking insolvency waiting to happen. It concerns the Ipswich and Blackwater Bank

(IB&B), the UK's 6th largest bank by assets; and the Celtic & European Banking Group (CEGB), which is Irish but owns a 25% shareholding in the IB&B. Signs are that all is not well at these two banks; yet to date, there has been no action – at least in public – either from the regulators or the Government, either in London or Dublin.

This newspaper believes that the British public has no more appetite for bank bail outs. It would be reckless for the government to accept more banking assets on the public balance sheet. The government must not only halt further bank nationalisations but also urgently establish measures that force banks to ring fence high risk trading strategies, and also return to sound lending practices.

Banks are not reforming their trading practices, continue to ignore systemic risks and are over-leveraged. In the specific case of the Ipswich & Blackwater Bank, Reddy exposes their dramatic undisclosed losses from proprietary trading, estimated to be in the region of £ 1,2 billion.

The fundamental problems causing weakness of banks have not yet been addressed. To name a few: non-transparency of risks in the derivatives markets, especially in securitisation; overstretched leverage in relation to banks' capital and reserves; maturities mismatches in borrowing and lending practices; continuing non-separation of banks' retail businesses from their proprietary trading.

To the man in the street, the revolution in financial innovation and banking over the past fifteen years is almost incomprehensible. They are not alone. Governments, regulators, central banks and policy makers are behind the curve; while banks' own top executives rarely have any fundamental grasp of the risks inherent in *the derivatives products that their traders sell. Even the "quants", the banks' employees who design these products, do not understand the objective risks of their own inventions once unleashed into the markets.*

If today one asks what useful economic function do these banks perform, then the cynical reply is: to provide unheard of remuneration and bonuses to their top management while enslaving their clients in debt. Multinational businesses long ago gave up on banks as a source of lending; instead they retain profits to build war chests of cash for their own investment and growth. The banks themselves meanwhile have cut lending to consumers and small businesses because of credit default risks and low margins.

Large banks target the derivatives markets for a reason: ultra high margin returns, financed with leveraged funds. That casino-style risk taking should be a concern for their shareholders, because crippling losses and insolvency are an ever present danger.

This newspaper is a firm believer in the power and effectiveness of markets, not of central planning which history shows does not work. But today there is a deep-seated malaise in the way that the big banks operate with the implicit assumption of 'too big to fail' taxpayer-funded bailouts."

Angelov then turned to page 12 to read the article:

Another bank insolvency ?
Craig Reddy

This week has seen the high profile resignation of a senior Government Minister because of differences over policy for the banking industry, and also publication of the Financial Services Authority's Turner Report into the recent financial crisis in banking.

These events come on the heels of massive interventions by the Government in 2007 & 2008, nationalising Northern Rock, Lloyds Banking Group, Royal Bank of Scotland & HBOS, all of which potentially were on the verge of insolvency.

While the politicians debate and the regulators analyse, the banking industry itself remains largely unchanged. Risk taking in derivatives trading is poorly understood and controlled; leverage is far too high; inter-bank lending remains largely frozen due to uncertainty over counter party risk; deposit-taking is faltering; bad loans, particularly to the property sector, are increasing; and balance sheets hide large losses as assets are not marked to market.

The prevailing fragilities in banking are systematic and international. That is why politicians' and governments' reflex response to date has been to bail out financial institutions considered 'too big to fail' (TBTF). Like rabbits caught in the headlights, they are scared of contagion effects. The problem however with this response is that it rewards wrong behaviour; it creates "moral hazard". The signal transmitted to the market is that banks' managements can continue with irresponsible trading and lending since in the worst case they will be bailed out by the government.

Our investigation into the Ipswich & Blackwater Bank (IB&B) lays bare an imminent insolvency and knock-on risks to customers, shareholders and associate companies not only locally and nationally, but also internationally. It may come about through any number of possible concatenated events, but in our assessment the IB&B is at high risk.

The Main Trends

The IB&B is the UK's sixth largest bank by assets. Its growth in assets has been been an average 15% between 2004 and 2008,according to its last full year's accounts. This compares to only 6% between 1998 and 2003.

The dramatic step change in growth was occasioned by a change in the Bank's strategy in 2004, due to the arrival of a new CEO, Thomas Cartwright, parachuted in by the largest single shareholder, the Celtic & European Banking Group (CEGB).

While remaining a leading provider of residential mortgages, the IB&B began diversifying into new areas. It expanded commercial loans, notably to housebuilders. It entered into the wholesale market for funding as mitigation for slowing growth in net deposits. Most recently, in 2007, it opened a proprietary trading office, making trades in a variety of derivatives products. As a result, the sources of the IB&B's profits altered significantly. Comparing 2004 with 2008, profits from retail mortgages fell from 85% to 41%; commercial lending increased from 12% to 33%; proprietary trading soared (in two years) from 0% to 15%; and fixed income rose from 3% to 11%.

In parallel, the Bank's balance sheet became fragile. Between 2004-08, leverage has inflated from 14 to 1 to 31 to 1. Core tier 1 capital reserves have not been adequately replenished as the balance sheet has expanded, the ratio is down to under 5%; profits have been dissipated in large dividend payouts and bonuses to top management and (most recently) the trading team.

These trends have been supported by the Bank's main shareholder, the CEGB. Although not holding a controlling stake, the CEGB is the effective master of the IB&B's strategy. It succeeded in having it's candidate appointed as CEO back in 2004. Since then, the growth and diversification activities of the IB&B have had the CEGB's seal of approval. Institutional shareholders have until now sat back for the ride, content to take the dividends. Another CEGB-backed executive – Mary Donoghue - arrived at the Bank as CFO in 2006 and master minded much of the Bank's financial engineering. This heralded not only the initiation of the new proprietary trading office, but the reinforcement of aggressive selling and moves into higher yielding, higher risk, lending.

Persuaded by the IB&B's success formula, the CEGB gave permission to Thomas Cartwright in 2005 to spearhead its thrust into commercial property in central and eastern Europe, using a subsidiary, CPI GmbH based in Vienna. That move has left the CEGB exposed to high risks and resulted in serious overreach by the IB&B's top management. Thomas Cartwright committed suicide last week end, jumping to his death off the Orwell Bridge near Ipswich. The circumstances of his death are still the subject of a police enquiry. My investigation of his work for the IB&B and CPI GmbH, lead to the conclusion that the critical matters he was accountable for may well have been material factors in his death.

The Crisis and its Consequences for the IB&B

Geared for growth, the IB&B's executive team were ill prepared for the 2008 financial crisis. With their feet full on the accelerator pedal, they were not only loath to apply the brakes; they had forgotten where they were. The risk management function at the Bank was not upgraded or adequately empowered as the Bank's shift into riskier ventures intensified. Conflicts of interest between prudential supervision and risk-taking in lending and trading were ignored. Risk models were maintained only for each functional silo of the Bank's commercial activities. An integrated view of the combined risks under highly stressed market conditions was all but absent.

Yet the warning signs were there. The IB&B's last published annual accounts − to 31 November 2008 − show that profits fell 5%. Provisions for bad loans were increased 25% to £ 2,45 billion. Net deposits turned negative for the first time, down 3% to £ 125 billion.

The annual figures hide however the worsening trend. In the last quarter to end February 2009, as interest rates fell, net deposits fell 8%. Mortgage loan applications, down 12% for the year 2008, were down 26% for the final quarter. As house prices fell during the second half of 2008, so too households who had bought from the Bank loan to value mortgages in excess of 100%, suffered negative equity. The IB&B's own figures reveal a startling increase in the proportion of retail mortgages in excess of six months' arrears from 3% to 9%.

To fuel growth in commercial lending, the Bank started borrowing funds from the wholesale markets back in 2005. Interest rates at the time were high and the term structure of the loans predominantly from one to five years. In

2008, the accounts report wholesale borrowing of £ 78 billion, 52% of which has maturity of less than 1 year. The cardinal rule for commercial banking is prudential management of maturities on borrowings relative to lending, since significant maturity mismatching can be the Achilles heel of a bank's solvency.

The IB&B has not adhered to this rule. This year it has to repay its' wholesale creditors £ 40 billion; a fact that has already brought increases in the yields that it is being asked to pay by creditors. Furthermore, anecdotal evidence from the markets indicates that some of the Bank's wholesale lenders recently have required increases to the base collateral they originally took. While in one case this year, a lender abrogated their loan entirely; a move that reverberated amongst other institutions and which is having knock-on effects as other lenders seek revised terms with the IB&B.

These initially small movements are now accumulating. Since the IB&B's wholesale funding is now equivalent to 65% of retail deposits, it is evident that a bank run by wholesale lenders would bring the Bank to insolvency in very short order. Needless to say, a run on retail deposits would accomplish the same thing, as the Northern Rock experience in 2007 reminds us. Depositor withdrawals of 10% for example would be equivalent to £12,5 billion cash leaving the bank. Skittishness amongst retail savers should not be ruled out. Reports earlier in the week said customers in the bank's home town of Ipswich were making increased withdrawals.

To add fuel to the fire, I can now confirm that the bank has suffered an undeclared loss of at least £ 1.2 billion from high risk bets placed by its' proprietary trading team. Whether or not this loss is due to one or two 'rogue traders', or rather a pervasive 'casino' culture of *speculation sanctioned by senior management remains to be seen.*

Lack of Governance

Overreach by the IB&B, in terms of its rapid growth and diversification, has not been countered with strengthened risk management, tier 1 capital ratios, and management supervision. On the contrary, management's focus and prudential duties have been either lost or diluted. Even accounting rules may have been broken.

This corporate culture, alien to the IB&B before the arrival of Thomas Cartwright as CEO, is now engrained within the new divisions of the Bank, aided and abetted by the Board, and passively accepted by the main shareholder, the CEGB.

The results are to be seen far away from these shores on the Black Sea coast where CPI GmbH – the CEGB's vehicle for property investments in central and eastern Europe, and also managed by Cartwright – is active in many holiday home and luxury resort developments in conjunction with local partners known to have connections with mafia crime.

That could be considered a minor aberration were it not for the fact that at least one of these same partners appear to have been encouraged to bring their business practices to the UK. My investigation has uncovered that one of the partners in CPI GmbH is now a significant shareholder in Redwood Country Homes, via a Panama-based nominee company.

The CEGB has profited handsomely from its minority holding in the IB&B. Its' long term plan is believed to be to acquire a controlling holding. However, to do that, it would require approval from the Financial Services Authority, the regulator responsible for banking licenses in the UK.

My investigation has not found any evidence of a formal request having been deposed by the CEGB with the FSA. Which is not to say that unofficial soundings have not been made. In light of the damaging allegations that we have regarding the CEGB's CPI GmbH subsidiary in Austria, and the sudden unexplained resignation of a Board member last week from the CEGB, it is possible that the FSA's current view of the CEGB as a "fit and proper" holder of a UK banking licence is to reserve judgement.

Let the Private Sector Take the pain

Capitalism as a resilient and successful economic system is based on the effective functioning of markets. That applies too to the banking industry. Risk taking in the financial investment industry must have consequences, including on the downside. "Moral hazard" type policy initiatives by the government and the regulators, socialise onto taxpayers bank managements' risks.

The outcome of round one of the financial crisis in the UK has been a resounding victory for the state interventionists and for the bankers. Bail outs have been "de rigeur", foisted onto the taxpayer on the grounds of "too big to fail".

The problem is – and this is what my investigation has uncovered in the case of the IB&B – that almost nothing has changed in the ways that banks and bankers go about their business, other than the fact that they are now trying to cope with the consequences of a deleveraging phase in the credit cycle. My contention is therefore that there are further

*bank failures out there and that neither the
banks' owners nor the authorities are well
placed to deal with them.*

*Absent possible Bank of England emergency
liquidity funding, the IB&B may soon
experience accelerating calls for redemptions
on its wholesale borrowings and withdrawals of
its deposits. A private sector solution to the
bank's solvency problems could be engineered.
It is not too late; however it would involve
radical surgery to sell non-performing assets,
replace and strengthen executive management,
deleverage, raise core capital and change the
business strategy. All of which means being
taken under new ownership.*

*The resumption of effective market forces in
the banking industry can only occur when the
shareholders and other lenders take
responsibility for their actions. Which means
managing the risk of losses and its
consequences. The next banking failure in the
UK, which may be imminent, will show us
whether or not this lesson has been not only
understood but applied.*

*Part 2 of this investigation will be published
next Tuesday, 24*th *March*

Angelov sat back in his seat and put the newspaper down. He had
struggled to read the article. While his conversational English was
good, he was unaccustomed to reading it and the subject matter of the
article was not easy. He had worked slowly through it with a mounting
sense of unease as he began to see who the article was about. He
was unsure what 'crony capitalism' was, but in context it read like bad
news. The facts describing the IB&B were a disconcerting new
development. If correct, the Ipswich and Blackwater Bank was in a
bad financial position too. That gave him pause for thought. Yesterday
evening at dinner with Mary Donoughue she had disclosed nothing to
suggest that the bank also might be in difficulties. When eventually he

reached the paragraph which talked about RCH and its shareholders and debts he became alarmed.

The train started to decelerate and he saw out the carriage window that they were passing through the outskirts of a town. Checking his wrist watch he concluded that this was Colchester as the time was ten twenty. The arrival was scheduled for 10.22.

Incensed at the possibility of being exposed by the article, Angelov decided that this journalist Reddy needed to be 'educated' in some way. He, Angelov, might be playing away from home but that did not mean that some jumped up free thinking scribbler could compromise his operations by carelessly using the press to slander and abuse people at will. This guy was going to have to learn respect the hard way.

As the train pulled into the station, he gathered up the newspapers and his coat. He had arranged for Vladimir to collect him directly outside the station's exit.

Sure enough, as he left the station's main building, the headlights of a white Toyota Land Cruiser parked a few metres away, flashed him. The driver was Vladimir. Angelov hurried over, opened the passenger's door and climbed in.

"Dobre den, boss. The trains seem to run on time in this country" Vladimir said. "We've got Bourov still out for the count. And of course there's the money."

Vladimir pulled the vehicle out and executed a sharp U turn to head away from the station. He was dressed entirely in black and wore tinted shades. He waited a few seconds for Angelov to speak, expecting that he couldn't resist asking "how much ?". Yet Angelov remained resolutely silent, his face set in a grim pose as he stared sightlessly at the passing urban landscape. Finally, he spoke:

"Vladimir listen. Before we get to Bourov, there's a new problem to deal with." Agitatedly, he waved the folded copy of the Messenger, still open at the page carrying Reddy's article, at the Toyota's windscreen. "I want you to trace a journalist by the name of Craig Reddy. He works for this newspaper, 'The Messenger'. He's written an article in today's paper that says damaging things. It doesn't name me, but potentially it could expose me if there is any follow up. I intend to teach this guy about respect. Fast. Before he can inflict real damage."

Vladimir was a safe pair of hands. He was used to his boss' challenging demands. How do you find this guy ? he thought to himself. We don't know what he looks like or where he lives. He asked:

"OK, I understand. You want me to get started on that immediately, right ?"

Angelov was flipping through the newspaper's pages. Finding the Editorial article, he took the page between the thumbs and forefingers of both hands, tore it free and placed it on the armrest between the two front seats.

"Take this. It's got the address and phone number of the newspaper. Drop me off now at Bourov's place. Then find a public phone and place a call to them. Say you're from a courier firm or something and you have a package to deliver to Reddy. If you get through, ask him where you can deliver and that you need him to sign. If he's not there, try and get put through to their Human Resources people and obtain his private address. We need to find this nutcase and deal with him in short order. Got it?"

"No problem" Vladimir responded confidently, hiding his doubts that they could find the journalist. "Bourov's place isn't far from here. I'll drop you off there and then place a call. If I remember, there's a street phone box in a neighbouring road, as well as a pub. By the way, don't you want to know how much money Bourov has on him ?"

"Tell me"

"Six hundred and fifty thousand pounds ! Cash."

Vladimir kept his eyes peeled on the road but allowed a smile to creep into them as he sensed that Angelov, master of concealment, was taken by surprise at the amount. Neither of them spoke.

He decelerated the Toyota and turned it left into a side road. A black and white sign attached to a building near the corner identified it as Clarendon Way. He drove a short distance further and then turned right. They were in a small residential area of curving roads lined with relatively new terraced houses of buff coloured bricks and slate roof tiles. Each property had a narrow frontage but with individual parking spaces immediately outside. He pulled the vehicle over and parked in an empty space in front one of the houses, number nine.

"We've arrived. Igor is inside guarding Bourov. He should still be unconscious for a while, we gave him another dose of GHB this morning."

"What the hell is that ?" Angelov quizzed.

"Better known amongst the lads as 'Easy Lay' " Vladimir explained. "What the media call a 'date rape' drug."

Angelov already had his hand on the switch opening the car door, but half turned to his security guard: "Good, because he'll be well fucked by the time I've finished with him ! Get yourself back here as soon as you've found where to find Reddy. And don't take all day."

He grabbed his coat off the back seat, opened the passenger door and climbed out, taking the newspapers with him. He looked back at Vladimir who was busy manipulating the keypad on his mobile phone.

"Just texting Igor that you're outside. He'll open the door for you directly."

Angelov nodded his approval, closed the door and headed for the small house's front door. There was only one thing on his mind right now: Bourov. Disloyalty in Angelov's world had a fixed price. He was going to have to kill Bourov.

The window curtains were drawn but there was light entering his bedroom anyway because the curtain material was too thin. Bourov felt numb and his mind was groggy. For self preservation he neither moved nor opened his eyes.

He was lying on his own bed. That was where Vladimir and Igor had left him yesterday evening. He assumed that they had drugged him because of how he felt now. Although he was clothed they had taken off his shoes and socks and tied his wrists together with cord.

Slowly, his mind began to clear and his memory to return. The events of yesterday afternoon filtered back into consciousness. On returning to his terraced house they had taken him by surprise from behind as he entered the front door, bundling him inside. Although he himself had formidable strength, his unpreparedness for an assault and their combined and coordinated power had overwhelmed him. They had knocked him about and rapidly tied him up. From that moment till this he knew that he was in imminent and perilous danger. The drugs that had sent him into unconsciousness were a tyrannous reprieve since they had told him beforehand that Angelov personally wanted to 'talk' to him.

That moment had more or less now come. For while he feigned continued unconsciousness, he heard noise through the partially opened bedroom door which announced Angelov's arrival.

"Show me him" Angelov had said immediately, on entering the front door.

"Yes boss. He's down there in the bedroom. Still out. Those pills are strong even for a bull like Bourov."

There had been approaching footsteps down the tiled corridor, then the bedroom door opened wide.

"We've tied his wrists and leave the door ajar. One of us looks in on him every thirty minutes just to check."

Bourov remained motionless, concentrating to keep his breathing regular and slow. He heard movement towards him. Angelov stepped up to the bed and studied him minutely. Then he turned and departed without a word. Igor followed, leaving the door half open.

From the muffled sounds, Bourov concluded that they had both gone into the living room at the opposite end of the corridor. So far as he could tell, Vladimir was not with them. He knew it was Vladimir who had left earlier to collect Angelov at the station, yet apparently he had not returned.

What to do ? Bourov had the discipline not to panic. Nevertheless, with Angelov now arrived, he was certain that unless he found a way to escape he was living his last day. Angelov would interrogate him, probably torture him and then kill him at his pleasure.

As his strength and awareness improved, he reflected on how much he hated Angelov. Angelov treated him as his slave. Even if he had selected Bourov amongst his clan as the one to come to the UK and become closely engaged in Angelov's UK plans, it was expressly as a loyal peon. He was allowed no aspiration other than unbounded loyalty.

Bourov realised this train of thought was self indulgent. His sole aim had to be to execute his escape. Which meant acting before Vladimir returned. Two against one might succeed. Three against one struck him as impossible.

Imperceptibly, he started to run checks on his body. He wriggled his toes to confirm that he could feel them; then revolved his feet one at a time to see if he could control them. One after the other he opened his eyes to gauge if his vision was clear or distorted. His wrists were tied in front of him, not behind his back. Blood still circulated well in his hands and he bent his fingers. Last, he flexed his arm muscles for strength.

While enacting these quiet routines, his ears were peeled back for any sign of movement either from the living room or the front door. There was none, although he could hear the low murmur of voices as Igor and Angelov talked together in the living room.

A few minutes passed by. Then the living room door opened. Angelov came out, walked a few foot steps down the corridor and entered the toilet. With lighting speed, Bourov noiselessly slid from the bed and stood on his bare feet. The two men were now separated. This was his chance.

He found to his relief that he was steady on his feet. Without touching the bedroom door, he squeezed by and glided down the corridor. He went left into the kitchen. Ranged all the far wall besides the cooker, were cooking pots and frying pans hanging from an aluminium rack. He had almost no time to choose, as he heard the flush of the toilet cistern. Although constrained by his tied wrists, he succeeded to take a grip on the long handle of one of the heavy pots, and lift it from its' hinge. He retraced his footsteps back into the corridor and stood motionless to one side of the toilet door.

The door swung open and Igor emerged. With his head down in thought he started to turn to his right back towards the living room. Behind him, Bourov swung the cooking pot in an arc from above his own head, smashing it into the back of Igor's skull. The bodyguard collapsed to the tiles and remained there.

Bourov skipped over him and ran to and past the door to the living room, expectant that the noise engendered would rouse Angelov to investigate. He glued himself stock still to the corridor wall on the opposite side of the living room doorway to that leading to the toilet. He fought to steady his breathing.

Within seconds, the door swung open and Angelov appeared. He stuck out his head into the corridor to see what had occurred. Bourov was on him in an instant. With his two hands joined as a combined fist, he swung them ferociously at Angelov's chin. The man's head jerked up on the impact and his knees sagged. Bourov danced agilely around and kneed him viciously in the groin. As Angelov doubled down in pain, Bourov executed the coup de grace with another arced swing of his fists down onto his foe's neck. Angelov crumpled to the floor, hitting his head on the tiles. He too remained still.

Bourov jumped over him and returned to the kitchen. From a drawer next to the sink he withdrew a sharp carving knife. He drew out one of the pinewood chairs from the kitchen table; sat down and clasped the handle firmly between his knees. With Herculean concentration and precision he progressively cut through the white cord in a couple of minutes, freeing his hands. Then he went to another drawer and found the original ball of cord from which his hands had been tied. He cut two lengths from it. Back in the corridor, he used the cord to tie the wrists of Igor and Angelov.

Safe in the knowledge that the two men were incapacitated, but wary of the possible imminent reappearance of Vladimir, he conducted a search of the living room and then the spare room to find what he needed. The keys to the rental car were on the living room table. The suitcase with the money was placed upright next to a bookcase. His mobile phone remained where he had left it in his coat pocket, and his shoes were down the corridor near the front door.

By the time Bourov opened the front door to leave, five minutes had elapsed from the moment he had slammed the cooking pot onto Igor's head. There was still no sign of Vladimir and to his relief the Ford Fiesta was still parked outside.

He had no clear plan other than to put distance between himself and these would be assassins. Ten minutes later he drove onto the A12 in the direction of Ipswich. For the first time he began to think about where to hide over the week end.

Chapter Twenty Eight

11.55 Thursday 19th March 2009.   Giles' Statue, corner of Princes' and Queens' streets, Ipswich

Reddy walked briskly down Tavern Street amongst the late morning shoppers. He was anxious to be on time for his meeting with Elaine Cartwright, for fear that she might change her mind. Based on the short conversation that they had had on the phone yesterday, he surmised that she might use any excuse to convince herself not to keep the appointment.

He had parked the Mondeo in a public car park on Upper Barclay Street, as it afforded him both easy access to the town centre and a quick departure route back to his Marina apartment later.

Before setting off for the Giles' 'Granny' statue at the top end of Princes' Street – their agreed meeting place – Reddy first retrieved from his briefcase on the back seat of his car, the small package containing the Len Deighton book that he had bought for Natasha Medvedev. He needed to post to her today. Then he switched on his mobile phone, which he'd turned off prior to his earlier encounter with Russell Westlake. Checking for missed calls and text messages, he found a text message of congratulations on the success of his Messenger article from Peter Houseman and then an irate voice message from Samantha Cavendish accusing him of lack of authorisation to publish with a competitor. She said she needed to talk to him, urgently.

Houseman's words of encouragement reminded Reddy that he still had not purchased a copy of The Messenger in order to see his article. He resolved to buy one at a newsagents' on the way over to Princes' Street. The call from Cavendish was a salutary reminder to him that his meeting later with Edmund Burleigh, to ascertain his legal position vis à vis the Courier, was timely as Cavendish's lightning quick accusation didn't bode well.

Spotting the newsagents' he had had in mind, Reddy nipped inside and purchased a copy of the Messenger. Leaving the small shop with the paper, he was about to rifle through the pages to find his article, when his phone rang. He put the folded newspaper under his arm and took the call. It was from Pandit Singh:

"Hi Craig, how are you stranger ? You're building quite some notoriety around the office here since getting yourself suspended. Nice article for The Messenger though."

"Pandit, morning. Truth be told, I've only this minute bought the paper to see it for myself. I've been too busy with other things. Not so sure that I need more notoriety though. Is there flak coming from the 37th floor ? Am I in the firing line from Sinclair and Cavendish ?" he asked innocently.

"Craig, you know me. I'm not hard-wired into the rumour mill. But I think you'll find that your article is one of the hot talking points today amongst the media commentariat. That kind of 'success' doesn't go down too well here. You've published what's rapidly becoming a scoop, but with a competitor."

Reddy was astonished to hear all this. Yes, he had seen the early morning tv programme where his article had been mentioned, but he hadn't anticipated that that might morph within a few hours into a 'hot talking point', as Pandit had termed it. He had no time now either to discuss it or think it through. He chose instead to find an exit from their exchanges:

"You can't keep a good man down" he said, lightening the tone. "I'll have to follow up on it later, Pandit. I've a meeting starting in a couple of minutes. Tell me, did you see my email about your smart phone ? You forgot it when you left the sports centre after our squash game yesterday ?"

"Yes, thanks for that. I wasn't too worried. I'm able to monitor its' whereabouts as I've got GPS tracking installed on my notebook PC. As soon as I realised I'd forgotten it I checked where it was. I assumed that you had it. Your email was reassuring though. I need the thing back. Your suggestion sounds good."

"You agree to come up and stay the week end ? Watch the game at Portman Road with Simon Farley and me ?"

"Absolutely. I'll catch a train up to Ipswich Saturday morning. I'll let you know later when I'm arriving."

"Then the match ticket is on me. I'll tell them you'll collect at the ticket office before the match."

With that agreement in place, they closed the call. Reddy now had no time to browse his Messenger article. He quickened his pace and within a minute approached the 'Granny' statue from the north side of Queens' Street.

A woman probably in her late thirties was ambling back and forth by the statue. She was diminutive like Granny, but that was their sole likeness. She wore her brown hair short in page boy cut, and had on a light brown coat unbuttoned. A matching darker brown leather bag hung from her shoulder. In her hand she held a lighted cigarette which she dragged on nervously. Reddy went up to her.

"Mrs. Cartwright ? I'm Craig Reddy"

 She looked up at him, tremulously. Her eyes were hazel-coloured and their surrounds darkened by eye shadow. There was no responding welcome from her. Reddy proffered his hand, which she shook only reluctantly and with the briefest of touches.

"I've only got twenty minutes. I'm meeting my mother outside the Butter Market shopping centre for twelve thirty."

Reddy perceived that Elaine Cartwright was not only nervous but also stressed, tired and emotional. He first had to win her confidence, so he accepted her time constraint without demur. When she suggested they take a coffee at a coffee shop nearby, he fell in with her request.

"I appreciate very much your time, Mrs. Cartwright" he said, a little too stiffly, as they walked side by side.

"Elaine. Call me Elaine. Just be direct and ask what you want. I'll answer what I want to answer. Don't try to force me into subjects that I don't want to discuss. Those are the rules. Understood ?" Her explanation was an amalgam of assertion and defensiveness, perhaps a manifestation of her unstable mental state.

They turned into St. Stephen's Lane and arrived at the small coffee shop. It had a bright blue façade and window frames. Aluminium legged tables and hard-backed chairs were arranged along the frontage on the pavement outside. It had a quaintly toy town feel to it. Reddy had never been there before.

The weather was clement enough to convince them to sit outside. Only one other table was occupied. An elderly couple hunched forward in their chairs sharing a pot of tea; their recent household purchases in plastic bags resting at their sides.

Having ordered two cappuccinos with a waitress who came out to take their orders, Reddy tried to open up the conversation onto Thomas Cartwright:

"Although your husband was a busy man, he very kindly afforded me an interview. I'd wanted to have a follow up meeting with him but of course that wasn't possible. Let me say, again, my sincere condolences to you."

Elaine Cartwright ignored Reddy, fidgeting instead with her bag. She withdrew an expensive lighter and a pack of cigarettes. "I'm going to smoke. I hope you don't mind ?" She proceeded to light up without awaiting Reddy's response. She turned her head away from Reddy and blew the inhaled smoke out of the side of her mouth. Reddy indulged her with a smile. There were no other customers around to object. He said:

"I think you might be able to help my investigation Mrs Cartwright....."

"Elaine. Just Elaine, please" she interjected. "What do you want to know ? What is this 'investigation' about ? I don't understand."

Her peevishness, Reddy saw, was a veneer. He sensed that she might welcome the opportunity to unburden herself. With patience and cool deliberation he explained to her in plain terms his investigative dossier on the Ipswich & Blackwater Bank and how that had evolved to consider also associated factors like the role of the CEGB. She sat silently through his discourse, inhaling frequently on the cigarette, her eyes darting here and there like summer dragonflies skitting across the surface of a lake. When he finished, she put out her cigarette on the pavement with the heel of her shoe.

"It's very simple" she said, suddenly galvanised, as if the ritual of completing another cigarette had provided her power to rise into action. "My husband led a dual existence. He made frequent trips abroad to Europe. In addition to being CEO of the Ipswich & Blackwater he ran a company based in Austria. It was doing business in property. The CEGB encouraged him and put up the money. Things were booming in eastern Europe apparently. It was taking up more and more of his time. I used to go with him just occasionally. I loved the shopping and the museums. Far better than being a bored housewife in suburban Ipswich. He just let me spend money. I hardly ever saw him even though we stayed together. He was up to his neck in problems."

Reddy asked: "The business' activities started going bad ?"

She laughed ironically. "I suppose so. We never discussed that. But the work took its toll on him. He slept less and less. I think that it was more to do with people. He was having trouble with some of his partners maybe ? Anyway, I just indulged him."

"You weren't worried about him then ?"

"Yes, at times. He wasn't happy with some of the business contacts he made out there. But we didn't discuss the details. Mr. Reddy, I loved my husband. I didn't want just a businessman in my life. We adopted a rule that business things were left at the office. At home or out together we were a couple."

"So you were happily married ?"

"Like I said, I indulged him. We didn't have children; there were some complications. I didn't ask and he didn't tell, but there was another woman."

"You're sure ? You knew the person ?" Reddy failed to hide his curiosity.

"As sure as a wife can be. Mary Donoghue, his Finance Director at the Ipswich and Blackwater. She's a bitch and a predator. Thomas was concerned about the evolution of the Bank because he had become dependent on her for the sophisticated stuff the Bank did. She simply took advantage of him."

"You knew this yet did nothing ? Weren't you jealous ?"

She paused a second and sat back in her chair, giving Reddy a searching look. She demanded bluntly: "Are you married Craig ?"

"No, I'm not" he conceded.

"Well then, you probably don't understand the difference between having an affair and being in a loving long term relationship. Mary Donoghue forced herself on my husband to achieve her own ends. But affairs exhaust themselves naturally. My husband was too intelligent not to see what she was about. Their affair fizzled out before he died.

So he didn't commit suicide because of her. All I had to do was be there for him and remain patient."

She glanced ostentatiously at her wrist watch and then took up her cup and finished her capuccino. Her revelations were neither what Reddy had expected nor particularly valuable in respect to his investigation. He had hoped that Elaine Cartwright might be a mine of inside information about her husband's dealings with business partners and his management struggles steering the fate of the Ipswich and Blackwater. What he had obtained instead was an exposé into the man's private life, one in which two women had competed for his affections. One aspect of the story Elaine had told left him dubious: the apparent lack of jealousy, the flimsy bitterness for Mary Donoghue. With her looking already to terminate their meeting, he asked disingenuously:

"I don't suppose you knew one of your husband's customers at the Ipswich and Blackwater by the name of Russell Westlake ? He's the CEO of a house building firm called Redwoods Country Homes."

After a momentary pause with another bout of rapid eye movements, Elaine said brightly:

"Sure I know him. He and Thomas were firm friends. The Bank was a creditor to Redwoods. To him as well, I think. He'd come to the house sometimes. I only knew him through Thomas though. They'd do some boys' stuff together occasionally ? You know, like motor sports ? I tried it too once, but hated the noise."

"Did Thomas perhaps express concern about the extent of the Bank's lending to Westlake ?"

"There you go again. Off in the wrong direction. I really can't help you on the business side. In any case, my time's up. You may not realise it, but the funeral is tomorrow, I've still got a hundred things to do. Sorry I have to leave to meet my mother now."

She gathered her bag, pushed back her chair and stood up.

"Good day. I hope you succeed with your investigation. My husband wasn't perfect. He's committed suicide and even I can't fathom why. We never really know the truth about one another, do we ?"

On that enigmatic note she stepped away and departed with hurried steps. A forlorn woman, Reddy concluded, but one still fighting to survive.

As he looked for his wallet to pay the drinks, his mobile phone rang.

"Mr Reddy ? DS Adams, Ipswich Police, speaking."

"Yes ?" Reddy remembered the burly officer, built like a rugby player. Not the type to get into a maul with. He hoped this was not an 'invitation' for more quality time at Police HQ.

"DI Wright my boss asked me to call you, sir. We think it might be productive to have another discussion with you. Could you find the time to meet tomorrow afternoon ? I understand you spend time in and around Ipswich these days ?"

Reddy was bemused. Was Adams' observation made because he knew that he and the Courier were at loggerheads ? Regardless, he could think of no compelling reason not to accept.

"In principle, that's fine. Is there something specific that you want to ask ? We did cover a lot of ground last time."

"Probably better not to go into detail on the phone Mr Reddy. Can we agree on 14.30 tomorrow ?"

The young waitress, wearing a white apron over stone-washed jeans and pink T shirt, appeared at the café doorway and Reddy signalled to her with his free hand to pay.

"I'll be there, Detective. "

Chapter Twenty Nine

12.25 Thursday 19th March 2009. Driving east along A137, past Manningtree station

"This had better be right." Angelov fumed, watching the roadside scenery flash by.

He was seated in the front passenger's seat of the Toyota Land Cruiser, a road map open on his knees. Igor was driving, sullenly silent and still nursing his injuries. Vladimir was relegated to the back seat. His reputation with his boss was still intact. He had not been present during Bourov's escape from the apartment house, plus he had succeeded in the task allotted him of locating where the journalist Reddy lived. Nevertheless he kept diplomatically quiet unless spoken to. He had returned to Bourov's apartment house only minutes after Bourov's escape, to find Igor slightly concussed and with a cut on his head, and Angelov recovering from the precision punches Bourov had inflicted.

Bourov had made off in the rented car, taking the money and his mobile phone. In the rush to evade them, he had forgotten his personal computer, passport and the rental car's contract.

"You keep on this road", Angelov instructed Igor as the Land Cruiser approached the Ipswich to London railway line. "Go straight under the railway bridge." Igor obeyed.

In his original plan, Angelov had expected to have done with Bourov within an hour; terminally. Then he planned to go to Ipswich. First thing Friday morning, he intended to meet Mary Donoghue at the Ipswich and Blackwater's headquarters. Taking with him the money confiscated from Bourov, he would secretly deposit it in a newly subscribed private client safe deposit box. Thereafter, he planned to accompany Donoghue to Thomas Cartwright's funeral scheduled for nine forty five. He wanted to pay last respects to a man with whom he had worked extensively. Also, hopefully, he could seal the support of Donoghue in a new era of cooperation.

That done, he intended to "educate" the journalist Reddy. If he put the fear of God into him, that ought to ensure that he never again would do anything to compromise Angelov's business activities. With all that accomplished, he intended to leave Saturday afternoon for Madrid. Destination Panama.

However, Bourov's daring escape required immediate response, putting Angelov's 'plan A' on hold. The goal now was to find Bourov at all costs. A first step in that direction came when Vladimir found the rental contract for Bourov's car lying on the living room table. This furnished them with the vehicle's make, model and license plate number. It showed too that the car was due back close of business that day in Colchester. Angelov rejected Vladimir's suggestion to stake out the rental company's premises and await Bourov's return. He knew absolutely that Bourov would avoid returning.

Against his instincts, Angelov plumped for a course of action which had risks but which, he surmised, would probably yield results. He configured his smart phone to withhold caller ID and phoned Simon Farley the guy who, according to Russell Westlake, Bourov was now working for. Farley answered the call:

"Farley. Hello ? Who's calling ?" he said, irritably. He was standing next to Elvin Brown and Mark Hancock in the latter's builders' merchants yard. He took a few steps away from them both to gain privacy just in case the call required it.

"Good morning, Mr Farley. Sorry to disturb you. My name is Velchev" Angelov lied, invoking the name of a Bulgarian mafioso he knew from Varna. "I have your number from Russell Westlake. You know him I think ?"

"I know him" Farley responded, his voice weighted with indignation, "but I wish I didn't". He had had his fill of the man. Even now, talking to Mark Hancock, Westlake's name had been pejoratively on the tip of his tongue. He wondered who in hell's name this Velchev was.

"I see" Angelov said, although he didn't see at all and didn't want to. If there was a problem between this man Farley and Westlake, he wasn't interested. He switched tack: "I'm calling you not about Mr. Westlake. I'm a close friend of Georgi Bourov's ? He's working for you these days I believe ?"

"That's correct. At least, he works when he feels like it" Farley lamented, the sarcasm lost on Angelov. Bourov's recent unannounced absence from work at the Stratford construction site had been instrumental in Farley's team falling behind on their scheduled deliverables. In his current stressed state, Farley overlooked the positive experiences he had had with Bourov's contributions at work. He had finally seen Bourov again only half an hour ago, at Dears' brickworks, when going there to collect Elvin before his current meeting with Mark Hancock.

Angelov avoided entanglement in diversionary discussion. "Mr Farley, I simply wanted to know where I can get in touch with him quickly. I've called his mobile phone but he's not responding. Do you happen to know where I can find him ?"

Welcoming a rapid closure of the call so he could return to more pressing concerns, Farley acceded to the request:

"Sure I do. I was speaking to him myself just fifteen minutes ago. He's over at Dears' brickworks just up the road from here. The A137 on the way to Brantham. Doing some work there."

Angelov had no clue where Brantham was. He thanked Farley for the information and switched off his mobile. A quick perusal of the road map in the Land Cruiser's glove pocket had been all that was needed to find the A137 and Brantham. Using Bourov's notebook PC, they had run a search on Google maps and pinpointed the brickworks' site between the A137 and the river estuary.

The Land Cruiser approached and went around a small roundabout. They were now only a few kilometres south of Brantham. Vladimir and Angelov both had their eyes peeled, looking for a sign to the right off the A137 to the brickworks. But after a few more minutes and fruitless searching, they found themselves passing a street sign announcing their entry into Brantham.

"Turn her back. We must have missed it." Angelov said. He kept the frustration out of his voice but below the surface he had trouble containing himself.

Igor effected a U turn using the front drive of someone's house and they drove back slowly in the direction of Manningtree. The lack of speed generated a small queue of cars stacking up behind them.

"There's a turning off left ahead. Try it !" Angelov announced agitatedly, pointing with a finger at the windscreen.

Igor decelerated and turned the vehicle off the A137 onto an unsurfaced track, to the relief of the drivers in the vehicles behind them.

The track was potholed and narrow. There had been no indication at the roadside that the brickworks existed. After four hundred metres or so, they arrived in front of rusty security gates which were open. No one was in attendance and Igor manoeuvred the Land Cruiser slowly ahead and stopped close to a wooden office building on the left. He cut the engine. No one came out of the office building.

To their right were dilapidated timbered outbuildings, open at the sides. At the far end of the property newly-made bricks were stacked alongside the perimeter fence. Beyond that was a huge expanse of water meadows running down to the river estuary. The three men climbed out of the Land Cruiser. There was an eerie silence but for the occasional screech of seagulls circling above the river. Angelov signalled Vladimir to check inside the office to see if anyone was working there. Vladimir returned within seconds, shaking his head.

Angelov and Igor meantime had discovered Bourov's Ford Fiesta parked out of sight around the far side of the office building. It was empty and locked. However, tucked down between the back of the driver's seat and the rear seat was a black briefcase; the one in which Bourov kept the money.

"Assuming that there's no one else here, we get this done at once" Angelov insisted. "No fucking around. Understood ? Then we clear everything out, including the car and the money."

He waved Igor off to his left to the far end of the kilns, while he and Vladimir walked slowly away from the office building towards the nearest of the outbuildings. They were in poor condition and there was dust everywhere. It looked abandoned. There was no one to be seen. Iron rails ran along the ground from the inside of the open walled building towards the kilns several metres distant. Noiselessly, they moved off down the track.

The first kiln had been bricked up, presumably in preparation for firing the moulded clay. The second was open. Outside it on the rails was a wheeled metal container carrying pallets of unfired bricks. Occasional muffled sounds came from inside the kiln.

Angelov halted, causing Vladimir to do likewise. At the far end of the rails, Igor had appeared adjacent to the last of the four kilns. In sign language, Angelov communicated to him to take precautions. Igor disappeared behind the side wall of the third kiln.

Angelov too moved aside from the rails, positioning himself next to the corner of the kiln wall. Vladimir backed up onto the other side of the rails from where he had a clear view of the entrance to the kiln, unimpaired by the position of the wheeled container.

With both hands gloved and a leather smock tied around his stout figure to protect his clothing, Bourov emerged calmly through the kiln entrance, engrossed in his task. He lifted both hands to the sides of the uppermost pallet to pull it out off its' metal shelf on the container.

In one movement, Vladimir withdrew a handgun from the inside pocket of his jacket, raised it towards Bourov's head and fired a bullet through his brain. In the split second that Bourov's unconscious mind registered a man's movement, his face registered surprise, fear and resignation in a single last kaleidoscope of awareness. He was dead before his body reached the ground.

Chapter Thirty

12.50 Thursday 19th March 2009. *Library, Constable Country Club, south of Hadleigh*

The three men were each seated comfortably on Louis XIV style armchairs, facing each other in a tight circle. Conversation between them was intense and animated but underwritten by mutual respect. The topic of conversation was politics, but there was no wild declaiming or playing to the gallery. This meeting was, by consent, *in camera* so that differences of opinion could be discussed honestly.

To host the meeting, Mitchell Havering had booked, at very short notice, the Club's Library-cum-reading room for an hour starting from 12.00. Lunch in the Club restaurant was booked for 13.00. The two others with him were his brother Neill, one of the leading backbench Tory MPs; and the recently resigned Lord Preston, better-known to his friends and the Havering brothers as James Sturridge. Sturridge had accepted the location, away from the Westminster cauldron and the intrusive questioning of the media, because the subject under discussion – the IB&B's insolvency problems - had enticed him. He had been hard pushed to arrive on time from his home near Amersham.

The Library offered an ideal setting for their talks. It was utterly private, totally quiet, elegantly comfortable, and with in-house service available via a call to Club reception. The room fitted into a converted farm outbuilding, the original walls and roof of which had been left untouched. Inside the building, the room rose up uninterrupted to the roof, giving a sense of volume. The roof timbers were exposed. At first floor level, a wooden walkway had been built around all four walls, providing access to bookshelves lining the upper wall space. The shelves teemed with books of every description.

Most of the ground floor was also occupied with filled bookcases, all of seasoned timber in sympathy with the building's original materials. To the far end of the room was an area reserved for reading. A dozen or so comfortable armchairs and accompanying reading lights were at the visitor's disposal, ranged in small circular groups over an enormous Persian carpet.

It was now 12.50 and the three men had been arguing relentlessly.

The conversation had revolved around the problems still affecting the UK's banking sector in the aftermath of the nationalisations of Northern Rock, Royal Bank of Scotland and Lloyds' Bank. Yet all the participants knew and understood that the heart of their meeting was the subject of the Ipswich & Blackwater Bank in light of that morning's exposé published in the Messenger.

Neill Havering, ever the pragmatic politician, raised the topic of moral hazard:

"It's a free lunch, and its fundamentally wrong James. The banks are allowed to ride roughshod over everybody, including their clients, in the pursuit of profits. Yet when they mess up and become insolvent they are bailed out by the government at the taxpayers' expense.

I don't think that the government should get itself on the hook for the risk. There is no reason why bank restructuring cannot be managed perfectly well by the market place. Banks that make poor loan decisions should suffer the consequences. Banks' creditors, with the exception of retail savers, should not have any automatic or inferred protections from the state. Let them manage their own risk. After all hedging risk is what they're supposed to be experts at."

Lord Preston looked doubtful. Havering moved forward in his seat, leaning his elbows on his knees and clasping his hands together. With studied stillness he won Lord Preston's undivided attention:

"James, as a personal friend, let me tell you about some critical aspects of the IB&B case that may have evaded you and which I think were instrumental in the failure of your approach to the IB&B's problems being adopted."

Lord Preston was taken by surprise. This was not a development that he had countenanced. He sat back in his chair, straightening his back, and gave Havering a nod of his head:

"Go on, Neill. I'm listening".

"There is more in the Irish angle to the Ipswich and Blackwater case than meets the eye."

Lord Preston's curiosity was rising. He kept silent.

Neill Havering resumed: "As you know, the Ipswich and Blackwater's main shareholder is the CEGB. They have just over twenty five per cent

313

of the share capital. Which is not, under normal circumstances, a controlling interest."

"That's all terra cognita, Neill. What's new ?"

"Two things. First, the Irish Central Bank opened an enquiry into the lending practices of a number of Irish banks last year and recently added a new dossier on the CEGB to that enquiry. Unofficial word from sources in Dublin is that some of the directors at the CEBG may not be "fit and proper persons" to be Bank directors. One is being advised to resign immediately or face prosecution. He is linked to accounting irregularities and unauthorised loans. Second, the CEGB does not have a banking licence in the UK. It has exercised effective control of the Ipswich and Blackwater until now by having it's representative appointed as CEO. That was Thomas Cartwright, who committed suicide last week end."

Lord Preston arched a sceptical eyebrow:

"So you're saying that there is now a crisis of confidence internally over the governance of the Ipswich and Blackwater ? No news there Neill. It was precisely to avoid such uncertainty that I pushed for a quick intervention of the CEBG to inject capital into the Ipswich and Blackwater and consider a takeover. They have the financial muscle to do that."

"On paper they do, yes. In practice, they may also be in financial difficulties themselves. My Dublin informant tells me that they are over-leveraged and also suffering from an increasing portfolio of bad loans. The uncertainty in that assessment is due to the arcane accounting the investigators are uncovering and lack of internal controls over a subsidiary's activities in eastern Europe. Apparently there are significant investments that the subsidiary made that never went onto the balance sheet."

Lord Preston interjected: "If that is correct, and the CEBG's executive team are aware of the facts, that would explain their reluctance to envisage a takeover of the Ipswich and Blackwater. That was their initial feedback to me when I broached the matter with them. They were extremely cagey too about what information might leak into the market."

Neill Havering smiled wryly. Lord Preston, he could see, was beginning to understand the picture. Now he could deliver the *coup de grace*, albeit with friendly intent:

"The point here is this: the principal CEGB subsidiary in question is one based in Austria and its' executive representative on the Board was one Thomas Cartwright."

Lord Preston's jaw dropped. Momentarily, rays of sunlight shone through the library's windows casting an arc of brightness over the three seated men. He said:

"Are you implying that Cartwright's suicide may be more complicated ? Is the Ipswich and Blackwater implicated ? "

"It's a possibility. My sources have told me that the Financial Services Authority has been given information about Cartwright's activities on the continent. I suspect that the FSA has its' own inquiry ongoing into the Ipswich and Blackwater as a result of that disclosure."

"Fascinating Neill. You know, when I was preparing my Ministerial options and action for the IB&B last week end, the FSA representative never pitched up for the scheduled conference call. Should I put two and two together here ?"

"Probably. The FSA has full responsibility for banks' compliance to UK banking regulation. If they conclude that there were not 'fit and proper persons' operating the bank, then it could lose its licence. They have a reputation for staying quiet when they're undertaking such enquiries. I think though it is safe to assume that your FSA man's absence was a good indicator that something's cooking."

"Are you implying that there was a short circuit directly into number 10, alerting the Prime Minister to impending disaster, leaving me beached like a whale ?" Lord Preston pressured.

He was well and truly taken aback by Neill Havering's revelations, having had no inkling of them. For the first time unencumbered by Ministerial responsibility and constraints, he now let his political imagination run ahead of his logical mind, envisaging a plot designed to oust him.

"That I can't say. You will have to get back to Westminster and dig a little to discover whether or not that was so."

"James forgive me here, I'm just thinking out loud. In your current position, I'm wondering what you have in mind to do next. A man of your abilities isn't going to let an untimely resignation slow you down.

315

Are you staying in political life or rather thinking about a role in business somewhere ? Excuse me if that is an invasion. But Mitchell and I wanted to ask you today. Because we have an urgent opportunity presenting itself."

"Neill, my feet haven't touched the ground since I quit. What happens next, I don't honestly know."

"I understand, but let me seed this idea in your mind. The Prime Minister may want to nationalise the Ipswich and Blackwater but there are others who see it differently. I mean the City, the Bank of England and the shareholders of the Ipswich and Blackwater."

"Is there something afoot ? A private sector buyer ?"

If Neill Havering was a veteran politician, adept at the chess game of measured and elliptical disclosure, his brother Mitchell was none the less so. He hadn't spoken, listening instead attentively to the exchanges between the other two. Now he leaned forwards, towards Lord Preston, and commented:

"Jim. You know, don't you, I'm a non-executive director on the Board of the American International Investment Bank ? And you ? You've got insider knowledge of the whole Ipswich and Blackwater debate. Neill and I think that constitutes a great rescue team to pull together a private sector resolution of the bank's insolvency crisis."

Chapter Thirty One

12.45 Thursday 19th March 2009. Carr Street, Ipswich

Before leaving the café where he had talked with Elaine Cartwright, Reddy switched off his mobile phone. With Samantha Cavendish intent on arguing with him, it would be prudent first to have Edmund Burleigh's feedback on the legal position. Burleigh's office was his destination.

He walked first though to the nearby post office on Carr Street, where he bought stamps and then posted the small package containing Len Deighton's book 'Berlin Game', together with a note of invitation, to Natasha Medvedev. She was instrumental in his success with the Ipswich and Blackwater investigation, so he owed her. Additionally, he now had the intuition that she was expecting something else from him. In his letter he had invited her out for the evening in London next Wednesday.

Leaving the drab Post Office, he put out of his mind the worry that Natasha might refuse. In a couple of minutes he arrived at the law practice offices of Edmund Burleigh in Northgate Street. It was 12.45 pm, so he was late.

Burleigh's law practice occupied a sixteenth century building in Northgate Street. He and Reddy's father, when starting the partnership together back in 1998, had chosen to buy the property and today, even in current market conditions, it was worth nearly twice what they had paid for it.

It was a typical one storey town house of the period with half timbers and white-washed plaster walls and a gabled roof. Inside, the law offices had been decorated in sympathy with the original interior, keeping the plan of rooms and enhancing the whole with tasteful antique fittings and regency style furnishings. There was no attempt to create a modern atmosphere. For that, they could have simply rented out new office suites in purpose-built premises on a business park somewhere on the Town's periphery.

What Burleigh and Reddy's father had created within the walls of this solid 16th century burgher's house was a sanctum of calm confidentially. An environment where their clients' legal problems, whether mundane or labyrinthine, could be rationally but sympathetically dealt with. Privacy and integrity were the guiding principles in everything the partnership did for its clients. This recipe, and the particular spirit of care and attention in which it was applied, had proven itself over the years. An extremely high retention rate of clients was a symptom of this.

Reddy was no stranger to the premises, having been a regular visitor in the days when his father worked there. Yet after the hustle bustle of the town centre, even he could not fail to observe the oasis-like calm and poise that pervaded the place the moment you stepped inside. This was in part a function of the modern insulation and double glazing that had been installed, which radically dulled the noise from outside. But it was, more particularly, the ensemble of natural light and subtle choice of colour combinations of ornamentation and furnishing.

At the reception desk, he found the receptionist Lisa was befriended by an ornamental vase of effulgent orchids.

"Mr. Burleigh is just finishing with a client" she informed him. "Would you like to take a seat ? "

She ushered him into the adjacent waiting room. It was a study in bourgeois comfort and solidity. In its' middle was a beautiful antique oak round table on which a crystal vase held freshly cut yellow roses. A traditional wrought iron fireplace dominated the centre of the wall opposite the entrance door. The walls above hip height were painted a pastel shade of green, and fitted lights were positioned at intervals. In the far corner of the room an old grandfather clock, still in working order and made in London by Vulliamy in 1828, stood steadfast. When there was quiet in the room, its' gentle rhythmic tick provided a reassuring sense of continuity to whoever cared to listen.

"Make yourself at home Mr. Reddy. You're most welcome. Congratulations on your article by the way. It seems you're now a celebrity."

"Am I ? What on earth gives you that idea Lisa ?" Reddy inquired.

The last thing in this world that he wanted was to be associated with the celebrity culture, the admission criteria for which, it seemed to him, consisted in having appeared on television in a reality tv programme or to have had your photo published for salacious reasons in a gossip magazine.

"We're all wondering how you knew ?"

"How I knew what ?"

"First you publish the article in today's Messenger saying that the Ipswich and Blackwater may be insolvent and then their shares get suspended on the Stock Exchange. Well done ! You're a real sleuth !"

"The shares of the Ipswich and Blackwater are suspended ?"

"You mean that you didn't know ? It's already been on the national and local radio news at mid day. Everyone knows. Mr. Reddy don't tell me you're the only one in Ipswich who's not aware !"

Flabbergasted, Reddy was on the verge of finding some form of reply when a silver haired figure in a three piece tweed suit appeared in the doorway.

"Ah there you are !" Burleigh exclaimed, advancing towards Reddy. "My goodness, what have you done, Craig ? It seems your article has caused quite a stir. Will you take a drink ?"

"Edmund, good to see you. Yes, an espresso please."

"Good. Lisa make that two espressos please. Come this way to my office Craig."

Lisa gave Reddy a truly winsome smile, her blue eyes sparkling as she flashed her eyelashes before departing on her errand. This media celebrity business, Reddy noted, has some curious side effects.

Burleigh's office was at the back of the building, with bay windows giving a view onto a small Japanese style rock garden. The room itself was more study than office. Two of the walls were lined from floor to ceiling with fitted wooden bookcases stocked with legal tomes. Burleigh's desk was an antique cherry wood table inlaid with marketry around the edges. There was no computer on the table, just an angle poise lamp and a dark green leather protective cover. Two burgundy coloured chairs in regency style were positioned at angles in front of the table.

"Take a chair" Burleigh said. He himself settled down in the chair behind his desk and looked across at Reddy.

"I want your legal opinion Edmund on my employment contract. That's the reason I asked to see you today. On the other hand, I'd also like to get your view on a couple of other things that have come up, so long as you've got the time."

Burleigh gave Reddy an avuncular smile, as if signalling that he always had time where Reddy was concerned.

"I hope you don't mind me saying so, but it does conjure the old saying about locking the stable door after the horse has bolted. Never mind, we can come to that in a minute. What about your article though ? Why don't we first discuss that ?"

Reddy began: "I've been out of Ipswich most of this morning interviewing Russell Westlake, the Redwoods CEO. After that I met up just now with Elaine Cartwright. That's the widow of Thomas Cartwright ? The Ipswich and Blackwater's CEO who committed suicide last Sunday. So I'm not up to speed on what's been happening Edmund. I get the impression from Lisa that the article has caused created ripples ? "

"Understatement of the day" Burleigh said softly, his eyes giving Reddy a pertinent stare over his half glasses. "The fact is that the London Stock Exchange suspended share trading in the Ipswich and Blackwater at 11.25 am, after its' share price plummeted by over 10 per cent. Lisa happened to hear about it on the radio news at twelve. "

Reddy sat back in his seat. He did not wish to be deflected by events. He continued:

"The article is in two parts, Edmund. Have you read the first one in today's Messenger ? I've been too busy myself. Look," he said unfolding his recently purchased copy of the Messenger, "pristine. Still unopened !"

"I think you underestimate the impact that this is going to have Craig. Look, the fact that your article goes into specifics about the Ipswich and Blackwater, the CEGB, Redwoods and also this dubious connection with east European gangs, is going to be setting off alarm bells all over the place. I suspect that you're touching on some raw nerves. And that's not all. Don't forget the Lord Preston resignation this week. With the G20 Finance Ministers meeting here at the week end, I doubt that the Prime Minister was entirely enamoured of having that controversy in the papers."

"Well, the whole point of investigative journalism is to uncover the truth, isn't it ? Even if it is unpalatable or exposes misdeeds. I've put great effort into showing the risks hidden behind these people and their activities."

"Quite so, quite so. And therein lies the danger to you Craig. Believe me, you are attacking some powerful people. They won't take this lying down. Expect a backlash."

"I've still got the second part to write and publish next Tuesday. What are you proposing I do Edmund ? Back off ? That's not an option. I'm committed with the Messenger to do it. In any case, for my own integrity and credibility, I have to follow through."

"I'm not advocating that you don't fulfil your obligations Craig. What I'm saying is that you need to be far better prepared than I think you are currently, to handle the coming storm."

Reddy, flushed with enthusiasm for his investigation and confident in sharing it with his trusted friend, failed to register the import of what Burleigh had advised and continued:

"The second part is in some respects the more important. All the talking heads are pushing for regulatory reforms after the Northern Rock, Royal Bank of Scotland and other nationalisations. Well, part two will argue that what's *not* needed is more government and regulatory intervention. What *is* needed is market forces. Which means an end to bail outs and "to big to fail". It means too a return to sound money principles. I've unearthed a professor at London University, his name's Professor Bernstein. He's an economist and an expert on banking. He's promised to assist me on part two. The aim is to blow wide apart this consensus on so-called "stimulus" and money printing."

Burleigh's concentration had lapsed momentarily, but he quickly recovered his poise. With careful deliberation he said:

"Be that as it may, I think you need to see the clear and present danger in what has happened. Malicious interests may seek to spin this turn of events against you. For instance, they may claim that you had insider information. You'll need to declare that you have no direct or indirect interest in the Ipswich and Blackwater's stock. Another claim will probably be that you have precipitated the crisis. That the fall in the bank's share price this morning was caused by uncertainty generated by your article and that you are guilty of irresponsible journalism. Be prepared to defend yourself against attacks in the media of that kind. Believe me, it could get very nasty."

Burleigh had shifted forwards in his chair and clasped his hands in front of him on the table. He hoped that Reddy appreciated the risks he was facing. These quiet moments together in his study might be the only chance he had to prepare his friend in battening down before the eye of the storm swept over.

Reddy saw the good sense in Burleigh's advice. He had difficulty though with the idea that he himself would become an actor in the story. While he had no illusions about powerful interests and their ruthless instinct for self preservation, as an investigative journalist he saw himself merely as the messenger. That he would become a protagonist ? This was decidedly new territory.

"I appreciate your comments Edmund. You're my trusted advisor, you know that. I'll prepare my defence against those kinds of arguments. Right now though, what I would like to hear from you is your legal opinion on my contract with the Courier. I've been putting off talking to my boss about this. If I'm to have defences in place, I think you'll agree that this is a good place to start ?"

"Quite so, quite so" Burleigh began, taking off his spectacles. "But I'm not a specialist on employment law. I can seek further advice from another lawyer friend of mine who is. However from my reading of your contract it appears that freelancing with third parties is not expressly forbidden. Journalists at the Courier can and do write for other titles from time to time, isn't that so ?"

"Correct. Although the custom is that this is communicated with your boss. Which, to be honest, I haven't done in this case as I'm suspended."

"Well, in that case I suggest the following. First, send an email immediately to your boss explaining what you have done. Apologise for any possible 'oversight' in not having communicated earlier. Second, I think you should add that, since you are suspended, you are not working expressly for the Courier and that the article was written and published after your suspension. That should be enough to put them on the back foot. Just make sure you get that sent to your boss before she gets to talk to you."

Reddy considered these steps wise and agreed to take them. He then remembered his promise to Simon Farley to raise the matter of that morning's SOCA raid.

"Edmund, I've a further favour to ask. Do you recall my friend Simon Farley ? You did the legal work to get him set up with his own company ?"

"Indeed I do. Big fellow. Used to be a professional player with Ipswich Town ? Fine young man. Does he need assistance ?"

"There's potentially some very bad news. You know, last year he started importing some building supplies, roof trusses, into the Ipswich Docks. He teamed up with Russell Westlake to share the shipping costs across from Antwerp. The bad news is this. Simon was down at the Docks' warehouse at dawn to load up some of his consignment and there was a police raid in search of drugs. They gave Simon a hard time. Then their sniffer dogs found some traces of what they claim is cocaine. It's been sent to the labs for testing. They didn't arrest Simon but he's under suspicion. He needs a lawyer. There's no question but that he's innocent. Can you please call him and see what can be done ? He was round at my apartment early this morning, clearly stressed by the experience. I promised him that I'd talk to you about it. "

Burleigh listened with profound attentiveness. When Reddy finished, the lawyer's face was clouded with disquiet.

"Of course I'll help. Fast action is needed I think. Did he say anything specific about who on the Force conducted this raid ? I do know the Chief Constable, but I'll need all the facts before contacting the police."

"That's the queer thing, Edmund. According to Simon the raid wasn't by the Ipswich police. It was the responsibility of SOCA. It stands for Serious Organised Crime Agency. Have you heard of it ?"

Burleigh shook his head. "They're new to me. Nevertheless I'll follow it up. Leave it to me."

Their conversation drifted from there for a few minutes more. Then Reddy took his leave of Burleigh, the lawyer putting a hand on his shoulder as they parted at the reception and repeating: "Get your arguments ready Mr Reddy ! Don't let them hound you."

Reddy hurried down Northgate Street and back to his parked car on Upper Barclay Street. He had work to do back at his apartment. Before driving away, he again switched on his mobile phone to review who might have called. Since having been at Burleigh's offices, he had been inundated with missed calls and text messages, mainly from media people wanting to speak to him. Amongst others, he identified calls from a contact at Sky TV, Radio Suffolk and even Guy Almond for BBC TV news. Did they want to pick his brains for sources, on the back foot because of his scoop ? Or rather were they acting like bloodhounds intent on the kill ?"

Amongst the voice messages, one from Stan Cerny asking Reddy to return his call urgently regarding the IB&B. His curiosity piqued as to what interest Stan might have in the IB&B, Reddy placed the call. After two rings Stan answered:

"Craig, hi. Thanks for calling. Listen, I wanted you to be the first to know. Your article in today's Messenger has stimulated interest here at the AIIB. Things are moving and I'm involved."

Caught for words, Reddy remained silent, trying to fathom the import of what Stan had said.

"Craig ? Are you there ?"

Reddy recovered: "Yes, Stan. Go on, please explain."

Cerny recounted the call he had had with the AIIB's CEO Larry Acheson. Acheson himself had been catalysed into action by a call from Mitchell Havering, a non-executive director of the AIIB. Havering had convinced Acheson that there was a great opportunity to buy some valuable assets from the CEGB at knock down prices. He was leading an initiative for a private rescue operation for the IB&B. There was to be secret high levels discussions and negotiations starting tomorrow between the CEGB and the AIIB. He, Cerny, was instructed by Acheson to participate because of his deep knowledge of the central and eastern European banking market. The target asset AIIB were interested in was CPI GmbH, owned by the CEGB, and Cerny's job was to advise Acheson on the acquisition.

"The bottom line is this, Craig. I'll be able to provide you with some unique details of the events. Confidentiality will have to be respected but there would still be enough details to have another scoop relating to your IB&B story for the start of next week."

Delighted by the news, Reddy offered to make himself available to meet Cerny somewhere close to, but offsite from, the negotiations during the week end. They agreed to firm up the details later and ended the call.

He was about to turn off the phone when it rang. The number showed on the LCD screen; it was Natasha's private number. He took the call.

"It's me" Natasha said, breathlessly.

Reddy was surprised that she was contacting him during her working time. He hoped that she was not putting herself at risk making the call.

"Hi. How are you ? Have you seen my article in the Messenger ?"

"Yes, its good. There's been a huge reaction already in the media, hasn't there. But I haven't got time for that."

Conscious that Natasha might have grabbed a couple of minutes privately somewhere to make the call, Reddy stayed focused:

"OK. What did you want to talk about ?"

"Sean O'Connor" she shot back. "Did you phone him yet ?"

Reddy was perplexed. The name meant nothing to him. He asked:

"Who is he, Natasha ?"

"You didn't see the details I provided about him on the flash disk ? He's waiting your call."

"Sorry, no. I must have missed it. I don't have his details. Who is he ?"

"My whistleblower at the IB&B. He works there on the proprietary trading desk."

Reddy paused. Finding his voice again he said:

"That's fantastic. Is he willing to talk to me ?"

"Exactly. The sooner the better. I've told him that he can trust you. Anyway, don't worry. I'll have him call you instead. I've got to go. Make sure you get to see him within the next 24 hours."

Reddy said "I will."

But she had already cut the connection.

Chapter Thirty Two

14.45 Thursday 19th March 2009. Daily Courier HQ, Universal Tower, Canary Wharf

Guy Almond, the BBC journalist, was standing on the pavement holding a sheet of paper in front of his chest. Behind him across the busy street was a modern office building, on the ground floor of which was a branch of the Ipswich and Blackwater Bank. Almond, wired for sound, was talking to camera:

"The London Stock Exchange suspended the Bank's shares at eleven twenty five this morning after the price fell as much as twelve per cent in two and a half hours of trading on rumours that the bank may be insolvent. An article published in one of this morning's papers raising questions about the Bank's financial health appears to have been the catalyst. The bank's senior management are refusing to speak to the media for the moment but they have issued a press statement, which I have here. Basically, it says that the Bank will not comment on market or media rumours. However it reassures its customers that all branches and cash dispensers are open and operating normally. Customers' deposits are insured and safe, it says."

A female voice over, the tv studio's news presenter, asked:

"Guy, can you give us a sense of what is happening on the street ? You are in Ipswich which is the historic home of the Bank. Are customers calm or is there a sense of panic ?"

"Layla, I've talked to several of the customers visiting this branch this morning. Opinion is divided. Certainly there are some who are withdrawing money. On the other hand, others either hadn't heard about the rumours at all or else were not fazed by them. These last say that they're confident that the deposit insurance is credible. I think that people's perception is influenced by the recent memory of Northern Rock, Layla. None of their retail clients lost any money because of the Government's robust intervention and reassurances about deposit insurance."

"And your Westminster contacts Guy ? Are there any signals yet that the authorities might be make a pre-emptive move to calm the markets ?"

"That's a great question, Layla. The markets hate uncertainty and the Stock Exchange will want to know very soon when the Ipswich and Blackwater's shares can be safely traded again. My sources tell me that the government does want to normalise the situation latest over the week end. I would expect that the Triumvirate – that's the Treasury, Bank of England and the Financial Services Authority – will be meeting in the very near future to come up with a solution."

"Finally Guy, what can you tell us about the Ipswich and Blackwater's next moves ?"

"Well, as you know, the Bank has suffered the grievous loss recently of its CEO, Thomas Cartwright, who committed suicide last week end. His death is currently the subject of an investigation by the Ipswich Police. However they are remaining tight-lipped about the status and nature of their enquiries. There is little doubt that the untimely loss of the CEO has caused difficulties. The succession isn't yet clear. The incumbent Finance Director, Mary Donoghue, was made acting CEO last Monday. We wait to see whether or not she will be confirmed in the post on a permanent basis. There is some speculation I understand, that the Bank's main shareholder the Celtic and European Banking Group, may be under pressure to strengthen the top executive management team at the Ipswich and Blackwater."

"Thanks for those insights, Guy", Layla said, the tv picture image now reverting to her. "

"Let's now go to…………."

Sinclair Monroe, remote control device at hand, zapped Layla from existence and switched the tv set onto CNBC.

"If they've sent Guy Almond to cover the story, then the Beeb see it as part of their headlines, at least for today" Monroe asserted. "They'll probably lead with it on tonight's six o'clock news unless there's other major breaking news in the meantime."

"That's the first time I've seen Almond outside of central London this year" Samantha Cavendish observed caustically. "Anything beyond a one kilometre radius of Westminster and he's invisible."

Monroe gave her a formidable stare from under his eyebrows. "Listen Samantha, we have our journalist Craig Reddy providing the basis for a scoop, only for the television people to be first on the scene providing live coverage. And where from ? From Ipswich for heaven's sake. Slap bang in Reddy's home territory ! They've thrown down the gauntlet."

The two of them were together in Monroe's office, sitting side by side in the two upholstered chairs in front of Monroe's desk. They had turned both chairs around one hundred and eighty degrees so that they could watch the television, a wide flat screen device attached high up on the opposite wall.

Monroe it was who had called an impromptu meeting. Both he and Cavendish were aware from the moment they arrived at the Courier's HQ that morning that Craig Reddy had published an article in the Messenger raising questions of insolvency about the Ipswich and Blackwater Bank. Cavendish's attempts to reach the journalist by phone had so far failed. During the day, each of them had monitored separately developments in the story on the television news. Now they were together for the first time that day and Monroe had already laid out his strategy to Cavendish. It amounted to 'double or quits'. Either Reddy had to be sacked with immediate effect or else reinstated and brought back into the charmed inner circle.

As a precursor to making that decision, he and Cavendish were assessing the potential damage done by Reddy's article. They were also watching events unfold on the television, to ascertain the 'narrative' that the story was being given by their media competition. As Editor of the Courier, Monroe's heart was with print journalism. However his head knew that the war was lost. Television news called the shots these days. Not just in terms of amplification and projection of 'the message'. But also in the way that a subject is, or is not, chosen to be a headline. The conclusion that he was tentatively beginning to draw was that Reddy's article, far from being castigated as reckless speculation, was starting to become a *cause célebre*.

CNBC's on air programme was still coming from its' London studios, although with US markets already open, it was coming to a close. Paul Astor the presenter, renowned for his knock about style with programme guests as well as his ironic sense of humour, was interviewing a City analyst specialising in the finance sector:

"Tell me Stuart, and we've only got thirty seconds left I'm afraid, what is your view on the Ipswich and Blackwater Bank ? This article in today's Messenger newspaper claims that it may be insolvent. Mismatches between loan maturities, non-performing property loans, huge losses on hedging trades. You name it. A catalogue of calamities

? Are we looking again here at casino banking ? Is it a 'too big to fail' bank that the authorities will have to rescue ?"

"Paul, the last full year financial results of the Bank were unspectacular. Its' share price has been under serious pressure, but so has the whole banking sector. The Ipswich is, I think, the sixth largest bank in the UK. I'm not able to comment on the specifics of the article as I personally do not cover this particular stock. What I can say though is that the general public's perception of the Bank as an old fashioned retail bank with a strong legacy business in mortgage lending is definitely at odds with the reality. Analysts who do follow the stock tell me that in the past few years the Bank has moved swiftly to open up new avenues of lending and borrowing, as well as proprietary trading. In that respect I consider the Messenger's article to be absolutely on the money. Of course, the article goes further than that, claiming that losses are being kept off the balance sheet. That remains to be seen."

 "So, if you're a betting man Stuart" Paul said with a cheeky grin, "another bail out on the cards ?"

Caught with a question he hadn't expected, yet which cried out for a simple 'yes' or 'no' answer, Stuart the analyst hedged, slipping into a Scottish vernacular: "Betting's a mug's game, Paul. Anyway, I'm a Scotsman, so I'll keep ma monnaie in ma pocket."

Monroe, himself a Scotsman, zapped the programme and switched off the television with the remote. He scoffed:

"These youngsters are getting too canny with their interview techniques. They've learnt how to avoid answering questions. Just like the politicians."

He arose sprightly from the armchair and stretched. His shirt sleeves, characteristically, were rolled up above his elbows. A sure sign, Cavendish knew, that he was in clansman warrior mode. Ignoring the panoramic view afforded through his wall to wall office windows, he returned to the seat behind his desk.

 Cavendish was obliged to reposition her own chair so that they faced one another.

 "So, what's your view Samantha ? Is this a re-run of the Kerviel saga at Societé Generale ?"

Uncertain of where her boss wanted to establish the Courier's 'take' on the IB&B news, and at the same time keen still to pursue the dismemberment of Reddy's career at the newspaper, Samantha answered:

"You mean, a 'rogue trader' story, as opposed to a pervasive culture of risk taking in the upper echelons of the bank's management ?"

"Yes, precisely. We need to define the approach. Are we going after top management for negligence and possible fraud, or rather only looking at the downfall of another Nick Leeson or Jerome Kerviel. Individuals who exceeded their authority and ended up with fatal losing bets that couldn't be unwound ?"

Having read carefully Reddy's article in the Messenger, Cavendish was aware that it fired criticisms at the IB&B on a number of counts, leaving open a variety of interpretations what the fundamental causes of it's precarious position might be. Further, she had been shocked to read reference to Redwood Country Homes' plight as a borrower from the bank. Although, they were no longer close friends, Cavendish had genuine sisterly feelings for her younger brother, Russell Westlake. There were unspoken sentimental bonds between them. At some stage during the next 24 hours, she wanted to call him and discover if he was coping with things. Now, largely unconsciously, her protective instincts for her brother coloured her attitude to Reddy and his IB&B story. None of this, naturally, could she afford to mention to Monroe. She said:
"Monroe, I think this story is still evolving and has a number of threads. Couldn't we break it down into its' component parts and have a couple of my journalists run with them ? That way, we hedge our bets ?"

"Alright Samantha, do that. However, I want to hold the story together as well. I think this material Reddy has put together is a case of the whole being greater than the sum of the parts. I don't want to lose that edge. That means we need Reddy."

Monroe was already on the phone to his PA:

"Jennifer, get Carrington on the phone for me please."

He pressed the button placing the call on speaker so that Cavendish could also hear Carrington's voice when he came online. As they both waited, Monroe rubbed his chin reflectively then said:

"The big picture for this newspaper is unchanged Samantha. I've got the interview with the Prime Minister upcoming tomorrow afternoon in Downing Street. That's still Plan A. You've got an appearance on the television on Sunday, followed by an interview with the US Treasury Secretary, I think next Wednesday. However, we can't ignore events. And events are turning Reddy's way."

"Hello ? Carrington here, Mr Monroe" the silky smooth voice of Oliver Carrington emitted from the speakers.

"Yes, Carrington. I've got Samantha with me. We're looking at the question of Craig Reddy and how to solve it. Tell us, what's the latest you have from the IT boys ? Did they find anything significant or incriminating on Reddy's laptop computer ?"

Carrington logged the fact that today Monroe was calling him only by his family name, but that did nothing to dent his natural self confidence.

"Not yet, I'm afraid sir. They tell me that analysis of the logs show that Reddy deleted all his work files before handing in the machine. I guess he put everything onto another device. Maybe he suspected something ?"

"I see. So we've got nothing to pin on him ?"

"Too soon to say. The IT techie I spoke to explained that even though he's taken off the files, they may be able to reconstruct the information. Apparently when we think that we wipe clean our data, it remains fragmented in various places on the hard disk. It takes time though to find and reconstruct. I've instructed them to get to it with top priority, as I understood you wanted actionable information against Reddy in short order. Isn't that so ?"

"That was the plan, Carrington. However, events have overtaken us it seems."

"You're referring to Reddy's article in the Messenger ? Isn't that the final nail in his coffin ? Writing a lead article for a competitor without formal authorisation ? If you need an argument surely you have it right there. We can go nuclear on him today. End of story."

"Carrington, when I want you to make executive decisions I'll tell you, understood ?" Monroe admonished. "I want 'damage limitation' here with regards to Reddy. That means first, no fall out with Downing Street. The interview with the PM must go according to plan. But it also means we need to keep Reddy on a close leash. He's the one that has made this Ipswich and Blackwater story into a potential scoop. I'm damned if I'm going to have that lead destroyed by our competitors. Samantha, you must find Reddy today. I don't care how. But I want to make sure he is back in the fold and working for us. With immediate effect get it to him in writing that he is no longer suspended. Is that clear ?"

"Perfectly, Sinclair" Cavendish replied emolliently. "You want him back on the case too, I take it ?"

"Conditionally, yes. First though, we need to understand that his investigation is accurate. If there are going to be challenges to the truth of what he claims then we must have credible defences. Second, he's got to work in a collegial manner. Get it into his head that he's not the Lone Ranger. He works for the Courier. Because of the sensitivity of the subject, further publication is subject to proper Editorial scrutiny."

Samantha remained silent, mindful of the implied criticism. She didn't look forward to the prospect of having to switch tactics in her next conversation with Reddy and appear forgiving and emollient. Certainly not after having gone after him verbally that lunchtime like a rampant pitbull. Monroe was still talking:

"My instinct on this Samantha is that the Courier can and must get the scoop. But without alerting other media competitors. Explain to Reddy that he is re-instated on condition that he gets the scoop on what the authorities are up to on the Ipswich crisis. Tell him that I'm not interested in the ancillary issues, just the headline of whether there is a rescue for the Ipswich or if it will be allowed to fail. Samantha sort it out, please. Remember what Guy Almond said a few moments ago ? The Triumvirate are already cooking something up in Whitehall or somewhere. If Almond has just reported it, then there's no time to lose."

"That suggestion is downright dangerous" Cavendish retorted, feeling as if she was teetering on an emotional precipice.

Oliver Carrington, suave and assured, sat with legs crossed in the seat opposite from her desk, smiling back at her.

"It's the logical next step, if you're committed to Reddy's demise at the Courier" was his calm riposte. His lips betrayed a seductive smile.

Cavendish, seated in the chair behind her desk which was immaculately tidy, swivelled around and looked out through the ceiling-to-floor windows at the cityscape across to the Millenium Dome. Everything was still physically the same, yet her emotions were playing havoc with her habitual managerial calculus.

The hiatus created by having her back to Carrington offered a momentary breathing space in which she had to make a momentous decision. Either protect her own family interests, or her own career. Reddy's scoop in the Messenger had exposed difficulties affecting her brother's company. So far, the media reaction to the article had not picked up on that. But it weighed heavily on her. Then, in addition, her husband was also now pressuring her to do something to silence Reddy. He had told her yesterday evening of word from the Whitehall grapevine that the forthcoming Audit Commission Report on mismanagement of local government finances had been leaked to opposition party MPs. It was rumoured that Reddy was being positioned to write an exposé on the Report which would undermine his position in the Government as junior minister for Local Government. Cavendish had let herself conspire with her husband, that 'something' must be done about Reddy. She too had had the same line of thinking as him until this meeting with Monroe. She was exasperated with Reddy's non conformism and evident bloody mindedness. But now, having watched the unfolding events on television with Monroe and parsing her boss' comments, it had become clear that he was not 'on board' for Reddy's sacking.

She swivelled her chair back, away from the window. Carrington sat motionless, patient, apparently care free. For the first time, she sensed Carrington's vindictiveness. Keeping her own counsel on her real motives, she instructed:

"OK, Oliver. You do it, on condition that its on your own head. I'll claim no knowledge if the matter comes out. Is that understood ? Officially, I am pursuing a reconciliation with Reddy, as per Monroe's instructions."

"Leave it with me" Carrington purred, contentedly. "I'm on the case. I just need to find the right opportunity. I'll keep you in the loop."

With that, he arose languidly from the chair, and left her office. He had accomplished his goal to convince Cavendish to break in to Reddy's apartment to find the confidential information that he necessarily must be hiding.

Cavendish watched him depart, still struggling to contain her emotions. For the first time too, she was apprehensive about Carrington.

Chapter Thirty Three

10.26 Friday 20th March 2009. Outside the Non Conformist Chapel, Ipswich Cemetery, Ipswich.

Her ordeal was not yet ended. Elaine Cartwright hated being the centre of attention. Yet as the distraught young widow, all eyes had been on her as she walked veiled in black, down the aisle of the small chapel accompanied by a black suited Russell Westlake.

Beforehand, she had been terrified by the thought of the funeral service. She didn't know how, but with her father to one side of her, and on the other Russell Westlake, she had summoned the fortitude to sit, stand and pray at the appropriate moments.

Westlake and Thomas Cartwright's father had taken the responsibility to go to the lectern and read from the Bible. Her brother Jack had made a short memorial speech to Thomas. The vicar had spoken of God's work and the mystery of life and prayed forgiveness for Thomas that he had taken his own life. God would understand, he had said.

She had sat, wearing black from head to toe; veiled and motionless. Looking at the closed coffin; numb to her soul. Because this shouldn't be happening. Thomas was still alive; still part of her. She could hear his voice, feel his warmth, see his mirthful eyes, know his thoughts, imitate his laughter.

Now she and Westlake passed through the chapel's porch and the opened tall wooden doors onto the asphalted driveway. Outside it was overcast. Wind occasionally gusted, swaying the branches of the trees nearby. The hearse was parked a few metres away. Pall bearers had already brought out the coffin and placed it into the vehicle's rear. It remained for the chauffeur to drive the hearse slowly, in cortége with the funeral party, up the narrow road to where Cartwright's grave had been prepared about a hundred and twenty metres away.

The vicar, in white pleated gown and black cassock, approached her and Westlake. He was nearly totally bald but for wisps of grey hair around the back of his head. He wore tiny rimless spectacles, behind which his irises were mere pin pricks. In one hand he still held a black prayer book. The wrinkles and blotches on the back of his hands revealed his age. He had a gentle and respectful manner.

"Mrs. Cartwright, if you would like to wait here please a few moments while the guests leave the chapel ? Then we will follow the coffin to its appointed resting place."

She nodded her acquiescence, unable to find words. The vicar was someone known to Thomas' parents but a stranger to her. He looked at her with sympathy, wanting to lift her despond. But her eye lids fell to the ground like collapsed tombstones and the moment when he might offer words of healing evaporated. He looked instead at Westlake, standing dutifully at her side. Their eyes met. Westlake, a man of action by nature, took the unspoken hint in the vicar's eyes:

"I'll be looking after Mrs. Cartwright vicar, don't worry. We'll do fine. Just let us know when to move."

The vicar, short and rotund, thanked him and moved away, a little too willingly, to chaperone the funeral guests as they emerged in ones and twos from the arched porch of the chapel.

Westlake knew that Elaine was suffering badly. He knew too that she would like to be held and comforted by him. But they both knew that that was taboo. That was for another day. They stood together side by side untouching, each cocooned in isolation. She found fleeting escape watching a songbird sitting in a nearby tree. The tree's leafless branches left the creature easily exposed and vulnerable yet it chirruped and tweeted as if convulsed by Spring. Yet to Elaine, it's songs sounded like elegies.

As the other guests continued to emerge from the chapel, Elaine's elderly parents gathered around her to offer moral support. Westlake had shared a few words with her father prior to the service. He'd noticed that Thomas' parents, after formally polite exchanges with Elaine's, had kept their distance. Whether because of a preference for private grief or other more complicated reasons he did not know. If any of these people took exception to his presence and closeness to Elaine, it was not overt.

Among the last of the mourners stepping out from the chapel, he saw Mary Donoghue. Her red hair burned bright, refusing to be quietened by her black woollen coat, trousers and shoes. To Westlake's surprise, at her side she was accompanied by Radomir Angelov. Angelov, Westlake remembered, had told him that he was not going to attend the funeral yet here he was nevertheless. Donoghue and Angelov must have been late arrivals for the funeral service as Westlake had not seen them before the funeral service.

Seeing Westlake with Elaine, Donoghue waved very discreetly at him and then nudged Angelov. He was in the process of extricating a pair of designer sunglasses from the top pocket of his dark suit. He hesitated in raising them to his eyes and looked across in the direction Donoghue was now pointing. When his eyes alighted on Westlake, he waved the sunglasses briefly at him in acknowledgement, without producing a smile.

A half formed question came into Westlake's mind about how Angelov had come to be teamed up with Donoghue this morning and what might have changed his mind to attend Cartwright's funeral. He had no opportunity to develop it further though as the funeral director had signalled to the vicar that everyone was ready. He nonetheless made a mental note to quiz Angelov later when they met.

The vicar had now taken up position behind the hearse, and invited Elaine and Westlake to walk with him. Elaine took Westlake's arm. The four parents followed on behind them as the hearse pulled away at walking pace up the straight road that led away from the chapel towards the plot prepared for Cartwright's grave.

The distance involved was only one hundred and twenty metres but for Elaine the time it took felt interminable. She was oblivious to the muted sounds of footfalls behind her or the low hum from the hearse's motor. The well-tended cemetery grounds populated with mature trees, which in different circumstances might have appeared serene, were blotted out from her cognition. She was weighed down by a dull anger and despair at the finality of death. To her, the entire external world at this moment was monochrome.

Westlake sensed Elaine's deep malaise. It manifested itself in the frailty of her movements and her absolute silence. She needed his arm to hold not just for physical support. Alone, she might melt away, he thought. He tried to focus on the things around him as a way of keeping in touch with life, with normality. To each side of the tarmac road, headstones and graves lined the way. Unintentionally he found himself reading one or two of the headstone inscriptions......"in loving memory"........."born 12ᵗʰ September 1982, taken from his loving family in the bloom of his youth 23rd April 2002"..............the effect of their death dates being to galvanise Westlake's spirits, as this promenade with the dead released new life-giving determination.

The hearse pulled to a stop just in front of a crossroads. The funeral director alighted from the vehicle and opened the back door. He marshalled the pall bearers and oversaw their efforts to extract and lift out Cartwright's coffin. Elaine and Westlake stood to one side watching the proceeding. The cortége of mourners moved off the road and between the headstones towards the open grave which was positioned ten metres away. Hardly anyone spoke.

Looking beyond the hearse and down the straight road that ran through the cemetery and eventually to the exit, Westlake's focus on the events was distracted by the advance of a black car headed towards them. It was still some way off and moving rather quickly; certainly in excess of the twenty mile an hour speed limit. Was someone arriving very late to join the mourners ? He didn't know. The car came closer and he saw that it was a Mercedes 'S' series occupied by a driver and a passenger in the back seat.

The pall bearers had arrived beside the open grave and lowered the coffin by it's edge. Twenty or so friends and acquaintances were congregating around the other side so that the vicar, Elaine and the parents could occupy the space next to the coffin while the vicar uttered last words of salvation.

Angelov too had taken note of the oncoming vehicle. He had removed his sunglasses and easily identified its' make. After all, there were more 'S' series black Mercedes in Sofia than in the whole of Bavaria. He let Donoghue walk across the cut grass to join the others, and hung back on the verge. His curiosity held him to the spot.

The Mercedes slowed almost to a halt at the cross roads and then executed a U turn so that it faced away towards the exit. A tall man in black slacks, black shirt and grey jacket climbed out of the verge side rear door and walked briskly towards the hearse. He wore sunglasses even though there was no sunlight. Westlake didn't recognise him. He turned to the Elaine:

"Who is that, do you know ?" he asked, identifying the advancing black figure with an inclination of the head.

Elaine had difficulty to talk, consumed with other thoughts. Barely perceptibly she shook her head from side to side in response. Westlake turned to the vicar who was close by them:

"Please can you accompany Mrs Cartwright ? I'll join you in a moment. "

He indicated to Elaine to proceed to the graveside with the vicar which she did. Then he stood his ground near the hearse with the intention of intercepting the individual and checking who he was. At all costs he wished to avoid some disruption that might impact the proceedings and possibly fragilise Elaine's already febrile state.

The man in black was moving deliberately and confidently towards Westlake, perhaps to identify himself and offer apologies for a late arrival. He certainly didn't seek to avoid an encounter and creep anonymously off into the group of mourners. From two metres away he fixed Westlake with a resolute look and said:

"Mr. Westlake, isn't it ?"

"That's me, yes" Westlake responded, detecting an accent in the voice "Are you invited to this…….."

Angelov had kept a watchful eye on the newcomer as he rapidly narrowed the distance to Westlake. He had a clear view of his face which was clean shaven and swarthy in complexion. He looked about mid thirties and carried himself upright. It was as if he looked like……

The man put his right hand inside his jacket. When he withdrew it again he was holding a handgun. He levelled it at Westlake and shot him twice in the chest.

As he saw the shot fired and Westlake collapse to the ground, Angelov finished his thought: the black clad figure looked like a professional killer. Also, the gun he had used was familiar. Angelov had one, the same make and model, back in Sofia.

The man instantly turned away and ran for the waiting Mercedes. The driver had never cut the engine. By the time Angelov himself started to run to the scene, the gunman was at the car, opening the passenger door.

Reaching Westlake, Angelov saw no movement. He lay on his back partly on the grass, but with his legs splayed across the verge. There was blood seeping through his white shirt. Angelov knelt down and took his right arm. He thrust back the sleeve of the jacket and felt for his pulse. He was aware of cries and shouting behind him but ignored it all. Still holding Westlake's wrist he looked up and saw the Mercedes gathering speed in the direction of the cemetery exit. He could find no pulse. It had ceased. Westlake was dead. The assassins were free away.

Chapter Thirty Four

10.45 Friday 20th March 2009. Public park, near IB&B HQ, Ipswich

DS Adam was in plain clothes. Wrapped in a black raincoat and hands dug deeply into his pockets, he had left the unmarked police car in the empty parking area and walked down to the small lake in the middle of the park. He found an empty park bench and settled down to await the arrival of Harry Keogh. He idly watched the ducks swimming on the water, occasionally dipping their heads into it in search of food.

Keogh had phoned Adam half an hour previously and urgently demanded an offsite meeting. He had sounded tense, with an undercurrent of excitement. For an ex policeman, Adam reflected, that probably meant that he had genuinely important news. Since having been forced to cooperate with DI Wright's investigation, Keogh had apparently resurrected some of his old policing values.

An elderly woman walking her dog on the far side of the lake came into view. The dog, a young spaniel, was intent on exploration. The owner's attempts at a leisurely and ordered stroll were continually defeated by the animal's instinctual imperatives.

From behind his right shoulder, Adam heard footsteps close in. It was Keogh. He had taken a short cut across the grass rather than the longer route using the tarmac footpath from the road.

"Good morning" he said, brightly.

Adam nodded and invited him to sit besides him on the bench. Keogh did so, placing a black canvas bag that he had been carrying on the bench between them. He glanced at the shaven headed detective and said:

"Its Thomas Cartwright's funeral this morning. They're all there."

"Not you though ?" Adam queried.

"No. Cartwright didn't have time for people like me. Just expected the security side to care of itself."

"You've read this article about the bank published in yesterday's Messenger ?"

"Sure. Someone showed me it" Keogh admitted, cautiously.

"If there's so much dubious stuff going on at the bank, wouldn't the top man want to know ? Wouldn't he be talking to the security boys continually ? Wanting to have his finger on the pulse and be able to put out the flames ?"

"That's not how it works in banks these days. Control is all about technology. Trading is automated. Us guys in security ? We use technology too, for video surveillance, that kind of thing. But when you're talking about the bank's lending and trading, then you have to be in IT. It's them that are responsible for the security of the information systems."

DS Adam, a mere casual user of IT applications, had no desire to explore that area. He asked:

"So as the wise head of security, what offerings of frankincense and myrrh are you bringing me ?"

Keogh opened the zip along the top of the canvas bag. He pulled out a plastic package.

"These devices store copies of video images provided by our security cameras in the proprietary trading room. Cartwright had me install them there about six months ago."

"Do they show anything revealing ?"

"I've copied some images from last Tuesday evening and again from yesterday. They show episodes where Mary Donoghue has entered the trading room and started haranguing a couple of members of the trading team."

"Is that so unusual ? No reason why a top executive can't bite someone's head off to keep them in line."

"Agreed. A touch of discipline with the troops can work miracles. But think about the context. Donoghue's bosses in Dublin are on her back. At their meeting with her in London on Wednesday they insisted on sending in a specialist team of two analysts to run a due diligence on certain areas of the business. I know because I met them when they started this morning. They needed security access IDs."

"That's news, but still. What can I get from these videos ?" Adam repeated.

"I'm not sure. But the camera angle reveals her face. An expert would be able to read her lips and tell you what she's saying."

Adam thought about that. He was still looking out across the lake. The old lady with the spaniel had stopped and was feeding bread to the ducks. Was Keogh feeding him pap, he wondered ? Or was he perhaps on to something?

"OK. Thanks. I'll get our specialists to see what they can come up with."

He made to take the package from Keogh's hands, with the intention to terminate the conversation. Keogh made no effort to hand the package over.

"One more thing before you go" he said.

"I'm listening."

"There was a foreign visitor with Donoghue this morning. He left with her for the funeral."

"And ?" Adam asked, anxious to get back to police headquarters.

"Before leaving he took possession of a new safe deposit box. I took him to it personally. He left money there."

"Do you have his name ?"

"Yes, I do. Angelov. I thought perhaps it might mean something to you."

Reluctant to demonstrate any evident interest, Adam restrained his rising curiosity.

"It might. It might."

Chapter Thirty Five

14.50 Friday 20th March 2009. Home of Lord Preston, between Amersham & Hertfordshire border

Lord Preston was seated alone in his study, deep in thought. The house was quiet, all his guests had either repaired to their rooms or gone off outside for a post prandial stroll in the gardens and grounds. No further meetings or discussions were planned until four o'clock.

It had all started so well, and he had been optimistic that Mitchell Havering's plan could work. Once the various guests had arrived at his home around nine that morning, he had arranged for the golf players among them – namely Declan Moroney, Larry Acheson and himself – to make the short trip over to the Chilterns Golf Club for a relaxing round of golf; also to act as an amicable 'get to know you' session. Stan Cerny, an adviser to Acheson; Fraser Campbell, an 'unofficial' visitor, and Blessing Hall, Lord Preston's private secretary, had teamed up to play tennis on the Court situated at the far end of the grounds.

Now though, having seen the volatile chemistry between Declan Moroney and Larry Acheson, he had serious doubts that he could turn things around.

For one thing, the clock was ticking down. All the participants were agreed that the initiative to find a private sector solution to the Ipswich and Blackwater Bank/CEGB crisis only had until Sunday morning to succeed. The Bank of England, the London Stock Exchange and the Government all required that a formal decision on the next steps for the IB&B be made public by Monday lunchtime. Already, media speculation was rife that a meeting of mandarins in Whitehall was stitching together another nationalisation, with the implicit imprimatur of Downing Street. If they were to succeed, then it was paramount that their talks finish by Saturday night or latest Sunday morning so leaving time to arrange press releases and media events for Sunday evening before the markets opened for business Monday morning.

The other aspect worrying Lord Preston was whether Larry Acheson's startling offer to Declan Moroney was mere grand standing or the first shot across the bows for a bloody negotiation over the value of the commercial opportunities to hand. In any case, he had only a brief window of opportunity to repair the damage and get things back on

344

track. The question was, how to break the deadlock in the context of a rupture in personal relations between Moroney and Acheson. As he sat and pondered alone, his wife half opened the study door and looked in.

"How are you James ? Would you like a cup of tea ? I understand things are, how can I put it ? Simmering ?" she observed cautiously, trying to test her husband's disposition.

James Sturridge looked up from his reverie and sighed. Even if his wife remained diplomatically in the background, she nevertheless was fully apprised of the reigning atmosphere. It hung like a heavy Flemish tapestry.

"Thanks. Earl Grey, and a dose of pure honey please Dorothy. I need sugar to re-energise."

"James ?" she began, "I know you want this to succeed, but don't take it personally. It's not your fault if two grown men behaved like kindergarten miscreants."

"Except that sometimes a firm hand is needed, isn't it Dorothy ?"

In their history of shared parenting bringing up two boys, now young adults and flown the nest, it had been a cardinal rule that corporal punishment was the last resort in bringing the youngsters back into line. It was used exceedingly sparingly, because the threat of its use was real, and so effective. Dorothy smiled with her eyes and replied:

"Sometimes. Usually though the threat is enough."

"Yes, but in this situation I don't have an effective sanction Dorothy. I'm just acting as 'honest broker'."

"That shouldn't stop you tipping the scales a little bit should it ?" she suggested, in complicity, "I'm sure everyone's looking for a positive outcome here James. If they weren't why come in the first place ?"

"Seduced probably by your exquisite cuisine, my dear ?"

"Stuff and nonsense, James" she rebuffed, intent on keeping her husband on the subject at hand. "Listen, James ?"

She stressed the interrogative in her voice to secure his full attention.

Lord Preston was mindful of the fact that he had invited Declan Moroney to join him for a walk in the garden at three o'clock for a private one on one discussion. He was reluctant now to get mired in a longer debate with his wife. Nevertheless, he knew her tenacity all too well.

"Yes, my dear ?"

He gave her a regard which he prayed she would interpret as his full attention.

"James, maybe you need a *deus ex machina* ? You know, an unexpected catalyst from outside to change things around ? Help you get out of the hole; move things forwards ?"

Lord Preston wondered whether he was ever going to get his cup of Earl Grey tea. He persevered:

"Dorothy, Moroney's going to be joining me here in a few minutes. Quickly, please, who or what are you talking about ?"

"Darling, that clever man Mitchell Havering. He put you up to this didn't he ? Shouldn't he share the pain ? Give him a ring. Tell him that I personally welcome him to stay and that 'no' is the wrong answer to my invitation." She added, impishly, as she made to leave: "Apart from that, he is rather charming !"

Lord Preston found himself about to speak to an empty doorway. He stopped himself. What was it she had said ? Why come in the first place unless you're looking for a positive outcome ! Dorothy, God bless her ! He began to feel animated for the first time since lunch.

The hint of an idea began to form in his mind. First, a positive outcome had to mean positive on all sides, with no fear among the participants that the negotiations were a zero sum game. Second, the personal chemistry conflict between Acheson and Moroney had to be unravelled. Who better to catalyse that than Mitchell Havering ? As a non-executive director of the American International Investment Bank he was a trusted advisor of Acheson. At the same time, knowing the man well, he could assist Lord Preston in managing him. As for Moroney, while he may not know Havering, nevertheless as chairman of the Tory Party constituency for Blackwater, he was personally engaged in the mission to save the Ipswich and Blackwater Bank from insolvency. It was that engagement indeed that had instigated Havering's meeting Lord Preston yesterday at the Constable Country Club, urging him to accept the role of 'honest broker' in a Havering-inspired initiative to find a quick and robust private sector deal to save the bank. They both wanted to avoid another damaging bank nationalisation.

Unconsciously, Lord Preston's hand found its way onto the cordless telephone sitting on the low table to the right of his armchair. Havering's mobile number was stored in memory. He dialled. After four rings it answered:

"Mitchell Havering"

"Mitchell, afternoon. This is James. Have you got a few moments ?"

"Absolutely. Listen, I was meaning to phone you. Find out how the talks are evolving. Anything I can do to help ?"

"Yes, to be frank. We have a time out from the proceedings. It's caused by some personality issues between Declan and Larry. The Texan came out all guns firing at poor Declan. He declared that the CEGB's banking and investment business in central and eastern Europe is rotten. Then added insult to injury by telling him he could think himself lucky if AIIB took it off his hands for one euro."

There was silence on the other end of the call. Lord Preston asked:

"Mitchell ? Did you hear me ?"

"Yes James, I did. Tell me, how did Declan respond ?"

"Well it was Irish pride well and truly hurt. For about ten minutes he would hardly talk to either me or Larry – we were out playing a round of golf at the time ? – he curled up into his shell so to speak. It took all my diplomatic skills to keep the pair still playing. As you can imagine, the atmosphere was poisoned for the rest of the game."

"And no sign of reconciliation from Larry. Am I right ?" Havering asked, apparently knowing in advance the answer.

"Correct, you obviously know your man."

"Still hasn't gotten over being a fighter pilot in Vietnam. Plus being Texan, nuance and compromise aren't key components of his negotiating toolkit."

"Mitchell, listen. You've put me up to this and I for one definitely want to see a successful result emerge this week end. But I need your insights into Larry. I'd like to invite you to come over and join us for the week end. As I 'm the host and *maitre de ceremonie* I have the freedom to do that. Will you join us ? By the way Dorothy insists that you come too. She says you're charming."

"James, please tell your wonderful wife that I most graciously accept. Listen, I'm not surprised this hasn't started smoothly. Not to worry. That's Larry upsetting the apple cart to see how people react. He puts them on the back foot. We just need to reel him in a bit. Leave that to me. When should I be there ?"

"As soon as you can get yourself down the A12 and around the M25 ? Say in two hours. We have a resumption of talks scheduled for four o'clock and dinner at eight."

"James, some advice, if I may. Meet at four by all means but don't discuss business. Let's do that tomorrow morning. I'll be over for six and you and I can appraise the way forwards privately before dinner. Let's get everyone back around the table enjoying themselves first."

Lord Preston was amenable to the suggestion. They ended their call. Next on his agenda was Declan Moroney. He checked his watch. Already five past three. He climbed out of his armchair, took the thick navy blue Polo pullover hanging off the back of the chair at his writing desk, and put it on. The weather outside was dry but cool. He didn't want to catch cold, nor lose the 'smart casual' style that all guests had adopted for the week end.

Leaving his study door ajar, he went out into the corridor in search of Moroney. He had suggested to him earlier to meet at three in his study. Yet his nineteen thirties built house was on a grand scale and newcomers did on occasion get themselves disoriented and lost. He went down the corridor past the dining room towards the main entrance hall. It was illumined by large windows both in the front door and to each side. The windows themselves held colourful art nouveau style mosaic window panes.

Declan Moroney had been between a rock and a hard place many times before in his career. He'd learnt the black arts of political improvisation, subterfuge, shameless lying and predator-like business negotiation.

Right now, Moroney was between the rock of the CEGB's lack of ready cash to fund a rescue of the IB&B, and the hard place of having his bluff called in a time-boxed game with Larry Acheson. Acheson's American International Investment Bank was the only immediately available buyer of the assets that the CEGB could sell to raise the full amount of required funds.

Moroney paced around his bedroom, like a caged tiger. The room was on the first floor of Lord Preston's house at the rear side, with a view over the gardens and beyond to the rolling hillsides of the Chilterns.

With Reddy's Messenger article having already published a figure of £ 1,2 billion of trading desk losses, Moroney knew that at least 1.5 billion euros cash was needed to demonstrate to the markets on Monday morning that the CEGB had the financial muscle to rescue the IB&B. From the cancellation of the Dublin commercial centre project he'd agreed with Sir Peter Westlake, he had £500 million. He still needed another £1 billion. In normal circumstances, CPI's business was worth around 2.8 billion euros. But Larry Acheson knew that this negotiation was not 'normal circumstances', it was a fire sale.

Which was why Moroney was upset with Acheson's offer. Acheson had in effect signalled from the outset that the game was up. He surmised that CPI's assets were up for grabs at pennies to the pound.

Ceasing his repetitive pacing from door to window, Moroney took his mobile phone and placed a call to Cieran Connolly, the senior person of the due diligence team at the IB&B.

"Cieran, its Declan. Give me a head's up on what you've found. Any more black holes in the IB&B's accounts ?"

"Hello Declan. We've gotten ourselves set up here at the headquarters this morning. Mary Donoghue's gone off to the funeral. Everyone else is cooperative but the atmosphere is electric. Damien and I have access to the trading and financial systems. We've defined strategies how to proceed with the due diligence. It'll need at least a week to prepare initial findings. We haven't even yet spoken to Donoghue."

Moroney said, his patience worn thin, "But what's your gut feeling ? Is this loss likely to be far bigger or is the £ 1.2 billion figure in the right ball park ? I need to know."

"I've gone into other financial organisations with these kinds of losses. Experience says that the first approximate figures mentioned are usually underestimates. Particularly where the losses are part of a culture of excessive risk taking encouraged by management."

That was not what Moroney had hoped to hear. He closed the call in exasperation. He sat down on the bed and slipped on his brogues. On the bedside table was a decorative green-glazed clay four leaf clover. Moroney smiled ironically.

'Time to dissimulate' he said to himself.

He rose from the bed, opened the bedroom door, and headed for the staircase to go downstairs for his planned one on one with Lord Preston.

There was a noise of heavy footsteps above his head to his left. Glancing through the wooden stair banisters, Lord Preston saw Moroney descending.

"James, God bless, what a fine house you have" Moroney enthused. "To be sure, it's like home from home. Was it your wife who put the four leaf clover in my bedroom ? You know, I'm not a superstitious man, but it's reassuring to have a token of good luck to look after you."

Unprepared for this outpouring of homespun bonhommie, Lord Preston recalibrated his thinking. Had his wife really put a four leaf clover in the bedroom ?

"I'm delighted to know you feel at home Declan. Are you up for a stroll around the grounds ? The weather's holding up for the moment. Good opportunity to have a private chat perhaps ?"

Moroney nodded his assent as he stepped off the staircase into the hall. Lord Preston opened the front door wide open and invited him through. As Moroney passed outside, Lord Preston saw his wife approaching from the far end of the corridor. She was carrying him his cup of Earl Grey tea. He threw his arms up in the air, shrugged, and went outside to join the chairman of the CEGB.

"Does the man have no manners ?" Moroney exhaled. "God help us all if he is the best that the American banking industry can send to Europe these days. Or is it just me, James ? Am I old fashioned ? Can't we have politeness and respect any more in business ? Is it all only pushy egotism and avarice now ? To be sure that's not the way we do business in Ireland. Not even today. May the Devil take him's what I say !"

They were walking side by side, Moroney with his hands tucked deeply into the pockets of his green windcheater, a replicated version of the national rugby team's kit. Lord Preston guided him across the gravelled house frontage towards the tennis court at the side.

"I agree with you Declan. Politeness and respect can go a long way in building solid business relationships.   But let's be honest, self interest and its' prosecution is what drives human nature isn't it ? Adam Smith based the Wealth of Nations on that assumption didn't he ? He was the first to argue that self interest was in fact in the social good, that it drives isolated individuals to cooperate together in exchange. Hence the effectiveness of markets."

"Aye, there's nothing wrong with the profit motive. I'm on common ground with you there James. My problem is the way this Yank goes about his business as if he can run straight over you. He doesn't care who or what he destroys in the process. I can't understand really why he's here. To be handed a privileged opportunity to steal some of the CEGB's assets at derisory prices ? "

"Declan, I want to be transparent and I want to see a positive outcome to the problems we need to solve with you to keep the Ipswich and Blackwater Bank solvent. You'll remember it was Mitchell Havering, the brother of Neill the Tory MP, who instigated this initiative ?

Moroney nodded his head, then allowed his chin to sink contemplatively, his eyes pinned to the ground as they were now walking down an uneven paved path at the side of the house.

 "He's a solid man, Mitchell. It was the fact that you and he set this up that I accepted to come. What I didn't expect is this Larry Acheson. Why is he here, James ?"

"You're probably not going to agree with this at first hearing, but in our view he's here to enable you to do things which, in this very tight spot the CEGB is in, you won't be able or possibly even allowed to do."

351

Moroney scoffed dismissively at the proposition. He countered:

"This man has nothing we need, and the idea of cooperating on any joint efforts is anathema. If he thinks he can get control of the Ipswich and Blackwater Bank in a fire sale then he's pissing in the wind."

They had reached the back of the house. Before them was a broad expanse of lush green lawn. Beyond, a low continuous privet hedge with one entrance point from the lawn ran horizontally the length of the lawn's edge. On the other side was a rose garden. Lord Preston guided his guest towards the entrance. In the sky above, the sun was making weak efforts to break through the carpet of grey cloud.

"Ok, Declan, I understand your position. So let me ask you this. What is CEGB's number one business priority in all of this, bearing in mind the circumstances and constraints ? You have difficulties ongoing back in Ireland which consume much top management time, I understand. Now the shares of the IB&B are suspended and the markets expect a clear statement of direction latest Monday morning. If not, this Government has form as you know. They'll nationalise the bank. You have no choice but to act now. What's your game plan ?"

The rose garden was rectangular in shape. Paved paths were laid around all four sides of the internal perimeter, as well as two more traversing perpendicularly into the centre, dividing the rose garden into four segments. At the centre, where the two paths met, was an ornamental stone sundial with a vertical wrought iron needle rising in the middle. Without a word the two men gravitated towards the sundial.

Lord Preston pulled up in front of it. Moroney naturally did likewise, staring disinterestedly at the object. With no direct sunlight in evidence, the device wasn't performing its function. Into the silence caused by Moroney's own inner struggles with conflicting impulses and perceptions, Lord Preston cajoled:

"Declan, I understand this isn't easy. But you're the leadership of the CEGB. What's your bottom line ?"

Moroney smiled ironically and, for the first time since they had left the house, looked Lord Preston in the eye. He confessed, tongue in cheek:

"You English, you'll be the death of us Celts to be sure ! You're Roundheads to us Cavaliers. But so be it, we can't change that. James, listen. The IB&B was supposed to have been our spearhead into the UK market. That's why we put Thomas Cartwright in there a few years back. He was English and so understood the mentality and the market, but he was also 'one of us' ? He'd grown up in Ireland and been with the CEGB for some time. He knew our culture and way of working. The problem is that the original plan got derailed. Or rather, side-tracked.

Because we had implicit trust in Thomas, we also let him head up our expansion into central and eastern Europe. Even that's not quite right. We *encouraged* him. Of course, we sent Mary Donoghue over to Ipswich to provide Thomas with top management support and additional financial engineering expertise. But other than that, we basically gave them *carte blanche*. In retrospect, that was a massive management mistake."

Lord Preston sensed that at last Moroney was zeroing in on what mattered. He sought to guide him further, asking:

"So is holding on to the Ipswich and Blackwater the CEGB's bottom line ? And if so, what price are you willing to pay to achieve it ? As things stand, the bank is heading for insolvency and the regulators and politicians are hovering like vultures. You're not in a strong position currently. The CEGB doesn't even have a banking licence in the UK, it's awarded to the IB&B independently, after it demutualised from being a building society."

"The UK banking market is important for us, James. Looking ahead beyond this stock market crisis, it has enormous potential. The CEGB sees the IB&B's banking license as one of its crown jewels. We desperately want to keep it; not least because the Irish market is in turmoil. So, to answer your question. Finding a durable solution to the IB&B is our bottom line. The problem is that we simply do not have the cash flow available to fund a recapitalisation. Going cap in hand to the markets with bond issuance or new equity also isn't likely to be greeted with enthusiasm by the markets."

"I fully agree Declan. So that, if I'm not wrong, leaves you with but one option, doesn't it ?"

Moroney had taken a hand out from his windcheater pocket and fingered the tip of the sundial needle. He said:

"Asset sales ?"

"Precisely"

"CPI GmbH ?"

"Seemed the most likely candidate to me and Mitchell Havering, to be honest."

"Hence the participation of the Texan !"

Lord Preston saw from Moroney's expression that the penny had dropped finally. It was important that Moroney see that Acheson was not in the business of trying to take away the IB&B. His earlier tee shot on the golf course, mentioning CEGB's CPI Gmbh subsidiary had been genuine, even if the price he offered was absurd. To press the point home he continued:

"Declan, the AIIB has its main banking business on the continent. Acheson wants to strengthen its' presence there. He has no remit to enter the UK market. AIIB are cash rich. Do a heads of agreement deal with him this week end that will provide the CEGB with the funds to recapitalise the IB&B. Add into the mix a completely new management team at the top of the IB&B. Give that team an explicit commitment to clean up the bank in alignment with the wishes of the regulatory authorities. A package of that nature announced with the backing of the full CEGB Board plus a few key institutional shareholders ? Then, a formal request to the Bank of England for temporary emergency liquidity to be repaid in full after the IB&B has been recapitalised through the sale of CPI. How does that sound ?"

Moroney, dissimulation uppermost in his mind, felt that he had now caught Lord Preston on his hook:

"I'm not sure, James. You see, the IB&B needs at least 1.5 billion euros. The book value of CPI is about Euro 2.8 billion, but that's without write downs and mad Texans bidding one euro ! Added to that, our succession plan for the IB&B isn't in place. We don't see Mary Donoghue as a permanent replacement for Thomas. Yet we don't have an alternative name in the frame. That is unless...."

"Unless what Declan ? "

Moroney slowly lifted his finger from the top of the sundial needle. As he did so, some rays of sunlight at last broke through the clouds and lit up the rose garden. The sundial needle for a few moments created a shadow to reveal the time.

"Unless you, James, would accept an offer to become the IB&B's new Chief Executive Officer ?"

Chapter Thirty Six

14.30 Friday 20th March 2009. Police HQ, Civic Drive, Ipswich

The frenetic activity he had seen on arrival at Police HQ a few minutes earlier had alerted Reddy to the fact that something important had happened, although he had not fathomed what. Now, seated again in the interview room with DS Adam, he was learning the facts.

"DI Wright won't be able to join us, I'm afraid. This meeting too will have to be shorter than I'd hoped " DS Adam explained. "There's a press conference this afternoon at five o'clock and DI Wright and I have a scheduled meeting with our Chief at 15.00 to plan that."

Reddy exhibited no emotion. Inside though, he was irritated by the change. He'd foregone the opportunity to drive down to Amersham and profit from Stan Cerny's presence at the secret rescue meeting for the IB&B being run by Lord Preston. For what ?

DS Adam was still talking:

"We have a new crisis. In fact, we're downright overstretched with this… " DS Adam paused for dramatic effect, locking eyes with Reddy's, before adding: "killing of Russell Westlake."

His words almost knocked Reddy out of his chair.

"Westlake's dead ? How ? What happened ?" he asked, in disbelief.

"He was shot this morning while attending the funeral of Thomas Cartwright by an unknown gunman who fled the scene and has not yet been apprehended. Needless to say, with a murder enquiry now on our hands, you'll appreciate that DI Wright has other priorities right now."

The news left Reddy's speechless. The lost opportunity of another scoop for his own investigation together with the travails he still had with the Courier, the fabric of his thoughts while on his way to the Police station, faded from his mind.

Yesterday he had been with Westlake and the experience was still fresh in his memory. He had vivid images of the man and his behaviour traits, especially at the end of their meeting when they had had a spat over the SOCA raid. Now, Westlake was probably lying on a gurney somewhere in a hospital or morgue, awaiting a forensic assessment before being placed into a freezer. Reddy swallowed involuntarily, his mouth suddenly having dried. He said:

"Sorry, you've completely thrown me off balance. I interviewed Westlake only yesterday. For further material for my own investigation ? Do you remember ? I told you about it last time we met ?"

"Indeed I do, Mr. Reddy. That is why DI Wright and I wanted to speak to you again. We concluded that there were more questions we need to put to you."

"That's not a problem. You have my full cooperation." Reddy declared, wondering to himself whether or not it would be wise to mention his discussion with Westlake on the topic of the SOCA raid and its impact on his friend Simon Farley.

"We expect nothing less. So let's get to it." DS Adam the rugby player liked to get 'stuck in' to test the mettle of the opposition "Tell me, what would be the motive for someone to kill Russell Westlake, in your opinion ?"

"Cui bono ? Who benefits from his death ?" Reddy responded, surprised by the question. With no reply from Adam, he continued: "Go to the heart of the matter to find a reason. I would look into Westlake's activities abroad. I don't know if you are aware, but he was a joint owner in Sirocco Property Investments which was developing property on the Black Sea coast. He couldn't have realised those ventures without local partners and they may have been less than wholesome. At least, that's what I learnt talking to the Courier's journalist in Bulgaria."

"Are you implying that Westlake was engaged in criminal activity out there ? Maybe financial crimes ?"

"That, I'm not sure. All I can say is that the last annual report and accounts of CPI GmbH, the main vehicle of the CEGB in continental Europe, show that sirocco is an associate company operating out of Bulgaria with construction projects on the Black Sea coast. The key shareholders in that firm, apart from CPI itself, were Thomas Cartwright and Russell Westlake. I believe there were local businessmen too."

DS Adam was both surprised and embarrassed by Reddy's declared source of information. That it was already in the public domain for those who cared to look, made him feel *gauche*. He asked:

"So, you think Westlake may have created enemies abroad while developing his business interests there ? Perhaps he stood on too many toes without realising it ? But if that were the case, why not kill him there ?"

"Perhaps that would be too obvious ? An extra territorial killing would throw local police off the scent ?"

"Or killing someone at their friend's funeral is making a statement ?" DS Adam conjectured.

"Yes, I hadn't thought of that. But if so, what statement does it make Detective ? And to who ? I'm afraid I'm out of my depth with such speculations."

"So tell me instead about possible motives back in the UK. You met Westlake yesterday and interviewed him. What was your take away from that ? In the light of what's now happened ?"

Curiously, Reddy discovered that he was able to conduct these thought experiments with ease. The ideas flowed:

"All is not what it seems at Redwood Country Homes, in my opinion. Of course, as CEO, it was in Westlake's interest to present me with a picture of harmony and normality. Who in the right mind would expose to a financial journalist the weaknesses and risks facing their company ?"

DS Adam was beginning to warm to Reddy. His account had affinities to the conclusions he and DI Wright had drawn following their own meeting with Westlake on Tuesday. He ventured a witticism:

"Mr. Reddy with your reputation for shutting down businesses, I'm sure that's true ! The Ipswich and Blackwater Bank is still suspended from the Stock Exchange isn't it ?"

Reddy smiled briefly at the detective's quip, but let it perish unanswered. He continued:

"My take is that Redwoods may be in serious financial trouble. They have loans outstanding of nearly £ 1,2 billion, principally with the

Ipswich and Blackwater Bank. Personally, I suspect that there may be other loans concocted somewhere off the balance sheet too. I spoke yesterday to Elaine Cartwright. One of the results of that conversation was her confirmation that her husband and Russell Westlake were not only close business partners but also firm friends. They did "boys' stuff" together, she said."

"You met with Elaine Cartwright ? Mr. Reddy you are a resourceful man it seems. How did you find her ?"

Reddy's disclosure of a meeting with Elaine Cartwright caught DS Adam on the back foot. Despite their best efforts, the police had so far failed to get to see her to talk about the circumstances of her husband's suicide. They had no mobile phone number for her and she did not respond at her home number. When a squad car had been sent around to her house, they found it locked up and apparently empty. Only after being called to the scene of this morning's murder had he and DI Wright met her and taken a statement. But that had covered only the immediately preceeding events.

Reddy said casually, "Journalists have their methods you know. It's not that difficult these days to trace people's mobile phone numbers you know. But let me resume, if I may ?"

DS Adam nodded.

"Now, with Thomas Cartwright dead," Reddy continued, "I think that Westlake would have been a very worried man. The future of Redwoods is in the hands of it's creditors. They're over-leveraged and there's a major downturn in the house building market. Throw into the mix the cancellation of that huge Loxwood Park development near Colchester – that would have accounted for about 25% of Redwoods' total projected house sales over the coming three to four years - and you can see that Westlake looks increasingly like a trapped man. The only outlets to resolve his dilemma would be either to sell off some assets, which effectively means the firm's land bank, or else renegotiate the repayments on his debts."

This picture of a harassed and desperate Redwoods CEO, running from pillar to post in search of solutions to insuperable constraints, appealed to DS Adam. Having met Westlake at the man's offices, he was less than convinced himself that the man's polished exterior and self confident aura were much other than camouflage for a wily business operator. One willing to take audacious risks to achieve profits and success.

"That's a compelling scenario you've constructed" DS Adam enthused, "however, why would any of those financial problems cause his murder ?"

"I'm not saying that they would. At least, not directly. But I do think that the future was looking bleak for Westlake and his company. Think about it, detective. He would now have to deal with a new management regime at the Ipswich and Blackwater when renegotiating his debts. Debts, by the way, that are looking increasingly unsustainable."

DS Adam's experience of negotiating debts was limited to decisions about paying off his monthly credit card. That was cause enough for stress, given his take home pay. He conceded that being responsible to repay £ 1,2 billion could cause nightmares if you knew you were unable to pay. Reddy, observing the detective's occluded expression, pressed on:

"If I may, I want to draw to your attention to one more piece in the jigsaw which may have influenced how Westlake lived his last days ?"

"Go on, I'm keen to hear your view."

"I think that Redwoods was vulnerable to a take over and that would have been anathema to Westlake. As founder, entrepreneur and CEO, Redwoods was his baby. He would never let go without a fight."

"You think the firm was vulnerable because its share price is low ? I'm not a stock analyst, but that puts it in the same category as about most other publicly traded companies in the UK these days" Adam countered sceptically.

"It's not just that. Rather, the combination of all the factors: over-leveraged, poor revenue prospects, very low share price, loss of confidence by it's chief creditor and, this is the perhaps the most telling: poor defences against any potential predator wishing to acquire the shares on the open market. Westlake didn't have an alliance of shareholders with a majority stake."

"And, to your knowledge, were there any predators prowling around Redwoods Mr Reddy ?"

"Yes, I suspect that there were. Detective, you know the saying 'keep your friends close, and your enemies closer' ? There is a Panama-based nominee company that had accumulated a share holding of 12 per cent in Redwoods by the last published accounts and which has been aggressively adding to that position since. I asked Westlake about it when we met, but he waved away the question as irrelevant. My instinct with Westlake is to assume the opposite of everything he told you. He was the master of disguise. That probably helped him become an effective risk taker and entrepreneur. I think he knew who is behind the money in that Panamanian investment vehicle. If I'm right, that's because they were established friends. What we have to consider though is this: could this 'friend' potentially sucker Westlake ? Could this person strategically outmanoeuvre Westlake ? For example, by cosying up to his creditors and doing a deal behind Westlake's back ?"

"Mr. Reddy," DS Adam said, deeply intrigued, "you have a devious mind. But I think you may have something. You know, the Police too have their methods, including connections to our international colleagues. This Panamanian company you mention attracted our attention too. We know who owns it…….."

DS Adam's sentence was interrupted as there was a knock on the door and DI Wright entered. Both men were taken aback by her unexpected arrival. Although she still looked athletic and meticulously dressed, Reddy thought she looked harassed and weary. The added stress of handling this morning's dreadful events was taking its toll.

"Charlie, I was looking for you. Reception told me I'd find you here. Good morning Mr Reddy. I'm sorry that I couldn't join this session as intended. DS Adam has no doubt explained to you the circumstances ?"

"Yes, he has. I'm….."

DI Wright was in hyper drive, not waiting to hear Reddy's reply:

"Good. Look, Charlie, something's come up. I've received an updated list of names of people attending the funeral. The first draft we obtained wasn't complete. It turns out that Angelov was there ! In his statement to us which I've only received a few minutes ago, the vicar described a man who he'd seen outside the chapel after the service and then again after Westlake had been shot. He said that this man was the first person on the spot to reach Westlake and checked his pulse. The vicar didn't have a clue who it was but confirmed that the man was with Mary Donoghue. I've just spoken by phone with Donoghue. She's confirmed that Angelov was with her."

"So where is he now ?" DS Adam queried with animation. "Let's talk to him immediately."

"That's the point. He absconded. No one remembers seeing him leave the cemetery, not even Donoghue. I think we should put out an alert for him at once and pull him in for questioning."

"As a suspected accomplice ?"

"Potentially. I don't know. What I do know is it's an offence to leave the scene of a crime like that. We've got an a priori case for arresting him on sight."

Wright stood still for a moment. Then, as if a light went on in her mind, she asked Reddy:

"Does the name Angelov means anything to you, Mr. Reddy ? A Bulgarian."

"No, but that he is Bulgarian is possibly important. Russell Westlake had business interests on the Bulgarian Black Sea. And there's something else, now I remember it. Until recently there was a Bulgarian working at Redwoods. He seemed to have privileged access to Westlake. I'm trying to remember his name....... Bourov. That's it. Georgi Bourov. I've even met him myself once. Strong as an ox. Used to be a weight lifter back in Bulgaria I was told."

DS Adam took note of the name. He wanted to discover how Reddy had come to meet this man Bourov but DI Wright took over the meeting:

"I wanted to have an extended conversation with you Mr. Reddy about the Ipswich and Blackwater Bank and possible financial crime. Unfortunately I'm going to have to defer that to another day. This morning's events have caused turmoil to our plans. We were expecting to talk again to Mr. Westlake about some of his activities. With his murder, obviously our priority is to shift the focus our investigation to find his killer. So I'm afraid I'm going to have to bring this particular session to a close. DS Adam will brief me."

DI Wright opened the door of the interview room to demonstrate that Reddy's exchanges with her colleague were terminated. The two men quit their chairs. Reddy made to leave, but turning sideways at the open door he offered a parting comment:

362

"Inspector, when you return your investigation to Thomas Cartwright and his activities, I'm at your disposal. I believe financial crime was central to what he and Donoghue were doing. I have plenty of circumstantial evidence plus some of the financial facts surrounding his operations with both the Ipswich & Blackwater and Sirocco Property Investments, his operating vehicle for the central and east European region. I'd be happy to talk you through them. I'd suggest to you though that police resources are insufficient to fight financial crimes in banking. There's a significant amount of fraud, around. Look at the case of Bernie Madoff on trial now in the US ?. That shows that the biggest heists in the banking industry are those which remain entirely hidden until or unless the casino bets that were placed blow holes in the balance sheet so egregious that even banksters cannot conceal them."

On that note, Reddy turned on his heels and was gone.

DS Adam and DI Wright exchanged looks. This last version of journalist Craig Reddy was not one that they had seen before. DS Adam observed:

"The man's on a mission. I have the impression he's upped his game since he's made the headlines. What do you think, Paulie ?"

"He'll need to. Look at us, we're also in the eye of the storm. Haddock's going to be on my back real soon if we don't find Westlake's killer. Did you glean anything new from Reddy ?"

"Yes. He thinks that Russell Westlake was running around in ever more desperate rings because of financing problems with Redwoods. Essentially the same line that I tried to test with him when we interviewed him Wednesday. The added value in Reddy's analysis though is he thinks there is a predator investor out there working hand in glove with the Ipswich and Blackwater. Reddy said there are some Bulgarian interests working with Westlake on the Black Sea and he concludes these are the same people that have been buying up Redwoods' shares through that Panamanian firm ? What he doesn't know is that it is Angelov ! "

"Charlie that's ammunition to the argument that Angelov is an accessory to murder. The motive being to destroy confidence in the company by killing the founder and entrepreneurial guru behind its' growth ?"

363

"And when the markets crater the firm's shares further, step in and buy them out for peanuts, offering to do a deal with the creditors."
"But why take the risk of being at the scene of the crime ?"

"It's a perfect alibi."

"But not yet a water tight argument for our investigation, Charlie. There are too many loose ends and the Super won't buy this line without more evidence. First, we've got to be on the alert for that S series Mercedes. No one present at the funeral succeeded to read the car's number plate. Second, we must notify someone from Westlake's family of his killing and have them come to identify the body. Third, before Haddock fires us, we must interview Elaine Cartwright and explore with her the relationship between Westlake and her husband."

"Or indeed her husband's relationship with Mary Donoghue ?" Adam added. "Don't forget, the feedback from Intelligence on the list of client names. Four are known ex Irish provisional IRA. I communicated that information to the CEGB in Dublin yesterday. That, plus this scoop article by Reddy in the Messenger appear to be the triggers for the due diligence team to be sent in to the IB&B headquarters ?"

"Which Mary Donoghue will be most keen to thwart, if there has been any wrong doing. Latest Monday morning Charlie, I want her in here for questioning." DI Wright insisted, with stern determination.

Chapter Thirty Seven

16.48 Friday 20th March Seafront, Undercliff Road, Felixstowe

Reddy found Sean O'Connor, as planned, sitting at a table on the terrace outside a restaurant café on Undercliff Road. He wore a high quality brown leather coat, buttoned up against the chill wind blowing off the sea. Incongruously, he wore John Lennon style round rimless spectacles, as if intent on conveying an image of a down at heel bohemian intellectual.

After the shortest of introductions, O'Connor insisted on leaving the café to walk together along the seafront back towards the pier and his parked car. They were face on into the bracing wind; one which encouraged the seagulls to circle and glide above the grey North Sea.

Underway side by side for a couple of minutes, and with not a soul around them to overhear their conversation, O'Connor began to tell his story.

"We're called the 'Irish Tigers' " he explained. "There's only ten of us, all guys, all Irish, all hand-picked by Mary."

"And all supposedly fiercely loyal to her too." Reddy put it as a statement but was looking at O'Connor for confirmation.

"Correct. We were all selected by her on three self-reinforcing criteria. First, having proven Irish nationalist sympathies. Second, having successful financial trading experience. Third, being willing to swear loyalty to Mary. She was the Queen Bee. We were the worker bees."

"So the quid pro quo for your connivance in her schemes was the incentive of huge bonuses. Is that it ?"

"Not only, but yes that played a role."

"What sort of bonuses were on offer Sean ?"

"Enough to turn young guys' heads. I mean, your salary might be a mere £100,000 a year, whereas bonuses could be easily six times that. Some guys pulled in well over £ 1 million a year."

To Reddy, these earnings figures were astounding. He had difficulty contemplating the effect such windfall wealth might have on young men. So he asked:

"The entire Tigers team is young men, you say ? What kind of team culture did you build ?"

"Yeah, well we're all roughly the same age. Between 30 and 38, not older. On the trading side it was fiercely competitive. Every man for himself. But socially we had a mad time together, being single and all."

"You had some 'bonding' sessions and the like ?" Reddy speculated. His mind conjured an image of boisterous, testosterone-fuelled alpha males revelling in some lap dancing bar.

"And some !" O'Connor ejaculated, laughing to himself at some private experience remembered. "We'd run down to London at the week ends. Spend money like water in the clubs on champagne and hookers. Bonding ? Yeah, there was definitely bonding."

"Sean, I need to understand something. What's your motive to play whistleblower ? I mean, have you had some kind of conversion ? Are you aware of the risks ?"

O'Connor halted abruptly, and turned to face Reddy, hands dug deeply into his coat pockets. He said:

"Self preservation. Pure and simple. You bet I know the risks. All the guys can see the future. The good times are over. With Cartwright gone and the trading losses now coming out into the open, Mary's toast. None of us want to end up serving jail sentences."

Reddy felt a spasm of disappointment. Naively perhaps, he had thought O'Connor's motives might be more honourable. Immediately, he cast the misconception aside. 'Deal with the reality' he told himself.

"Are there definitely financial crimes to be revealed ?" he asked.

"Of course" O'Connor responded, with equanimity. "And the point is this: it started at the top. Mary Donoghue was the prime mover."

Not unaware that O'Connor probably was positioning the story to lay the guilt at top management's door and achieve maximum exculpation for himself and fellow traders, Reddy sensed that this was the moment to discover whether or not the quality of O'Connor's testimony would stand up to scratch.

"Tell me, Sean, in simple language, how was the trading environment set up ? How was it fraudulent ?"

With clarity, O'Connor explained:

"There is a dual system in place. The official one, which is monitored by risk managers and the compliance guys; and the informal one. For the latter, Donoghue has system administrator rights. That means she can manage the configuration of the system at will."

"Go on. What does that mean in practice for you traders ?"

"Isn't it obvious ? We all have user access to the second system as well. That allows us to execute trades that ignore the rules and constraints operating on the official system."

"With no links between the two systems ?"

"Yes, there are connections. They're defined by Mary and involve the connivance of a few engineers in the IT Department."

"Do you understand how it's set up ?"

"Not in detail no. It's Mary's closely guarded secret. What I do know is that both the application software and the database run with separate instances for the official and the informal systems. Then there's some custom software written that permits some of the successfully executed trades on the informal system to be migrated to the official version."

Reddy was no software expert and felt himself on uncertain terrain. Nevertheless, the layman in him wanted to ascertain the business implications.

"Does that mean then that the informal system was where the losing trades started accumulating ? Is that how the proprietary trading desk ran up £1,2 billion of losses ?"

"The losses may be higher than that, but basically, yes. Although it was more complicated. Mary herself was also skimming. Plus, she rewarded us with ad hoc payments as an incentive to keep quiet."

367

"In short, both conspiracy and fraud then ?" Reddy concluded.

They had arrived a short way before the pier, where the road widened and there was space for car parking behind the sea front promenade they had walked along. O'Connor's black Porsche was parked at the curb.

"Definitely. And now Dublin has sent in a couple of guys to investigate what's been going on. Mary's already lost it too. There was a major blow up between her and the guys yesterday when she came back from meeting Moroney, the head of the CEGB, in London."

"You think she's seen the writing on the wall ?" Reddy inquired.

O'Connor, car keys in hand, pressed the remote to unlock the Porsche. He opened the driver's door.

"Reddy, she's toast. I have to survive. Remember this when the police come calling: I'm the man who supplied the intelligence. Don't forget."

He climbed down into the driver's seat and fired up the engine. It had a throaty roar as he touched the accelerator pedal. The car door window slid down and he looked out at Reddy. His face exhibited no sign of remorse or regret; green brown eyes staring unyieldingly through the rimless spectacles at Reddy.

"No longer an 'Irish Tiger' then ?"   Reddy concluded.

"Tigers are an endangered species. Adapt or die."

O'Connor backed the Porsche out into the empty road, changed gear and sped away.

Chapter Thirty Eight

07.50 Saturday 21st March 2009. Sports Centre, Grafton Way, Ipswich

There was a definite 'feel good' factor to early bird activity in the gym, Reddy thought, congratulating himself on having arrived at the Sports Centre just after the six thirty opening time. The barely populated gym at that hour, left you free to roam and choose whatever exercise machines you fancied or which were part of your regular training routine.

It was ten to eight in the morning and he had been training since six forty five. He had begun with some light stretching, using an individual floor mat to lie on. Then he chose one of the high performance running machines and did a steady twenty minute jog. It was that which had attuned his mind and body. The 'feel good' factor, he knew, was a naturally occurring phenomenon when endomorphines kicked in. Thirty five minutes running was the tipping point at which, for him personally, this happened.

With no pause, he switched to a rowing machine and executed a strenuous four kilometres in two, two kilometre sessions. That second session had induced a copious flow of perspiration and necessitated a cool off and rub down, accompanied by a healthy dose of mineral water from the bottle he had brought with him. The endomorphines were doing their thing.

Wandering around the still almost empty gym holding the bottle and with a towel draped over his shoulders, Reddy looked through the large sheet glass windows that formed much of the sports' centre's external wall. Dawn had already broken and streaks of pale orange and yellow light were emerging horizontally across a dark grey sky.

To top off his work out, he returned again to the rows of running machines, selected the same one he had used before and programmed a five kilometre distance. By now, the Sports Centre staff had gotten around to turning on the amplifiers and motivational music was now blasting forth. To Reddy, this was 'noise pollution'; one of the many useless invasions into the modern quality of life. He tuned himself out and focused on inner concentration.

Having established a steady pace, he let his thoughts turn to matters confronting him. On the personal front, he acknowledged that unconsciously he had decided not to make any effort to repair and restore his broken relationship with Julie. He had made no effort to reach her since he found her voice message on his answer phone last week end. If her claim that they were finished was a tactic to stir him into winning him back, it had backfired. If, on the contrary, it was a plain statement of fact, then his silence had endorsed it. He ought to call her to seal the deal, yet he knew that with other pressing issues to handle, he would probably let it bury itself.

What certainly would not be buried was the dilemma with his boss, Samantha Cavendish. Reddy had been unprepared for the *volte face* on her part yesterday. The more he pondered her action, the more convinced he became that it was an initiative engineered by the Editor Sinclair Monroe. Samantha, expectant that her current status as "Acting" Deputy Editor would soon become formalised on a permanent basis, was His Master's Voice. She had manoeuvred herself into a position of close and effective working relations with Monroe. He apparently trusted her, although with his peerless experience of the media industry he stood head and shoulders above her, in Reddy's opinion. The conclusion he drew was that, in this matter, Samantha was merely the marionette, and Monroe was pulling the strings. If that was so, then personalising the issue as a conflict of style and personality between himself and his boss would get him nowhere. He saw the stark truth: this week end he would need to take a decisive view on his future. Did he intend to stay at the Daily Courier, yes or no !

Toying with that dilemma triggered in Reddy's mind the memory of Immanuel Bernstein. The professor, having indicated his willingness to assist Reddy with part two of his article, had sent him some ideas by email late yesterday. Reddy had taken only the briefest of glimpses at the input but was greatly enthused by what he read. Bernstein was proposing a radically opposite approach to the litany of bank 'bail outs'. He proposed the resolution of failing banks by harnessing the resources of the market, allied with effective transparency rules to accelerate debt write downs and allow recapitalisation. To Reddy, the proposals seemed both plausible and potentially effective. On returning to his apartment from his work out, he would devote time to understanding them fully and then commence the drafting of part two of his article.

That effort would be time boxed by his appointment to meet up with Pandit Singh and Simon Farley and watch Ipswich Town's home game against Watford. He'd agreed with Simon on a rendez vous near the stadium for 14.15 but was still awaiting to hear from Pandit when he'd arrive at Ipswich. That left three hours ahead of him to devote to his work.

Maintaining his steady training pace on the running machine, Reddy's thoughts returned to the IB&B's insolvency. Time was running against a rescue or resolution. There remained much sensitive material from Natasha's flash disk that he hadn't published. That, together with the conversation he had had yesterday with Sean O'Connor from the 'Irish Tigers' team, demonstrated that the financial plight of the bank probably was far worse than even he had assumed. If that were true, then a further article composed with Bernstein's help was equivalent to fiddling while Rome burned ! Wouldn't it be better to call Stan Cerny and talk to him ? Or even, call Havering and caution him on the risks of negotiating a deal between the CEGB and the AIIB. He had Havering's business card back at his apartment. Intervening somehow in the 'secret' IB&B rescue meeting near Amersham looked like the right thing to do.

The LCD screen on the running machine indicated that he had but one hundred metres to run to complete the programmed distance. Reddy's white T shirt was now thoroughly wet with perspiration and sticking to his chest. He felt in fine fettle. The work out in his head examining the matters immediately in front of him had been as important as the physical work out on the gym equipment. He knew from experience that it was the latter that provided him with the foundation for the former.

The machine slowed and came to a halt. He picked up the towel, then the water bottle and locker key from the plastic moulded pocket positioned at the front of the machine. He stepped off the rolling carpet. Wiping his perspiring brow with the towel he crossed the polished wooden floor in the direction of the changing rooms. The gym was now alive with mainly young adults going through their individual exercise routines.. People, Reddy suspected, who lived by a carpe diem philosophy. Or as the sports shoe company said 'just do it !"

"Good morning, Mr Reddy" a female voice said from nearby.

Instantly, Reddy recognised the voice. Looking right he saw DI Wright approaching, kitted out in a black sleeveless T shirt and matching lycra running tights. Her long hair was tied tightly back behind her back and she wore minimal make up. She too held a towel and had evidently already been doing some exercise. 'Bloody hell' Reddy exclaimed inwardly 'what a stunner'. Unburdened of her professional attire and clothed in figure hugging sports gear, Wright presented a shapely, athletic figure.

"Hello. So you do in fact use this gym ?" Reddy said, keeping the surprise out of his voice. "When we first met at Police HQ last Tuesday I had an inkling that I had seen you before somewhere. It was here."

Wright wiped the moisture out of her face and laughed. "Funny that ! I had the same thought as you but didn't think it the right time or place to ask."

Her friendly response gave Reddy the feeling that there was no need to maintain a composed professional profile. It was Saturday morning and she was not, presumably, on duty. He ventured:

"Call me Craig, please. So are you a regular this time of day ? You take your fitness seriously ?"

"I have a regular training programme. No half measures with me. However, the work comes first. This morning I'm in early because I go on duty for nine. Don't forget we're up to our necks in a murder investigation, I'm doing overtime all week end. This is my only chance to get some exercise."

"I don't envy you. Although we do have another thing in common apart from early morning training."

"What would that be ?" Wright asked, curious.

"We're both hounded by the media for news of our investigations, right ? I saw the local evening news on television last night. You and your boss received prominent treatment. I hope you can handle it better than me. To be honest, I'm trying to keep a low profile."

"My boss, Haddock ? He takes most of the media pressure. The bad news is, he's on my back big time to get a result. He was already fired up by the suicides of Cartwright and McAuley. The murder of Westlake has left him fuming. Especially the spectacular nature of the killing. Great for sensationalist tabloids and tv chat programmes. A nightmare for me and the investigation team."

"No sign or sightings of this Angelov character or the car used for the killing ?"

"None. No one recollected the vehicle's license plate number."

"Are you working on the assumption that all three events are related, perhaps parts of a wider criminal network ?"

"We're still ruling nothing out, Craig. On the other hand we have to keep a tight focus on the facts associated with each individual case. My experience in policing crime is that concocting complicated theories is usually a waste of time and effort."

"So you wouldn't envisage the possibility that I shared with DS Adam yesterday that the Westlake murder is perhaps 'making a statement' ? Perhaps a mafia-style killing ?"

"Certainly the location and circumstances provide some ground for that speculation. We know too that Westlake had business in Bulgaria. But he also had a meeting scheduled with Angelov at his firm's offices for yesterday afternoon. If they were that close, it seems unlikely to me that Angelov would have him killed. That said, I want Angelov in for questioning ! We have issued an alert to stop him leaving the country."

Reddy sensed Wright's unflinching determination. She was every inch a professional when focusing on her work. 'Integrity' was a word that played in his mind to describe her.

He seized the moment:

"I don't want either of us catching cold standing here talking but one last thing, if I may ? Are you aware of a raid conducted the other day by SOCA on a warehouse at Ipswich Docks ?"

The irises in Wright's eyes narrowed and her body tensed up:

"Yes, I'm informed. How do you come to know about it ?"

"My best friend, Simon Farley, was apprehended during that raid. He came to visit me afterwards when he was set free. He told me what happened. The officers took away some traces of a substance they say might be cocaine."

"Its not my case Craig and I shouldn't really be discussing it with you. However, the procedure is it will be tested at the labs. Your friend may well be in difficulty if the test results are positive."

"Simon is innocent Inspector. I've known him since schooldays. He's not a drug user and I'm willing to stand as a character witness in his defence."

"That is your choice. The issue I think from SOCA's perspective is not whether he is a user, but whether he has been illegally importing and selling it ? I know that Mr Farley has no criminal record, which speaks in his favour. However, SOCA may well press charges if the tests are positive."

"SOCA are missing something in all this" Reddy insisted. "According to Simon, these traces of substance they found were located by the sniffer dogs in the storage areas reserved for product imported by Russell Westlake ! You should be running a toxicology test on Westlake's corpse."

Reddy felt himself over animated and in danger of saying too much or even the wrong things. He took his leave of Wright and departed for the mens' changing rooms to shower and change.

DI Wright had been determined to put in a short training session at the gym. Today it was less her fitness regime that had impelled her and more the need to clear her head of yesterday's mayhem and prepare herself for clear-thinking prior to going on duty at nine o'clock. The pace and pressure of the investigation was unrelenting and she was the lead investigator. Under no circumstances did she want her male colleagues to see her wilt or stall. An early morning session in the gym was her antidote to work stress.

Meeting Reddy had been unexpected, even if she did remember having seen him in the past. Their conversation had enlivened her initially, only to depress her at the end. When he took his leave, obviously disappointed in her attitude to his friend Farley, she had quickly returned to her running machine to immerse herself in a final fifteen minutes of high performance running. The physical exertion was both purifying and challenging, a combination that left her feeling good. A dose of invigorating self confidence would help her fight through the coming day.

After completing a distance of over four kilometres in the fifteen minutes she had climbed off the running machine to cool down. Her footsteps took her over to the large pane glass windows on the far side of the gym shaped in a half circle. There were five windows that ran from floor to ceiling interspersed along the wall. Wright wandered aimlessly over to the corner window. She looked out onto the car parking below. The dawn light had given way to nascent daylight. Off along Grafton Way, the vehicle traffic was still sparse.

As she watched, regaining her normal breathing rhythm, she saw a figure emerge from below and walk away down the pavement heading to the road. It was Reddy, obviously intent on walking home since was crossing the car park with no evident intent of looking for a car. He wore a blue denim jacket and jeans and carried a blue sports bag. His movement was lithe and light. She guessed he was feeling pleased with himself for having put in an early morning gym session. She knew the feeling. What, she wondered, was his motivation ? How was he coping with his own pressure ?

A white Toyota Land Cruiser, which had been parked close to the Sports Centre exit, pulled out of its parking space and slowly headed to the Grafton Street exit. It halted besides Reddy. A man climbed out from the front passenger's seat and called Reddy. He stopped walking and faced the man. To Wright it looked as if the man wanted to ask for directions and was lost.

As the two men began to talk, the back passenger door of the Toyota also opened. A second man emerged. He wore sunshades and a black leather jacket. He approached the other two calmly. Reddy took a step back, perhaps to get a better look at the second man. As he did so, the first grabbed his left arm, twisted it behind his back, and moved around him. The second smashed his fist into Reddy's jaw. The impact knocked Reddy off balance. As Reddy fell backwards, the first man wrapped his arm around his throat. The other hit him again, this time in the stomach. Reddy's sports bag fell from his shoulder as he collapsed to the ground. The two men picked him up with apparent ease. He didn't struggle. They quickly bundled him into the back seat of the Toyota. They jumped back into the vehicle and the driver pulled out immediately onto Grafton Way without waiting for them to close the car doors.

In the few seconds from the second man alighting from the back of the Toyota to the two men grappling with Reddy, Wright's awareness transformed from being a casual observer of a person who intrigued her, to an alert police officer intent on action. She turned and ran for gym's exit. At reception, people watched as she hurtled past towards the stairway, calculating that it was quicker to reach the ground floor exit that way than awaiting the lift.

Taking the steps down two at a time, she bumped into a guy arriving through the glass entrance doors, ignoring him. Outside on the pavement and facing the parking area, she slowed and looked towards the place where the Toyota had been moments before. It was nowhere to be seen.

Wright put her hands on her hips and recovered her breathing. She swore under her breath, realising that in trying to reach the men by running outside, she had missed the opportunity to capture the vehicle's license plate number. Annoyed with herself, she walked over to the place where she thought the events had occurred. Lying on the grass verge was Reddy's blue sports bag. She picked it up, and disconsolately turned back for the Sports Centre.

Reddy had been kidnapped. She'd call it in immediately to HQ from her mobile phone. Her day's work had suddenly gotten worse.

Chapter Thirty Nine

14.30 Saturday 21st March 2009. Iberia flight to Madrid

The flight had been airborne about twenty minutes when the pretty air hostess asked:

"Can I offer you something to drink sir ? A glass of champagne perhaps ?"

She was a most satisfying sight in the centre of Radomir Angelov's field of vision as he leaned back in his comfortable first class seat. He rarely touched alcohol during the day time. Right now however, the occasion and the context conspired to tempt him. He smiled back at her, a response which brought out a radiant sparkle in the woman's eyes.

"Yes, that sounds perfect" he enthused.

The air hostess left to prepare his drink, leaving Angelov to relax while looking absently at the puffy white clouds sailing outside the cabin window. He had the luxury of no neighbouring passenger and so could spread himself languidly and expansively in the available space.

The air hostess promptly returned carrying the filled champagne glass and a folded paper napkin on a tiny silver plate. Angelov submitted to her ministrations as she took the liberty to open and arrange the table that unfolded from his arm rest.

"There you are Mr Dimitrov. Enjoy !" she encouraged, "Please don't hesitate to ask if you would like a refill, or other refreshments."

He adored that, the personal touch in first class. Angelov thanked her, turning on one of his most charming smiles. He could tell, as she turned to go and attend the few other guests occupying the first class cabin, that he had left an impression not so much on an air hostess, but rather upon a female psyche.

Picking up the champagne glass by its stem he studied momentarily the bubbles rising and bursting effervescently. He savoured a little of the drink. It melted and tickled the inside of his mouth then left a distinct but fleeting bitter taste on the sides of his tongue. Champagne was an amusing if fragile temptation, Angelov decided.

'Mr Dimitrov', indeed ! Angelov smirked at his own adaptive resilience. His UK sojourn had been brought to an abrupt end. Yet, when travelling abroad, he always carried with him a second passport, courtesy of his privileged contacts in the Bulgaria Passport Office. From the moment that he had acted to extract himself hurriedly from the crime scene that was Thomas Cartwright's funeral service and Russell Westlake's murder, he adopted his new persona.

Leaving behind the cemetery and the confusion caused by Westlake's death before the police arrived had been essential. He feared that the police might open inquiries into his background which could lead him into difficulties. A rapid exit had been easy, as Vladimir was present in the cemetery's car park acting as chauffeur in the rented Land Cruiser. They drove directly to his Ipswich hotel and Angelov checked out. Vladimir then drove them out of town and onto the A12 heading for Colchester. Igor was still there, based in Bourov's apartment. Angelov placed a call to an airline and booked his seat to Madrid, with final destination Panama City. He gave Igor and Vladimir instructions to leave the country separately back to Bulgaria via Vienna also on Saturday.

At ease and free, Angelov took stock of the strategy. Was it now in tatters ? Where to go from here ? His 'plan A', cozying up to Sir Peter Westlake with a view to partnering on lucrative construction contracts for the London Olympics 2012, had not been progressed. At least, not on the face of it. He'd had to cancel their re-scheduled Friday morning meeting. On the other hand, with Russell Westlake dead, Angelov did not rule out exploiting that as an opportunity. Maybe he could leverage his own business relationship and knowledge of the son to garner empathy and interest from the bereaved father ? Angelov warmed to that idea; the classic 'turn a problem into an opportunity' formula. Except that that would require his early return to the UK, a return that would be contingent upon firm knowledge that the police had identified Russell Westlake's killers and so had no interest or energy in talking to him. Since Angelov himself had a good idea who was behind the killing, he believed he could arrange discreetly for the Ipswich police to be fed intelligence that might lead them to the perpetrators.

Of course, Angelov had had Vladimir kill Bourov, but that didn't worry him. Once Bourov's corpse was discovered, he expected the police investigation to wind down quickly once they learned that it was a foreign manual worker. There was no possible way they could find linkage back to him, as Russell Westlake could not tell his story. The Bourov crime scene at the brickworks had been left impeccably clean; Vladimir having even found the bullet embedded in the kiln wall. The

378

disposal of Bourov's corpse had been effected wearing gloves and wrapping the corpse in plastic during its transport.

The financial issues surrounding Redwoods Country Homes, particularly their loans from the Ipswich and Blackwater Bank, were elements outside of Angelov's immediate control. He was coming to the view that a few weeks' pause and patience were called for to see how the cards fell. Would Mary Donoghue remain at the Ipswich and Blackwater Bank and if so, would she be able to renew Redwoods' loans ? How would the markets respond to the loss of Redwoods' CEO ? Who was Westlake's likely successor ? Imponderables, all.

The air hostess passed down the cabin again. Angelov caught her eye:

"That is so good" he explained, waving the empty fluted glass, "I think I can be tempted to have another."

This time, as the young woman retreated back down the aisle to fetch the champagne, Angelov treated himself to a view of her rear. Another of life's small pleasures, he reflected.

Why, he didn't know, but at that moment a thought association brought him a mental image of the journalist, Reddy. That kidnap episode had been pure entertainment. Angelov let linger the image of the blind folded, bound and roughed up Englishman laying spread eagled on the ground. Respect. Maybe the Englishman would understand the word now.

By the time the hostess returned and re-filled his glass with champagne, Angelov had put on the available in-flight headphones and chosen a music channel. It was playing a programme called 'Crooners' Classics'. The image of the Englishman's sufferings faded as Angelov let himself be entranced by Frank Sinatra, singing 'I did it my way'.

Chapter Forty

15.50 Saturday 21ˢᵗ March 2009. North Stand, Ipswich Town football stadium, Portman Road, Ipswich.

Pandit Singh had his small laptop computer open and balanced on his knees. The blue plastic seat he was in was less than ideal, and so too the environment, for working on the machine. He was receiving strange looks from some of the people around him.

It was half time in the match between Ipswich Town and Watford, a match that so far was goalless and short on entertainment value. On a pitch now devoid of the teams' players, an assortment of youngsters were now taking turns to try and kick a ball through a rubber tyre strung up from one of the goal's crossbars. Some of the entertainment-starved crowd cheered and jeered as, one after another, the would be goal scoring heroes slammed the balls everywhere except through the required hole.

Singh's attention was devoted to the computer screen for a good reason. Craig Reddy had not shown up to meet him and Farley before the game as planned. Neither had he called them. Attempts to reach his mobile phone ended up on his voicemail. During the first half, Singh had had the idea to check on his computer for the whereabouts of his own smart phone. The machine ran a GPS locator application linked to the phone. If the phone was switched on, Singh could track its' precise geocoordinates on an electronic map.

"Hey, what's that ?" Farley asked, as he squeezed down the row of seated fans with two cups of tea. Regaining his empty seat besides Singh, he handed him one of the foam cups and leaned across to look at the screen.

Pandit explained: "I forgot Simon. Maybe I can find where my smart phone is with my GPS locator. It runs here on my laptop. My guess is, wherever the phone is, that's where we'll also find Craig."

Farley had never seen such a thing before. He observed Singh attentively as he tapped on his keyboard and then searched to expand a map.

"The phone's on and transmitting" Singh explained. "Just a second."

As Singh fiddled some more, Farley's sense of expectation notched up a couple of levels. He was anxious about Reddy's absence, although he wasn't sure exactly why. That his friend had hit the news this week and been the subject of considerable media attention disturbed him.

"Here, it is" Singh said, "I've magnified the map to street level. The phone's located here in Ipswich on Civic Drive. Do you know it Simon ? It's somewhere in the central area."

Farley stared at the screen. A street map was visible on which at the centre he could see a red icon flashing.

"Is that it ?" he asked, pointing his finger at the flashing icon.

"Yes. Civic Drive."

"But that's probably the Police headquarters" Farley objected, disquieted. He'd had enough of dealings with the police for a long time. He had no wish to meet them now.

Singh too was surprised but not fazed: "The application doesn't lie Simon. That's where my smart phone is right now. It's stationary too. I need to go and get it while I can. It's a company device. Chances are that Craig is there too. What do you want to do ?"

"Do you have your number ? Let me first call it and see who answers."

Singh recited his smart phone number from memory. Farley withdrew his own device from his inside coat pocket and dialled.

"Hello, who's calling please" replied a man with a Scottish accent. It wasn't Craig Reddy.

"Hi, good afternoon. Name's Simon Farley. I'm phoning on behalf of my friend who's beside me here. You see, you're using his phone without his permission and we're wondering why ?" he said with pugnacious politeness.

"I see, sir" came back the level reply. "May I ask then to talk to the owner myself, since he's with you ?"

Farley sensed that he had misread the situation, having expected to find himself talking either to Reddy or else to some delinquent who had stolen the device. He surprised himself by submitting meekly to the anonymous Scotsman.

381

"He wants to speak to the owner" he said, passing his phone to Pandit, at the same time as there was a roar and rising applause from around the football ground as the players of Ipswich Town and Watford took to the field again to start the second half.

"I'm Pandit Singh, the owner of the smart phone you have" Singh shouted above the mounting crescendo of noise.

"Mr. Singh, I'm Detective Sergeant Adam, Ipswich Police. We have your phone in safe keeping. Can you tell me how you came to lose it ?"

"Sure. I was playing squash earlier in the week and left it behind after the match. My playing partner picked it up and was keeping it until I could collect. His name's Craig Reddy. He's a work colleague. Tell me, why is it now with the police ?"

"Your phone was one of the contents found this morning in Mr Reddy's sports kit bag by my boss DI Wright. She retrieved it early this morning outside a Sports Centre where she and Mr Reddy had both been training. Mr Reddy was apprehended by some men in a Land Cruiser after leaving the Centre and bundled into the vehicle. We are working on the assumption that he has been kidnapped. They all made off leaving Reddy's bag by the kerbside."

Pandit's brown eyes widened progressively as he listened to the detective's story. His body stiffened, stricken by the unlikely reality he heard. His anxiety fed to Farley who disengaged from the activity on the football field when he saw Singh's alarmed reaction.

"Listen, Officer, can we come to see you now ? We're in fact not far away from your headquarters, watching the football game at Portman Road. We're both close friends of Craig Reddy. We'd expected to meet him and see this match together but he never showed up. Perhaps if we come we can help each other find Reddy ?"

"What the hell's up ?" Farley interjected, exasperated at not hearing what was being said, yet understanding that something was seriously wrong with Reddy.

"I'm here and available to see you both, if you can come now Mr Singh" Adam offered, "Let's hope indeed that we can find Mr Reddy."

DS Adam was alone in his office, seated at his desk, his hands toying with Pandit Singh's smart phone. Before him was a short typescript report, prepared by a police constable that morning. It made interesting reading. By fortuitous circumstance, it had been circulated around the CID detectives that morning by an assiduous member of the administrative staff. DS Adam perused the text a second time. The name mentioned had caught his attention.

Anglia Auto Rentals reported on Friday evening a blue Ford Fiesta presumed stolen, its' return overdue 24 hours and the renter not responding to calls. The name of the renter, one Georgi Bourov. His passport was Bulgarian. On Saturday morning, the landlord of the Crooked Billet at Tatterstone near Alton Water phoned in to report a parked blue Ford Fiesta in his car park. It had been there overnight Thursday and Friday. Still parked there this morning, the landlord had grown suspicious and called it in. A police patrol car team had visited the abandoned vehicle. They had reported its' registration number. The back office team had checked with the stolen vehicles database and confirmed it as the missing Anglia Auto Rentals car.

"Bourov. Georgi Bourov." Adam said out loud, as if testing it. A Bulgarian, and the name mentioned to him yesterday by Reddy as working for Westlake at RCH.

He was about to put his feet up on his desk when his phone rang. Lifting the receiver, Reception announced the arrival of Farley and Singh. They were awaiting him downstairs in one of the interview rooms. DS Adam replaced the phone receiver on its base. He arose from his chair, still holding the smart phone belonging to Singh. As he prepared to leave his office, there was a knock on the door and DS Clarkson poked his head inside.

"Got a minute ? I've something that might interest , Charlie."

DS Adam halted, unprepared for interruption.

"Make it short, I've visitors."

He opened the office door wide open and occupied the space as a statement of intent to Clarkson not to enter.

"It's the McAuley suicide case. You and I need to talk. We've found a handwritten note. Apparently written by McAuley before his death. I'd like you to see it."

"Unusual. I thought suicides don't write notes ?"

"Mostly true, but this one did."

"Does it reveal anything material ?"

DS Clarkson sensed he'd caught Adam's curiosity. He smiled knowingly.

"It's rambling and incoherent but accuses a "Mr. Fix It" of many things, including being the supplier of his cocaine."

"Took you a long time to find Des. The man died last Sunday night. Why the delay ?"

"The note wasn't found when the police were called last Monday, Charlie. A family member called us Wednesday afternoon. She'd come across it locked away in his desk."

" 'Mr. Fix It' ? That's a bit elliptical isn't it ? Who do you reckon it is ? "

"How about Russell Westlake ?" DS Clarkson suggested. "According to McAuley's estate staff he visited McAuley last Sunday afternoon."

Adam threw a sceptical frown at his colleague, but he took the bait:

"Sounds promising. OK, I'll pass by your office after my meeting."

He sidestepped Clarkson as if evading a rugby tackle and set off down the corridor with the smart phone, leaving his colleague stranded.

'Christ !' he thought to himself, "young Des has excelled himself. This might strengthen the case for Westlake's involvement in drugs trafficking and put a motive on his killing. I must tell Paulie."

Chapter Forty One

A large red orb floated in his mind. It changed shape slowly, growing larger then smaller. It looked like some distant planet viewed through a telescope that was slightly out of focus. There was nothing else but darkness. He sensed that there was pain too, but he hadn't the strength to identify it or assess it. He dropped back into unconsciousness.

Later, perhaps much later, he became aware again of light. Not strong, but diffused. He could feel that his eyelids couldn't open. He was blindfolded and the material was tied tightly behind his head. His hands too were bound, behind his back. As he slowly regained more awareness, the pain and aches awoke and intensified all over his body. His mouth was parched and gagged; swallowing was difficult and his tongue couldn't move freely. He tried to move his legs, only to discover that his ankles too were tied. Then the cold took over and the shivering began. He was cold to his bones.

Worse was to come, because his memory slowly returned and with it, fear. Fear of the physical violence inflicted while blindfolded. Fear of not knowing where or when the next blow would fall. Fear of not knowing the intentions of his captors. Was he living his last hours or moments ? A kaleidoscope of distorted and intermingled images now cluttered his brain; patterned in ever changing combinations as a sense of impending doom weighed down on his shredded nerves.

Elvin was alone. With his thoughts and his work. Sundays were lonely at the best of times. Now, in the certain knowledge that the brickworks would close at the end of the month, he was conscious that time was precious. He might not have achieved much in life but he was proud nonetheless of the way he had kept Dears' bricks a high quality product down the years. Theirs was a reputation respected far and wide. The bricks were used at the Queen's residence in Sandringham and also on Prince Charles' property down in the West Country somewhere.

He had taken it as a personal challenge to ensure that, down to the last order, the necessary production schedule would be maintained regardless. The other two workers on the kilns, become friends down the years, had let their disappointment become resentment. Last week they had been off 'sick'. Their hearts were no longer in it; they didn't care, and the owners didn't care either.

Elvin cared. That was why he was here now. He intended to complete the loading of kiln number two and block it up. On Monday, with the other guys, he would then complete the loading of kiln number three. Then the firing of the bricks in the two kilns would begin simultaneously.

He had come to the site dressed in his habitual working gear, shabby and dirty but fitting like a glove. The peaked cap he wore was tilted back at a jaunty angle on his forehead. Having parked his fifteen year old Vauxhall car alongside the wooden cabin that was the site offices, he walked across to the nearest brick kiln, kiln number one, which was in its second day of cooling down. He'd be opening it up to retrieve the fired bricks on Monday afternoon once he and the others had closed kilns two and three.

He turned left and followed the iron rail track past the still warm kiln to kiln two which was still open. A wheeled metal trailer was standing on the rails outside, laden with removable trays of moulded unfired clay bricks. Everywhere around was thick with clay dust.

He peered inside the open kiln. The stacking of bricks was about two thirds completed. Still another one thousand three hundred bricks to go. To Elvin, the prospect of accomplishing that today was neither daunting nor boring. The routine of physical labour would be a therapy. He put on his dilapidated heavy duty gloves, pushed up the sleeves of his dusty blue work jacket, and then pulled the top tray of moulded bricks out from the trailer.

As his body adjusted to the steady rhythms of pulling, lifting, carrying and placement of the bricks his mind began to roam. Or rather, it was ensnared in a closed loop of worry. He was worried about Simon Farley and worried too about Bourov. What he couldn't fathom, he told himself, was Bourov's further disappearance. One minute he'd arrived at the brickworks Thursday afternoon and had insisted to get stuck in to helping load the kiln; then later, when Elvin returned from the meeting with Simon and Mark Hancock at Hancock's yard, there was no Bourov to be found. He'd vanished and so too his car, without a word or a message left anywhere as to where or why he'd suddenly left. From having established for himself a reputation as a highly reliable worker, Bourov had transformed into a mercurial mystery.

Which was why Elvin was now at work. Completing the task that Bourov had said, on Thursday, that he'd be happy to do. So, why hadn't he ? Elvin was pondering that question, turning it around in his mind as if moulding some clay into the required shape. Elvin was a good judge of character. From people's behaviour he could discern usually their motives. Bourov's about turn in behaviour was not consistent with the person Elvin knew. Except for one vital fact. Elvin had not forgotten the conversation in Flemish he had overheard earlier in the week in the pub. Could it be that Bourov's new found unreliability was caused by his involvement in the deal that the two Flemish men spoke about ? If so, what might have happened since to generate Bourov's skittishness and deliberate dissembling with his colleagues and acquaintances ?

Elvin continued to unload and stack the bricks at his own pace, comfortable with the work routine. All the while ruminating, letting his thoughts turn around and evolve.

As he emerged once again from the kiln to collect another tray of bricks, he heard a vehicle engine in the distance approaching the brickworks. No one would drive down the track from the main road on a Sunday morning unless lost or up to mischief. Elvin interrupted his routine, pulled off his gloves and walk back up the rail track past kiln one and out into the open space leading to the wooden office building.

A dirty white open backed truck bumped and clattered through the main entrance to the brickworks and ground to a halt besides the offices. Small dust clouds swirled around the tyres momentarily. At the wheel was Simon Farley, together with a passenger whom Elvin didn't recognise but who was dark skinned.

Elvin was not surprised to see Farley. With his bricks now delivered, Farley would be keen to make up for lost time by starting on the repairs at his parents' summer house. But with other problems on his mind too, perhaps he wanted to have chat. The discussions they had had with Mark Hancock had been inconclusive. Hancock had provided a reasonable account of the exchanges he had with the SOCA officers, but nothing he said added significant insight into Farley's understanding of why SOCA was targeting him. Elvin was aware of Farley's suspicion that this was some kind of conspiracy, possibly involving the boss of Redwoods. At least, that was how Farley had explained it to him later. Farley, Elvin worried, was seething with anger like an active volcano preparing to blow.

Elvin stood his ground, watching as the two men climbed down from the truck cabin. The second person was an Indian; tall, with jet black hair and dressed in smart designer clothing. Farley by contrast wore old work clothes, threadbare blue jeans, a labourer's collarless shirt, and his trademark leather bomber jacket. Farley approached Elvin.

"Hi Elvin. I thought we'd find you here. Tried your house number first but no reply. By the way this is Pandit Singh. He's a colleague of Craig Reddy's."

Pandit remained silent but shook hands with Elvin. Elvin turned back to Farley:

"You down to work on the house today ? Are the bricks ok ?" he enquired, unsure what topic of conversation was appropriate in the presence of this stranger. He was studying Farley minutely, keen to gauge his mood.

"No they're not. Your guys have messed up. You remember the loaded lorry here when I came down last week end ? You told me that that consignment was for another customer. What do they do ? Deliver it to me ! "

Stupified at this carelessness, Elvin adopted an apologetic tone. He hadn't checked that the right bricks had been sent to Farley's parents' place. he'd only been informed by the office staff that they'd gone. In an effort to make amends he said:

"Look, Simon, I'll tell you what. Your bricks are definitely ready. If you're up for it, then drive your truck down there" he pointed down the site beyond the last brick kiln to where the new bricks were stored and paletted, " and the three of us can load them now."

Farley interrupted:

"Elvin, thanks. We can do that. What I wanted to tell you first though is this." Farley looked askance at Singh, wanting him to affirm and be implicated in the story. Elvin waited, nonplussed.

"Craig Reddy has been kidnapped" Farley blurted out. "Yesterday in Ipswich."

The news left Elvin dumbfounded. He understood the long history of friendship between the two of them. This week Reddy had been in the national and local news. Elvin hadn't paid much attention, since the subject was beyond his realm of comprehension. The media and politics was a world apart from the one in which Elvin made his daily round.

"How do you know that ?" Elvin asked, gently.

"The Ipswich Police confirmed as much to us yesterday afternoon. A detective happened to be training at the gym Craig uses and saw him being manhandled into a car. Three guys, and they used force."

"So what's happened since then ?"

"There's an alert out for the vehicle. No sign of it or his assailants. I phoned the police again this morning before coming up here to see you. We're really worried about Craig. You know he's been in the media headlights this week with an article he published ? Apparently it made waves. I told the police that there's probably a link to that. I reckon Craig's ruffled a few feathers somewhere."

Elvin slapped together his two gloves in frustration. A small cloud of dust escaped from them. He felt powerless. If this kidnapping was true, then Reddy might be in serious jeopardy; which in his darkest thoughts translated as 'Reddy could be dead'.

"It seems to me then, we're in the hands of the police to find Craig" he said lamely, "unless you guys have some leads ?"

Farley and Singh both shrugged despondently. They too were frustrated at their powerlessness to intervene or solve the crisis. Reddy's mobile phone was found by the police in his sports kit bag so that avenue was closed. In a display of desperation Farley splayed out his arms, palms of his hands open, in Elvin's direction.

"We're at a loss what to do, Elvin. Any suggestions ?"

"Yes, don't idle away the time. It'll kill you. Let's get those bricks of yours loaded up. Gives you something useful to do instead of eating yourself up on speculations and anxiety. Come on !"

He turned away and plodded in the direction of the kilns, not waiting for their response. Singh and Farley glanced at one another. Neither had a better proposal. Farley said:

"Follow him down Pandit. I'll bring over the truck."

Singh deferred to Farley without a word. As Farley went off to the truck, digging out the keys from his bomber jacket, Singh set off after Elvin. Catching him up as he reached the first kiln and turned down the iron tracks, Singh spoke for the first time:

"Unusual place you have here Elvin. I've never been in a brick works before. It looks like the place could do with a face lift ? Seen better times I would guess ?"

Elvin had arrived before the entrance to kiln number two, with the metal trolley and trays of moulded bricks. He stopped, took hold of the trolley with one hand and pointed into the open kiln with the other.

"These are the last bricks to be fired. I'm loading the kiln now. This one and the next one" he pointed at the adjacent kiln number three. "The firm's closing at the end of the month."

Natural curiosity taking over, Singh stepped across the iron rails and between the tray and the kiln entrance to take a look inside. Bricks were stacked filling the available space. He would have liked to ask Elvin some questions about the firing of the kilns, but the man had already moved away down the track, oblivious. Singh followed on. He heard Farley's truck drawing closer on the other side of the kilns, and then pass on by. Curiosity not quenched, at the next kiln he pulled up outside the open entrance and glanced inside.

It was gloomy, dusty and empty but for an amorphous dark object or bundle dumped in the dust in the far left corner of the kiln. Singh let his eyes adjust to the gloomy light. The bundle looked like a crumpled body. Then the legs shifted slightly. His instincts were screaming 'fight or flight' ? but he mastered his momentary immobilism:

"Elvin" he shouted insistently, "come here. Look."

Elvin, now five metres away, reluctantly retraced his steps, as Singh explained:

"It looks like you've a tramp or an unwanted guest in here. There's some guy sleeping."

As Elvin reached the entrance to the kiln, Singh finally advanced cautiously towards the body. It was only at close quarters that he saw the blindfold and the cordage tying the person's feet.

"He's been bound and gagged !"

Elvin, quick to understand and react, withdrew a pocket pen knife from his jacket pocket, knelt to one side of the body and starting cutting through the cord tying the hands. Singh adopted a similar stance and undid the knot tying the blindfold at the back of his head.

There were heavy footfalls outside the kiln and then Simon Farley appeared.

"What's up guys ?" he quizzed.

Then he pulled up suddenly, seeing the person's face.

"God damn it ! That's Craig !"

Chapter Forty Two

11.15am 22nd Sunday March 2009. * *Accident & Emergency, Ipswich Hospital, Heath Road, Ipswich*

"That's not an option." Reddy asserted "I've work to do. Just let me have back my clothes back, please."

He was sitting sideways on the elevated medical examination bed, naked but for his boxer shorts. He had received stitches above his left eyebrow, which had been cut open by the blows of his assailants.

Dr Bandarasingha, a chubby man with skin as dark as peat and a bald pate that shone pearl bright under the ceiling lights, held on to the lapels of his opened white coat and gave Reddy his solemnest stare.

"Mr. Reddy, on your own head be it" he admonished. "As I told you before, you have suffered from concussion having taken a bad blow to the head. You are still dehydrated and exhibit symptoms of trauma. If you wish to depart against my advice then so be it, but please sign yourself out without my concurrence. Good day."

He turned peremptorily to the nurse standing at his side and handed her the plastic clip board containing the patient's admission and treatment records. Then he was gone.

Feeling vulnerable in his naked condition, Reddy attempted a placatory smile at the nurse. She was having none of it. She pulled a biro from the top pocket of her uniform and extracted a sheet of paper from the clip board:

"Sign on the dotted line" she instructed. Pointing at a battle grey metal wardrobe in the corner of the room, she said: "Your clothes are there."

Nose in the air, she too then turned on her heel and left the room in theatrical style. Reddy lowered himself gingerly to the floor. "Old battle axe" he murmured.

Dressed, he found his way down a long corridor filled with the walking wounded to the A & E reception area. Simon Farley, who had driven him in his lorry to the hospital for treatment, was still sitting there next to the water cooler, engrossed in reading yesterday's local newspaper.

Determined not to succumb to the aches and pains that troubled him, Reddy exhorted:

"Come on Simon, let's get moving. No time to lose."

Farley looked up in surprise from the opened newspaper. Seeing the repairs effected to Reddy's brow, he asked:

"Nothing broken, just some stitches ? They're letting your out then ?"

"There was a minor difference of opinion" Reddy conceded, "but liberty is not to be trifled with. Listen, first I need to get back to my apartment to wash and change. Then I need to talk to DI Wright at Police HQ and brief her about the whistleblower at the IB&B."

Farley was reassured that his friend had a clean bill of health. Earlier, while driving him to Ipswich hospital, he listened avidly to Reddy's account of his abduction and beating at the hands of a gang whose motives, according to Reddy, remained uncertain. Farley didn't contradict him for fear of missing the story. However, it was clear to him that the events were a warning to Reddy that his investigation had stepped on the wrong people's toes. He had resolved to stick close by Reddy for the time being. Accidents happened in threes. He lifted himself stiffly from the uncomfortable moulded plastic seat and they headed for the exit side by side. He said:

"The wagon's outside in the car park Craig, I'm at your disposal. By the way, it says in yesterday's paper that the police have put out a four corners alert for a Bulgarian guy called Radomir Angelov. He was at Cartwright's funeral on Friday but then disappeared before the cops could interview him. You think he might be implicated in Westlake's murder ?"

"I have a good idea who he is, Simon. A Bulgarian entrepreneur and business partner of Westlake. He owns shares in RCH and has construction interests with Westlake on the Black Sea coast. If I'm right, then it's difficult to see why he would be complicit in Westlake's murder."

"Well, running away from the police doesn't do his case any good." Farley observed, conscious of his own recent history with SOCA.

They went out of the A&E building and walked along the pavement towards the visitors' car park. Farley's dirty truck was already visible, incongruous amongst the family saloon cars.

An approaching white Ford pulled over to the curb besides them. Its' passenger side window slid open. The driver called out:

"Mr Reddy !"

Undeterred by a possible reoccurrence of his kidnapping, Reddy bent down to see who had called his name. To his astonishment, he saw not one, but two faces he knew staring back at him. The driver was DS Adam; his passenger, Samantha Cavendish. Reddy blurted out:

"What on earth are you doing here, Samantha ?"

Her face was uncharacteristically blotchy, with heavy shadows under the eyes and hastily concocted make up. Reddy thought she appeared leaden and distracted. Her hair was tied back at the nape of her neck and she looked strangely austere.

"Hello Craig" she said, colourlessly. "I've been to identify my brother, Russell at the morgue. He's been murdered."

Reddy caught his breath, thrown off balance by his boss' reply. Recovering, he said politely:

"I'm sorry. My sincere condolences. Whatever happened ?"

Cavendish kept looking ahead into the distance, unable or unwilling to countenance further exchanges. DS Adam, disconcerted to find that his passenger also knew Reddy, leant across from the driver's seat to intervene and take control. He redirected the conversation:

"Mr Reddy, what are *you* doing here ? Ipswich police are on alert trying to find you. Does headquarters know that you are released ?"

Turning his attention to the policeman, Reddy explained:

"I've just been in A and E, officer. Can I come down to see you at headquarters in about an hour to brief you ? I need first to get cleaned up at my place."

"I'd appreciate that you do that. Say, one o'clock ?"

The rendez vous agreed, DS Adam pulled the car away and was gone. Confounded, Reddy watched as the vehicle departed.

"That was my boss, Samantha Cavendish" he explained to Farley.

An attentive witness to the exchanges, Farley observed:

"The only murder I know about is Russell Westlake's last Friday."

Reddy was dumbfounded. He had perceived the connection at once. As if having to wake himself up, he exclaimed to the heavens:

"Samantha is Westlake's sister !"

Chapter Forty Three

13.42 pm 22nd Sunday March 2009.   Police HQ, Civic Drive, Ipswich

DI Wright approached the closed door with trepidation. Having listened for the past half hour to Craig Reddy's exposé of the fraud prevailing at the IB&B's trading desks, she knew this was a make or break moment for her investigation. She wanted authorisation to raid the IB&B's headquarters. She knocked firmly and opened the door.

"Come in Wright" said the familiar voice.

DI Wright stepped into Chief Inspector Haddock's office. To her surprise, she found him standing in the middle of his office in conversation with a casually dressed Commander Dullingham, the SOCA officer.

"Just wrapping up with Dullingham here, Inspector. He's been briefing me on SOCA's investigation. They're closing it down. Their results have impact on our work."

Addressing Dullingham cordially, Haddock invited him:

"Maybe you can rehearse the main points again for DI Wright before you go ?"

"Good day, DI Wright. Yes," Dullingham acknowledged, not having offered his hand, " the UK side of the investigation is being closed. The main suspect is dead."

DI Wright sensed that the atmosphere was far more congenial than the last time these two men had met. Suspicious that some deal had been done, she surmised:

"And the main suspect is the deceased Russell Westlake ? "

"Correct. On balance, the evidence stacks up against Westlake. The laboratory tests returned a positive result for cocaine on the substance traces found at the warehouse. We've revisited the question of the Farley and Westlake business association. In light of the facts at our disposal, we've concluded that Farley is a bit player. He was probably only a gullible building supplies importer, but valuable to Westlake as a smokescreen."

DI Wright digested the news. Fixing Dullingham with a sharp stare, she said incisively:

"Westlake was murdered. It appears he had some dangerous acquaintances. The cartridge retrieved at the crime scene came from a CZ 75, a Czech 9 millimetre handgun. We are actively looking for a Bulgarian named Angelov who was at the funeral when the killing occurred. Do SOCA know of this man ?"

Dullingham allowed a slow smile to play on his face. He stretched his back up to his full height and looked down his long nose at Wright, with an air of unconcealed superiority. He spoke with annoyingly calm authority:

"We hold the view that Westlake was involved in importing cocaine and was aided in doing so by an east European drugs gang. Intelligence colleagues in MI6 have implicated him also in a scheme to provide IRA terrorists with retirement homes on the Bulgarian Black Sea coast. We believe the reason for Westlake's murder was a failure to meet some obligations he made with the Varna mafia. Your man Angelov is not, so far as we know, an active part of the Varna mafia. He runs his operations out of Sofia. However if you're looking for a definitive view on him, I suggest you get in touch with MI6."

DI Wright's expression became progressively grim and her posture taut as Dullingham's suave expansiveness took wings. Her Chief, fully aware of the SOCA man's grating style and its effect on his protegé, allowed him to finish. With seasoned ease he then negotiated his rapid departure, all the while maintaining an even handed amiability and good grace. Once the man had left, hubris intact, Haddock appraised Wright. She was crestfallen, but trying damned hard not to show it.

"Pauline" he said, in a conciliatory tone, "sometimes it's necessary to take it on the chin and move on. I want you to close the inquiry into Cartwright's suicide and leave the Westlake murder case to one side, unsolved for the time being. There's other important work to do."

She had never before heard Haddock use her Christian name. Still seething at the perceived defeat at the hands of SOCA, she was momentarily blind to the opportunity it presented. Failing to find her voice, Haddock's filled the gap:

"Don't you want to proceed with the case against Donoghue at the IB&B ?" he cajoled. "The evidence from those video tapes DS Adam has obtained are damning. Reddy's Messenger article puts the argument that crimes have been perpetrated: financial fraud and conspiracy. Let's bring the miscreants to account."

Heartened by Haddock's stance, which coincided with her own goals, DI Wright felt the pressure on her relax. Proceeding against the IB&B, a possibility which earlier she highly doubted, now looked likely.

"Chief, if that's your view, then I've got a proposal and a request" she announced with new found confidence.

"Tell me."

"I propose we conduct a raid on the IB&B headquarters first thing Monday morning. The purpose being to search for, and confiscate, incriminating materials exposing financial fraud and possibly related offences. The request is that before you make that decision, you join me now in the interview room to hear for yourself the latest testimony from Mr. Reddy. He has reappeared and has new information on the IB&B obtained from a whistleblower working at the bank. It substantially reinforces our case. I think it also justifies the arrest of Mary Donoghue."

Chief Inspector Haddock, cognisant of the delicate diplomacy deployed to repair relations with SOCA after having denigrated their failed raid earlier in the week, knew that risky operational projects necessitated careful planning. That was reason to proceed with exceeding care. Equally, he knew too that the prize of success was 'winner takes all' professional recognition.

"Lead the way, Inspector. I'm keen to meet this Mr. Reddy. If you're right about the quality of his disclosures, then we set up our Projects Room immediately for a full scale raid planning session."

Chapter Forty Four

16.12 pm 22nd Sunday March 2009. "The Yorker" Pub, Sarratt, east of Amersham, Hertfordshire.

The rain had been incessant since they had left police headquarters in Ipswich. Farley was at the wheel of Reddy's Ford Mondeo, having insisted that his friend not drive. Mercifully, they had navigated the M25 without major hold ups, although the quantities of rain water washed up onto the car by the innumerable freight lorries was enough to baptise a nation.

Their destination was a pub in Sarratt, a bucolic village inhabited by the urban well to do, for a meeting with Mitchell Havering. While waiting at Ipswich Police headquarters for DI Wright to return from her visit to Chief Inspector Haddock, Reddy had retrieved his mobile phone from DS Adam and called Havering to arrange it.

Wrapped up in his favourite Burberry's raincoat, Reddy had used his freedom as a passenger to staunch his ravenous hunger. A chunky cheese and branston pickle sandwich, that he'd hastily prepared at his apartment, was devoured in lightning speed. Then he placed a call through to Stan Cerny.

"Stan, Craig Reddy calling. Are you able to talk ?"

"No problem. I'm alone in my room. The talks have been interrupted. What's going on with you ?"

"Listen, I've got disconcerting news about the IB&B. It's pertinent to the rescue efforts and negotiations between your boss Acheson and the CEGB. I'm going to explain everything to Mitchell in a few minutes when we arrive at Sarratt."

"Well, it seems I'm not invited" Cerny lamented, "so what do you me to do ?"

"You're advising Acheson on the value of CPI, the firm owned by CEGB. I need an insider's take on the situation. You've done the number crunching analysis. What's Acheson going to be willing to offer when it goes down to the wire ?"

"That's a hell of a question Craig ! I'm his advisor not chief negotiator."

"OK, I appreciate that. But you're best placed to make a judgement. You know the problems on the CPI's balance sheet and you know Acheson's strategy and style."

Cerny laughed. It was measured, not hearty.

"Craig, a guy like Larry keeps it simple. Did you know that his opening gambit on Friday was to offer Declan Moroney one euro to take the burden of CPI off him ? What a masterstroke ! It completely took the wind out of Moroney's Celtic sails. He was speechless. "

"Stan, please. What's his game plan ? Does he want CPI or not ? If yes, what is he likely to be willing to pay ?"

"Easy champ, easy" Cerny teased. "Look. Last Friday's market closing CPI was valued at 2.8 billlion euros. Last year's earnings per share were at a multiple of only eight. Since then the retail mortgages market in central and eastern Europe has deteriorated badly, so this year's earnings are going to be worse. My guess is Larry smells blood and won't offer in excess of 40 cents to the euro. He'll start as low as 500 million and possibly have 1,1 billion euro as his last offer."

That was all Reddy had wanted to know.

While he had been talking to Cerny, Farley had been negotiating winding country lanes not wide enough to support more than a Fiat 500. He expressed mounting frustration as locals in over-sized four by four vehicles bore down on the Ford at alarming speeds, careless of the lanes' diminutive widths.

"Good God, it's Sunday" he cried, banging the rim of the steering wheel with the palm of his hand, "are these nutters intent on meeting their Maker ?"

The relief Farley felt from having been told unofficially by Ipswich police that he no longer was under suspicion from SOCA, had not vanquished his appetite for invective.

As they were both growing frustrated at being late for the meeting, Reddy stabbed a finger at the windscreen in the direction of the village green: "There it is, over there."

'The Yorker' inhabited a structure consisting of three different edifices all joined into one establishment, an odd assortment of red brick and white washed exteriors.

Farley found a parking space on a road to the side of the village green and a short walking distance from the pub. As they approached it, Reddy noticed the pub sign hanging above the front entrance. It illustrated a batsman down on one knee swinging across the line of a cricket ball as the wickets behind him flailed and the stumps arced into the air. 'Every ball requires an appropriate stroke', Reddy mused.

Entering through the front door, they found themselves enclosed by low ceilings, a flagstone floor and traditional half timbered white washed walls. The bar was straight in front of them, stocked to the rafters with every conceivable variety of alcoholic beverage. A large blackboard on the bar counter displayed the day's menu in chalked handwriting. Off to the left was a tastefully decorated restaurant, its' tables largely depleted of tableware except for their white tablecloths, bestrewn with the flotsam and jetsam of long departed Sunday lunch diners.

A cosy sectioned off room to the new arrivals' right was furnished with a large wooden table surrounded on three sides by a wooden bench made comfortable with soft cushions. It had space for six people but was occupied only by two. Reddy immediately recognised Mitchell Havering and 'Wes' Hall.

"Come and join us" Havering invited, with an encouraging smile and wave of the hand. "Wes tells me that you've met" he said, standing up and shaking hands vigorously with Reddy.

Reddy and Farley divested themselves of their coats and joined the couple at the table. Taking in details of their sectioned off space, Reddy's attention was drawn to a worn out cricket bat attached to the wall beside the entrance to the main bar.

"Signed by members of the English cricket team back in the sixties" Hall said, noticing Reddy's efforts to decipher the cricket bat's hieroglyphics. "Brian Close, Freddie Truman, Ken Barrington. Remember them ?"

"Before my time, Wes. But wasn't that the same era as when your namesake was knocking down the English batsmens' wickets ?"

"Spot on" Hall exclaimed, a gleam of pride in his eyes.

The enlarged group settled in their places. Havering and Hall then launched into solicitous enquiries of Reddy's kidnapping and release. He insisted on curtailing any story telling, remonstrating that they focus exclusively on the challenges facing the IB&B rescue mission at Lord Preston's house. Agreed on this, Mitchell Havering exploited his natural leadership to sum up the prevailing status back at the house:

"Negotiations are temporarily halted. Only Lord Preston is aware of this meeting. Wes is here to represent him. Lord Preston remains at his house fulfilling his role as host. In practice that translates as the unenviable task of entertaining Larry Acheson and Declan Moroney, the incompatible protagonists."

Interrupting, Reddy asked:

"Is the chemistry really that bad between those two ?"

"Yes and no, Craig. Yes, the gap in style and substance is evident. No, the two men are both devils for subterfuge. Acheson specialises in being laconic and shot tempered. Moroney deploys bombast and Celtic charm."

"Surely that's nothing that two eminent businessmen like yourself and Lord Preston can't handle ?" Reddy countered, a mischievous smile curtailed by pain shooting across the stitches above his brow.

"It's classic chess playing, agreed" Havering admitted. "However, this evening's negotiation is our 'last chance saloon'. Moroney and Acheson have to find a mutually acceptable deal. If there's nothing tangible flowing from this evening's session, then we're empty handed. Remember, tomorrow morning the markets expect a clear announcement."

"Which might end up coming from the government" Hall interjected. "The tv media earlier today were speculating on a deal having been stitched up in Whitehall during this week end."

"Meaning, in effect, another government bank bail out ?" Reddy asked.

"If the shares remain suspended on Monday, then it is likely the government will act with a bail out, yes" Hall confirmed. "Don't forget, Number 10 wants this story off the front pages. There's the upcoming G20 here in the UK at which he stars as Super Mario."

Hearing about the stalled rescue efforts, Reddy's resolve to relate his insights into the IB&B's evolving insolvency dynamics was reinforced:

"I don't want to be the bearer of bad news, but there's now more to contend with following the latest developments. Let me brief you."

With attentive silence from Havering and Hall, he recounted all he now knew, spanning from his conversation with O'Connor the 'Irish Tiger' whistleblower, to his presence at Ipswich Police headquarters where he'd heard Chief Inspector Haddock authorise a raid on the IB&B offices for Monday morning. His interlocutors listened intently, their expressions progressively more worried.

"So the bottom line is this" Reddy summarised, "the proprietary trading team has blown a hole in the IB&B's balance sheet to the tune of at least £ 1.2 billion, maybe more. My whistleblower has the facts and wants to trade evidence for immunity. But there will be worse losses to come. For example, Redwoods Country Homes, which will be in disarray with the death of Westlake it's CEO, is all but insolvent yet owes the IB&B roughly £¾ billion. Either the CEGB's own due diligence team, or else the police, are going to get their teeth into the data and discover the true extent of the mess. On top of that, comes Mary Donoghue's credit default swaps dealings with CPI."

Hall, not a finance expert, interjected: "There you've bowled us a googly, Craig. Run that one about credit default swaps across me again. I need to get it right to report to Lord Preston."

"Sure Wes, " Reddy responded "Donoghue prepared credit default swaps to sell to CPI as protection for their multi-currency mortgage business in central and eastern Europe. Those insurances blew up in the past few months as repayment defaults rocketed in countries like Poland and Hungary due to their currencies collapsing."

Havering, beginning to feel, like the Ancient Mariner, a 'sadder and a wiser man', had heard enough. It was time to decide how to act:

"Craig, your revelations are hugely valuable. However, as concerns this rescue, there are things we can control and others we cannot. The police raid of the IB&B headquarters on Monday is not something we control. Advance knowledge of its' occurrence is an advantage however. I can profit from it during our closing negotiation session this evening as a tool to pressure the protagonists. The same can be said with respect to the whistleblower. In effect both developments put a premium on the parties seizing the opportunity now before it is terminally lost."

"I agree," Reddy concurred "just so long as Moroney and Acheson still both see you and Lord Preston as 'honest brokers'. The moment they lose confidence in that assumption the rescue attempt is a dead letter. Are you sure that your active presence in these negotiations doesn't compromise things due to a conflict of interests ?"

Mitchell Havering was not one to take umbrage, but his response forthright:

"Nothing to fear in that regard. I made it plain to Larry from the outset that my mission is to see the IB&B effectively rescued at no cost to the taxpayer. That's my political commitment. In addition, as a non-executive director of the AIIB, I have already rendered a business service by drawing his attention to CPI GmbH as an acquisition opportunity that fits with the bank's strategy. Beyond that, he has an expert advisor with him to weigh in with an assessment of the target's valuation."

It was a card up Reddy's sleeve, that Havering had no knowledge of his friendship and recent communication with Stan Cerny. Fast forwarding from Havering's robust self justification, he asked:

"So how do you envisage 'closing the gap' between Acheson's derisory offer and the amount that Moroney needs to bring a viable rescue proposal to his Board and the markets on Monday ? With £ 1,2 billion of unofficial losses already in the public domain, my guess is he'll need to have at least that on the table by tonight."

"And that's do-able" Havering insisted. "He told Lord Preston yesterday that CEGB already have £ 500 million saved from shelving an unstarted property development project in Dublin. That means he only needs another £700 million. Lord Preston told me privately, he believes the Bank of England is willing to step in with emergency liquidity assistance for the IB&B if the CEGB itself comes up with that £ 1.2 billion."

"In euros, that £700 million is nearly 1.1 billion. CPI's market value is 2.8 billion. Acheson thinks he's at a fire sale. He's punted 1 euro, presumably just to upset Moroney. Does he have an acquisition fund sizable enough to buy CPI at say, a 50% discount ? And even if he does, is he willing to part with the money ?"

"That's where the art of negotiation comes in Craig" Havering asserted. "My role with Lord Preston will be to lead the two men towards a common destination. We think we can do that if we know in advance what both players need and are willing to concede."

"So you think 1.1 billion euro for CPI will do it ?" Reddy asked inquisitively, remembering his phone conversation with Stan Cerny .

"I do" Havering affirmed, "on condition that we also find a face saving formula for Moroney. He can hardly return to his Board on Monday proselytising an asset disposal at less than 45 cents to the euro."

Reddy was about to acknowledge this, but Havering was in full flight:

"Bear in mind too that raising the £ 1.2 billion is only a means to the end of keeping the IB&B solvent. The CEGB definitely wants to accomplish that. But the rescue must itself stand muster before the critical eye of the markets and the regulators. Remember, the Stock Exchange expects the IB&B's shares to be back trading again tomorrow."

"Is there another building block you can add to the solution to improve the rescue's resilience, apart from maybe obtaining the Bank of England's emergency assistance ?"

"Indeed there is, isn't there Wes ?" Havering revealed, with a conspiratorial smile. "Lord Preston has accepted Moroney's offer to take on the CEO's role at the IB&B if the regulators and the BoE accept the rescue package."

Chapter Forty Five

12.15 Wednesday 1st April 2009. Parliament Hill, Hampstead Heath, London

The weather was blustery with towering clouds billowing across the sky. As it was also dry, young mothers were out with small children and babies in lightweight buggies, taking some fresh air. Dog owners were being hauled around the heath by their demanding mastiffs. The inviting gusts of wind had caused a few teenagers to attempt flying kites at the top of Parliament Hill.

Standing atop the hill were Mitchell Havering and Professor Bernstein. Both were wrapped up in warm overcoats, hands dug deeply into pockets. Bernstein sported a black cashmere scarf and French style black beret. They had met each other at Hampstead Heath tube station and walked together onto the heath, climbing to the top of Parliament Hill. Having arrived about five minutes ago, they surveyed the scene while watching out for the arrival of the others who also were invited for lunch; Edmund Burleigh, Craig Reddy and Reddy's new girlfriend name unknown.

"Your appearance before the Select Committee on Banking at the House of Commons on Monday caused something of a stir, Immanuel ? I assume that was deliberate ?" Mitchell Havering asked, giving Bernstein a conspiratorial grin.

Bernstein had planted his feet wide apart, the better to assure his stability in the face of unpredictable gusts. He kept his gaze firmly on the horizon and his expression remained inscrutable. In his field of vision was a wide sky suspended over an immense expanse of variegated greys that was central London's built environment. Off to his left, were the familiar shapes of prominent office buildings in and around the City of London financial district.

"It was intended as a wake up call, Mitchell. You know, at my age I've nothing to lose. I say it as I see it. I always have done to be honest. This generation of professional politicians are extremely poor. They are sleepwalking into disaster with their profligate spending and escalating debt mountains. How to break them out of their torpor ? So, to answer your question: yes, I told them some home truths. I suspect I won't be invited again in a hurry after that."

Havering had known Bernstein for a few years. It had taken time for him to attune to the Professor's wavelength. Now that he had, he recognised that he was dealing with an individual with profound, and profoundly important, knowledge: what he called 'Austrian economics'. Havering and his brother Neill were cultivating the relationship with Bernstein in the hope that one day he might become the economic policy advisor of a future Tory Government. In response to Bernstein he observed:

"The media reaction was somewhat ambivalent though. The financial journalists and business editors couldn't find an easy way to slot you into a category for the sound bite machine. They mostly damned you with faint praise and focused on the entertaining exchanges you had with some of the Committee. Did that surprise you ?"

"Not at all. Anyone who explains their economic views from a theoretical position that is not Keynesian is faced these days with an audience that is ignorant. Certainly the political class in this country doesn't have a clue. And that applies equally across the mainstream media. None of the Committee knows anything at all about Austrian economics and its insights into the current crisis. If you want to find genuine alternative perspectives you have to look elsewhere. Which is what I've been doing all my academic life."

"You've undoubtedly found a convert in Craig Reddy" Havering averred, curious to discover what the professor's thinking about the journalist might be.

"Yes, a remarkable young man. He grasped the main tenets of the approach quickly. I think that was because he was already looking around for more powerful and effective explanations for what's happening. His investigation of the Ipswich and Blackwater was exemplary. You see, it is the power of ideas that change the world. I take my hat off to him !"

"Well, you changed the course of history yourself Immanuel. Probably you're unaware, but my brother Neill and I approached Reddy with material for a scoop on a different topic earlier that week. He'd agreed to write an article immediately, but that all fell aside once he'd met you."

"I see. No I was unaware that you'd approached him" Bernstein conceded.

"It's a long time I think since an article has had such an immediate impact in the public domain as his Ipswich and Blackwater article in the Messenger. I'm the first to admit" Havering revealed, "when I myself read it, I saw at once the need to act."

"I'd wondered about that and was going to ask you" Bernstein admitted. "If you hadn't taken the initiative for a private sector solution to the crisis, the Ipswich and Blackwater would have become yet another nationalised bank ? Another millstone round the neck of the taxpayers."

"Precisely. Of course, it was a risky undertaking but I felt it my duty to try. Luckily, I was successful in outmanouevring old Larry Acheson. Then, out of the blue, Declan Moroney offered the CEO job to Jamie Sturridge, which he accepted, and the whole thing fell into place as if it was destiny. The markets really took to the idea of having Lord Preston at the helm of a rescue operation for the IB&B."

"I wouldn't underestimate either the unofficial support you received from the Governor. Word from my contact at the Bank of England was they were delighted with your initiative. Just damned worried it would blow up in a messy failure and then a nasty run on the bank, perhaps worse than with Northern Rock ?"

"Agreed. That was the nightmare scenario I had to avoid. The Government is replete with inveterate interventionists. Most of them were on the far left in their student days. The idea that banking can put its own house in order doesn't align with their statist ideology."

Havering broke from his comments. Taking a hand from his pocket, he pointed down the hill towards the Highgate entrance to the heath, near the tennis courts. There was a group of three people heading up the hill towards them. Bernstein squinted and stared in the direction Havering was pointing. Havering declared:

"If I'm not mistaken that's Edmund and Reddy."

Bernstein concurred: "So it would seem. I see Reddy has a female holding his arm. Who would she be, any idea ?"

"None at all. We shall discover soon enough."

The two men stood in silence watching the approaching threesome, invigorated by the blowing wind. Within five minutes the group was within hailing distance. Burleigh took the lead over the couple as they arrived. His sparse silver hair had been woven into knots by the wind.

"Turbulent conditions, what ?"

He proffered his hand, first to Havering then Bernstein.

"The Met Office forecast is for a brightening outlook." Havering replied.

"Never believe forecasts or forecasters." Bernstein quipped.

Reddy and his girl friend then gathered round and introductions were made. Bernstein noted a scar on Reddy's brow but said nothing.

"Allow me to present, Natasha. Natasha Medvedev." Reddy announced with obvious pride, tinged with nervousness.

Natasha, the only female present and an eminently elegant one, became the centre of the men's attention as each sought to compete for her attentions with old fashioned gallantry and charm. She took it all calmly and in good faith. It wasn't the first time she'd encountered old men vainly countenancing that they could capture the attention of an attractive young woman.

Pursuing a meteorological metaphor, Burleigh commented:

"The turbulence extends to what's going on in London today. We've just left the protesters rallying at Hyde Park. All manner of opposition to the G20, capitalism, the bankers. You name it. There are other rallies going on in the City and in the East End the police told us. Apparently, the protesters have named today 1st April Financial Fools Day."

"Great to see you back in circulation again Craig" Bernstein observed warmly, "You had a harrowing experience the other week."

After a short convalescence from his nightmare kidnapping, Reddy had found the fortitude and energy to get back to his work. Re-visiting the details of his sufferings at the hands of the gangsters was not a subject he wished to dwell on. With irony he replied:

"After having had threats from my boss at the Courier that I would be fired, I'll admit that the prospect of getting fired in a kiln was indeed harrowing ! Although, to be honest, I had no clue where I was until my friends rescued me."

The others listened attentively. All had been shocked and worried when the media communicated that Reddy had been kidnapped. That the kidnapping was linked in some way to Reddy's investigation, no one doubted. Yet, after a debriefing with the police and the elapse of ten days since the event, the identity of the attackers was shrouded in mystery. Reddy himself had considered and reconsidered the permutations and possibilities privately and was keeping his own counsel.

Edmund Burleigh couldn't resist the temptation to ask:

"Is there any resolution yet to your arguments with your employer Craig ? Do your bosses still want you out ?"

"I suspect so yes. Samantha Cavendish took bereavement leave last week following the death of her brother, but she bears a grudge against me for having published criticisms of his company. Monroe Sinclair gave me a call which was marginally conciliatory in tone though. We agreed to talk at the end of this week."

"That's good. It keeps your options open doesn't it ? And by the way, how did you react when you discovered that your investigation into Redwoods meant you were investigating your boss' brother ?"

"Edmund, I missed that completely until I met Cavendish by chance at Ipswich hospital where she'd visited the morgue to identify his body. It never occurred to me that her maiden name was Westlake. That's a cross I'll have to bear I guess. If we reconvene for talks, that is."

Bernstein interrupted them, extemporising as *maitre de ceremonie*:

"Ladies and gentlemen, may I suggest that if you've had your fill of this revitalising wind, we get down off the Hill ? I've a table reserved for us all in a Thai restaurant for twelve forty five over in Hampstead, so we need to get our skates on."

The proposal found unanimous support, and the party of five set off down the Hill westwards in the direction of Hampstead Village. Bernstein took the lead, with Burleigh beside him, the two getting to know one another for the first time. Reddy, Natasha and Havering brought up the rear.

"I want to take the opportunity" Havering said to Reddy, "to thank you personally for the sterling work you did in publishing that article. It was the catalyst behind the initiative to put in place a private sector rescue of the Ipswich and Blackwater Bank."

"Thanks. When I wrote it I never imagined that might happen. The big questions is, is the rescue going to succeed, Mitchell ?" Reddy asked. "There are formidable challenges ahead. Not least, the police criminal investigation. The raid they conducted on the IB&B headquarters won plaudits from the press."

"You're right. However, with Lord Preston appointed as the CEO and the Bank of England agreeing to emergency liquidity assistance on condition of the rescue plan being implemented, the markets have been calmed and time has been won. Customers have stopped withdrawing deposits. Now the heavy lifting transformation programme begins. As for the police, well, that will drag on for months I expect. We'll have to see how strong a case the director of public prosecutions can build. However, the presumed culprits are no longer in control at the IB&B. Lord Preston is the new broom."

"You're close to the AIIB and Larry Acheson. Is the purchase agreement for CPI GmbH from the CEGB going to go through ? That's the short term key to the CEGB being able to raise the IB&B's capital reserves."

"After Larry took back to his Board the memorandum of understanding he had signed that week end with Declan Moroney, there was foot dragging initially. But he and I together won the argument. The Board accepted the deal and have recommended it to shareholders. Shareholders should vote their approval within the next week."

Reddy admired Havering for his suave ability to operate effectively in the highest echelons of the corporate world, without apparently compromising his core values. In this affair, his energy and commitment to achieving a resilient rescue operation for the Ipswich and Blackwater had won him plaudits in the opinion columns. Reddy observed:

"That gives Lord Preston a fighting chance then. Still, the devil's in the detail and I suspect he'll find more nasty surprises before he finishes the clean up. Thomas Cartwright and Mary Donoghue had a lot to answer for."

Havering observed:

"What is it Shakespeare said : "the evil that men do lives after them; the good is oft interred with their bones ?" Yes, there's a litany of bad, and also illegal, financial transactions and liabilities to clear up. Still, let's have faith in the new man at the top."

Overhearing the conversation, Bernstein looked over his shoulder at them:

"There'll be no 'brave new world' in the banking industry yet Mitchell. Your man Lord Preston may be a capable fellow but this crisis is not over by far, believe me."

Havering, cognisant of Bernstein's bearish economic views said:

"You're a perma bear Immanuel. According to the media and the political elites, all's for the best in the best of worlds. The US administration has announced $ 1.7 billion of spending stimulus and the Federal Reserve will keep interest rates low. Stock markets are responding positively to the medicine."

Bernstein scoffed:

"Bromides and obfuscation, Mitchell. Mark my words, these Keynesian 'stimulus' measures never will accomplish their intended goals. Tell me in nine or twelve months' time if we have a sustainable recovery. I tell you now: we will not. The fundamental problem is going to remain, and that is the massive debt overhang. Everyone in the western world is over leveraged – banks, governments, municipalities, consumers, corporations. You name it. The politicians and central bankers have their heads in the sand. Or worse, up their backsides. Monetising the debt is only going to make matters much worse in the near future."

"What a game, eh ?" Havering said to no one in particular.

"Is that a '*Berlin Game*'?" Natasha queried Reddy, nudging his arm conspiratorially.

"A what ?" Havering asked, mistakenly thinking the question was directed at him.

Reddy jumped to Havering's rescue: "It's a coded message between Natasha and I. It means changing sides and joining the opposition. Natasha has changed sides with me and we're both avowed students of the Austrian economists' explanations of the crisis."

"It sounds to me then," Havering averred, "that Professor Bernstein has been conjuring his magic again. I myself had no peace from him until he'd permeated my thinking with von Mises ! Anyway, looking ahead what are your plans, Craig ? Stay with the Courier if you can reach an accord ? Branch out and work freelance, perhaps ?"

"I'm struggling with that decision Mitchell. Although it may get made for me. I need to make money, if for no other reason than to pay the mortgage !" He raised his voice so Bernstein could hear him:

"Immanuel, you're the economist," he egged "Can you offer advice on making money ?"

"An economist Craig, not an investment adviser! But since you ask, I'd say 'Go long the banks'. Buy bank shares. With all this central bank money printing, it's a sure thing the banks will make money from it. We economists call it the Cantillon effect."

Reddy jested, "Is that a 'banker' ? A sure thing ?"

"Of course. At least, until they become insolvent."